THE TRADE

James Martingell is a self-made explorer, hunter and prospector, and few men know war-torn Southern Africa better than he. He also sells guns to whoever can afford them. Offered a fortune to deliver a huge stock of weapons to would-be Boer rebels in the Transvaal, he supposes his fortune is made. Instead, he finds himself facing betrayal, imprisonment, open warfare and eventually murder as he becomes involved with international traders. Will he survive long enough to become the best known, and most feared, gun-runner in the world?

THE TRADE

THE TRADE

by

Christopher Nicole

Magna Large Print Books
Long Preston, North Yorkshire,
England.

British Library Cataloguing in Publication Data.

Nicole, Christopher
  The trade.

A catalogue record for this book is
available from the British Library

ISBN 0-7505-1333-0

First published in Great Britain by Severn House Publishers
Ltd., 1997

Published in Large Print 1998 by arrangement with Severn
House Publishers Ltd.

Magna Large Print is an imprint of
Library Magna Books Ltd.
Printed and bound in Great Britain by
T.J. International Ltd., Cornwall, PL28 8RW.

CONTENTS

'Such as do build their faith upon
The holy text of pike and gun.'
Samuel Butler, *Hudibras*

Prologue

'Well, Martingell? Well?' Charles Rudd, florid and handsome, was impatient. As well, perhaps, as apprehensive. The day was hot, as only days in Central Africa could be hot. The sky overhead was an unclouded blue. To either side, the land undulating from hill to valley, dotted with the occasional acacia, was parched and therefore brown and inhospitable, but by all accounts rich, in what white men wanted.

Rudd's problem was that there was no more than a score of white men standing behind him, with their black servants and their half-dozen black guides, while around him stood the massed ranks of the Matabele, warriors of renown, together with their women and their children; the kraal behind them was empty save for the snarling dogs. Not a hundred years ago the Matabele had cut loose from their erstwhile masters, the Zulu, during the reign of the redoubtable Shaka, and sought their own fortunes in the highlands beyond the rivers. Now the kingdom they had carved for themselves was in turn being sought,

9

by a less febrile but more implacable foe than even the Zulu. In this spring of 1893 Charles Rudd had no doubt that Cecil Rhodes would be remembered long after Shaka the Zulu was buried in history. Shaka had lived for revenge and military glory; Rhodes lived for dreams, than which there is no more potent force in humanity, where the dream is driven by ambition and naked force.

But here the naked force was all on the other side, at the moment. He watched James Martingell leave the King's side and return to his. The King, his name was Lobengula, was a somewhat mild-looking man, absurd to European eyes in that he wore a voluminous, brightly coloured skirt and black boots; in that he was naked from the waist up, yet had an English bowler hat on his head; in that his bare chest was adorned with a necklace of worthless beads, and that he sat in an English-made armchair. But he was the King. He was unarmed, but the warriors who surrounded the court and its guests bristled with knife, spear and bow and arrow; with their shuffling feet they sent a constant wisp of dust into the air. That they as yet possessed no rifles was, Rudd knew, the ace in his hand. An ace he now had to play. For Martingell had reached him.

James Martingell was tall and well-built. His lean face was sun-browned and stress-lined, but he had the clear eyes and confident demeanour of a man who had spent his adult life in these hills and valleys, along with the perpetual watchfulness of a man who has long known his life has hung by the thread of his own courage and experience. Thirty-two years old, despite his years of adventure among the black people, he retained an essential determination to be true to his race and his caste. James Martingell shaved every morning, even his moustache, worn by every other member of Rudd's party, and his clothes were invariably clean; the bandolier he wore across his chest was polished to a high sheen by his servant. His broad-brimmed hat sat squarely on his head. Yet there was no man prepared to call him dandy, much less something worse. He was as quick at drawing and sighting the revolver hanging from his waist as any Wild West hero of legend, as accurate with a rifle as any Buffalo Bill ... and besides, it was what *he* had found in these hills close by the legendary city of Zimbabwe, in particular the golden nuggets he had shown to Rhodes himself, which had brought Rhodes' emissaries here. 'Well?'

11

Rudd asked a third time. 'Tell me what he wants.'

'The price is high, Mr Rudd. The King wishes above all else security.'

'We will provide that for him.'

'He would prefer to provide it for himself. His people are surrounded by enemies. He would have his enemies fear him, as they fear the white man, because of the white man's weapons. He wishes rifles for his warriors.'

'I am sure that can be arranged.'

'Martini-Henry breech loaders,' Martingell said.

The men at Rudd's back moved restlessly.

'What, does he seek to take on the British Army?' someone muttered.

'Martini-Henrys,' Rudd said, half to himself. 'All right. How many?'

Martingell cleared his throat. 'One thousand.'

Once again Rudd was temporarily speechless.

'This half-naked savage wants a thousand modern rifles?' Starr Jameson demanded. As a close friend of Rhodes, he was second-in-command of this expedition.

'That's what he wants.'

'One thousand,' Rudd muttered. 'Very good, Mr Martingell.'

'Each rifle to be accompanied by a

12

hundred rounds of ammunition,' Martin-gell said.

Rudd grinned, briefly. 'Is that all?'

'I doubt he can count to more than a hundred,' Dr Jameson remarked.

'He seems able to count to a thousand, doctor,' Rudd pointed out. 'Very well, Mr Martingell. It's a hard bargain, but if he will agree to our proposition ...'

'That is not quite all, Mr Rudd,' Martingell said. 'The King also wishes a gunboat to patrol the river.'

'A gunboat? On the Zambesi?'

'How does he suggest we get it there?' asked Harry Salt.

'I imagine in pieces,' Martingell said.

'Did he specify how big a boat?' Rudd asked.

'One big enough to carry two guns.'

Rudd frowned. 'What sort of guns?'

'He has in mind a couple of four-pounders, mounted bow and stern.'

'So ... thirty feet will do. I think we can provide that. The guns will be smooth-bore muzzle-loaders, of course. He's not asking for RBLs, I hope?'

'I doubt the King knows it is possible to rifle a cannon, much less load it from the breech,' Salt suggested.

'Is that the end of it?' Rudd inquired.

'Not quite. There is also the matter of rent.'

'Rent?'

'You wish to dig in his soil, Mr Rudd. He feels that a rent should be paid.'

'In addition to sufficient arms and ammunition to start a war?' Salt shouted. 'The man's effrontery is ridiculous!'

'You wish to dig, Mr Salt,' Martingell pointed out.

'How much rent?' Rudd, as usual, remained cool.

'Two hundred pounds.'

'It's steep. Very well, Mr Martingell. Two hundred pounds a year.'

'A *month*,' Martingell said, and could hardly suppress a smile at Salt's expression; he felt there was some danger of the mining engineer having a seizure.

'A month?' Rudd repeated. 'As you say, Harry, the bastard is clearly ambitious. But we have come here to get what we want. Two hundred pounds a month, one thousand rifles with ammunition, and a gunboat. Is there anything more, Mr Martingell.'

'Those are what the King wants, Mr Rudd.'

Rudd nodded. 'Then tell him he will have those things, if he will sign the paper. You have read it?'

'I have,' Martingell said.

'Will he sign it? Give me your opinion.'

'I believe he will sign it, Mr Rudd. But

14

you will need to deliver.'

'Oh, we shall deliver,' Rudd assured him.

'Then may I say it is my opinion you are getting the best of the bargain.'

Rudd smiled. 'You would say that, Mr Martingell. But I am assuming you are correct.'

'I am not speaking only of what you may be able to dig out of the ground,' Martingell said. 'These people do not want you here. They would cheerfully resist you. The young men, certainly. It is the elders, and especially those three ...' he nodded to the three men who stood around the King's chair, 'who seek a peaceful future.'

'Then let's get to it. Take the paper, read it to him, and have him sign it.' Martingell took the paper, returned to the King's side.

'This is madness, Charles,' Jameson said, taking off his hat to wipe sweat from his brow. 'You heard what Martingell said. These warriors wish to resist us. And you have just given them the means to do so. What happens if the King were to die?'

'He looks healthy enough to me,' Rudd remarked.

'I was thinking of assassination.'

'We will have his signature on that agreement, doctor. We will show that to the world. Thus we will have the legal right to come here and look for gold and diamonds. No one can gainsay that once he signs. Least of all the Boers.'

'To hell with the Boers,' Jameson said. 'They are nothing but a pack of farmers. So they duffed our boys up at Majuba. That was because they had modern rifles. Now you are giving these born fighting men the same power.'

Rudd scratched his chin as he watched Martingell bending beside the King, reading the paper. 'A thousand rifles,' he said. 'Let me tell you what Colley did *not* have at Majuba Hill, doctor: Maxims. A thousand rifles, in the hands of untrained and undisciplined troops, will be like chaff in the wind when confronted with a Maxim gun, or as many as we think necessary.'

'You'd bring machine-guns up here?' Salt was astounded.

'We certainly mean to protect our people, Harry. And that includes you. Once the King signs that paper this country is ours.'

Martingell had finished reading, and Lobengula was nodding. 'Read those last words again, Martingell.'

Martingell read, 'You are granting the Company full power to do all things that they may deem necessary to seek and procure the minerals.'

'Tell me what that means.'

'You will permit them to import such machinery as they deem necessary, to dig mines as and where they consider it necessary, to enter your country in as great numbers as they consider necessary, and ...' Martingell took a deep breath, 'to oppose any opposition they may encounter with force, if they consider it necessary.'

'But the King has said that your people will not be opposed, Martingell,' said one of the elders behind the chair.

'Then neither of us have anything to worry about,' Martingell said.

'Did you ever see a chameleon catch a fly, Martingell?' Lobengula asked. 'The chameleon gets behind the fly, and remains motionless for some time, then he advances, very slowly and gently, first putting out one leg, and then another. At last, when well within reach, he darts out his tongue and the fly disappears. England is the chameleon, and I am that fly.'

'Then you will not sign?' Martingell was almost relieved.

'Oh, I will sign,' Lobengula said. 'It is the will of Heaven.'

PART ONE

Building

'Conscience has no more to do with gallantry than it has with politics.'
Richard Brinsley Sheridan, *Pizarro*

Chapter One

The Trap

'Martingell,' Charles Rudd said. 'How good to see you again. You remember Dr Jameson?'

Martingell shook hands. In his circumstances there was nothing else to do; if neither he nor King Lobengula had had any doubt that the Company intended to rule Matabeleland and Mashonaland, neither had expected it to happen by naked force within two years. 'You've been busy since last we met, doctor,' he remarked.

'The Matabele provoked that war, Martingell.'

'I have no doubt of it. But you always knew they would, didn't you? And the winning of it was made the easier by your knowledge of exactly how they were armed, and how much ammunition they had.'

Jameson pulled the end of his waxed moustache and glanced at Rudd. 'Water under the bridge,' Rudd said, jocularly.

'Or over the Matabele,' Martingell suggested. 'And it was blood rather than water.'

It was Rudd's turn to give him an old-fashioned look, before his ready smile returned. 'It is simply impossible for the black nations to stop the aspirations of the white, and particularly the British, from realising their goals,' he said. 'The sooner the natives learn this simple fact, the better for us all.'

'And Lobengula?' Martingell asked.

'He has a monument. I should point out that he did not die in battle.'

'But of a broken heart no doubt. Although he knew what was coming. Well, gentlemen, I am sure you are satisfied with our progress. And your prowess. I have a ship to catch.' He looked through the open window of the office over the rooftops and church spires of Cape Town and the broad expanse of Table Bay, dotted with both sailing and steamships.

'Bound for where?' Rudd inquired. He had invited the hunter to visit him, and knew that Martingell would not leave without learning the reason.

'My brother's business in Beira,' Martingell explained.

'Shipping arms,' Jameson said.

'Dry goods, Dr Jameson.'

'But you still go into the interior?'

Martingell shrugged. 'I'm a salesman.'

'Dammit, man, be straight,' Rudd said. 'You're a scout and a prospector. And I will say this, you are the best damned scout I have ever come across. As for prospecting, we're in Rhodesia because of what you found there.'

Martingell raised his eyebrows. 'Rhodesia?'

Rudd flushed. 'Well, it's a name we talk of. Appropriate, wouldn't you say?'

'No doubt. Although I have never heard of a vast country being named after the prime minister of another country.'

'There are great things afoot,' Jameson said, showing signs of impatience. 'Your, ah, travels take you across the Vaal, do they not, Mr Martingell?'

'Aye, doctor, they do.'

'Then you know the people there.'

'Some. The ones you once described to me as ignorant farmers.'

'And the land?' Rudd put in.

'I would say so.' Martingell frowned. 'I hope you're not thinking that President Kruger is as easily confounded as King Lobengula? Or that his people are that unacquainted with rifles. Your average Boer farmer, be he sixteen or sixty, can shoot the eye out of a monkey at a hundred yards with a modern weapon. And they all have modern weapons.'

'You deal in enormities, Martingell,' Rudd said. 'If you travel in and out of the Transvaal, then you know the plight of the Uitlanders.'

'I would not call it a plight, Mr Rudd.'

'Dammit, man, they are deprived of all political power, and in many cases are treated as second-class citizens.'

'Mr Rudd, those people, whether they have come from Manchester or London, have gone to Johannesburg for but one reason: to find gold and become rich. Good luck to them. But the fact remains that they are uninvited strangers in another man's land, that there are a great number of them, who thereby are straining the infrastructure of the Transvaal state, and who, if they were allowed to vote, would probably overthrow the present government.'

'That is called democracy, Martingell.'

'I have observed that the meaning of democracy is usually as interpreted by the party in power. May I ask you gentlemen what the British reaction would be if, for instance, gold in huge quantities was suddenly discovered in Wiltshire, and Frenchmen and Germans and Dutchmen and Russians flocked to England in their millions and then demanded the right to vote in British elections?'

'Hypothesis,' Rudd commented.

'Gentlemen,' Jameson said. 'Arguing the rights and wrongs of the case is pointless. *Civis romanus sum*, Martingell. Those people are British citizens. They are in need of protection. Are you going to say they should not have it?'

Martingell frowned. 'You mean the British Government is about to take action?'

Rudd snorted. 'They won't, and there's the truth.'

'But Mr Rhodes will.'

Rudd and Jameson exchanged glances. 'Mr Rhodes knows nothing of our plan,' Rudd said.

If you expect me to believe that, Martingell thought, you must take me for a fool.

'I take it you are a man of your word?' Jameson asked.

'I always have been, doctor.'

'Then you'll understand that every word spoken here today is confidential. This is one of those cases where it is necessary to seize time and opportunity by the forelock, as it were. There are some 40,000 Uitlanders, mainly British, in and around Johannesburg. They are in a desperate situation, whether you care to acknowledge it or not. We regard it as our duty to assist them.'

'We?' Martingell asked, softly.

'Myself, Mr Rudd, and a group of like-minded patriots. We know that neither the British Government nor the Government of Cape Colony can take overt action. That would be an act of war. But if the

Uitlanders, foreigners, were to refuse to be browbeaten by Kruger's thugs any longer, and rise up in revolt, then our various governments would have to support them; no government in Westminster would last five minutes if it was learned that British men were being murdered and nothing was being done about it.'

'Even if these same men had in the first place provoked a civil war?'

'Once it's begun, the circumstances of its origins will become meaningless. Now, the Uitlanders are on the boil; we have communicated with their leaders. But they are also, understandably, afraid of the possible consequences should they act and fail. They wish a sign that they will be supported. It is our intention to give them that sign.'

'You intend to invade the Transvaal? Without anyone knowing?'

'No one knows our plan, outside of a handful of dedicated men. In which you are now included, Martingell.'

'And I assume you have an army standing by, not knowing where they are going or who they are going to fight.'

'We have damn near 500 men who will follow us to the gates of hell,' Rudd declared. 'Every man an expert shot.' He grinned. 'And they have well over a hundred rounds each, as well as Maxims.'

'And you're not likely to be opposed by more than 70,000 Boers. Who are also all sharpshooters.'

'Oh, come now, Martingell. There is no Boer army.'

'That is because the nation is the army, Mr Rudd. You'll be poking your finger into a wasps' nest.'

'The Boers have no proper command structure, no military plans,' Jameson asserted. 'Forget Majuba Hill, Martingell. We've been through all that. Colley's people were inadequately armed, they were fighting over country they did not know and did not understand, in red jackets and white topees and, frankly, they were poorly led. We have 500 men who know the country and the conditions, who will wear khaki and, if I say so myself, they will be well led. Because we know our objectives, sir. And our limitations. We know we cannot take on the Boers once they have been allowed the time to mobilise themselves. It is not our intention to give them that time. We cross the frontier, and we ride like the devil for Johannesburg. Three days, sir. Three days. When we get there, the Uitlanders will rise with our support. Johannesburg will be in our hands before Kruger can draw his breath.'

'And then?'

'The Uitlander leaders will put forward

their demands, which will necessarily be accepted, and we will withdraw. There, sir.'

'And my part? You surely do not require a guide for such a venture.'

'We need arms for the Uitlanders. You and your brother import arms through Beira and sell them to the blacks. Don't attempt to deny it, man. What we wish you to do is ship arms down the coast to Delagoa Bay and disembark them at Lourenco Marques. From Lourenco Marques the Portuguese railway runs to Pretoria and thence Johannesburg. But we're not asking you to leave Portuguese territory for more than an hour. At Komati Poort you'll be met by interested parties who will complete the payment and take over the shipment. All you have to do is return to Beira.'

'Complete the payment?'

'There'll be half down, as soon as you agree, and half on delivery.'

'Of what, exactly?'

Jameson picked up a sheaf of papers from the table and held them out. Martingell riffled through them and blew a soft whistle. 'We're talking of a quarter of a million.'

Jameson nodded. 'That's our costing.'

'You gentlemen have that kind of money?'

'We can obtain it. Will you do it?'

Will I start a revolution? Martingell wondered. Cause people, perhaps innocent people, to be killed. Perhaps destroy a country. He was a pragmatist. His family had been bankrupted in England when dealing in horses. His brother William had fled the country with his teenage sibling and what little they possessed, to seek their fortunes in Africa. They had soon recognised that while fortunes *were* to be made in Cape Colony, they would not be made by an undischarged bankrupt, unless they happened to stumble across a diamond mine, and these were less easy to come by than was supposed by the British press. Portuguese East had been a better proposition.

And they had prospered. Portuguese colonial rule was lax. White men came and went into the interior and returned without questions being asked. They had begun selling rubbish to the Africans north of the Zambesi, but soon realised they would do better with guns. Then they had prospered even more. William Martingell was now a wealthy and highly respected man in Beira. He had so far turned his back on the Britain that had rejected him as to marry a Portugese wife, and was a father three times over. His younger brother had always been, and remained, a more restless personality. James Martingell prided himself that his forays into the bush, both as salesman and prospector, had fuelled the family wealth. That one African tribe might, indeed would, use their new weapons to conquer another African tribe had not concerned them a whit. They had never anticipated that the white man's insatiable lust for precious metals would take them north of the great river; the Boers of the Orange Free State and the Transvaal had always been farmers and nothing more. Now they were about to suffer the fate of the Africans they despised. Martingell had no love for the Boers. He disliked their treatment of their African subjects. But that they were a proud, courageous, intransigent people was proved by their history, by their very survival in the midst of so much antagonism.

'Well?' Jameson demanded. 'By my reckoning you'll clear not less than ten per cent.'

Martingell nodded. 'You'll understand I must obtain the agreement of my brother.'

'Do that,' Rudd said.

'But don't take too long,' Jameson recommended. 'We want those guns by the beginning of November.'

'Six months?' Martingell mused. 'Tight.'

'Can you do it?'

'Oh, we can do it. The moment Will agrees we'll put the order in hand. But we'll need the purchase money.'

'You shall have it by wire,' Rudd promised. 'The moment you let us know you are going ahead.'

'Well, then, gentlemen, I'd best catch that ship,' Martingell said.

'Shake on it,' Rudd invited.

Martingell hesitated, then clasped the proffered fingers.

'You've sworn secrecy,' Jameson said, also shaking hands.

'I'll keep my word, doctor. I always do.'

'Well,' Jameson said, 'you could look a little more happy about it, Mr Martingell. You'll be making a fortune.'

'I think what you're planning is criminal, Dr Jameson. But ...' Martingell shrugged. 'There's a profit.'

Beira was a new town, founded only four years earlier, although on the site of an older Arab city. The Portuguese, in the person of Vasco da Gama, had first touched this coast in 1498, but penetration had been slow; the Portuguese had been more interested in the huge tract of land known as Angola, on the west side of the continent, from whence slaves could easily be obtained and then transported to Brazil. The tribes on the east side of the continent were more warlike and had farther to travel, as slaves.

Thus Beira, if the first real indication that the Portuguese were here to stay, remained very much a frontier, for all that it was also a seaport, flanked by sandy beaches. Because no one really knew what they were talking about when they spoke of Portuguese East. The mapmakers in Lisbon, who had attended the various international gatherings engaged in dividing Africa, had naturally laid claim to as much territory as possible, stretching their boundaries to the borders of the Transvaal and Matabeleland, or Rhodesia, Martingell supposed it should now be called, in the south, and to an indeterminate distance in the north until it become an adjunct to the equally vague German claim bordering the great lakes. But not even James Martingell really knew what lay out there. There had never been any organised exploration, much less penetration or establishment. The Portuguese authorities were more interested in the railways they had carved through the jungle to reach the landbound states of the interior, and of these the Boer state of the Transvaal was the most important. The Boers had to have access to the sea, and they preferred that it should be through Portuguese territory rather than

British. The railway meant money for the government.

Thus it had been left to individuals, of whatever nationality, to make their way through the vast forests to the north-west. James Martingell had been one of the first, just as he and his brother had been one of the first companies set up in Beira itself. They had prospered, but never yet to the extent that was now promised. William Martingell whistled as he read the list. 'This is big time, James. I doubt we can do it.'

'I'm thinking of Count Adolf von Beinhardt,' James said. 'We've been good customers of his for four years now.'

'Fifty rifles a time,' William pointed out.

'So, now we want quantity. He's a businessman. Chances like this don't come very often, Will.'

William Martingell continued to stroke his chin. Seven years the elder, he was a shorter, more stocky version of the family. He also carried the burden of the family guilt in that it had been his careless speculation that had bankrupted the firm in England, driven his father to suicide and his mother to an early grave. He had always felt protective to his little brother, even as he had recognised over the past few years that of all the men in the world James

Martingell least needed protecting. 'I think one of us should go to Cologne,' James said. 'This is a man-to-man business. And time is short.'

William was nodding, slowly. 'And France. Creuzot guns. My God, is the man thinking of starting a war?'

'Aye,' James said. 'I have a notion that is just what he's thinking of starting.'

They lunched in the open air, behind the house, shaded by enormous umbrellas from the heat of the noonday sun; it was considerably warmer in Beira than in Cape Town, or even the highlands of Rhodesia; the afternoon sea breeze was blowing in from the Indian Ocean, but it was a hot breeze. 'Willi tells me you are only staying a few days,' Maria Martingell remarked, slapping the hand of her eldest child, a four-year-old terror named Joachim.

'Business,' James explained. 'I need to go to Germany.'

'I should love to visit Germany,' Catherine said, and flushed as she dropped her head to study her plate.

William winked, and Maria patted her sister's hand. 'So you shall, one of these fine days.' She gave James a hard look.

James was well aware that it was Maria's dearest wish to tie the family entirely together by having him marry her sister.

He was also aware that Will thought it might be a good idea. But it was not *his* idea. Catherine was pretty enough, in a mousy fashion, with straggling brown hair and a poor complexion, and she had the full figure of most Portuguese women. But he felt they were too close to the Delgados already. He knew just how much they owed Antonio Delgado. When they had been penniless refugees in Lisbon, Antonio Delgado had befriended them. Just appointed Captain of the port in Beira, then being built, he had invited the two young Englishmen to accompany him and seek their fortunes under his aegis.

By then Will had already been interested in Maria, and in fact they had been married in Lisbon before departing; by the time they had reached Mozambique Maria was pregnant. In 1891 Catherine had been just fifteen, and not yet in the marriage stakes. Now she was very marriageable indeed, but acceptable husbands were thin on the ground—except for the remaining Martingell. But there was more than freedom in it for James. Almost from the day they had set foot on this soil he had explored, encouraged by both his brother and the Delgados, seeking new markets, new people, perhaps even new frontiers. It was the twelve years that he had spent, travelling with a single servant, far beyond even the supposed borders of Mozambique, penetrating through the Transvaal into Matabeleland and even north into the Congo, that had made him so valuable to the South Africa Company. Just as it was the gold he had found in Matabeleland that had drawn Rhodes' attention to the country, and brought about the horrible crime of the virtual destruction of a people.

James felt only a modicum of guilt about the Matabele War. He had been given a job of work to do, and he had done it, without fear or favour. He had warned Lobengula of what he was risking, just as he had told Rudd of the crime he was contemplating. He had gained a reputation for honesty and plain speaking, among natives as well as white men. Which was why Jameson was now trusting him with his plans for his wild scheme. But James remained a man. One does not wander through the bush, virtually alone, for twelve years, and merely eat, drink, wash and sleep, when not walking. Women had certainly been available, the African concept of morality being different to the European. But the fact remained that he had never slept with a white woman. It was not something to be contemplated lightly, especially where the horrors of the marriage bed (as perpetrated by a white man who was all but an African himself, on a white girl who was presumably as virginal, in mind and body, as all proper white girls), could be so quickly and devastatingly revealed to a sister who was also a sister-in-law. 'Visit Germany?' He smiled. 'Of course you shall, Catherine. When you are older.'

'Mausers?' Count von Beinhardt stroked his chin. It was a large chin, in keeping with his large nose, the pair separated by an even larger moustache with waxed ends. 'Five thousand Mauser rifles? This is an army for whom you are working?'

'I am working for a man who wishes to form an army,' James said.

He was nervous, and had been smoking very quickly, as Beinhardt had observed. Now he pushed the box of Havanas across the huge, ornate desk. The desk fitted the office, which was as large as the Martingell house in Beira, and high ceilinged, with portraits of past Beinhardts to either side, the whole dominated by the huge painting of the Kaiser on the wall behind the desk. He was wearing uniform, his withered left arm as always carefully disguised, staring out across the room in a perpetual challenge to the world. James clipped the end of a second cigar, lit it. Beinhardt was completing the reading of the list. 'I must ask on whose behalf you are making this purchase,' he said.

'And I cannot tell you, Herr Count.'

Beinhardt raised his head to gaze at him.

'However, if it will put your mind at rest,' James said, 'I can assure you that they are not to be sold to any African chieftain or king, adjacent to German East Africa.'

'That would indeed reassure me.' Beinhardt got up, walked to the huge map of Africa that occupied part of one wall, and studied it for several seconds. 'It will reassure our people in Dar-es-Salaam even more.' He continued to study the map, and James knew he was making some calculations. The Transvaal Boers used Mauser rifles, but they had no need to import them clandestinely by means of a sub-agent. The British in Cape Colony and Natal were armed with Martini-Henrys, but they too merely needed to place an order, openly and above board. The same went for such Portuguese troops as there were in Mozambique. 'You give me your word on this?'

'Willingly,' James said.

'Then your order will be filled. As this is to be a clandestine operation ...' he paused, but as James did not comment, continued. 'I suppose you require cover?'

'Farm implements,' James said.

Beinhardt nodded. 'I need to inquire about financing.'

'Present your bill, and if the goods are to standard, as I know they will be, Herr Count, you will be paid in full. I have letters of credit to certain bankers who will be known to you.'

'And you and your brother will become wealthy men. I congratulate you.' Beinhardt returned behind his desk and sat down, carefully folding the tails of his frock coat across his lap. 'Where from here, eh? You will, at a stroke, become the biggest arms dealer in Africa.'

'I'm afraid this is a one-off,' James said. 'I doubt it will ever be repeated.'

'There are only so many private wars to be fought, eh? Even in Africa. Nonetheless, I am sure your feet are now set on an always ascending ladder.' He tapped the list. 'It will take a month to assemble this. Will you remain here in Cologne?'

'I have business in France. But I will be back in three weeks time.'

'Capital. Three weeks ...' Beinhardt turned the pages of a gold-bound desk diary. 'June 6. Yes. Why do you not come to dinner.' James had never been invited to Beinhardt's house before. But buy enough, and one is acceptable anywhere. 'White tie,' Beinhardt said.

Adolf von Beinhardt's house was merely an extension of his office, in size, in appointments, in sheer grandeur. It was set in Bavarian parkland and occupied several hundred acres. Reached by a winding drive between rows of poplars it glowed with light and heat and excitement. James reckoned he was the only non-German guest, and found himself in the midst of a black-suited minority among the glittering uniforms of the soldiers and the gleaming bare shoulders of the women, hair universally upswept into overhanging pompadours, *décolletages*, fingers and ears dripping with brilliants. But even if his suit had hastily been made for him in Paris—he did not normally mingle with the aristocracy of Europe—he was very much an honoured guest, greeted warmly by Beinhardt himself, introduced to his wife and two daughters, and then to everyone of importance in the room, while at table he found himself on his hostess's right, and on the left of the eldest of the daughters, Cecile von Beinhardt.

'Papa has been telling me of you,' she said, sipping wine. She was, he estimated, about twenty, taller than average and with glowing auburn hair inherited from her mother. Her features were small, her bone structure delicate, but her figure

40

was attractively full.

'Nothing bad, I hope,' James replied in his best German, which was quite acceptable, as he had been dealing with Beinhardt for several years.

'So romantic,' she said, with a slightly condescending smile. 'Walking through the African bush, all by yourself.'

'Never by myself, Fräulein. I always have a servant.'

'Hardly company,' she suggested.

'True enough. I have tried teaching him to play chess, but he prefers poker.'

'Don't we all!' she remarked, surprisingly. 'And now you are rushing back to Africa?'

'I'm afraid so, as soon as I have taken delivery of some goods from your father.'

Now she turned her head to gaze at him. Of course she had to be aware that her father was an arms dealer, and thus any goods he might sell would have to be arms. 'To South Africa ...' she mused.

'To Portuguese East Africa,' he corrected.

'I think you must live a very interesting life, Herr Martingell. You are staying in Cologne?'

'For the next three days.'

'I go riding in the park most mornings. I shall be there tomorrow. I should be pleased to continue our conversation.'

Well, well! he thought. 'I shall be there too, Fräulein,' he said. She smiled, briefly, and turned to engage the man on her right in conversation.

To James' disappointment, Cecile was accompanied both by her younger sister, Clementine, and by two grooms. But what had he expected? Cecile von Beinhardt was most definitely a lady. 'Is not spring the best time of the year, Herr Martingell?' she asked. 'Do you have good springs in Africa?'

'We have nothing that can really be called spring,' James said. 'Certainly in Portuguese East. But then we have nothing that can properly be called winter, either. Just a wet season and a dry season.'

'It sounds very boring.' They galloped for a few minutes, then reined their steaming horses, panting themselves. 'Why do you live there? I mean, you are not Portuguese.' She glanced at him but the pink in her cheeks was surely just exertion. 'Or am I being impossibly inquisitive?'

'Not at all. I live there because my brother and I have an import-export business in Beira.'

'The Portuguese do not mind this?'

'Not in the least. Besides, my brother is married to a Portuguese.'

'Ah,' she said. 'Yet I sense a mystery.

Oh, forgive me, I shall not probe further. Shall we have another gallop?'

Was she interested in him? James wondered. Or had her father set her to find out something about his background, in view of the scale on which they were suddenly doing business? But despite Beinhardt's considerations of the future, James knew this *was* a one-off, if Jameson's plans were successful, he would have no further need to order weapons clandestinely. If they were unsuccessful ... he would not be in a position to. Meanwhile, he stood beside William as his brother carefully ticked off each item. They were requiring the use of two box cars, and William had travelled down to Lourenco Marques to see the cargo being unloaded from the ship and back on to the railway. 'I do not think I have ever seen so many guns in one place at one time,' he remarked.

'Nor will you have ever seen so much profit as when we are paid by the Uitlanders,' James pointed out.

'Yes,' William said thoughtfully. He was a pessimistic man, but the down payment had been made promptly and without question. 'Are you satisfied, Antonio?'

Delgado had also come down the coast to see the goods for himself. 'I'll be happier when you return with your profit, James,' the Portuguese commented. 'The thought of these guns falling into the wrong hands quite disturbs me.'

'No one knows they are here, except us three,' James reminded him.

'And a few Germans, to be sure. Well, God speed!'

The train was puffing, the guard was waving his flag. James stepped aboard, and they pulled out of the station, leaving William and Antonio waving on the platform. Once they were out of sight, James made his way forward to sit with Msamli, his servant, and the two other Africans who worked for the Martingells and were there to oversee the shipment. But like everyone else, to them this was farm machinery bound for Pretoria, as was indicated by the manifest; the top layer in each car was indeed farm implements. It was just over 50 miles to the Transvaal border, and Komati Poort, but progress was slow, as the thickly forested land slowly rose from the coast, and as the train stopped often enough to put down or pick up passengers. It was nearly dusk when they at last pulled into the frontier town.

It had been a steaming hot day and, as the train would not be returning to the coast until the next morning, James looked forward to getting to the one hotel the little town offered and having a bath. But first he had to find his Uitlander customers. The station was as usual crowded, the arrival of the train from the coast promising new goods for the shops, newspapers and mail, indications of what might be happening in the outside world. There were as always customs officials, but these were disinterested. As James had anticipated, they wanted to inspect the manifest and asked for one of the boxes to the opened, to turn over the rows of hoes inside.

The customs officer wandered off again, while James supervised the unloading, wondering where his clients were. He had no idea whether they intended to reload the gear on to the Transvaal train waiting in a siding—which seemed unlikely—or whether they meant to take them off into the interior by wagon. There were certainly more wagons than usual waiting in the yard behind the station. But where were the clients? Suddenly he had uneasy vibrations. He couldn't believe that Jameson and Rudd had spent all that money without meaning to fulfil their part of the bargain, or that the Uitlanders who were in the plot would not also wish to complete the deal. For them not to be here …

The cargo was now fully unloaded. And he saw three men leave the wagons and walk across the yard to the steps leading up to the platform. Relief flooded his system. Then Msamli muttered, 'Boss!'

James turned his head sharply, and saw six more men standing on the other side of the track. These men were armed. He swung back again, as the first three men reached the steps. On a trip like this, James carried no weapon, but his revolver was in his attaché case. He reached for it, and was checked by the man nearest to him.

'Don't do that, Mr Martingell. I am Commandant Steen,' the man said. From his accent as well as his brick red colouring and the sandy hair that seeped out from beneath his flat hat, James had already deduced that he was a Boer. 'And you are James Martingell, are you not?'

'I am he,' James acknowledged.

'I have to tell you, Mr Martingell, that the men who were supposed to meet you are under arrest. As are you, now,' Steen went on. 'Together with your boys.'

'On what charge?' James demanded.

'Smuggling arms, Mr Martingell. It is a very serious offence.'

Chapter Two

The Victim

'Wake up,' the man said. James stretched, and disturbed the cockroach which had been inspecting him; it scurried over the side of the cot and on to the floor. 'Breakfast,' the gaoler said.

A woman was standing in the doorway with a tray. Woman? She was hardly more than a girl, and James could tell at a glance that she was a mulatto. 'No need to rise,' the gaoler said. 'Martha don't know no gentlemen, save in bed.' He guffawed.

The girl's brown cheeks were pale enough to show her flush. She had aquiline features and lank black hair which hung in a wiry profusion past her thighs. She seemed to be wearing a single chemise-like garment, and her feet were bare. Her figure was full, although he did not not think she was a day over sixteen. She placed the tray on the floor beside the bed, then stamped with her bare foot on the first cockroach that would have attacked the food. 'You better eat quick,' she said, in English.

He was certainly hungry, although more

47

thirsty, and gulped at the mug of coffee, nearly scalding his mouth. The girl withdrew to the far side of the cell, but remained there, watching him. 'The commandant wishes to see you,' the guard said, standing in the doorway, arms folded, revolver holster exposed.

'I'm looking forward to that,' James agreed, while he tried to think who could have betrayed them.

The commandant's office was across the compound. 'Sit down, Mr Martingell,' Steen invited. 'I hope you are well?'

'I'd be better for a bath,' James said.

Steen's smile was cold. 'You could be having one within the hour. Just tell me who those guns were for.'

'I have no idea. My instructions were to deliver them to the border.'

'Five thousand modern rifles, 300 revolvers, four Maxim guns, two dismantled Creuzot breech-loaders, ammunition, cordite ...' Steen flicked the pages on his desk. 'My men have been up all night making out this list. You knew what was in your cargo, Mr Martingell. Apart from the farm machinery, I mean.'

There would be no point in lying. 'Yes, I did.'

'So, you conduct enough weapons to start a small war to our border without knowing to whom they were to be delivered?'

'I was to be met by agents of the principal, who would take delivery and complete the payment.'

'Then tell me the name of the principal.'

'I am not in a position to tell you that, Herr Steen.'

Steen gazed at him for several seconds. 'I think you need to understand your position, Mr Martingell,' he said. 'You are, as I understand it, an Englishman for whom England no longer has any use. Therefore you operate out of Mozambique, with the connivance of the Portuguese authorities, certainly, but do you really suppose they give a damn whether you live or die? You have no consul to whom you may appeal for help. You are a will-of-the-wisp, wandering across the face of southern Africa. Oh, we have had our eye on you for some time, Mr Martingell. Will-of-the-wisps are often visible for short periods, then they disappear and are never seen again.'

'I think you may find that the Portuguese are more interested in me than you suppose, Herr Steen,' James said, more in an effort to maintain his confidence than because he actually believed it. 'They will certainly find out where I am, as will my brother.'

'Correction, Mr Martingell. They will find out where you have *been*. But where you will *be,* when they find that out, will be another matter altogether. It is a question to which you hold the answer. Tell me the name of the man who financed the buying of these guns, and you can be on a train back to Lourenco Marques tomorrow morning.'

'You expect me to believe that?'

Steen gave another cold smile. 'You had better believe it, Mr Martingell, because if you do not, then the future is grim indeed. His name?'

'I am not in a position to give you that,' James repeated.

'You are serving very little purpose,' Steen pointed out. 'And doing yourself more than a grave disservice. Those guns can only have been meant for some of the more discontented Uitlanders. Now there are a great number of these people. Many are discontented, others are not. We know this, but we do not possess actual names and identifications. The importation of sufficient weaponry to start a revolution is a serious matter. We intend to take it seriously. That means that life may now become very hard for *all* the Uitlanders, many of whom have their wives and children with them. Whereas, if it became possible for us to identify the dangerous

50

troublemakers, the men who paid for your shipment, Mr Martingell, we could deal with them, and allow the rest of their people to continue an untroubled existence. Surely that makes sense to you?'

'My business exists on confidentiality,' James said.

Steen sighed. 'Senseless,' he said. 'Do you know, Mr Martingell, I can send you outside to my people and have them beat you to a pulp. No one would ever know, no one would ever care. If you died, it would have been in attempting to escape. Do you really wish me to do that?'

'Of course I do not,' James said, feeling tension creeping over his body.

'But you will not reconsider your position?'

'I cannot.'

'Very well. However, at the moment I am not going to beat you up, Mr Martingell. I am going to give you a little time to reflect. In the meantime, papers will be prepared for your prosecution as an arms smuggler. This is what you need to reflect upon. If you are brought to trial, there can be no doubt that you will be found guilty, in which case you will be sentenced to a long term of imprisonment in one of our more remote and severe establishments. Places where we send our black rapists and murderers, men who would love to

51

have a handsome young white man as permanent company. Think about that, Mr Martingell. Take him back,' he told his sergeant.

'I wish to know what has happened to my people,' James said.

'They have already been dealt with.'

'Just what do you mean by that?'

'What I have said, Mr Martingell. They are no longer in Komati Poort.'

James Martingell would not have survived for as long as fourteen years, over periods of extreme stress and considerable danger, had he not been an optimist who faced every crisis by first counting his assets, and only then worrying about his liabilities. But assets on this occasion were hard to discover as he lay on his cot and stared at the low ceiling, and occasionally flicked a cockroach away from his chest. He felt sick at the thought that Msamli and the other two might already have been executed, or at least already confined to that hell with which he had been threatened. While he ...

Of course, William and Antonio would know what had happened by now; news travelled through the bush faster than by any telegraph system yet invented. But if that was an asset he did not know how it was going to help him. The Portuguese had a certain clout with the Boers, as the Transvaalers depended upon the Portuguese railway for the importation of most of their goods, as well as for the export of their saleable produce. But as Steen had pointed out, it was extremely unlikely that the Governor in Beira would make an international incident out of an illegal arms dealer being held on the frontier, especially as the arms dealer in question was not even Portuguese. Antonio's influence did not extend that far. Nor would William dare bring Jameson and Rudd into it. He knew as much as James that it would mean the end of any further business with South Africa.

What, then, was left? Beinhardt had been paid for his arms, therefore he had no further interest in the affair. And Jameson would simply have to write off his money. If any good came out of the whole miserable business, it would lie in the cancellation of the mad scheme to raise the Uitlanders and seize the Transvaal. But it would probably also involve several of the Uitlander leaders being shot, guilty or innocent. The only salvation he could see would be to get out of this cell, certainly before he was transferred to Pretoria or Johannesburg for trial. But it seemed almost impossible, simply because it was not a prison. It was a cell in a police compound; between himself and the open air there was an office always occupied by two armed guards. He would need help. A great deal of help. So where would he find that?

There was only one possible source. Martha visited him twice a day, with his food and drink. She seldom spoke, showed no interest in him; there were several other men in these police cells, awaiting trial—he saw them when he was exercised, although he never had the opportunity to speak to them. As for Martha, as he daily grew more filthy and his beard sprouted, he did not blame her for her lack of interest. But as the days drifted by, and he showed no tendency to violence, she began to come unaccompanied by a guard, although the guards were never far off.

But in the cell, they were alone, while she waited for him to finish his meal. 'Do they beat you?' he asked.

She had been studying the floor, seeking cockroaches to stamp on. Now she raised her head, sharply. 'What is that to you?'

'I just wonder why you put up with it.'

She gazed at him for several seconds, then she said. 'Eat your food.'

But he had made a point of contact, to which he returned the next day. 'Tell me about yourself,' he invited.

'Why?'

'Because I'm interested. I'm an educated

man, Martha. Try to imagine what it is like, lying here, day after day, with nothing to read, nothing to do, nothing to think about ... except you.'

Another long stare. Then she asked, 'You want to have sex with me? You have money?'

'They took all my money.'

She shrugged, and picked up his empty plate.

'But I could still make it worth your while.'

'How?' She actually smiled. 'You got extra big long one?'

He doubted he did, to her satisfaction. 'Do you have a mother and a father?' he asked.

'Everyone has mother and father,' she pointed out.

'I mean, are they about? In Komati Poort?'

'Daddy went off, long ago. I didn't see him.'

'But you know of him?'

'He was a white man, name of Alexander.' A shadow crossed her face; white men were obviously not her favourite people, except perhaps as clients.

'Would that have been a surname, or a given name?'

'Mummy always said she was Mrs Alexander.'

'Sounds Scottish,' James mused. 'And your mother?'

'She died four years gone. She coughed blood.'

'I'm sorry. You've had a rough time.'

Martha went to the door. 'I'm alive,' she said.

But he had her interest. The next day, she asked, 'How can you make it good for me, if you have no money?'

'Is that all that is important to you? What about the sex itself?' She seemed to ripple, from head to toe. 'You don't like that, eh? All right. What about being free of this place? Wouldn't you like that?' he asked. 'If I were free, I would take you to Portuguese East, find you a job. No sex, unless you wanted it. Good food. And freedom.'

'How can you do this?' she asked. 'You are in a cell.' She grinned. 'Then you go prison. For ever and ever.'

'Well,' he said, 'I could do it if I were no longer a prisoner.'

Her tongue came out and circled her lips, slowly. 'They would take the skin from my bones before they hanged me,' she said.

'Only if they caught you. The border is only a mile away.'

'The border,' she said scornfully. 'They

cross the border whenever they wish. Chasing runaways. They always bring them back.'

'No runaway from here knows the bush like I do,' James told her. 'We would not be caught.' She almost fled from the cell. Would she split? Somehow he didn't think so. But to his alarm she did not come back the next day, and he was served by a black boy, who did not speak English. 'Where is Martha?' he asked in his best Afrikaans.

'Martha sick,' the boy said.

Was she really sick? Or had she let slip what they had spoken of, and been locked up herself? Yet his own treatment did not vary. Then one morning, a month after his arrest, his door was thrown open and Steen stood there. 'Well, Herr Martingell,' the commandant said. 'Your friends have shown their hand.' James sat up. 'Three days ago, a body of 500 armed horsemen, commanded by Dr Leander Starr Jameson, crossed the Transvaal border, riding for Johannesburg. You know this man, Jameson?'

'We have met,' James said, cautiously.

'As you wish. His object was to rouse the Uitlanders into rebellion against the State of Transvaal. That is an act of war, Herr Martingell.'

'Then we are at war?' James could not believe his ears.

Steen chuckled. 'No, no! Only 500 men? Besides, we knew they were coming. They have been rounded up and are all under arrest. Including Dr Jameson.'

James swallowed. But hadn't he told Jameson it was a mad idea? 'And the Uitlanders?'

'The people to whom you were to supply guns? They did not move, Herr Martingell. Perhaps your failure ruined their ardour. Perhaps they just had more sense.'

'What will happen to Jameson and his people?'

'They claim to be prisoners-of-war. But their action has been disavowed by both the Cape Colony and the government in England. That makes them plain outlaws. We hang outlaws.'

'All five hundred men?'

Steen grinned. 'However many there are, actually. Plus one. You, Herr Martingell. You are one of them.'

The next day, to his great relief, Martha returned. 'They are going to hang you,' she said. 'They are going to take you from here tomorrow, to Johannesburg, and there you will be put on trial with the others.'

'And bang goes your chance to get out of this hell,' he said, with more levity than he felt.

She treated him to one of her long stares,

then glanced through the open door. But the guard was no longer even close. 'You will take me away, and take care of me?' she asked in a low voice.

'For ever and ever,' James said, meaning every word.

'You will not beat me?'

'Never.'

'You will marry me?'

'Ah ...' but now was not the moment to temporise. 'If that is what you wish.'

'You promise these things? You swear, by God?'

'I swear by God,' he said.

'You will kill for us?'

'If I have to.'

'Tonight.' She picked up the tray and his empty plate and left.

What have I done? James asked himself, as he lay on his cot and stared at the ceiling. But what else could I do? He thought it extremely likely that Jameson and his people would be bought out; however much he might deny complicity, Rhodes had to be involved, and friendship apart, he could not risk any last-minute confessions. But that did not apply to him. He had no friends in Cape Colony, and he had no friends in England. And the Boers would want their sacrificial lamb. But the escape! You will kill for us? How casual the question. The woman to whom he had volunteered to tie his life. A far cry indeed from Cecile von Beinhardt, in her satin and perfume; he did not suppose Martha had ever eaten with a knife and fork in her life, or used a napkin.

But he was answerable to no man, save William. And William would understand. He grinned. He was not so sure about Maria, while Catherine ... How slowly the hours passed, while the cell seemed to get hotter every moment. That was the blood pounding through his arteries, making his brain clamour for something to happen. He had no watch, but had a fairly good idea of what time of day it was from the shadows outside the barred window. His evening meal usually came about five, an hour before dusk. But the evening steadily drew in, and it was all but dark when at last he heard the guard say, 'What kept you?'

'There was a problem in the kitchen,' Martha said. 'The food was spoiled.'

'I reckon it was good enough for him,' the guard said, and unlocked the door. It swung in and Martha entered, carrying her usual tray. And this time the guard came in with her.

Martha set the tray before James. 'It must be eaten, now,' she said, and lifted the cover.

Both the guard and James saw the

revolver lying on the plate at the same time. But it was James who picked it up and levelled it. 'Speak and I'll blow your brains out.'

The guard hesitated, and Martha snatched his own pistol from its holster, at the same time pushing the door to. Then she drew the knife from the guard's sheath. 'God have mercy,' he muttered.

'No,' James said.

Martha glanced at him. 'He will give the alarm. You said you would kill for us.'

'Not in cold blood. Come here and lie down, Fritzie,' he commanded.

The guard crossed the room; he was very frightened and sweat rolled out of his hair. James made him lie on the cot and bound his wrists and ankles together in the small of his back, using his own belts. Then he gagged the man with his socks, tying them into place with his handkerchief. Lastly he tore the blanket into strips and with it secured the guard to the bed. Martha watched with glowing eyes; undoubtedly she felt that her solution would have been far simpler, and far safer too. James wondered if Fritzie had been one of her clients. 'Lead,' he told her, taking Fritzie's Mauser pistol from her hand and thrusting it into his belt, while keeping the revolver in his hand. At least he could go down fighting.

Martha cautiously opened the door, nodded, and stepped into the lobby. She held up one finger as she approached the door to the office. As there had been virtually no noise, there was no reaction from the other cells. James nodded; it was now dark outside. In the office a lantern glowed. 'What kept you?' the other guard asked as Martha stepped into the room.

'Fritzie wanted to talk with the prisoner,' she said.

'What's he saying?' The guard swung his chair round from the desk, and gazed into the muzzle of James' revolver. 'Jesus!' he muttered.

'Lie down on the floor,' James said. 'Keep an eye on the door, Martha.'

It took only five minutes to truss the guard as securely as Fritzie, and now James had two Mauser pistols, as well as a cartridge belt, to add to his revolver. 'Give me one,' Martha suggested.

'Later.' He had a suspicion that she might be trigger happy. He put on the cartridge belt and took the guard's cap. Thus equipped he would look sufficiently like a guard, in the dark and from a distance. 'Ready?' Martha nodded, and opened the outer door. James followed her into the night.

It was a perfectly straightforward business

to cross the compound to the wire fence and to get through it; it was neither barbed nor electrified. But it was intended to keep stray animals out, not people in; the Boers were protected to a large extent by their reputation for ferocious response to any criminal acts. Once through the fence, they were on the edge of the little town, with the forest only a few feet away. The border was not defined, save by the customs post at the railway station, and so they made their way through the trees as rapidly as they could, going downhill as in the forest it was difficult to see the sky and so discern their direction; it was basically downhill all the way to the coast.

Branches clutched at their clothes and hair, thorns scraped their arms, but they knew they had to hurry, and indeed they had only been on their way half-an-hour when they heard the sound of a whistle behind them, followed immediately by the barking of dogs. Martha stopped to look at James: she would not say it, but she counted them lost because of his humanity—they could not outrun the dogs. 'Water,' he said.

He could hear it, above the rustle of the leaves as the night land breeze commenced. Martha listened for a moment, then pointed, and a few minutes later they came upon the stream, rushing down the hillside. Now the dogs were very close, but James led the girl into the water, and waded down the centre. It was some 3 ft deep, and the bottom was uneven; several times one of them fell and had to clutch at the other to get back up—within seconds they were soaked to the skin, which was a great relief to James after his weeks of forced filth.

Now they could see the glow of the lanterns being carried by their pursuers, and hear their shouts and whistles, always accompanied by the barking of the dogs. But the barks had diminished in certainty; the dogs had lost the scent at the water. 'Downstream,' someone shouted. 'They can only have gone downstream.'

James touched Martha on the shoulder and gave her one of the Mausers. 'They'll hang us anyway, if they catch us,' he said.

She did not need convincing. He had a notion she had been waiting a long time to fire into her previous masters. Now she turned, identified the lead light, perhaps a hundred yards upstream from them, coming and going among the trees, and squeezed the trigger six times. The bullets crashed and crackled into tree trunks and off branches, but there were shouts of alarm from the pursuers, and from the sound of a cry someone might even have been hit. James grabbed Martha's arm and led her out of the water on to the east side of the stream. He reckoned they were already technically over the border, but he did not suppose the pursuit was going to end because of a few shots; his idea had been to slow them up. 'I liked that,' Martha panted,

'Great stuff!'

'But I need more bullets.'

'When we stop.'

The pursuit had actually ceased for the moment, presumably while the wounded man was tended, and if the dogs were again barking, they still had no scent. On the other hand, come daylight the fugitives' progress through the bush would be tracked easily enough. But James knew where he was going, if he could reach it. 'I have to rest,' Martha panted, falling to her hands and knees.

'Five minutes.' He used the time to take her Mauser and reload it. But he was pretty tired himself; lying on a prison cot for several weeks with only half-an-hour's exercise a day was no training for safari.

He got Martha up, and they continued on their way. 'I don't hear anyone behind us,' she said. Even the noise of the dogs had faded.

'They'll be along come daybreak,' James

said. 'They won't want to let us go.'

'Are we going to make it?'

'If we keep moving,' he promised her. They stumbled onwards, now needing to rest every half-an-hour, until the darkness began to fade. Almost immediately they heard a shot; it was perhaps a mile behind them, but it was assembling the posse; someone had found their trail.

'What can we do?' Martha asked.

'Keep going.'

She looked doubtful, but it was only another fifteen minutes, and broad daylight, when she suddenly stopped with a little shriek, at the apparition which appeared before her, large and black and naked, but armed with both spear and bow. 'Good morning!' James said, in Portuguese.

The African studied him for several seconds. 'M'gell? You shoot gun?' He also spoke Portuguese, after a fashion.

'The people looking for me shot gun,' James said.

'Not far.'

'That's it. We need your help.'

The African considered. 'Ngolo would wish to help me,' James pointed out.

The African came to a decision, and nodded. 'You hurry,' he commanded.

Weary as they were, they could not keep up with him; but James knew they would not have kept up with him in any event. Every so often the African whistled, to tell them where he was. Behind them the gun was fired again and again, and once more they could hear the dogs. Then a few minutes later they came upon the kraal, set deep in the trees. Their guide's whistle had been heard, and people came out to greet them, naked warriors, naked girls and boys, apron-clad matrons, and chief Ngolo, who wore the silk hat James had given him on his last, less exciting visit—when James had had half a dozen rifles and ammunition for sale; Ngolo was carrying one of the rifles now. 'M'gell?' he asked. 'You got trouble?'

'Plenty trouble,' James said.

Martha shrank against him. Her mother, or more likely, James thought, her grandmother, might have been pure African, but she had lived in white society long enough to be afraid of the men of the forest. 'I hear how you were arrested,' Ngolo said.

'If they take me, they will hang me,' James said.

Ngolo nodded. 'They will not take you, M'gell.'

'I must warn you, they have dogs; they will know where we have come.'

'How many men?' Ngolo asked.

'Six, maybe ten.'

Ngolo extended his arms, to include all

his people, but mainly the young men, of whom there were at least a hundred. And five of them, in addition to the chieftain, had rifles. 'They will not take you, M'gell.'

'Then you have my eternal gratitude.'

Ngolo grinned. 'We talk after, M'gell. Now you go.' He spoke his own language, rapidly, and two of the young women hurried forward, gesturing James and Martha to follow them.

'I didn't know you knew these people,' Martha muttered.

'I know just about everyone in this forest, on the Portuguese side,' James said. 'We have business together.'

They were led into the kraal, surrounded now by eager children and snapping dogs, and escorted to a hut. The girls gestured them inside. 'We need food and drink,' James said.

They giggled, but understood him; a few minutes later both were produced. Martha regarded the food suspiciously. 'What is it?'

The meat had been dried and was stringy and tasteless. 'Some kind of animal,' James said. 'It won't kill you.' There were also peppers, which made the mouth and eyes water, and ground nuts. 'Concentrated protein,' James assured her.

By now they could hear the barking of the dogs outside the kraal, and also voices raised in some agitation. Boer voices. The chief was keeping his low. 'Will he give us to them?' Martha asked.

'No. He wants the rifles I can give him.'

She finished her meal, drank some of the water. 'I am so very tired.'

'Me too. But we can sleep easy.'

Her eyes were liquid. 'You do not wish sex with me?'

'As a matter of fact, I do, desperately. But it won't amount to much until I've rested.'

'We rest together,' she said, and took off her tattered shift. 'You will not forget your promise to me.'

He stripped off himself, lay down on the blankets beside her, took her in his arms. 'I will not forget.'

It was impossible to sleep, exhausted as they both were, while the discussion was being continued at the gates of the kraal. But eventually it dwindled. By then they had been unable to stop fondling each other, and although they both fell fast asleep, it was with sex in mind. They awoke together, and a moment later she was on his chest, squirming against him, her dark hair flopping into his face.

She was a long distance from Cecile von Beinhardt. But he reckoned she knew more about what she was at, at that moment, having practised so often. Certainly she knew exactly how to arouse him, where she wanted his hands to be, and what she wanted him to do with them when they got there. Equally she knew how to prolong his strength to the last possible moment, so that they climaxed together. 'I please you?' she asked, kissing his face again and again.

'Very much.'

'You will see. I will make you a good wife,' she promised.

'I have no doubt of it.' Gently he eased her off him as he saw the door of the hut darken, and a moment later Ngolo joined them.

The chief was not the least embarrassed at the two naked and intertwined bodies. 'You have rest?'

James grinned. 'In a manner of speaking.'

'Pretty girl,' Ngolo remarked. 'Those Boers gone. But they know you are here. You must leave this night. My people will escort you until you are safe.'

James nodded. But one did not beat about the bush with Ngolo. 'What do you wish in payment?'

'Guns,' Ngolo said. 'Breech-loaders.'

James nodded again. 'How many?'

'One hundred. And bullets.'

James rubbed his nose. 'One hundred rifles. And ammunition. You value me highly, old friend.'

Ngolo grinned. 'You are my friend. But I must arm my people. Boers may come back.'

'If they do, knowing you helped me escape, there may well be more than a hundred. Armed with rifles.'

Ngolo's grin widened. 'Then we kill more than a hundred. You will bring rifles?'

'It will take some moons. What will you do till then?'

Ngolo shrugged. 'Boers come, we go in forest. Boers burn kraal, we rebuild kraal. Then when rifles come ...'

How to start a frontier war in one easy lesson, James thought. But he was in the mood for that. 'I will be as quick as I can,' he promised.

'Just like that?' Martha asked, as they were provided with food for their journey.

'He trusts me.'

'But you will surely not come back?'

'Of course I will come back. These people are my business.'

She made no further comment, but clearly she thought he was mad.

They were provided with an escort of

a dozen warriors for the first part of their journey, leaving the kraal at the dead of night. Sure enough there was a Boer encampment about a mile away from the kraal, and the dogs were restless, but the warriors knew their way and led them safely well out of earshot. Then they clasped James' hands, and melted back into the darkness.

It was just dawn. 'Can we rest now?' Martha asked.

'We rest when we are beyond pursuit,' James told her.

It was approximately 100 miles from Ngolo's kraal to the coast. The first half of this, through the bush, took them five days; Ngolo had allowed James to retain possession of his three sidearms, as his people did not know how to use revolvers or pistols, but progress remained slow, as they attempted to avoid confrontation with any dangerous animals, most important, snakes, that cropped up. The necessity to gather food occupied a good deal of each day, after their initial supplies had run out. Martha was obviously impressed by James' bushcraft, and made ever more extravagant promises of how good a wife she was going to be. James preferred not to consider the matter at all. He was a man of his word, and had every intention of honouring his promise, but he knew there were going to be problems, both social and domestic.

For the time being he led them southeast, making for the railroad, and on the fifth day they reached it. Next morning they were at a halt, and that afternoon the train came rumbling down the track from Komati Poort, stopping when James flagged it. 'You have stirred up a real hornet's nest, senhor,' said the conductor. He knew James well enough.

'Just take me to Lourenco Marques,' James said. 'I'll arrange payment when we get there.'

'Who will make this payment, senhor?'

'My brother. Our firm.'

'There is no longer a Martingell firm, senhor.'

James stared at him in consternation. 'What do you mean?'

The conductor shrugged. 'It is closed down, I have heard. Perhaps Capitan Delgado will pay for you, eh?'

'Ah ... yes, of course he will,' James agreed.

They found seats. James deduced that several of the passengers were Boers, from the hard stares they gave him, but then, with their tattered clothing and scratched faces and arms they must look like two long-lost absentees from civilisation, James thought. However, no one made any

attempt to interfere with them; James'
revolver and his Mauser pistol were
plainly in evidence, and Martha also
carried her pistol conspicuously. 'There
is trouble?' she asked, anxiously watching
his expression.

'I'm afraid there may be,' he said. 'But
we'll find out when we get to Beira.'
What the devil could have happened? So
he was not bringing back their anticipated
£25,000 worth of profit, but the firm had
been on a sound financial footing. To hear
that it was, in the words of the guard,
'no more' was as inexplicable as it was
alarming.

He encountered the same resistance when
he attempted to find a passage up the
coast. 'You have money, Martingell?' asked
the agent.

'Not on me. I will send you the money.
You know my word is good.'

'I know that, Martingell. But a good
word is no use without money, and you
have none.'

'I shall get to the bottom of these
rumours as soon as I reach Beira,' James
assured him. 'But I have to get to Beira.
Captain Delgado will settle my account.'
The agent pinched his lip. But there could
be no doubt that Captain Delgado had
money.

Martha had never seen the sea before, and she did not like the look of it, or the Arab dhow which was to be their transport. 'We will sink,' she declared. 'Why we not go in that one?' She pointed at a coasting schooner.

'Because that one costs more, and I have very little money,' James said.

'You have *no* money,' she pointed out.

'But I'm still going to marry you,' he assured her.

She looked doubtful.

With contrary winds it took them two days to beat up the coast. Martha spent the whole time being sick, while James brooded. But at last Beira hove in sight, and the crew of the dhow dropped their lateen sail and allowed the vessel to coast alongside one of the stone docks. 'I shall never go to sea again,' Martha vowed.

'Of course you will,' James said. 'It is just a matter of getting used to it.'

He led her up the dusty street, deciding against going to Delgado's office, which was on the front, until he had spoken with his brother. Martingell Brothers was only a street farther on, and he stopped in consternation at the sight of the boarded-up building; the upper floor, where the family had lived, was shuttered. 'This your home?' Martha asked.

'It was.' James banged on the front door, while a group of black children accumulated, soon to be joined by a Portuguese policeman, who chased them away, gave Martha an appraising look, then gazed at James standing on the verandah, hands on hips.

'Senhor Martingell? We heard you were in gaol, in Pretoria.'

'I happen to be here. Where is my brother and his family?'

'I cannot say, senhor. Your brother is not here.'

James almost ran back down the street to the Capitanerie, Martha hurrying behind him. He burst into the outer office, and encountered Antonio coming out of the inner. 'James?' Antonio was clearly astounded. 'They said you had been hanged.' He gazed at James' tattered clothes, and then at Martha's even more inadequate shift.

'Then I am even more fortunate than I supposed. Where is William?'

'Ah. You'd best come inside.' He glanced at Martha as she made to follow.

'I am his wife,' Martha said. Antonio's eyebrows shot up.

James would have preferred to break the news in his own time. 'It was she who got me out,' he explained.

Antonio held the door for them both, his brain clearly working overtime. 'You'll take a drink.' He poured whisky from the bottle on the table. 'And the lady?'

'I have never drunk whisky,' Martha said.

'Maybe now's a good time to start,' James said.

She took a sip, and made a face.

'You'll get used to it,' James told her. 'Just sit quietly, there's a good girl.'

Antonio sat behind his desk. 'You were taken, with the guns, by the Boers.'

'Correct.'

'But Jameson went ahead with his hare brained scheme, anyway.'

'Correct.'

'There has been considerable diplomatic activity.'

'So I believe. Is the good doctor still under arrest?'

'Oh, indeed! They mean to hang him. But you ... they knew who you were, of course. And made representations to the Governor here in Beira. I did what I could, James, believe me. But Pretoria carries considerable clout here, financially as well as diplomatically. The upshot was that William was declared *persona non grata* in Portugese East.' He gave a wry grin. 'No one supposed they would ever see you again.'

'So where is William?'

'I have no idea.'

'But ... Maria is your daughter.'

'Of course she is. And I am happy to say that she is well. I would not describe her as happy, but these are not happy times. We must hope for an improvement.'

James scratched his head. 'Forgive my stupidity, but do I understand you to mean that Maria is here in Beira?'

'Of course she is. This is her home.'

'And the children?'

'This is their home as well.'

'And she does not know where her husband is?'

'He said he would write as soon as he was settled, somewhere. But he has not done so. Mind you, it is early days yet.'

James stared at him. 'Maria let him go, by himself?'

'She had no choice. We hope to find a buyer for the warehouse and the stock, but one has not yet come forward. And he had no money, beyond the little I was able to provide. His bank account has been sequestered by the government in anticipation of a heavy fine. I am sorry, James, but it would appear that you and your brother overreached yourselves. God knows how much I like you both but ...'

'But you kicked him out without a penny.'

Antonio's eyes were suddenly cold. 'The Government kicked him out, James. I saw to it that he had a penny, at least.'

'But you would not care if you never heard of him again,' James said angrily.

'He is my son-in-law. I must care what happens to him. But my first duty is to my daughter. Now it is time for us to think of you. I am assuming no one knows you are back in Beira?'

'If they don't, they soon will.'

'Of course. The Transvaal Government will wish you extradited. You must leave immediately.'

'You mean I must flee, penniless, into the night behind my brother.'

Antonio threw out his hands. 'Do you suppose you are some demi-god who can challenge the world and say "Do your worst"? You are a convicted fugitive ...'

'I have never been convicted of anything, because I have never been tried.'

'That is a technicality. You are a fugitive from justice, which assumes that you are guilty, or you would have remained for the trial.'

'Do you suppose it would have been a fair one?'

'That I cannot say. My advice is to put yourself as far away from that justice as you can as rapidly as you can.'

'That is not as easy as you think,' James

said. 'I have obligations.' He could not stop himself glancing at Martha, seated in the corner. She might not be able to understand Portuguese, but she could tell the two men were having an intense discussion. She gave an anxious smile.

'To that bint?' Antonio asked.

'Were you not my friend, I would punch you in the nose,' James said. 'Or are you my friend?'

'Of course I am your friend, James. In so far as I am able.'

'Well, my principal obligation is to Chief Ngolo. I have promised him a hundred rifles, with ammunition.'

'Are you mad? Sell a hundred rifles to an up-country tribe?'

'I intend to give them. I owe him.'

'You mean he helped you escape. Do the Boers know this?'

'Certainly they do. That's why he feels he needs the rifles.'

'What are you trying to do, start a war? But of course, that *is* what you tried to do. Listen, my friend, I want you out of Beira on the next ship.'

'Going where?'

'I do not care, and I do not think you should, either.'

'I have no money.'

Antonio snorted, opened his desk drawer and took out a wallet, which he threw across the desk. 'That will keep you for a few days.'

'There is also the matter of my train fare to Lourenco Marques, and my boat fare from Lourenco to Beira.'

'I will settle them.' Antonio gave a brief smile. 'Now you can bear in mind how much you owe *me*, eh? Now go, and take your half-caste friend with you. And don't ever let me see your face in Beira again.'

James picked up the wallet, stood up. 'I will wish you a happy Christmas, senhor.'

Chapter Three

The Trader

'The woman must wait outside,' the clerk said.

'She is my woman,' James protested.

'No coloureds are allowed in this building,' the clerk pointed out.

James controlled his temper with an effort; but his temper had been on the verge of eruption for weeks now. 'We'd best not antagonise these people at the moment,' he told Martha.

'I will wait in the street,' she agreed.

He wondered what she thought of it all.

81

She had assumed she was fleeing to safety and even prosperity, instead of which she was living with an outcast and a fugitive. But she had never complained, although occasionally some of her questions as to what was going to happen next were disturbingly direct. His answer to every one was. 'Just let's get to Cape Town'. Well, now they were here.

'Mr Rudd can see you now.'

James stepped inside. He had spent almost the last of the money Antonio had loaned him on clothes, a dress for Martha and a suit for himself. The white duck did not fit very well, but it was at least clean, as was his shirt. That his boots were scuffed was unavoidable. Rudd, on the other hand, was as dapper as ever. 'You would appear to have nine lives,' he remarked. He did not offer to shake hands, but gestured James to a chair.

'And I've needed every one of them.'

'We must hope they have not all been used up,' Rudd commented. 'So what brings you to Cape Town?'

'Wouldn't you agree that the risk to my nine lives began right here, Mr Rudd?'

'*Your* nine lives, by God!'

'What is happening with Jameson's people?'

'Oh, we'll get them out. There'll be no hangings. But the consequences ...

you'll know Rhodes has resigned as prime minister?'

'I did not know. But that is the price of failure.'

'It might not have been failure had you delivered those guns, Martingell.'

'I did deliver them, Mr Rudd.'

'To the Boers.'

'We were betrayed. Someone got word to the Boers what was really in those crates.'

'Now who was that, do you suppose?'

'I have no idea. But I mean to find out.'

'You don't suppose your incompetence has caused enough trouble?'

'We were betrayed,' James insisted, again.

'That must remain a matter of opinion.'

'Fund me, and I will find out who was responsible.'

Rudd raised his eyebrows. 'My dear fellow, you have already cost us a quarter of a million pounds. Don't tell me again; you didn't lose it, you were robbed. That doesn't alter the fact. We have no more use for you, Martingell.'

James swallowed both his pride and his anger. 'My brother and I are destitute; the Portuguese have closed us down.'

'Then you will have to obtain honest employment, will you not?'

James decided against reminding him that he had just virtually condemned himself as dishonest. 'I may need your help to do that, Mr Rudd.'

'And I shall not give it you, Mr Martingell. Nor will you find it in Cape Town. Good day to you, sir.' James' big hands curled into fists. But assaulting Rudd would only land him in gaol, and leave Martha to starve. Only she wouldn't starve; Martha had the gift of survival, and the body for it.

'Mr Martingell.' James, stamping through Rudd's outer office, checked. 'Do forgive me.' The young woman was trim rather than pretty, but not the less attractive for that, if only because her yellow hair, which she wore in a pompadour, was slowly coming unpinned and drifting down on to her neck. She wore a high-necked white dress, and looked vaguely harassed.

'My pleasure.' He raised his hat. 'You have the advantage of me.'

She looked more flustered yet. 'My name is Anne Horsfall. I'm one of Mr Rudd's secretaries.'

'Ah,' James commented, looking around him at the otherwise empty office.

'Oh, Mary has just stepped out,' Anne Horsfall said. 'I just ... she bit her lip. 'I wanted to say that I'm sorry. I ...' she glanced at the door to the inner office, but it was securely closed. 'I think you have been very badly treated. If indeed you were betrayed.'

'Thank you, Miss Horsfall. It *is* "miss"?' She wore white gloves.

Anne Horsfall blushed. 'It is, Mr Martingell. If there is anything ... well ... I felt I should say it.'

'And I thank you. I shall not forget your kindness.' As he stepped outside into the brilliant sunlight, he thought how reassuring it was that there were still nice girls left in the world. Not that he supposed any of them would ever wish to be found too close to James Martingell.

'What we do now?' Martha asked, seeing from his face, as he reappeared, that the interview had not gone well.

'I'm damned if I know.' He took her to the waterfront to look at the ships. He had a little of Antonio's money left, possibly sufficient for one more sea passage. But where was he going to go, with any prospect of earning a living, much less finding William? His life, which only a few months ago had been so full of excitement, good living and good prospects, had suddenly come to a full stop. He had not been ready for that.

'Mr Martingell?' James turned, sharply, surprised to be addressed by a stranger twice in one morning, to look at a little man with a waxed moustache and a white topee to go with his freshly pressed white suit. 'My name is Bendt.' James would have said he was German before the introduction, although he spoke perfect English. 'It is very hot, standing here,' Bendt said, 'Will you take coffee?' James glanced at Martha. 'Oh, by all means bring your servant,' Bendt said. 'She is a pretty girl.'

'Who is not welcome in every establishment in Cape Town.'

Bendt smiled. 'Then we will take her somewhere where she *is* welcome.' Clearly he knew the port very well, and five minutes later the three of them were seated on a shady verandah being served coffee by black maids. Martha was delighted.

'How did you know my name, Herr Bendt?' James asked.

'It is my business to know things, Mr Martingell.'

'You live in Cape Town?'

'I run an agency. Imports and exports. For my German principal.' James waited, already certain of what he was about to be told. 'The firm is Beinhardt, of Cologne,' Bendt said.

James nodded. 'I am not sure what

86

interest Count von Beinhardt can have in me, now,' he remarked.

'Count von Beinhardt is interested in all men of talent, who also have local knowledge. Your local knowledge is unique, Mr Martingell, in that it comprises, I am told, just about all of the eastern half of Africa south of Lake Tanganyika.'

'You flatter me. My name isn't Livingstone.'

'Count von Beinhardt was very distressed to learn of your misfortune in the matter of guns for the Uitlanders. Especially as they were his guns. But he was impressed by the fact that no one has ever discovered that they were *his* guns. He regards that as business confidentiality of the highest quality, especially where you might have tried to negotiate your release by disclosing your backer.'

'As you say, Herr Bendt, business confidentiality.'

'Thus Count von Beinhardt would be willing to offer you a position in his establishment.'

James' heart pounded pleasantly. 'In Germany?'

'No, no, Mr Martingell! In German East Africa. Do the names Tippu Tib or Burghash mean anything to you?'

'Certainly. Tippu Tib rules the eastern

Congo, and Burghash is the Sultan of Zanzibar.'

'Correct. And for years Burghash has been supplying Tippu with his weaponry. But since the British have taken over Zanzibar from us, they have put a stop to this supply. However, it so happens that the government of German East feels that a strong Tippu is a stabilising influence in the Congo Basin.'

'I had heard that he was negotiating with Belgium.'

'*Belgium,*' Bendt remarked with contempt. 'A tiny nation populated by tiny people. What business have they to seek to rule an area about the size of all Europe? Bah! We prefer Tippu.'

'But you can't supply him with arms, openly.'

'It would be politically inexpedient for us to do so, Mr Martingell. However, we are a broad-minded people, dedicated to the furthering of trade throughout Africa. Throughout the world. In some contrast to your British, I may say, however much they may be prepared to debate the issue. We would have no objection were the well-known traveller and explorer James Martingell to set up a trading post in territory under our control. German East is a vast area, as I am sure you know, Mr Martingell, far beyond the capability of

88

any European power adequately to police. Thus I could give you my assurance, and the assurance of Count von Beinhardt, that you would not be interfered with.'

'I would need financing.'

'Of course. Count von Beinhardt would be your silent partner, as all the weapons would come from his factories. However, you must be very clear on one thing: the Count will also be the controlling partner.'

James nodded. 'I would also need to be clear on one or two other things.'

'Such as?'

'Are these guns I am to sell to Tippu Tib for use against the Belgians?'

'Hopefully not. They would be for his use to protect himself against anyone who encroaches upon his territory, without consent.' Bendt gave another of his secretive smiles. 'We would see that he got more, and better quality, than Rudd sold to the Matabele, eh?'

'And what about Rudd, and the Rhodesia Company? The territory they claim abuts the Congo, does it not?'

'We have no information that the Rhodesia Company plans any further expansion.'

'But suppose they did?'

Bendt's eyes were hooded. 'Then Tippu Tib would be entitled to defend himself, would you not say?'

James considered. He had no desire to supply an African chieftain with guns to shoot Englishmen. On the other hand, he had no reason to like the Rhodesian Company, which had just refused to support him now he was down and out —however charming one of its secretaries. 'There are other potential enemies of Tippu Tib,' he remarked.

'The Boers?' Bendt gave another snort of contempt. 'I think they are required to spend their time looking south, since the Jameson Raid. Besides, they are open veldt farmers, not penetrators of the deep forest. In any event, would you lose any sleep if a Boer got killed by a bullet you had sold to Tippu?'

'Probably not,' James mused.

Bendt pressed home the advantage he saw he was gaining. 'This operation will make you a wealthy man, Mr Martingell. It will entirely restore your fortune. I see a glittering future before you.'

James stroked his chin. 'There are two other considerations.'

'Tell me.'

'My brother. He was forced out of Portuguese East, and has disappeared.'

'And you wish to go looking for him? An admirable concept, Mr Martingell. But it cannot be. Tippu is urgently in need of guns. However, our agents will search for your brother, and find him, too. I give you my word.'

'I would be grateful. My other problem is Chief Ngolo. He saved me from the Boers. I promised him a hundred rifles with ammunition.'

'We can arrange that. But how will you get to him, if you are *persona non grata* in Beira?'

'As with German East, Portuguese East is too big an area to be policed adequately. I would come down from the north.'

Bendt flicked the end of his moustache. 'You are aware that there are British agents active in the north of Portuguese East? We suspect they may be thinking of accomplishing something for themselves there.'

'I'll keep out of their way. But ...' James frowned. 'There's no chance that my guns may be used by Tippu Tib against the British?'

'None at all,' Bendt assured him. 'Are you also aware that it is 1,700 English miles from Dar-es-Salaam to Pretoria? To reach Ngola, just inside Portuguese East, will hardly be less.'

'So it'll take time. But I can use the lakes. And if I break my word to Ngolo, I won't be worth a cent in the rest of Africa.'

Bendt nodded. 'I will see what can be arranged.'

'I do not like this place,' Martha muttered. There was indeed a considerable difference between Dar-es-Salaam and Beira. The German port was a huge, natural, land-locked body of water, utterly safe from the worst that the monsoon could throw at it, which was no doubt why the Arabs had named it 'Haven of Peace.' James suspected that the name was now history. Dar-es-Salaam was also even more of a new town; the Germans had only been here for less than half-a-dozen years. But because they were German, and not Portuguese, there was a great deal more building in evidence, and more uniforms, too. The native people, even the Arabs, of whom there were a considerable number, looked cowed; they had been taught their places.

Yet, as Bendt had said, the Germans were more liberal conquerors than the British provided always that one paid respect to them and to their imperial flag. And paid the necessary taxes, of course. Thus where Zanzibar, just off the coast, had for long been accepted as the hub of the African slave trade, the British had all but abolished that pernicious dealing in human beings where they governed. The Germans had seen no reason so to interfere with local custom, or local profitability, and slave gangs were to be seen on the streets of Dar-es-Salaam, whether waiting to board ships, or to be marched into the interior, or worst of all groups of young men waiting to be gelded before being taken into the households of wealthy merchants. As with Martha, James could say he did not like this place. But yet it remained the gateway to prosperity. Beggars could not be choosers.

He had letters of introduction and letters of credit, from Bendt, which were studied by Herr Fessnung, a large, stout man, manager of the House of Beinhardt, German East Africa. 'Welcome, Herr Martingell,' he said, 'Oh, welcome.' He gave the usual curious glance at Martha, resplendent in new green gown and broad brimmed hat, and shoes, purchased for her in Cape Town by Bendt, and now content to sit in a corner, and smile. 'I have been expecting you, of course, since receiving instructions from the Count. Indeed, I have been instructed to prepare your personal safari.' He flicked a page of the file on his desk. 'A hundred Mauser rifles and 10,000 rounds of ammunition. Is that correct?' James had never encountered anyone who fulfilled his agreements as rapidly as Adolf von Beinhardt. After the delays and machinations involved in doing business with either the Portuguese in Beira or the English in Cape Town, he found it a great pleasure.

'I will not ask you for whom these weapons are intended, Herr Martingell,' Fessnung went on. 'But I am instructed to tell you that this initial expedition must first be used for making contact with Tippu Tib and making a first delivery of arms to him. His need is urgent. The shipment is already packed up and waiting to go. You also need to choose a site for establishing your internal warehouse. For this you will in time require protection, and I am to provide a sufficient number of askaris for that purpose. Once these things have been attended to, you are free to make your delivery to Ngolo. Is this, satisfactory?'

'More than satisfactory.'

'Well, then, I am sure you will agree that, as I have the necessary goods, your safari should be commenced immediately. Time is of the essence.' He cocked his head and looked at Martha. 'Your servant is unwell?' Martha had appeared to have fainted, and was panting for breath. 'Perhaps it is the heat,' Fessnung said.

It was certainly much hotter than in Beira. But James had been about the place with his brother and sister-in-law

94

when Maria had first become pregnant. 'Shit!' he commented.

But he recovered from the shock more quickly than Martha herself. 'What am I to do?' she asked. Incredibly, considering the life she had led, she had never been pregnant before!

'How long is it since you passed blood?'

'I think about four months.'

'Jesus Christ! You could have told me before?' He felt that was late for an abortion, even if secretly he did not want the child.

'I thought it was all the going and coming, and sailing.'

'Well, I have arranged it with Herr Fessnung,' James assured her. 'He will find you somewhere to live, and provide you with funds until my return.'

'I don't want you to go,' she said. 'Please stay here with me, James.'

'I must go, Martha. I have to earn the money that Fessnung will be paying you. But I won't be away more than a few months. I'll be back for the birth.'

'Don't leave me, James,' she begged, clinging to his hand.

Much as he regretted having to abandon Martha, in her condition, James would have been deceiving himself had he not acknowledged his delight to leave Dar-es-Salaam and begin his mission. And it promised to be a worthwhile year, which would entirely put him back on his feet. He was guaranteed a ten per cent share of the profit from the guns, and he now knew that he could trust Beinhardt. He was also doing what he did best, and liked best, penetrating the forests and mountains of the interior. Had he any news of William he would have been a totally happy man, when only a month ago he had been utterly despairing. But of William there was no news at all; James suspected that his brother might even have gone back to England, supposing as he must have done that James was lost forever. But by the time he returned to Dar-es-Salaam he was certain, William would have been found and be waiting for him, and Martingell & Company would have been revived. And then, he was determined, they would return to Beira in triumph, and under German protection, and reclaim Maria and the children. And Catherine? He was promised to Martha.

But first the mission. The first 300 miles were easy enough, as the Germans, like the Portuguese, had constructed a railroad into the interior, crossing the coastal plain before climbing into the hill country of the Morogoro, carefully skirting the very high ground known as the Southern Hills to differentiate it from the even higher ground at the north end of the German claim, abutting the new British protectorate of Kenya Territory, and which culminated in the sky-scraping majesty of Kilimanjaro. That was unknown country to James, but not to Biltong, his assistant, a half-caste German who claimed to have climbed the god mountain, or at least part of it. 'Man, there is snow up there, all year round!' he boasted.

Biltong, James supposed, no less than Hammacher the bookkeeper, was an essential adjunct of the safari, and not merely to make sure that the Englander did exactly what he was contracted to do. Biltong knew how to deal with the natives. James had dealt with native Africans all of his adult life, but, except for his brief and unhappy sojourn in the Transvaal, they had always been free men, with pride in themselves and their culture. Even in Cape Town, where they were definitely second-class citizens, they had not been slaves. But this safari was composed entirely of slaves, nearly a hundred black men who were clearly regarded as belonging to an inferior species. Distressingly, this opinion was held even by the African guards and drivers, who used their whips freely and their tongues to curse and swear at the toiling carriers. Even on the train the drivers prowled up and down, using their whips on anyone who did not take their fancy. When James protested mildly, Biltong pointed out that these scum, as he called them, were used to no other form of treatment, and leniency would be interpreted as weakness, and a reason for desertion if not mutiny once they were out in the bush.

Certainly desertion was taken seriously. One man tried it from the train, was recaptured, and flogged mercilessly while the train waited. 'I am sure things could be better managed,' James suggested to Hammacher, who was there to take control once James had departed to the south.

'It is the custom in this land.' Hammacher was a stout, contented man who looked harmless enough, but James had quickly recognised him to be extremely tough and entirely pragmatic. 'And you must never forget that our safety, and the safety of the guns, and the ivory afterwards, is paramount. One rules best by instilling and maintaining fear.' James supposed he was right, but that didn't make him the least proud of what they were doing. What the other passengers thought about it he could not tell; there weren't many of them, and they were all Germans, in any event. And the punishment had its effect; there were no other runaways, at least until the train reached the railhead.

This was at Mbeya, a few miles south of the boundary of the country claimed by the Rhodesia Company. It was an area James had visited before, as an agent for that ambitious concern, but he had no desire to enter territory which could be claimed as British. Instead the 'stores' were unloaded, and he and his slaves, together with Biltong and Hammacher and their guard of askaris, set off on a trek to the north-west. This was heavy going, because only some 50 miles from Mbeya the land rose steeply to nearly 2,000 ft., while remaining thickly forested. It was a hunter's paradise, for game abounded, from fleet-footed gazelle to lion. These last were a nuisance, as despite the size of the safari they roamed round the camp, and two men were lost when carelessly wandering beyond the limits. However, the presence of the huge beasts acted as an extra deterrent to running away, and they progressed steadily, singing a mournful dirge as they trekked through the undergrowth.

Progress was slow, less than ten miles a day, and it was three weeks before they saw the glittering waters of Lake Tanganyika below them. This was its southern extremity; it stretched some 400 miles to the north. Here, at Kalambo Falls, where the river toppled down some 700ft, one of the biggest drops in the world, Tippu Tib was waiting for them.

Although he had passed through this region before, James had never met the great chief. Tippu was an Arab, a big, heavy man with a huge nose and flowing beard and moustache. Although he was nearly 40 he looked as fit and strong as any of his followers, and towered above the forest Africans who composed his bodyguard. His eyes, peering into James' as they clasped hands, were piercing and powerful. 'Martingell,' he said. 'I have heard of you.'

'And I of you, Mohammed ibn Hamid,' James said, using Tippu's real name.

That pleased the chief; his teeth flashed as he smiled. And he smiled even more as Biltong opened the boxes to reveal the rifles and ammunition and the machine-guns. 'This is good, Martingell,' he said as they sat together at dinner, eating with their fingers from the same pot. 'But I will need more.'

'To fight the Belgians?' James asked, as innocently as he could.

Tippu chewed for a few seconds before replying. 'I do not think that is practical,' he said at last. 'For more than a little while. They are many.'

'Belgium is a small nation,' James remarked.

'That may be so. But their people here are numerous, and they are well-armed. If I cannot be sure of winning, why fight them at all? If they will give me what I want.'

'Will they do this?'

Tippu grinned. 'They are more likely to give me what I wish when they realise the problem they may have if they do not. So, you see, when next the commissioner comes to me, I will greet him with a guard of honour. One thousand men, each armed with a Mauser breech-loader.' He stroked the gun he had chosen as his own, and which lay on the ground beside him. 'And outside my village, there will be four manned machine-gun ... what do you call them?'

'Nests,' James said thoughtfully. 'And what is it you wish?'

'Why, to continue as I am. I am quite prepared to acknowledge this Leopold as my king. I doubt he will ever come to Africa. But I will be his governor-general, here in the Congo'

'And the slave trade? The Belgians will wish you to stop it.'

Once again Tippu chewed for several seconds before answering. 'That will be difficult. The Arabs are my friends. More, they are my people. We all kneel to the East when we pray. In the direction of stopping the trade, we shall have to hurry slowly.'

The next day, when the guns had been carefully counted and stacked, the ivory was brought out, massive elephant tusks, each worth its weight in gold. The beginning of a new fortune for the House of Martingell.

The trek back to the railhead, carrying only the ivory, was accomplished much more quickly. At Mbeya, James and Hammacher parted company, Hammacher to return to the coast with the ivory, James to continue south. He had spent the past few weeks evaluating the men who had accompanied him from Dar-es-Salaam, and from these he chose four askaris and twelve of the slaves, as well as the most civilised of the drivers as his servant. The rifles for Ngolo had been left in the warehouse at Mbeya. These were now loaded on to the backs of the slaves, and he set off to the south. 'Give my love to Martha,' he told Hammacher. 'And bank my share of the proceeds, eh?'

'I look forward to your return, Herr Martingell,' Hammacher said. Then it was off on the real safari.

From Mbeya, they trekked south for 50
miles to reach the northern end of Lake
Nyasa. Here they embarked on boats
negotiated from the local tribe, with whom
James had had dealings before; the lake
was 400–odd miles long, and would carry
them almost to the borders of Portugese
East, while by boat they could travel much
faster and in greater comfort than walking.
James thoroughly enjoyed the voyage, even
if they had to take shelter from time to
time as sudden strong winds whipped up
the surface of the inland sea. But game
continued to be plentiful on the banks, as
were fish in the lake; crocodiles eyed them
as they paddled by, hippopotami snorted
in the shallows and threw up vast clouds
of water, monkeys chattered, lions roared,
and all seemed well with the world.

Having very deliberately left Biltong
behind, he spent much of his time teaching
his new servant, Mbote, to speak English,
and then to play chess—he had bought
himself a new set in Dar-es-Salaam.
Mbote found English hard going, but
proved remarkably adept at chess, while
the askaris would gather round to watch
in amazement as the two men pushed the
little pieces of wood to and fro. The slaves
were totally bemused, as although James
had allowed Biltong to equip him with a

bullwhip, it remained coiled and hanging from his belt. Apart from his distaste for its use, James also calculated, correctly, that now they were out of their own country none of the slaves would dare risk running away to find themselves in the hands of people who would certainly resell them, if they did not actually eat them. They were, in fact, terrified every time James called at a village. They realised that he, or his name, was known to most of the people they met and came to regard him almost as a god.

It took them only three weeks to travel the length of the lake. Once out of the boats they had to climb again, but once over this range, the Shire Hills, they were down into the coastal belt, where the going was easier, although the forest was thicker. Now they were actually in territory claimed by the Portuguese, but also being penetrated by the British, James had been warned. As he had no desire to encounter either nationality, he made his way warily. But the day came when he realised there was a party of men not far away, and approaching; they were firing rifles. 'Camp,' he told Mbote.

As always, the boxes were arranged in the centre of the camp, and the drivers armed themselves. The other party emerged an hour later, standing on the edge of the clearing to survey the unexpected people in front of them. There were four white men and some two dozen Africans. They discussed the situation among themselves for several minutes before one of them came forward, his right hand held up. James did likewise. 'We'd not expected to encounter any white people up here,' the spokesman said, in English, at the same time eyeing the boxes.

'We're for the coast,' James lied.

'With a good haul there.'

'We trade.'

'Are you saying that's not ivory?'

'It is not ivory,' James said.

The Englishman looked over his shoulder, and his companions advanced. One of them pointed. 'You're James Martingell. I saw you once in Cape Town.'

'Then you have the advantage of me,' James said. 'But I am Martingell, yes.'

'Then there will be guns in those boxes.'

'Whatever is in those boxes,' James said, 'is my business.'

The men glanced past him at the four askaris, each armed with a rifle, as was Mbote.

'Sure, well, we did not mean to offend you,' said the original spokesman. 'John Sutherland.' He held out his hand, and James took it. He did not trust these men, but he did not intend them to know that.

'Archie Bell,' said the man who had claimed to recognise him. 'Tom Proud and Billy McQuaid.'

James continued to shake hands. 'And you gentlemen are after ivory?'

'We're told there are more elephant than a man can count in the high country.'

'It's a long way,' James said. 'And you'll be entering the country controlled by Tippu Tib. Perhaps you've not heard of him.'

'A savage rogue,' Sutherland remarked.

'In his own domain, a great king,' James said. 'But as you say, also a savage who does not take kindly to strangers. I wish you success.'

'Well, we'll spend the evening over a bottle, eh?'

James shook his head. 'You'll keep your distance, Mr Sutherland. My askaris will be on guard all night, with instructions to blow the head off anything moving within 50 yards of my camp.'

Sutherland glared at him, and his hand hovered over the revolver holster hanging from his belt. But James also had a holster, and his flap was already unfastened. While behind him the askaris stood motionless, watching. 'By Christ,' Sutherland said. 'They told us you were a renegade, Martingell. Be damned to you.' James watched them retreat to their people, and turn off into the bush.

Next morning the ivory hunters were gone, and he could proceed on his way, It took him another week to reach the forest close by Ngolo's kraal. He would have supposed that the news of his coming would have spread, but the forest was singularly empty of people, and, during the past two days, of game as well. They did see one African, but he ran off at great speed before James could speak with him. He resisted the temptation to hasten, despite the apprehension which now consumed his mind. This turned to grim reality soon enough as he parted the last of the leaf screen and gazed at what had once been the chief's kraal. It had been quite literally stamped into the earth, after being burned. 'What happen with these people, bwana?' Mbote asked, while the slaves muttered at each other and even the askaris seemed to huddle together.

'They have paid a price for helping me,' James muttered. 'Let us leave this place.'

'And these guns, bwana?'

'We'll take them back. The Boers aren't going to get them.'

But even as he spoke he heard the click of rifle bolts. The askaris responded, then lowered their weapons as some 50 armed white men came out of the jungle. James' entire being was tense with anger and outrage as he recognised their leader. 'Steen!'

Steen peered at him. 'Martingell? My God! We did not expect to see you back here.' He pointed. 'Still running guns, I see. For Ngolo?'

'Unfortunately, a little late.'

Steen nodded. 'Not that a few rifles would have made a great deal of difference. Was this the price of your escape.'

'It was.'

'Well, I am sure you are hungry and thirsty. You'll join me for lunch. Oh, and your friends as well. Just tell them to lay down their weapons.'

The askaris obeyed without question; they were outnumbered by ten to one. And James knew that he could do nothing more than go along with Steen's transparent hospitality. He was a dead duck. Once again, just as things had been on the up. 'You have been here since my escape?' he asked, as he accepted a cup of Dutch gin. 'Camped in Portuguese territory, waiting for me to come back?'

'I told you, Martingell, we did not expect you ever to return. No, no, we do not occupy Portuguese territory, although we reserve the right to enter it in hot pursuit, when necessary.' He grinned. 'Or in—how shall we say—preparation? We were told four days ago that a party led by a white man was approaching from the north rather than the coast. We found this intriguing. So we thought we'd come across and wait for you, and see what you intended. It never crossed our minds that it could be *you.*'

'So what happens to me now? Off to Pretoria, and a hanging?'

Steen guffawed. 'Are you that anxious to die, Martingell? My dear fellow, this is Portuguese territory. We have no jurisdiction here.' James could not believe his ears. 'As long as we are certain that you do not mean to harm us. Well, of course you did mean to harm us, at least indirectly, but as Ngolo is no longer here to receive the guns, we will accept them as a gift from you to us. And then you can go back whence you came, and good fortune to you.'

James still could not believe his luck. 'And my crime?'

Steen waved his hand. 'History, Martingell. History.'

'Those are good people, bwana,' Mbote remarked, as they began their return journey; with no load to carry the slaves were even singing as they marched. 'They could have killed us all, and no one would ever have known.'

'Yes, they could,' James agreed. Good

109

people! Steen? Steen had been acting under orders. But then, when had he not been acting under orders? The very escape had been too easy, the Boers' acceptance of Ngolo's resistance had been too easy. They could have destroyed him immediately, but they had not. They had waited to be sure Martingell was safe.

But whose had been the orders? He felt like someone wading through a pool of dark water, unable to see where he was placing his feet, suddenly feeling a tug at his ankle, the threat of something, weed or snake or quicksand, that could hold him in a vice. Whose orders?

The party had nearly traversed Lake Nyasa on their way north before his mind, tormented with suspicion, reached another suddenly opening door—into darkness. If his escape had been wanted, and connived, then was not Martha part of it? Take the Englander to safety, and be free. His hands curled into fists. The mother of his child. The woman he had fully intended to marry, up to five minutes ago. But Martha could hardly be blamed for accepting the offer of freedom; she had not harmed him in any way. The important question remained, who had ordered his escape?

He had not got any nearer solving the problem by the time his party regained

Mbeya. Two days later he was in Dar-es-Salaam, just in time, as he had promised, for the birth of Martha's daughter. 'What will we call her?' she asked.

'Ah ...' James thought of his mother, who had died in despair as the family fortunes had dwindled, 'Anne.' And realised that he was also thinking of the girl who had offered him sympathy in Cape Town.

'Anne. I like, Anne. Oh, James, it is so good to have you back.' Right then was not the moment for awkward questions, and there was a great deal to do, apart from holding his daughter in his arms; being one generation closer to white than Martha, she was almost blonde, and had blue eyes.

'I'm sure she'll be a great beauty,' Fessnung said. 'Now, James, we have tremendous news. We have found your brother. In Portugal, believe it or not, where he was trying to raise funds to restart your business. Well, you have done that, eh?'

'Does he know this?'

'Indeed. He is on his way back to Africa now, to join you. Now, you have chosen a site for your warehouse?'

'Mbeya, obviously. We will need an office here in town for actually receiving the goods, but the railhead seems to be the obvious place for accumulating the

111

merchandise, especially as Tippu Tib is likely to remain our best customer.'

Fessnung stroked his chin. 'Tippu Tib may well be overtaken by events. They wait for no man. Tell me, did you see anything of the Boers on your safari.'

'Indeed I did.' James told him of the encounter with Steen.

'I agree, most mysterious,' Fessnung agreed.

'What is more important is how they feel free to come and go out of Portuguese territory,' James said.

'I suspect they have some secret agreements with the Portuguese. In which we are interested. Would you, or your brother, like to return to Beira?'

'We certainly would, if only to regain possession of William's family. But I imagine we would be arrested on sight.'

'I am sure you would not be, if you travelled as accredited representatives of the House of Beinhardt.'

'I thought our relationship was to be secret?'

Fessnung smiled. 'As I have said, events control men rather than the other way about. There seems no doubt that there will soon be another war in South Africa, between the Boers and the British.'

James frowned. 'That would be madness, on the side of the Boers.'

'Madness sometimes is a result of desperation.' Fessnung gestured at the huge map of Africa pinned to the wall. 'Since the Rhodesia Company has secured itself in Matabeland and Mashonaland, the Transvaal is shut in on three sides, by potential enemies, men who have not forgotten Majuba Hill. The British Foreign Office once claimed Transvaal and the Orange Free State as their own. They have not forgotten that claim. Now, of course, Jameson's Raid has exacerbated the situation. There is talk of moving an army to the Cape, and Natal. I doubt the Boers can sit idly by and watch that happen.'

'A pre-emptive strike? I still say that would be madness.'

'There could hardly be a better time for it,' Fessnung pointed out. 'The Cape Government is in total disarray, and total disgrace, internationally. They have broken all the rules of civilised conduct, and this is felt even in Whitehall, so we are informed. Were the Boers to take the initiative and gain a few victories before the British can increase their forces in South Africa, the British electorate might well decide they are doing only what is necessary for their freedom. A potent force, the British electorate, once aroused.'

'And you wish to supply arms to the Boers.'

'Well, you see, they need arms if they are going to fight British regulars with any hope of success. The average Boer rifleman is the best marksman in the world. And he is also not as unwilling to accept discipline as some people would believe. They are a nation in arms, or prepared to go to arms, certainly. But there are certain facts about modern warfare that are unavoidable. Artillery and machine-guns. The best rifleman in the world is at a disadvantage when opposed by a man with a Maxim gun. And the best concealed marksman in the world can still be blown to bits by a howitzer shell. They have got to obtain artillery. There is a fortune waiting to be made, James.'

'But you can't deal openly and directly.'

'Our government cannot, certainly. Let's not forget that the Kaiser is Queen Victoria's grandson. You cannot expect him openly to support the Queen's enemies. My God, when he went so far as to send Kruger a telegram of congratulations on so successfully coping with Jameson there was a political furore. In addition, there are other areas, soon to be made evident, where Germany and Britain will be in conflict, or at least dispute.'

'Such as navies,' James remarked. It was his business to keep abreast of any news involving armaments.

'Absolutely. I do not wish to enter with you into an argument as to the rights and wrongs of the matter. It is a fact that Germany intends to build a high seas fleet to equal the British, and that is what matters. No, no, Germany cannot be overtly involved in a South African war. Neither can Portugal, which is Britain's oldest ally. But neither Germany nor Portugal wishes to stand idly by and watch the entire map of South Africa turn red. The Portuguese have informed us that they will not object to the House of Beinhardt shipping farm materials through Lourenco Marques for Pretoria. And the Boers have informed us that they will bear no grudges towards any man who can bring them heavy guns and machine-guns.'

The penny dropped. 'Steen was informed of this.'

'But of course.'

'And did Count Beinhardt also arrange my escape from Komati Poort, knowing that one day I could be useful to him?'

'I think you can be sure of it. Count Beinhardt made his fortune by accurately foretelling the future.'

'Well, Herr Fessnung, I am very glad to have escaped the Boers, even if it was a put-up job. But I'll not be going back.'

Fessnung frowned. 'I do not understand

115

you, James. This is the opportunity of a lifetime, as I have said. Besides, you work for the Count.'

'I do, where it is possible. But as I think I made it clear from the beginning, I will not sell guns to be used against the British.'

'Oh, come now! The British?'

'They are my flesh and blood.'

'You are a renegade, not welcome in your own country. This is well known.'

'I doubt it is known at all, sir, except to me. I was employed to keep the Africans in weapons, to resist the encroachments of the Belgians, and the British, to be sure. I understood that this was for the greater glory of Germany, certainly. But as yet I have discerned no treason in what I was doing. Now you ask me to commit that treason, and to aid a side I abhor. I will not do it.'

Fessnung gazed at him for some seconds, then shrugged. 'You must make your own decisions, James. But I must of course inform Count Beinhardt that he needs another agent.'

'I understand that.'

'And you also understand that as against supplying the weaponry for a major confrontation between what are essentially European forces here in southern Africa, and supplying a few rifles for Tippu Tib, there is all the difference in the world. Indeed, that the latter may well sink so far into insignificance as to be out of sight.'

'I understand that, Fessnung.'

Fessnung snorted. 'An arms smuggler with a conscience. You may find the world a bleak place, James.'

Bleak indeed, James thought, as he returned to the modest house Martha had been allocated. Even the house was not his. He had been paid his share of the worth of the ivory from Tippu's first shipment, and was for the moment quite a wealthy man, but yet again that glittering future threatened to escape him. The future to which William was returning. And did it really matter whether or not he sold arms to the Boers? He might loathe them for their treatment of the Africans, and more than anything else for their destruction of Ngolo, but were they not as entitled as Tippu Tib to stake their ground and defend it?

Against the British, there was the rub. Tippu was not involved in that. But was not Fessnung right there too? His family had been virtually expelled from England. What allegiance did he owe to the Crown, and the old woman who wore it? There was not the slightest risk of there being a Martingell in the British soldiers who would be employed against the Boers.

Thus it all came down to a dream. Of one day being able to return to England, in wealth and splendour, enough wealth, if need be, to pay off his father's debts. Enough splendour to live as his mother had always dreamed. Probably they were only dreams. But they were viable as long as he remained British. They could never be viable if he was the cause of British soldiers being shot down or blown to pieces.

'You are troubled,' Martha said. 'I thought that now you were back our troubles were over.'

'Our troubles may only have begun,' James said. But he did not pursue the matter, endeavour to find out who had actually organised their escape, with her compliance. Almost certainly it was Steen himself—but on instructions from someone else. No doubt Beinhardt. And what did it matter? If Steen had appeared in his cell doorway, keys in hand, and said, 'Run for your life, Englander,' would he not have done so?

Pending an actual dismissal from Beinhardt, he needed to continue the operation for which he had been promised employment. Nor did Fessnung raise any objections when he said he was going up to Mbeya to begin establishing the trading post. Martha as usual was reluctant to let him go, but he did not feel a frontier post was the best place for a nursing mother, much less her child. 'I'll be back in a week,' he told her.

Two days later he, Mbote and Hammacher, all good friends now, were marking out the foundations for both the warehouse and the office; there would be living quarters above. 'I have applied for permission to live up here and be your bookkeeper,' Hammacher said.

James clapped him on the shoulder. 'I will like that. But you realise that I am not Count Beinhardt's blue-eyed boy at this moment.'

'The Count respects integrity,' Hammacher said. 'And you have that, James. He will not let you down, because of your integrity.' James hoped he was right, They worked hard for three days before James felt he should return to the coast. Hammacher nodded. 'I will remain here and get the work started.' They had already recruited a native work gang.

'I am sure you will do well. When I return, I'll have Mrs Martingell and the child with me.'

Hammacher raised an eyebrow. 'Mrs Martingell?'

'I intend to put that right on this trip.'

'You'll excuse me, but I think we are now friends, eh? I would say that may cause more of a difficulty than any difference you may have with Count Beinhardt.'

'Because of her colour? But then, Otto, as you have said, I am a man of integrity, am I not?'

Not believing that Beinhardt was interested in his domestic affairs, he was in his tent on the edge of the site when the train rolled up from Dar-es-Salaam that night. Hammacher went to greet it, and returned in half-an-hour with, it appeared, a great deal of company.

'We have a visitor,' he announced, perspiring and carrying his sun helmet in both hands.

In great consternation, James stared at Cecile von Beinhardt.

Chapter Four

The Chairman

Cecile von Beinhardt wore a linen dress, and not too much else, which was apparent as the sun pierced the thin material. Her auburn hair was upswept in a huge pompadour, and was worn beneath a broad-brimmed hat. Incongruously with the dress, she also wore brown boots, and gloves. She was far more beautiful than he remembered. 'I think you have forgotten me, Herr Martingell,' she said.

'I could never do that, Fräulein,' he assured her. 'But to see such a vision, in Central Africa ...'

'I am here to see how my father's affairs are progressing,' she said.

'Your father is in German East?'

'I am here, Herr Martingell. Will you not even offer me a chair?'

James snapped his fingers and Mbote hurried forward with one of the canvas folding camp chairs. He was equally astounded, none of the very few white women he had seen in Dar-es-Salaam had remotely resembled this apparition. Cecile sat down, and pulled off her gloves; her fingers were wet with sweat. 'I need something cold to drink,' she announced.

Hammacher hurried forward with a glass. 'Not very cold, I'm afraid, Fräulein.'

Cecile drank deeply. 'It is better than nothing. Does it contain alcohol?'

'A little. Do you mind?'

'Not in the least. Is this to be the site of your new business, Herr Martingell?'

'It is.'

Cecile finished her drink and got up. 'Show me,' she demanded. Hammacher had the sense to hang back, as James escorted his guest along the lines of string, pointing out the various features. 'Do these black people speak German?' she asked.

'Some of them have a smattering.'

'They will hardly follow a conversation, then. Fessnung tells me you refuse to ship guns to the Boers.'

He paused, to turn and look at her. 'You are very direct, Fräulein. Do you have a part in your father's business?'

'My father is not well, James,' she said. Another piece of directness that took his breath away. 'Therefore I find myself handling more and more of his affairs. Tell me the truth, are you not more pleased to see me than Papa?'

'I am delighted to see you, Fräulein, although I do not consider Central Africa, certainly in the interior, to be an appropriate place for a white woman. If she is a lady.'

'You mean because I may have to go behind a bush?'

'Or use a common outhouse. Very common, I'm afraid. There are no facilities for bathing; we use the creek.'

'I think all that is exciting. Why will you not do business with the Boers? I assure you that they have forgiven and forgotten that episode three years ago.'

'I will not do business with anyone who aims to fire my guns against the British.'

'A true patriot,' she remarked contemptuously. 'But if I may correct you, they are not *your* guns, James. They are my father's guns. More accurately, in the existing circumstances, they are *my* guns.'

'Are you telling me that our partnership is ended?' James asked.

Cecile gave a delightfully throaty little laugh. 'Our partnership has just begun, James. I think you should call me Cecile.'

Hammacher joined them for supper. By then a somewhat elaborate tent had been erected for Cecile, around and inside which the four black maids she had brought with her were fussing under the command of her German maid, a handsome raven-haired young woman named Lisette Uhlmann, who clearly did not take to Africa, or the heat. 'I believe in travelling comfortably,' Cecile remarked, James having counted the number of boxes she had with her. 'I have even a travelling commode. So you see I shall not have to use your bush or your outhouse after all. Bathing, now, tempts me. But I have also brought my bathtub.'

She was poking fun at him, making him uncomfortable. She was too much in control of herself and her life, and her surroundings. This offended his masculine sense of propriety; in Africa women were usually content to accept an inferior role because of the dangers to which they were exposed. Now she drank brandy with experienced sobriety, and once again managed to convey to Hammacher that he had completed his turn of duty. 'Is he good at his job?' she asked, when the book-keeper had left.

'Very.'

'I have a mind to make him manager here.'

'You mean I am being sacked?'

'Not at all. But I do not think this is the place for you. Our information is that Tippu Tib's days are numbered; the Belgians are very enthusiastic about the Congo. They like dark places. Now, if you were prepared to run guns down the lakes to the Transvaal, this would be the ideal spot. But as you are not, you would be wasting your time, and our money, by establishing yourself here. How do you feel about the Italians?'

'I admire their music.'

'I am speaking of their colonial ambitions.'

'Have they any, after Adowa?'

'Can you believe it? They had 20,000 men, armed with modern weapons, but surrounded by 90,000 savages and torn to pieces. More than 6,000 dead! No wonder General Baratieri committed suicide. There has never been a colonial disaster like it.'

'Would you describe Ethiopia as a colony?'

'It is populated by savages. Even Custer only managed to lose a couple of hundred. Oh, yes, the Italians are interested in a colonial empire, more than ever now. They are looking for revenge. For all of those penises cast to the wind, eh?'

Once again she surprised and shocked him by her language. In any event ... 'I had heard King Menelek treated his Italian prisoners humanely.'

'Perhaps he did, those he could get hold of. He has not that much control over his people. But as I say, the Italians will not give up. They have lodged themselves in Somaliland, and are making plans. Needless to say, these plans are not greatly appreciated by the Somalis.'

'More savages?' James could not resist gently poking fun at her in turn.

'Yes, James,' she said, without rancour. 'More savages. Both they and the Ethiopians would make good soldiers, had they the weaponry. Are you, then, reluctant to sell guns to be used against the Italians? There would be a full partnership for the man who could gain Beinhardt a foothold in the Horn of Africa. The foothold would have to be permanent, but the possibilities for profit are immense.'

James made no reply, although his brain was whirring. It was a way out from the unfortunate impasse his no doubt misplaced patriotism had got him into—no one in Great Britain had ever done anything for him or his family, and no one there cared whether he lived or died. Had he been perfectly prepared to sell guns to Tippu Tib because he felt the African monarch had a sense of honour himself? Then why not the Ethiopians, and their Somali cousins? Ethiopia was at least a Christian kingdom, and had been one for several hundred years. So it was reputed to be barbarous; there were quite a few European kingdoms which were hardly less so.

Cecile was unrolling a map of Africa. 'Is it not the dream of your Cecil Rhodes, or as he is finished, we could say *was* it not his aim, to see this map coloured red in a swathe from the Cape to Cairo?'

'He has no hope of that, with German East sitting in the way.'

'He would have even less hope were there an Italian East just north of Kenya.' She rested her hand on his arm. 'I must get away from these bugs. Think about it, James. We are speaking of your future.'

Her perfume remained hanging in the still air, and he could still hear the rustle of

126

her silk underwear even after she had disappeared into her tent. He had spent so much of his life in the interior of Africa that he could be as affected as anyone by the sight of a white woman in all her splendour, and when that white woman was also beautiful, and setting up to be his employer it was heady stuff as she no doubt intended. 'Some woman,' Hammacher commented, reappearing to sit beside him and refill their glasses with brandy.

'Do you know she is now virtually running Beinhardt? So what do you reckon?'

'I think that as long as she pays our wages she's as good as her father,' Hammacher said. 'I reckon ... holy Jesus!'

James swivelled in his chair. There were several lanterns lit in Cecile's tent and they could see her, standing close to the outer canvas, silhouetted against the light. There could be no doubt that she was naked. Or that she was posed, slender flanks exhibited against full breasts and flowing red-brown hair, which she had unpinned. Equally there could be no doubt that she knew that by standing there she would be exposed to the eyes of the entire camp, but more particularly to the two white men.

'How far are we from the border?' Cecile

von Beinhardt asked at breakfast. She had clearly slept well, had had a bath—all the camp had been aware of her maids filling her tin tub—and exuded good health and sweet perfume. Which was more than James could say for himself, or, he supposed, Hammerach.

'Which border were you thinking of?' he asked.

'German East, of course.'

'How long is a piece of string, Fräulein?' Hammerach said. 'Mbeya is as far as we have successfully penetrated.'

'Then what lies over there?' She waved her hand in the general direction of the west.

'There, west and north-west, are the lands of Tippu Tib, which you say may soon become Belgian.'

Cecile almost snorted. 'How can Belgium lay claim to Central Africa?'

'It does. Or at least, King Leopold does. He employed the great explorer Henry Stanley to pass through those forests, laying claim, in the name of Leopold.'

'You mean we are talking about flags on a map. Why does he want this land?'

James shrugged. 'Rubber. Minerals. There is much wealth in what the natives call Katanga.'

'Should we not also be interested?'

128

'You will have to ask his Majesty,' Hammerach suggested.

Cecile gave him a glare. 'Well, then, to the south?'

'The great lakes. Then Portuguese East.'

'And again we are to be constrained by a little nation?'

'The Portuguese were the first Europeans in East Africa,' Hammerach said mildly. 'They were here even before the Spaniards. Portuguese East was confirmed as within their sphere of influence at the Congress of Berlin, in 1878. Prince Bismarck himself agreed to it.'

'Prince Bismarck,' Cecile said, again contemptuously. 'That is history.'

'Nonetheless, to encroach too far to the south might cause a diplomatic incident, in which we might find ourselves isolated in the concert of Europe.'

The concert of Europe,' Cecile said, even more contemptuously.

'That is why we, the German government, your father, Fräulein, need to be careful about what we do,' Hammerach remarked.

'What he means,' James said, grinning, 'it is why you find it necessary to employ men like me, renegades, to sell your guns for you.'

Cecile gazed at him for several seconds while drinking her coffee. Then she said.

'You were to give me an answer to my proposal, today.'

'As I am outside of the concert of Europe, I think I will say yes to your proposal, Fräulein von Beinhardt.'

Cecile smiled. 'Excellent. I am so pleased. We will take the train to the coast tomorrow morning.'

'We?'

'You will accompany me, James. You may leave the building of this warehouse to Herr Hammerach.'

That night she did not again wander naked behind her tent flaps. James supposed that she regarded herself as having succeeded in what she had set out to do. So, she would use every weapon she possessed to achieve her goals, from money to her body ... and prospects? It was not a point of view with which he had come into contact before. But the prospects ... 'Tell me of this woman of yours,' Cecile remarked, as the train rumbled east. She had shown little interest in the extremely interesting country through which they were passing, with big game from giraffe to lion occasionally visible in the distance, even if they had learned to keep their distance from the roaring iron horse.

'She saved my life.'

'And you have shown her a proper

130

gratitude. I heard a rumour, when I was in Dar-es-Salaam, that you intend to marry her. Or perhaps you have already done so.'

'I haven't got around to it yet.'

'But you do intend it? Do you not suppose it might be a limiting factor, as regards your future, to be married to a half-caste?'

'Martha is the mother of my daughter.'

'And you are an honourable English gentleman, as you have exemplified. I still think it would be a mistake. I am sure she would do well enough as your mistress.'

'I think she would prefer respectability.'

Cecile smiled. 'The decision is yours, of course.' Now at last she looked out of the window. 'When will we reach Dar-es-Salaam?'

'Just about dusk.'

'Then you must dine with me, I am at the hotel. I would invite your fiancée as well, but I am sure she is not yet well enough for socialising.'

'Sweetheart!' Martha hugged him, and stood by proudly as he in turn held the babe in his arms. 'Will you be here for a while?'

'A while.'

'There was a lady here, inquiring after you. Very high and mighty.'

'She caught up with me at Mbeya. Cecile von Beinhardt. She is by way of being my employer.'

'A woman?'

'We live in a changing world. Now, I must hurry. Fräulein von Beinhardt wishes to entertain me to dinner.'

'Oh! I have nothing to wear!'

'The invitation is for me only.' He kissed her. 'Business. She is full of ideas.'

'Yes,' Martha said sadly, 'I can see that.'

'This is a somewhat primitive place,' Cecile remarked, as they sipped aperitifs. Although it was very hot, they were in the hotel lounge, for outside the bugs were swarming; fans rotated above their heads, but they still perspired.

'They've done the best they could,' James suggested.

They sat in cane chairs, and were attended by white-coated waiters while being eyed by the half-dozen other guests, all men. James did not know if they knew who Cecile was, but she was sufficiently eye-catching in a pale-blue evening gown with a deep *décolletage*, which left her shoulders and neck fully exposed, as her hair was again up in its pompadour. She wore a pearl necklace with matching earrings, and three extremely valuable rings—one, he noted, on her engagement finger; she had not worn that at Mbeya—protective armour?—and surveyed her surroundings like the queen she appeared. 'Now,' she said at dinner. 'You must explain to me what all of these odd things are.'

'The green fruit is avocado. We use it as a vegetable. Very nutritious. The fish is grouper. Those are peppers.'

'And these?'

'Ah, those are ground nuts. Again, very nutritious.'

'Does one eat them or swallow them?'

'I suggest you chew them.'

Cecile did so, and drank some wine. 'I wonder how these people's teeth survive! Now, James, plans. I wish you to return to Germany with me.'

'Eh?' James, also sipping wine, nearly choked.

'This Somaliland venture is not only productive, it is also dangerous. It needs planning to the last degree. And you must be in on the plans, do you not agree?'

'Well ... yes, I suppose I must. Is it necessary to make these plans in Germany?'

'Yes. In this instance, certainly. You must understand that there is a critical period ahead. I am not sure that Papa will ever be able to resume his position as Chairman of the company. Now, there is no risk of us losing control; we hold 70 per cent of the shares. But there can be no doubt that there will be, shall I say, some difficulties with the other directors. You know how it is; when the king dies, the nobles always wish to discover just how far they can manage his successor. And when his successor is a woman ...'

'I am not a director.'

'You are our principal salesman. You know Africa.'

'I have never been to Somaliland.'

'We will say that you have. None of them have been there either, so they will not be able to contradict anything you say, so long as you say it convincingly enough.'

'You are a devious woman, Cecile.'

She smiled. 'I am a determined woman.'

They returned to the lounge for their brandies. 'Am I allowed to bring Martha and the child with me?' James asked.

'I do not think that would be a good idea. We will make sure they are entirely comfortable here.'

'And how soon will I be returning?'

'That depends. A few months at the most. But in Germany. I wish you to be fully concentrated on the job in hand.'

'Somaliland,' snorted Herman Gruber.

'What will a bunch of savages pay us with? There are no elephants in Somaliland.'

'Actually, there are, Herr Gruber,' James said, having no idea whether there were or not. 'But there is gold in Ethiopia. That will be our principal source of revenue.'

'And the Italians?' inquired Joachim Speiren.

'It is a long coastline, Herr Speiren.'

James sat beside Cecile, at the head of the long table. They had travelled by way of Paris, and she had insisted upon fitting him out in several new suits, which made him look every bit as wealthy a gentleman as any of her co-directors. While she, as always, dominated the room in her pale colours and flaming personality, so overwhelmingly different to the drab greys, the clipped beards and moustaches with which she was surrounded. James had not been allowed to see her father, but he gathered that Count von Beinhardt was growing weaker every day.

'Is it then a unanimous decision that we proceed with this project, subject to the recommendations of our agent, Herr Martingell?' Cecile asked.

Someone snorted farther down the table, and someone else muttered *Engländer* disparagingly, but no one actually opposed the question.

'Thank you, gentlemen,' Cecile said.

135

She rose, and the men rose also, waiting while she left the room, followed by James. Outside, one of her male secretaries was hovering, 'Herr Guttmann is waiting to see you, Fräulein. He says you have a luncheon appointment.'

'Ah, yes. I had forgotten. I will be with him in a moment. Well, James? Are you content?'

He supposed that over the past few months they had developed the oddest relationship possible. They had spent most of those two months in each other's company, either on the ship from Africa, or in the train across France. She was a most beautiful woman, as she was well aware. She had also to be aware that he was sexually attracted to her. But she had never permitted him to cross the line of perfect propriety. They had slept in adjoining cabins and compartments, and never had she done more than say good night at her door before going to bed. While he ... sometimes he dreamed of her, still inhaling her perfume as he lay in bed. Of course he was betrothed to Martha, as she well knew, however much she might disapprove of it. But he did not suppose that would have inhibited her in the least had she wanted to have an affair with him. But she did not.

The plain fact was, no matter how

hurtful it might be to his masculine ego, that to her he was an employee and nothing more. But also, he thought, something of a toy, a prize poodle, to be displayed and for whose possession she should be congratulated. The great white hunter and explorer, now her personal agent for Africa. Why should he complain? So he said, 'Well satisfied. When do I leave?'

'We have to accumulate the goods.'

'That is not my province. I think I should pay a preliminary visit to Somaliland, just to make sure what we are about. We must make contact with this Mohammed ibn abd Allah chap, and make sure that he does have the money to pay us.'

'I think that is an excellent idea. Do you know, I think I may accompany you.'

'You? With respect, Cecile, the Horn of Africa is no place for a white woman.'

'They said that about the Congo. Now I really must rush, for lunch. I will have to persuade Guttmann, again, but that should not be difficult.'

'Who is this Guttmann?' James inquired.

Cecile gave one of her secretive smiles. 'He is the man I am going to marry.'

James felt as if he had been slapped in the face, even if he had seen the engagement ring. But what had he expected? That a beautiful young woman like Cecile von Beinhardt, heiress to a vast fortune and apparently determined to increase that fortune, would remain a spinster? She had indeed explained the difficulties of being a woman in such a masculine world as that of the arms trade. But it was nonetheless a shock, and not merely because the event would move her entirely out of his orbit for all time, but because he had to assume that her future husband would also wish to have a hand in the business. Would Cecile be able to manage him as easily as she managed her co-directors?

Feeling thoroughly out of sorts, he called for a horse and went for a canter through the woods after lunch. He was the only one at lunch; the Countess was at the hospital visiting her husband, and Clementine was out taking singing lessons; clearly Cecile had no intention of letting her sister have any share in the management of the company. The sun was setting when he walked his mount into the courtyard of the Beinhardt mansion, where grooms were waiting to take his reins, and Lisette was also waiting; he had left Mbote behind in Dar-es-Salaam and in the course of their journeyings he had come to know her almost as well as her mistress. 'Fräulein Cecile would like to speak with you, Herr Martingell.'

'Shall I not change, first?'

'She said for you to come to her the

moment you returned, Herr Martingell.'

James paused long enough to tap mud from his boots, then followed Lisette up a flight of side-stairs. This was a part of the house he had not been in before, as the guest apartments were in the other wing. He followed the maid along a well-carpeted and wide hall, to arrive before a pair of double doors, on which Lisette knocked. 'I have Herr Martingell, Fräulein.'

'Send him in,' Cecile called.

As if he were a servant, James thought. But then, he was a servant, in her eyes. Never before had he been invited into her bedroom. As Lisette opened the door her face was expressionless, but there were pink spots in her cheeks. James stepped past her, and the door was closed behind him.

Cecile lay on her stomach across the centre of a huge double tent-bed. She was wearing only a négligé, in the sheerest pale pink, and James' mind was overwhelmed by the curve of the buttocks at which he was staring. 'James,' she said, and rolled over. The negligee was not fastened, and now he was presented with a vision of thrusting breasts and thick-coated groin, while her legs, long and slender, were perfection; her hair was loose and flooded everywhere. 'Surely you are not shocked?' she remarked.

Of course he was shocked. 'Surprised, perhaps, Cecile.'

'You and I can have no secrets from one another,' she remarked enigmatically, and got off the bed, stalking across the room in a floating world of inexpressible femininity. She went to the table, on which there was an ice bucket containing an open bottle of champagne, and two glasses. 'You pour,' she commanded.

James stood beside her, and obeyed; it occupied his hands, which were demanding that he touch her. 'I have broken my engagement,' she said, taking a glass from his fingers and drinking. 'That fool forbade me to go to Somaliland. Would you believe it? My God, suppose I had been his wife?' James drank also. He didn't know what to say. 'So, I shall have to look elsewhere for a husband,' Cecile remarked. 'Don't you think that now, more than ever, you should rethink your relationship with Martha? I have said I have no objection to you keeping the girl as a mistress, or bringing up the child as your bastard.'

James was still lost for words; he had never encountered a woman, or expected to, who could determine for herself so completely what she wished, and say so.

'So,' she said. 'Let us first of all discover whether we can please each other.' She stood against him to loosen his tie, and was distracted by a banging on the door. 'I said I was not be disturbed!' she snapped loudly.

'Fräulein!' This was a man's voice, not Lisette's. 'There is news from Africa.'

Cecile frowned, then stepped away from James, and tied the cord to secure her negligee. 'What is it?' She opened the door.

'War!'

Cecile frowned at the butler, while James' head jerked. 'We are at war?' Cecile demanded. 'That is not possible.'

'We are not at war, Fräulein. England and the Boers. The Boers have invaded Natal. It has come through on the wire. The English are being defeated, everywhere. They say Durban will have fallen by the end of the week.'

Cecile gazed at James, her mouth open. 'It's not possible,' James echoed, 'for the Boers to beat the British.'

'It is what is happening, Herr Martingell,' the butler said.

'And the Boers did beat the British in 1881, at Majuba Hill,' Cecile pointed out.

James couldn't argue with that. But he still couldn't believe that the British would let it happen again. And there was another thing: 'If the Boers have attacked the British in Natal,' he said, 'they must know that there will be a massive response.'

'That remains to be seen,' Cecile said.

'I can assure you that there will be. And certainly President Kruger had to anticipate it, whether it happens or not. He must be very well equipped for a serious war.'

'I am sure he is,' Cecile agreed. 'Thank you, Johann. That was a most interesting piece of news.' She closed the door.

'Therefore he must be assured of a continuing supply of arms and ammunition,' James said, half to himself.

'I hope you are not thinking of rushing off to fight for the British?' Cecile asked, releasing the fastening of her négligé. 'You are not a soldier, James. And you are nearly 40. They would not want you, or need you.'

'You are selling weapons to the Boers,' he said.

'Yes.' She refilled their glasses. 'They are paying very well. As you say, they need those rifles. And those bullets. And those guns and shells.'

'I thought ...'

'You did not think anything, James, save that you determined you would have no part in it. I honour those sentiments. Thus I have made arrangements for you to use your talents elsewhere. But your talents are but an aspect of my father's business. We sell guns to whoever will buy them. That is the law of the marketplace.'

'Everyone who works for you shares a responsibility for what you do.'

'Do not be absurd. I take the responsibility for what I do. I do not expect anyone else to do so. I do hope you are not going to be foolish about this, James.'

God, to be able to speak with William, and find out what he thought! But this woman was his future, in so many ways. Their future, as well, of course. But the offer she had been about to make when they had been interrupted ... could any man refuse to accept Cecile, offered body and soul? But it would be his body and soul in response. She might be prepared to take full responsibility for the acts of her company, and her husband would obviously be associated with those acts. But what did he owe England? It had cast him and his family out. And he had not taken part in the selling of the guns to the Boers. Obviously people would point the finger, but he was innocent. And England and Germany were not at odds; in fact, the two countries had never been more friendly. 'As you say,' he agreed. 'I must make preparations to leave for Somaliland.'

She nodded. 'And I will accompany you. We shall make a grand safari.'

'Into the desert?'

'Why not?'

'What about all those severed penises?'

She smiled. 'I do not have one, James. Perhaps you had noticed that.'

The conversation was getting out of hand. 'I would like to return to Dar-es-Salaam first.'

She studied him. 'With what in mind?'

'I am still hoping for news of my brother. And I cannot just abandon Martha. And the child.'

'Of course not. Not physically, certainly. It is the other that concerns me.'

'Cecile ...' he hesitated. The fact was that while he considered her perhaps the most beautiful woman he had ever met, and every time he looked at her wanted to take her in his arms, which made her a woman he could very easily love, she was a woman he could never *like*. But she was the gateway to a glittering future. Besides, he wondered if she really liked *him?* She wanted a husband, but had been disappointed in her original German choice; now she sought someone who should bring her strength and experience of the business, and who would not be subject to the vagaries of German society or custom. And who she could utterly dominate.

Perhaps she could read his mind. 'I

know,' she said, 'I have been told, often enough, that I am a domineering bitch. How could it be otherwise? Had Papa had a son, things might be different. But I have known from when I was a little girl that I would inherit the business ... but also that custom demands I have a husband to rule it. So you see, I need strength without rivalry.' She herself refilled their champagne glasses. 'I will offer you a pledge, James. I will rule the House of Beinhardt, with you at my side. To do this successfully, we must promise each other that in public we will never differ on anything. Which means that you will accept my ruling on all public matters. But whenever we close that door on us, or any other door, for that matter, I will be your abject slave, to do with as you please. There, you see, I am being absolutely straight with you, as I will expect you to be absolutely straight with me. Will you agree to my proposal?'

She waited, standing absolutely still, while he gazed at her. Then he lifted his glass and drank.

James had never held a white woman naked in his arms before. But he suspected that even if he had, their memory would all have been swept away in an instant by Cecile von Beinhardt. She surprised him in so many ways. Whatever the vicissitudes of his family's recent history he had been brought up as a gentleman. White women were creatures apart. As a boy, he had doubted they possessed legs, as he had never seen any. He had never seen Maria's legs, or Catherine's.

They were not to be touched, except decorously by the hand. Their hair could only be admired, on their heads. To imagine hair on other parts of their bodies was impossible, a motley of unfulfilled dreams. Obviously they had to couple with their husbands, or the race would have died out long ago. But how this occurred was again unthinkable for a bachelor. The only married couple with whom he had ever been the least intimate was William and Maria, and they had never suggested that they used their bed for anything more than sleep and a certain required duty. Even to suspect that a white woman, a white lady, a member of the German aristocracy, could use her body as vigorously and sensually as Martha, would have left him breathless before today.

Then what of today? For compared with the sensuality of Cecile von Beinhardt, Martha was an ignorant and reluctant child brought up, even as a whore, in the strict sexual probity of the Boer ethos. Having released her négligé and allowed it to drift to the floor, Cecile had herself undressed him, revealing a detailed knowledge of male undergarments. As she stood against him, and his hands remained at his sides, she had said, 'You may touch me, if you wish, James. I *am* yours.'

Her skin had been like velvet. He had shuddered with anticipation as his hands had slid over those marvellous buttocks before coming up to cup her breasts. Then she had gently pushed him back across the bed to remove his boots and stockings and then his breeches. Then she had lain on him to kiss him, but before he could enter her she was away again, entirely twisting her body so that her head was between his legs, her lips seeking her goal, while he found himself in a similar position, for a moment uncertain what to do, what he dared do, before realising that, as she had promised, she was all his. When she did at last allow him entry, she seemed able to time her climax to his, another new experience, as he had not suspected white women allowed themselves such transports of joy and he suspected Martha always faked hers to please him. After, Cecile said, 'I think we should speak with Papa.'

Adolf von Beinhardt was clearly at death's door. James doubted he knew much of what was said to him, but that he raised his hand seemed to be accepted by both Cecile and her mother that he agreed to the proposed marriage. 'But when?' Hildegarde von Beinhardt asked, as they drove back to the house in a four-wheeler with a postilion in position. 'The doctor says he will not last the week.'

'Yes,' Cecile agreed, her tone conveying, what a nuisance.

James wondered if she was capable of actually loving any human being. Then he must be the same. They sought only profit, from each other as well as the world. Then so be it. 'So, we will arrange the marriage for next summer,' Hildegarde said.

'Seven months?'

'I am afraid that is what is required.'

'I shall probably be carrying all before me by then,' Cecile remarked. Her mother gave her a shocked look, and then glared at Clementine, who was hiding behind a fit of giggles. Then the glare was turned on James. 'Oh, don't take on at James,' Cecile said. 'I merely mean that it is necessary for us to go to Somaliland, and by the time we return, well ...'

'You cannot go anywhere while your father is in this state,' Hildegarde told her.

'This is business,' Cecile argued. 'Papa would wish me to go. If we do not take this opportunity, the Somalis will look elsewhere.'

'You would desert your father's death-bed?'

'Business,' Cecile said, in tones that left no room for further discussion.

'I think perhaps your mother is right,' James ventured, as he and Cecile sat together after dinner, both Hildegarde and Clementine having retired. 'You should stay for your father's last days.'

'And suppose he lingers for months? That is quite possible, you know.'

'Well, I can go on ahead. I am still not happy about you coming to Somaliland until I have checked things out. Or at all.'

'You mean you wish to get down to Dar-es-Salaam and that whore of yours,' she remarked. She was not in a good mood.

'You said I could do that. It would also be interesting to discover at first hand what is happening down there.'

The newspapers were still full of Boer victories, but also that the British were stirring themselves, and despatching more troops as well as their most famous General, Roberts, to sort things out.

Cecile snorted. 'You mean you wish to become involved. Your British blood is stirring.'

'Not in the least. But it is our

149

marketplace that is being torn apart. One of them. There is also my brother and his family. I really am bothered about them.'

'And Martha?'

'I think I need to explain the situation to her.'

'That you are going to marry me.'

'If you have not changed your mind,' he said.

She glared at him, then smiled. 'I am a bad-tempered bitch, am I not? We will consider the matter. Now come to bed.'

'With you? Here?'

'Have you not already done so? My dear James, I do not propose ever to sleep alone again, so long as you are available.'

James did not suppose there was any man who had so fallen on his feet. The world was his, so long as he remained Cecile's partner, and even more when he became her husband. If only he could rid his mind of the feeling that he had sold his soul for a mess of pottage. But if he had, it was to enter the very gateway of heaven on earth.

He lay on his side, in the dawn, gazing at her. She slept with perfect composure, as she did most things in life. Yet utterly relaxed, her face was no less strong than when alert, her lips tightly closed, her nostrils dilating gently as she breathed. She lay on her side, her legs spread like scissors, her hands clasped in front of her, her hair spread around her like a shawl. His wife! How could a man not love such a superb creature.

Downstairs a bell jangled. Cecile's eyes opened, flickered for a moment, then remained open, gazing at him.

Then she sat up, suddenly and violently, discarding the bedclothes so vigorously that he too was left exposed. She leapt out of bed, reached for her robe, just as there were footsteps in the hall outside and a banging on her door. 'Fräulein! Fräulein!'

'Cover yourself,' she told James, and strode to the door to open it.

Lisette was trembling. 'Fräulein! A messenger from the hospital. The Count is dead!'

'Has my mother been told?'

'She is being told now, Fräulein.' And at that moment from along the corridor there came a wail of anguish.

'Very good. Now help me dress. Oh, do not mind her, James. You must dress also. We must hurry.'

James got out of bed and reached for his underwear, while Lisette, sorting through Cecile's underclothes, hastily averted her eyes. 'I am most terribly sorry,' he said.

'Sorry?' Cecile frowned at him for a

moment. 'We knew it was going to happen any day.' Then she smiled. 'And now I am mistress of the Beinhardt Company. There is a dream come true!'

PART TWO

Reaching

'The devil's most devilish when
   respectable.'
Elizabeth Barrett Browning, *Aurora Leigh*

Chapter Five

The Mullah

It was not as simple as Cecile made out. Quite apart from the ceremonies surrounding the Count's funeral there were a hundred and one legal matters to be attended to, for, although the Count left his entire estate to his family, this was in the first instance to his wife, nor did he make any specific reference to Cecile taking over the running of the business, although he did make it plain in his Will that he expected the management to remain in his family. 'I imagine he assumed it would be placed in the hands of your husband, Fräulein,' Herr Dorting, the solicitor, suggested. 'Your father of course had no expectation of dying so young. But as you are not yet married, I think the best thing would be a—shall we say—type of regency, where the management is exercised by your mother and your sister and yourself, with suitable advice from the other members of the board.'

'That is utter nonsense,' Cecile declared. 'Mother has no wish to become involved in the business, and Clementine does not know how many beans make five. In any event, I am about to be married, the very moment it can be done with propriety.' She squeezed James' hand; he was seated beside her before the lawyer's desk, feeling extremely embarrassed.

'Ah!' Herr Dorting commented. 'It is your intention, then, to make Herr Martingell managing director of Beinhardt's?'

'He and I will run the company, yes.'

'You will have to have the agreement of the other directors.' Dorting's tone was sceptical.

'I will not. I will have to have the agreement of the majority shareholder, who happens to be my mother.'

Dorting tried another tack. 'There may be questions asked as to the suitability of Herr Martingell, with respect. His experience ...'

'Herr Martingell has been in the arms business as long as any member of this firm,' Cecile declared. 'Certainly longer than any of my co-directors. What is more, he knows the business on what might be called the shop floor. He goes out and sells the guns himself, not through an agent.'

Dorting looked scandalised. 'Well ...' he set up his last rampart. 'It would still be going against the implicit intention of your father's Will were Herr Martingell to be given an executive position within the company, and certainly that of Managing Director, before he became your husband.' He gave James another nervous smile. 'With respect, Herr Martingell.'

'Well, then, my mother and I will manage the company until then. It will come to the same thing.' She stood up with an immense rustle of black skirts.

'Lawyers!' Cecile said contemptuously, when they regained the house. 'Businessmen! All they know is how to create barriers, whereas you and I, my darling, know what needs to be done. One thing is certain: Father agreed to negotiating the Somali arms contract if it could be done. No one can gainsay that; and that is what we are going to do.'

'I entirely agree,' James said enthusiastically. 'Is Monsieur Le Barthe still about?'

'I understand he has gone back to Paris, no doubt looking for a new client. I shall wire him immediately that we are still in business. Then, I will leave mother to cope here, and ...'

'Cecile!' She glared at him. 'I do think that in our present circumstances we should add commonsense to propriety. The Horn of Africa is absolutely no place for a white woman. And the House of Beinhardt needs you here for its proper operation. I beg of you to be sensible and let me handle this.'

'What you mean is that you wish to return to Dar-es-Salaam and see your floozie without me hanging about.'

'We agreed that it was both necessary and correct for me to see Martha. I promise you it will be a short visit. Then I shall be up to Somaliland with the necessary samples. Meanwhile, you can be accumulating the actual shipment here. I will wire you the moment I have seen the colour of this Mohammed ibn abd Allah's money.'

She considered him for several seconds. Then she said, 'Perhaps that would be best. Just remember, the future is you and I. Neither one nor the other.'

James supposed there was no man who could be in a more fortunate position. He was loved with a consuming passion by a most beautiful and wealthy woman, who was intending to make him as wealthy and as powerful as herself. At Cecile's side, all the uncertainties of his youth would be buried forever. The problem was that it was a consuming love, and that his future depended upon his being at her side, not her at his. No doubt that was sheer male chauvinism rearing its head; he had lived all his life in a world where men were men and women fell into line behind them. That was not to say such a relationship as she intended could not work, especially as Cecile seemed prepared to follow his dictate, at least in public. And although they had not discussed it, he was certain she would find a place for William beneath Beinhardt's financial umbrella.

Then why was he feeling like a released convict as the steamer emerged from the Red Sea and began its journey down the West African Coast? Was it because he was returning to that part of the world he knew best? Or because he was going back to Martha—for the last time? But Cecile had also agreed that he could keep the half-caste as a mistress, if he chose. 'The Horn of Africa,' remarked Captain Bessers, standing beside him. The Captain was well aware that James was a representative of the House of Beinhardt, and was accordingly deferential, even if he did not know James' ultimate destination. Now he offered his telescope, and James levelled it across the sparkling blue water at the brown haze. 'Nastiest place on earth,' Bessers remarked. 'And I've seen a lot of them.'

'Is there a harbour?'

'Place called Mogadishu. The Italians control it. Well, they claim the whole country. Welcome to it, they are. Nothing but desert, scorpions, red ants and savages.'

'They must have a reason,' James ventured.

'Oh, yes! They want Ethiopia, and they have to have a sea base. Imperialism gone mad. But they're hell bent on avenging Adowa, whenever they can.'

'Have you ever heard of a Somali warlord called Mohammed ibn abd Allah?'

'Yes. He makes all the rest seem like saints, scorpions and all.'

'Why?'

'He's a fundamentalist Muslim.'

'Which surely merely means he's a puritan in morals.'

'Indeed. But there is more than that. As you said, he calls himself Mohammed ibn abd Allah. That's a kind of Mahdi. You know, the Muslim messiah, the promised one. He believes he's immortal, and it's off with the head of anyone who opposes him. You know what they call him? The Mad Mullah.'

'I imagine it's the Italians who call him that. Isn't the truth of the matter that he just wants them out of the Horn?'

Bessers gave him an old-fashioned look. 'No doubt, Herr Martingell. From what I've heard he's a cold-blooded murderer nonetheless.'

Something to be considered. But, James

reflected, any man fighting for his country will be considered a cold-blooded murderer by those he is opposing. And should he ever be captured by the Italians, he will no doubt suffer some cold-blooded murder himself, at the end of a rope. He looked forward to Dar-es-Salaam. And the port had hardly changed, except perhaps to grow. James supervised the unloading of the boxes of sample rifles but left them and his personal luggage at the customs house while he went into the town. It was still early in the morning, and although the inevitable crowds had gathered to watch the ship dock, most of the town was still asleep. Fessnung was one of those on the dock, however. 'James!' he cried in amazement. 'I did not know you were coming.'

'There's a lot to be done.'

'We heard of the Count's death, of course. We did not know what to expect. But there was a wire last week saying business as usual.' He frowned. 'That did not mention your visit, either.'

'It's rather hush-hush. I'll explain it later. But it is business as usual. Right now, I must see Martha.'

'Ah.' Fessnung scratched his ear. 'It might be better for you to come home with me and have some breakfast, and we will send a messenger to acquaint Martha with your arrival. Does that sound a good idea?'

'No, it does not,' James said. 'She is on my mind, and I want her off my mind before we get down to business.' He frowned. 'She's been getting her allowance?'

'Of course. Every week.'

'Right. I won't be long. Then, as I said, we have much to do.' Fessnung looked as if he would have said something more, but then thought better of it, and watched James striding up the dusty street.

He was at the house in ten minutes. This entire side street was still somnolent, with only an occasional dog slinking into the shadows. The blinds on Martha's windows were drawn, the house silent. The door was locked. He knocked, and as there was no response, banged as hard as he could.

'All right,' she called. 'All right! What you trying to do, wake the dead?' Then she said something else, but in a lower tone so that James could not make out the words.

A few moments later the door swung in, and she blinked at him. She wore a nightdress, which he surmised had only just been put on because it looked both clean and unrumpled, in contrast to her hair, which was scattered and soaked in sweat. She goggled at him. 'James? *James!*' her voice went up an octave.

'Sweetheart!' He swept her from her feet

162

and carried her into the house, kicking the door shut behind him.

'James!' she gasped, kissing him while panting for breath.

He set her down. 'Sorry I couldn't let you know I was coming. It's all a bit hush-hush. Now, is all well?'

'Yes. All is well.'

She was trembling, and now she gave a hasty glance up the stairs. James frowned at her, and suddenly realised what Fessnung had been trying to tell him. Martha licked her lips. 'It ... I must put some clothes on.'

'Not for me!'

'I must ...' she started up the stairs, checked when he would follow her. 'There is food in the kitchen ...'

'We'll eat together. Later. I wish to see the child first.'

She almost gave a sigh of relief. 'Of course,' then continued up the stairs, opened the door on the left of the landing. 'I do not think she is awake yet.'

James opened the door on the right, into the bedroom. It was gloomy in here, but he could make out the man, hastily dressing himself. He swung round as the door opened, and scrabbled for the holster on his belt, but James already had his hand on his holster, and was too quick for him. He levelled his revolver. 'Draw and you are a dead man,' he said.

The man raised his hands. He was no one James had seen before. Martha stood against the wall, shivering. 'Is your allowance not big enough for you?' James asked. He was more relieved than sorry that she had reverted to type, but he could not let her know that.

'He ... I was drunk.'

There was no smell of stale alcohol in the room, only stale sex.

'You.' James pointed at the man. 'Out!'

The man gathered his clothes in his arms and stumbled down the stairs. A moment later the front door banged. Martha began to regain her courage, for as yet James had not burst into violence. 'Are you going to whip me?'

'No doubt you'd enjoy that. No, Martha. I am going to make arrangements. You will remain here, with Anne, until someone comes for you. Do not attempt to take her away; there is nowhere you can go in Dar-es-Salaam, in all German East, that I can not find you very quickly. Then I *will* whip you, before I hang you. Remember this.' She gasped and sat on the bed. 'I will not be long,' James told her.

Fessnung sat behind his desk, looking embarrassed. 'You did not give me time to tell you,' he said.

'I agree. How long has this been going on?'

'Entertaining men, you mean? For some time. It is in her nature.'

'No doubt it is. Now, there are some things I need you to do for me. Where is my brother?'

Fessnung looked still more embarrassed. 'I'm afraid Herr Martingell is dead.'

James' head jerked. 'I was told he had been found, in Lisbon.'

'That is correct. And he returned here. But by the time he got here war had broken out between the British and the Boers. He immediately sailed down to Natal to volunteer. He was killed at the battle for Spion Kop, just before Christmas.'

'We seem to be cursed. Then tell me of his wife and children.'

'I believe they are still in Beira. But things are difficult there as well. Captain Delgado has lost his position.'

'But he remained in Beira.'

'I do not think he has the means to remove himself.'

'And the war? Before leaving Germany I heard that the British have checked the Boer advance.'

'Oh, indeed, and now they are pouring men and materiel into the Cape, and into Durban. This includes their most famous soldier, General Roberts.'

James nodded. 'I had heard that. So they will win?'

Fessnung shrugged. 'They have the power to win. But I think it will be a stalemate. The entire world is on the side of the Boers.'

'You mean Germany is on the side of the Boers.'

'The entire world,' Fessnung repeated.

'And good luck to them,' James commented. 'Now, here is what I require. I wish a coasting vessel, with an entirely reliable captain and crew, who will take me wherever I wish to go, clandestinely.'

Fessnung nodded. 'That will not be difficult. You seek a new customer for the house?'

'We have a new customer, or so I am informed,' James said. 'It is my business to confirm this. Second, I wish you to draw three drafts on the House. One will be payable to Captain Delgado, and will be sufficient to remove him and his family back to Portugal. The draft should be sent to him in Beira.' Fessnung frowned, but made a note. 'The second will be paid to Mrs Martingell, sufficient to remove herself and her sister and the children wherever they wish to go, with a rider that they are to be paid a pension for the rest of their lives by the House of Beinhardt.' Fessnung's frown deepened,

166

but he continued to write. 'The third will be payable to a suitable person who will take my child to Germany and deliver her to the care of Fräulein Cecile von Beinhardt. This should be payable in two parts, one for the expenses of the journey, and the other upon the safe delivery of the children.'

Fessnung regarded what he had written down. 'You are taking a great deal upon yourself, James. Can you be sure the House of Beinhardt will honour these drafts?'

'I can be sure. I will write a covering letter to Fräulein von Beinhardt now, explaining my dispositions.'

'And she will agree,' Fessnung said, thoughtfully. 'I will carry out your instructions, James. And wish you good luck.'

'There is one more thing,' James said. 'Where is Mbote?'

'Mbote? Why, he was here in Dar-es-Salaam when last I heard.'

'Find him for me. Tell him I wish to employ him again, as my servant.'

'Of course.' Fessnung was clearly relieved that Mbote was not also to be placed on a permanent pension.

'And find me that boat,' James reminded him.

James sat with Anne on his knee; she

was old enough to know him and love him. Martha sat on the other side of the room, watching them with smouldering eyes. 'Will you forgive me?'

'No,' he said. 'Because I have no doubt it would happen again, the moment I leave. And I must leave. I have made arrangements for the child. Do not attempt to interfere with them, or it will be the worse for you. Behave yourself and I will make over this house to you. That is, you will be able to sell it, if you wish, or remain here and practise your trade.'

She pouted. 'I saved your life.'

'So you did. And I am grateful, or you would not be getting off so lightly. Now remember, care for Anne until someone comes for her.'

'You think you can take away my baby?'

'That is what I am doing. She will be better off with me than she ever could be with you, Martha. You must see that.'

She pouted again. 'I ain't never going to see her again.'

'Right,' he said. 'You will not ever see her again. Now I am going out. I will use the spare room tonight.'

'You promised me you would marry me,' Martha shouted.

James, having kissed Anne, hesitated. 'Then I would have to kill you or divorce

you as a wife who betrayed her husband,'
he said.

'Bwana James!' Mbote said. 'It is good to
see you again.'

'And to see you, old friend. Will you
work with me again?'

'That is what I would like to do most,
bwana.'

James clasped his hand. 'The mission is
a dangerous one.'

Mbote grinned.

'There is a telegram for you.' Fessnung
held out the paper.

James read: *Goods despatched. Ship will be
in position south of Socotra one month today.
Signal by raising and lowering of flag. Good
fortune. Cecile.*

'Do you understand this?' Fessnung
asked.

James nodded. 'It means I have very
little time.'

'Your ship awaits you,' Fessnung said.

'Rudolf Barents, at your service, Herr
Martingell.'

The seaman was short and a bit stout,
but his shoulders were good and his eyes
clear. He was bald beneath his peaked cap,
and his blue tunic was well worn.

'He has worked for the House before,'

Fessnung assured him.

'Then you shall work for it again,' James said. 'You know what you have to do?'

Barents stood to attention. 'I am to sail my schooner wherever your worship wishes, and no questions asked.'

'That is satisfactory. How soon can we leave?'

'I understand there is a cargo, sir.'

James nodded.

'Then, as soon as it is loaded.'

'You have charts for the entire east coast of Africa?' James asked.

'Such as can be had, sir.'

'We'll load now.' James shook hands with Fessnung. 'My entire affairs are in your hands, Herman.'

'They will be taken care of. You have my word. But ... I cannot answer for what the House may do.'

James grinned. 'I can, Herman.'

Fessnung squeezed his hand again. 'Take care, old friend. I do not know where you are going, but this entire coast is unsafe.'

'And I am still alive,' James reminded him.

The schooner was called *Mannheimer*, because Mannheim was where Barents came from. She was 50ft overall and had a crew of six, apart from the captain; the deckhands were Arabs. Barents had his cabin aft, which he shared with James; Mbote, like the crew, slept on deck. 'Due east,' James told him, as they stood out of the harbour under shortened canvas.

Barents was obviously consumed with curiosity, but he had his orders and obeyed them, having to presume that his employer was making for the Seychelles, while James brooded at the dark water and the distant horizon. It had been a tumultuous few days since his return. Above all there lay the tragedy of his brother's death. William must have known things were looking up, but he had been haunted by his desertion of England, had been so anxious to redeem himself. And had died on a sunswept hillside. What a waste!

James had acted, as regards the Delgados, as it had been his duty. He had no doubt at all that Cecile would endorse what he had done to save them from poverty. For a white man, or woman, to endure poverty in Africa was a fate far worse than death. Equally, Cecile would have to be content with the outcome of his relationship with Martha. She had been prepared to accept the woman, but now that would no longer be necessary. She would certainly accept his child; she had already agreed to do so.

In real terms, therefore, matters had turned out as well as he could possibly have hoped. Yet he could not escape the feeling that he had not played a very gallant, or even manly, part in the business. Why, then, should he have gone south to Beira to see the Delgados' condition for himself? To maintain Cecile's unquestioning support, on which the Delgados now had to depend, he must carry out his duties, which to Cecile meant profit above all. The same went for his taking Anne back to Germany personally. Again, she would want to know why he was not in Somalia.

Should he have shot Martha's client dead, and then perhaps her as well? No one in German East would have charged James Martingell with murder. But he had only ever killed in self-defence, never in anger. Then perhaps he should have forgiven her. She had, as she had reminded him, saved his life. And he had, again as she had reminded him, promised her marriage. That was the point on which his conscience was really hung up, even if she been the most chaste of women in his absence. But it had had to be done, and he had to believe that she would be happier with the way things were, having as she did both the upbringing and the morals of a whore. It was time to look forward.

Next morning the schooner was alone on

an empty ocean. The wind had dropped during the night, and there was very little now. But it remained from the south, just sufficient to hold the sails taut, and the ship was making slow but steady progress to the east. 'You'll alter course, Captain,' James told Barents when the captain came on deck. 'Due north, until noon, when you can take a sight and establish our position.'

'Due north,' Barents agreed, and gave the necessary orders. Then frowned. 'The Horn?'

'Let's look at your charts,' James said.

These were spread on the cabin table. 'This course will take us directly into Mogadishu,' Barents said. 'You have business with the Italians?' He was sceptical.

'We will stand out beyond sight of Mogadishu,' James said, bending close over the chart as he studied it. 'We are making for Mareeq. There.'

'Mareeq,' Barents said thoughtfully. 'With a cargo of guns. Mareeq is beyond immediate Italian control, although that is not to say there may not be a patrol from time to time.'

'If there is, we will stand off until it goes away again.'

Barents brooded at the stiff paper. 'There is a harbour? I see no sign of one.'

'There is village, on the coast, and therefore some kind of shelter, I have no doubt. Just take me there.'

'You will sell these guns to Mohammed ibn abd Allah? Do you know of him?'

'I know of him.'

'He is a very terrible man.'

'So I have been told. But he is fighting a war, and he needs guns to do this successfully.'

'Half a dozen rifles?'

'These are samples.'

'He will cut your throat and take the guns, Herr Martingell. I do not wish to have my throat cut.'

'There is no need for you to risk anything. Just do as I tell you.'

With the wind astern they made a steady five knots; it took them a week to reach the latitude of Mareeq. It was a tense period, for while the weather held fine James was very anxious to avoid being stopped by any warship. They did sight a British cruiser, which raced towards them, belching black smoke, but she pulled away when she saw the German flag. In any event, they were sailing north rather than south, so even if the schooner was a gunrunner for the Boers, she had obviously delivered her cargo. James was more concerned about Italian interference. On the sixth day Barents closed the shore sufficiently for them to make out Mogadishu through binoculars, and James could see an Italian gunboat at anchor in the roadstead, but no one ashore seemed to have any interest in the schooner. Next day Mogadishu was behind them, and Barents could close the shore some more. Now James studied an empty brown beach, and empty brown land beyond. Sub-Sahara, he thought. He was used to the forest.

'What do you suppose that bugger wants?' Barents growled. 'Two of the bastards, by Christ! Pirates.' James levelled the glass to the north. Out of the shimmering horizon there were emerging two Arab dhows, each nearly as big as the schooner, and each carrying a vastly larger crew, armed, he rapidly made out. 'They're all pirates around here,' Barents grumbled. 'You'd best break out those rifles now, Herr Martingell.'

'Close the shore,' James told him.

Barents altered course to the west, and set a spinnaker, boomed out to starboard. The schooner increased speed, but the dhows were closing, slowly but steadily. Barents walked up and down his quarterdeck, snapping his fingers. 'They will cut our throats.'

'You have an obsession,' James pointed out, now studying the shore again as it

175

came over the horizon. A minaret to begin with, then a cluster of flat-roofed houses, painted in white and blues and yellows. No harbour, but an open roadstead where several dhows were anchored, and there was a reef, which would provide some shelter. He scrutinised the gently breaking water. 'Steer for that gap,' he told Barents.

'We will be wrecked,' the captain grumbled, but he did as he was told.

The pursuing vessels were no longer gaining, having shortened sail, clearly mystified that the schooner should be putting in. 'You'd best shorten sail yourself, and sound,' James advised.

Barents gave the orders, and a sailor went into the bow with the leadline. 'That reef is no shelter,' Barents complained.

'The weather is settled.'

'If it should come on to blow ...'

'Then I will tell you what to do. That water is green.'

Barents dropped his mainsail, and under jib and mizzen the schooner crept into the gap between the rocks. Now they could clearly see, the beach, where a large crowd had gathered, gesticulating and waving swords and spears; one or two fired muskets into the air. 'Close enough,' James said.

Barents had now taken the helm himself, and he spun the wheel to bring the schooner up into the wind. She held still for a moment, her sails flapping, then started to drift astern. 'Let go!' Barents bawled, and the anchor plunged into the clear water. 'Hand those sails,' the captain shouted, and the remaining canvas came tumbling down.

'Well done, Captain,' James said. 'Now put down a boat.'

Barents stared at the dhows entering the gap in the reef behind them; there were at least 40 armed men on each. 'We are abandoning ship?' he inquired.

'You are putting me ashore.'

'By the time you return, *if* you return, Herr Martingell, all our throats will be cut.'

'If those fellows try to come aboard, tell them you are in the employ of Mohammed ibn abd Allah. They will not dare touch you.'

Barents swallowed, he had no choice but to do as James suggested. A boat was put down, and James and Mbote were rowed ashore by two of the crew. Mbote was unarmed. James wore a revolver on his belt, but that was for show; he did not suppose it would be the least effective were he unable to establish himself. He also carried one of the rifles, unloaded. He sweated, but that was as much because of the heat as apprehension. He was doing what he had done a hundred times before in his life. Contrary to the general European view of the various African peoples—which arrogantly considered all the various tribes and nations as one people—he knew that they did not kill for the sake of killing, and were perfectly willing to accept friendship from any man. That they were universally suspicious, and often hostile to Europeans was because they had learned from bitter experience that the Europeans would kill, wantonly, in their pursuit of whatever they considered valuable. But he bore the most valuable gift in the world to an African warlord.

The boat neared the beach and the waiting crowd. The two crewmen backed oars, now looking distinctly frightened; almost every man waiting for them carried a sword or a spear. James sighed. 'All right,' he said, and stepped over the side into thighdeep water. 'I will signal you when I wish to return.' Mbote jumped in behind him.

James looked over his shoulder. The dhows were alongside the schooner, but there was no sign of any violence. The magic words must have proved effective. He waded ashore and was surrounded by people; these were no forest Africans but men as tall as himself, who stood very straight, and had brown rather than black skins. Their half-naked children swarmed about him; their women remained at the back. But were they not to accept him, their women would have their games—with parts of him.

A shiver, hastily suppressed, ran up his spine. Mbote's face remained impassive; he had total confidence in his employer. 'I seek Monsieur Philippe Desmorins,' James said in French; he had been told this was the lingua franca on this coast.

The people ceased their jabbering and stepped back from him. Obviously they understood only the name, and several pointed. James looked where they directed, and saw the Frenchman hurrying out of the village towards him. He was short and stout and soaked in sweat; he wore a dirty topee over dirtier clothes. 'Monsieur Martingell?' He peered at James from myopic eyes.

'I am Martingell.'

'My dear fellow. Le Barthe told me you were coming, but I had given you up.'

'I was delayed by domestic matters,' James explained. 'You have heard that Count von Beinhardt has died?'

'No,' Philippe said. 'I had not heard. But, *mon Dieu,* does that mean ...'

'Nothing has changed,' James said. 'If Mohammed can meet our terms, the weapons will be here in two weeks.'

'Your terms,' Philippe muttered, and looked at Mbote. 'This fellow is a forest African?'

'He is my servant,' James said. 'Where I go, he goes.'

'You'll come in out of the sun.'

He shouted at the onlookers, who fell away to make a path for them to go up the beach towards the house.

'My people are safe?' James asked.

Philippe looked at the schooner. 'They will be safe if those fellows know why you are here.' James nodded. They were in the village now, surrounded by growling dogs and even more vociferous children. Eyes peered at them from behind shuttered windows, while the main body of villagers trailed behind. James saw that behind the village there was a considerable area of cultivated land, irrigated by the meandering stream which seeped in from the rising ground behind. There was no desert here, although the land beyond the plantation was certainly arid. 'This is my store,' Philippe said.

James surveyed the surprisingly well-constructed stone building, which had been recently painted. As had the sign, *Philippe Desmorins*. The rest was in Arabic. 'What do you sell?'

'Anything that is saleable.' Philippe

parted a bead curtain to allow him into the shop.

'But where do you get your stock?' James asked, looking around himself at the miscellaneous collection of goods, stacked every which way, and varying from rolls of brightly coloured cloth to tins of paint, axes and saws—and one or two somewhat ancient firearms.

'I have a ship come once every other month,' Philippe explained. 'Out of Djibouti. That is French Somaliland, just round the Horn.'

'I know where Djibouti is,' James told him. 'But you cannot procure a supply of modern guns through there.'

'Well, no. The French authorities will not permit it. They regard Mohammed as much of a threat to them as the Italians. Or the British.'

'And you would not consider yourself a traitor, arranging for him to get the guns, anyway?'

'You'll take coffee?' Philippe parted another curtain and showed him into a darkened but comfortably furnished parlour. Here a young Somali woman, veiled to conceal her face but revealing a good deal else as her pantaloons were sheer, was waiting by the simmering stove. She did a double-take at the sight of Mbote. 'Then do you consider yourself a traitor,

in view of the fact that you are British?'
Philippe asked. 'Even if you work for a
German firm?' There was some contempt
in his voice.

'My information is that Mohammed
wars only on the Italians,' James said,
sipping the scalding hot, very strong black
liquid, and very aware of the presence of
the woman, who knelt beside him to hold
the saucer.

'My wife,' Philippe explained. 'One of
them. Her name is Atossa. I hope you
are right, as regards the British and the
French. These guns ...' he eyed the rifle.
'They are on your schooner?'

'I have a few more.'

'A few? Pouf! Do you not realise with
whom you are dealing?'

'It is necessary for Mohammed to
understand with whom *he* is dealing.
What I have with me are samples of what
we will supply, in as great a quantity as he
wishes ... once we have seen the colour of
his money.'

'Between them, the Germans and the
British feel they own the world,' Philippe
remarked, more in sorrow than anger.

'It would be very good for all of us if
Mohammed agrees with that,' James said.
'When can I meet him?'

'I despatched a messenger as soon as I
saw your ship entering the harbour. But he

will not come to the coast. You must go to him. We will leave tomorrow morning.'

'And my ship will be safe in my absence?'

'I guarantee it. Now let us relax, and eat and drink a little. Do you wish one of my wives for the night? They are all young, and clean.'

James looked at the woman Atossa, whose yashmak inflated as she smiled. 'I hope they won't take offence if I say no,' he said, reluctantly. And wondered why? The woman was certainly attractive, and Cecile could never know. And if she did, he did not suppose she would object. But it was necessary to keep his distance from these people and especially, he felt, from Philippe. He did not entirely trust the fellow. 'But Mbote may be interested,' he suggested.

'I do not give my women to forest Africans,' Philippe said.

Barents was unhappy at being abandoned, but as he had not yet been attacked and his throat remained uncut he was less depressed than usual. 'I shall not be gone long,' James assured him, as the guns were unloaded into the dinghy and carried ashore, where Philippe and his caravan were waiting.

'You have ridden on a camel before?'

the Frenchman inquired.

'I'm afraid not.'

'Ah. Well, this is one of our most docile beasts. What you do is this.'

James was installed, feeling distinctly insecure as his perch swayed in time to the beast's movements. Mbote also took some time to become accustomed to the strange seat. But eventually they moved off. They were a party of 12, Philippe bringing along two of his wives. 'For how may a man sleep in comfort, without softness at his side?' he asked.

They travelled almost due west, away from the irrigated and cultivated land—the stream meandered down from the north— out into a stony plain. 'They call this the Guban, the burned land,' Philippe explained. 'It is more fertile in the hill country.' He gave a brief smile. 'That is the land of Mohammed ibn abd Allah.'

The day grew hotter as the land gradually rose, and for the first time in his life James felt seasick. He was relieved when the caravan leader, Edoula, a heavy-set man who wore an ornately decorated dagger in his belt, called a halt and led them into a small depression. 'Italians,' Philippe said.

James accompanied the Frenchman and the Somali to the lip of the depression, where they lay on their stomachs and peered at the cloud of dust that rapidly became a body of some 40 horsemen, wearing blue tunics over khaki breeches, and armed with carbines, walking their mounts across the desert. 'A patrol,' Philippe explained. 'They are always a risk close to the shore.'

'Would they interfere with us?' James asked.

'Oh, yes, they interfere with everything. My women, pouf! And if they decided to search us and found those guns ... that would be very difficult.'

The horsemen passed by, at a distance of a quarter of a mile, and disappeared to the north. But Edoula would not let the caravan resume its journey until the Italians had been gone an hour.

To James' surprise, they lit a campfire that night. 'We are now beyond the normal limit of patrols,' Philippe explained. 'Besides, we must keep the lions off.'

'Lions, out here?'

'They range everywhere,' Philippe said.

But their sleep was undisturbed, and next morning they resumed their journey, the entire camp watching in amazement while James carefully shaved. 'In this country it is the custom to be bearded.' Philippe stroked his own bristle.

'But I am not of this country, and it would be best for everyone to remember that,' James told him.

The next day, after they had travelled all morning, they made camp at noon. 'Sheikh Daoud will meet us here,' Philippe explained.

James looked around at the brown stones and low hills. They had long left the river and it was difficult to see what was different, or sufficiently unusual to be used as a mark. But Philippe knew his man; they not been camped more than an hour when they saw dust to the west. The Somalis were so sure who it was that they did not even pick up their weapons. James stood up to watch the newcomers approach. There were 20 men mounted on camels, wearing flowing robes and armed with muskets, pistols and swords. Their leader was a somewhat little man, for a Somali, but had a big nose and strong jaw. He rode his camel at high speed and total expertise, brought the animal to a halt before the encampment in a flurry of dust, had it on one knee and was sliding from the saddle in almost the same movement. 'Sheikh Daoud,' Philippe said. 'May I present Monsieur James Martingell.'

He spoke French which was apparently understood by the Somali chieftain. Now Daoud looked James up and down, appreciating his height. But he was not about to be overawed. 'Where are the guns?' he demanded.

James gestured at the packs, and two of Edoula's party unwrapped the rolls to reveal the rifles. Daoud picked one up and examined it, again with a great deal of expertise, as he both looked down the barrel and along it, checked the trigger mechanism. 'This is good.' He looked to left and right. 'Where are the others.'

'There are five more here,' James said.

'Five?' Daoud's brows grew together.

'The remainder will be delivered when we have agreed payment.'

Daoud stared at him for several seconds. 'Where are they?' he asked again.

'On a ship off the coast,' James said, praying he was right. 'Not the ship on which I came,' he added hastily, not wishing either Philippe or Edoula to get the wrong idea.

Daoud continued to frown. 'This is not a game, Monsieur Martingell.'

'It is not,' James agreed. 'It is my livelihood.'

Daoud looked at Philippe.

'Monsieur Martingell's word is his bond,' Philippe hastily said. 'He is vouched for by my principals in Paris. He represents a German firm, famous for its arms deliveries.'

Daoud snorted. 'You wish money, before

you deliver the guns?'

'I wish to see your money,' James said. 'Then I will require a down payment. Then I will fetch the guns.'

Daoud considered some more. 'Mohammed ibn abd Allah would speak with you,' he said.

They continued their journey as soon as they had eaten. 'Now it is dangerous,' Philippe muttered.

'Did we not have to meet the Mullah, some time?'

'It would have been better with the guns. All the guns.'

They rode for the rest of the day, but did not break camp the next morning. Once again it seemed the Somalis would know where they were to be found. Now they were in a range of foothills, with higher land beyond. The ground remained parched, and open; there were few birds apart from the odd wheeling vulture, and no animals; apart from the humans, the only living creatures to be seen were ants and scorpions. James reckoned it would be very dangerous country for Europeans to campaign in, both because they would have to carry all their provisions, and all their water with them—unless they could persuade a Somali to betray his people and lead them to the various waterholes—and because their every movement would be overseen at some distance.

To his surprise, however, there was no shortage of water in the Somali encampment. 'We are close to a waterhole,' Philippe explained. 'That is why we are camped here.'

The well was just that, a hole let down some 50ft into the earth; blocked when not in use by a hand-planted bush, it could only be known to the denizens of the desert; another hazard for any invading army, as their enemies would be able to exist while they were on short rations. And when those enemies were all armed with Mauser repeating rifles ...! 'The Mullah comes,' Daoud announced.

The entire camp stood respectfully, as a vast crowd of camels approached. The army moved slowly, because an equal number of men were on foot, carrying folded tents and various other pieces of equipment. Behind them came the women, with food and cooking utensils. Both Daoud and Philippe performed the salaam, as the Mullah dismounted. James remained standing to attention, gazing at the tall, thin man in front of him, head concealed beneath his turban and features too, behind his beard. He did not think the Mullah was all that old, but he had an air of total command, and his dark eyes seemed to glow. 'James Martingell, your excellency,' James said.

Mohammed ibn abd Allah gazed at him for several seconds, then nodded. 'I have heard your name. You bring me guns.'

'These samples, my lord.'

Mohammed took one of the rifles and examined it as carefully and as knowledgeably, as Daoud had done. 'And the others?'

'Will be delivered upon acceptable terms.'

Another long stare, then Mohammed raised a finger. Instantly four men, who had been unloading panniers from the camels, hurried forward with an obviously heavy sack. This was placed on the ground, and at another gesture from Mohammed the neck was untied. Mohammed pointed, and James bent over it. The gold and silver coins winked at him. 'That is valued at one hundred thousand English pounds,' Muhammad said. 'It is the price we agreed.'

'I will take a thousand coins, as a deposit, my lord,' James said. Philippe hissed his terror at such presumptuousness.

'And the rest?' Mohammed asked.

'That I will take when I have delivered the guns.'

Mohammed smiled, a quick flash of white teeth. 'Then you will be an honest man. I will eat with you.' Philippe gasped in relief as the food was prepared. Mohammed gestured for James to sit on his right hand. 'When will this delivery take place?'

'Within two weeks. My ship is waiting for me.'

Mohammed nodded. 'At Mareeq?'

'Wherever you wish.'

'Mareeq will be best.'

'We saw an Italian patrol on our way here,' James said. 'I understand they sometimes visit Mareeq. If they should come while we are unloading the guns ...'

'It is my business to prevent them. Send word to me when you will be ready, and I will distract the Italians. But it must be done in haste.'

'It will be.'

Mohammed thrust his fingers into the pot of stewed lamb, and chewed, thoughtfully. James followed his example. 'I hope you are an honest man, Martingell,' Mohammed said. 'I have heard this, and now that I have spoken with you, I believe this. But so many men appear one thing and are in reality another.' He made one of his finger gestures. 'Take this man, for instance.'

From the crowd of Somalis waiting beyond the lunch party a man was dragged. He was a Somali himself, but his turban had been pulled off and he had been stripped to a loin cloth. Now, at another gesture from Mohammed, this was also stripped away. James suddenly had a violent attack of indigestion. 'This man betrayed us, or sought to do so,' Mohammed said. 'To the Italians. They paid him money. To betray those who have trusted you is the most heinous of crimes. Would you not agree, Martingell?'

James swallowed some lamb, with difficulty. 'I would agree, my lord.'

'Well, then ...' another gesture.

Instantly the doomed man was surrounded by Somali women, who proceeded to stretch him on his back on the ground. Several held him still by his arms and legs, while one of them, cackling in company with her sisters, produced a pot, with a spoon. With this spoon she proceeded to paint the traitor, from the navel to the knee, paying particular attention to his genitals and between his legs. The man writhed and struggled, but could not escape the weight of female flesh. As the women were all veiled it was impossible to tell their ages, but James did not suppose they were very old. His stomach felt light. 'Honey,' Mohammed explained.

When the man was thoroughly coated, Mohammed made another gesture. The women were now replaced by men, who pulled the culprit to his feet and marched him a few feet to a low mound on the earth. 'That is a nest of stinging ants,' the Mullah explained.

James' throat was absolutely dry. But he did not feel like drinking water—he would have preferred a large brandy.

The man was laid on his back, his naked buttocks in the exact centre of the mound. His arms and legs were spreadeagled, stakes were driven into the earth, and his wrists and ankles were secured, leaving him helpless.

Already the nest was starting to heave, and the man, up till now stoically silent, began to scream. 'The ants will eat the honey and beyond, first,' Mohammed explained. 'But then they will eat the rest of him.'

Chapter Six

The Transaction

'You'll understand why the Mullah is much feared,' Philippe observed, as they walked their camels back across the desert towards the sea. James made no reply. He still found it difficult to speak without his mouth filling with saliva. The man had taken a very long time to die; James was sure he could still hear his screams, the screams which had continued until the ants had reached his mouth. James did not suppose he would ever eat honey again. 'Can you imagine,' Philippe said, 'what it must feel like ...'

'I prefer not to,' James said. 'If you don't mind.'

'But you will deliver the guns.'

'I've accepted his money,' James pointed out. He would not admit the Mullah had terrified him as much as anyone. Easy to say that once he embarked he was safe ... but one never knew. What he did know was that an enemy like Mohammed ibn abd Allah would be as implacable as the Furies themselves. That was not something that could be risked. Equally, there was no question but that he possessed the money to pay for the guns. Just as he also possessed the power to take them, if he wished, without payment, once they were on Somali soil. But that was what this business was all about, risk and a trust in the future. If he really intended to press his war to a successful conclusion, Mohammed ibn abd Allah would need more guns and bullets, soon enough; why should he antagonise the man supplying him with those essentials?

194

And the Italians? James reminded himself that he was a businessman, not a moralist. He had nothing going for the Italians. As regards them, as regards all the white people in Africa, and that included the British, his sympathies were with the natives. By what God-given authority did the Europeans claim the right to divide up a continent between themselves, simply for prestige and wealth? There was morality for you.

They regained the coast without mishap, and without sighting any Italians either, and enjoyed the luxury of a bath and a sand-free meal. To James' great relief the schooner still rode at anchor, and as soon as he was cleaned up he signalled for the boat to pick him up. 'No trouble?'

'No, sir, Herr Martingell,' Barents said. 'But I am glad to see you back. Now we leave this place, eh?'

James shook his head. 'No, we must wait for the arrival of the steamer. You will be needed to ferry the goods, as there is no way she could get in here.'

'Jesus!' Barents muttered. 'If we are caught, Herr Martingell, we will all be hanged.'

'We won't be caught,' James assured him. 'Now come ashore and have lunch with Monsieur Desmorins.'

Barents relaxed over the wine, and even more in the company of the females, while, the meal over, Philippe retired with two of his women. The others looked at James and Barents expectantly, Philippe having again indicated that his friends could use any, or all of them if they chose, and were disappointed when James preferred to return to the ship, although Barents remained on shore. The execution of the Somali traitor might have turned Philippe on; it had quite put James off sex altogether, certainly with a Somali woman. But in truth he was too anxious to relax at all. It was now more than three weeks since he had been in communication with the Company, or with Cecile. There were so many things that could have gone wrong ... certainly the ship was due. But although he used Barents' telescope, the horizon remained empty of shipping, save for a few dhows and a distant glimpse of an Italian gunboat. There was a constant worry, although surely, like that British cruiser, the Italian navy was not going to interfere with a ship flying the German flag on the high seas.

Next morning he was awakened by a terrified captain. 'We have trouble!'

James dragged on his clothes and hurried on deck, to listen to the clatter of hooves and the rattle of *accoutrement,* as a squadron of Italian lancers trotted into the town, their pennons fluttering in the dawn breeze. The Italians clearly regarded themselves as being in hostile territory, for they had flankers out and the men had drawn their carbines from their scabbards and carried them on their knees. 'We must get out of here, Herr Martingell,' Barents said. 'But the wind is onshore.'

'Then we can't move. Nor should we. There is nothing to incriminate us.' The down payment was securely hidden in the schooner's bilges. 'Have the boat made ready.'

He was rowed ashore, just as Philippe staggered to the doorway of his shop, rubbing sleep from his eyes. 'Ah, Signor Desmorins,' called the captain, taking off his topee to wipe sweat from his forehead. 'Is all well with you?' He spoke French.

'At the moment,' Philippe muttered.

The captain signalled his men to dismount, and did so himself, stamping dust from his boots as he came into the shop, eyeing the women appreciatively, and then raising his eyebrows at the sight of James, who had followed him inside. 'Who are you?' he demanded, continuing to use French.

'This is Signor James Martingell,' Philippe explained. 'He is an agent from my company.'

'That is your schooner?' the captain demanded.

'That is correct, signor,' James acknowledged.

'It is flying the German flag.'

'We are a multinational company,' Philippe explained, sweating.

'Ha! To trade with this dump? I wish to search your schooner, Signor Martingell.'

'You're welcome,' James agreed.

'The reason I am here,' the captain said, importantly, 'is because we are patrolling the entire coast, looking for a German vessel, a steamer. She passed through the Suez Canal several days ago.'

'You are at war with Germany, signor?' James asked innocently.

'No, we are not at war with Germany. We are at war with this madman who calls himself the Mullah. And we have reason to believe that this ship may be carrying arms for the rebels.'

'Ah,' James said. 'The rebels. Who are they rebelling against, signor?'

The captain glared at him. 'Why, the Italian government of course.'

'But this is Somaliland, is it not? And this Mullah regards himself as the lawful government. Therefore would it not be true to say that it is you who are rebelling against him?'

Philippe was virtually jumping up and

down in terror. But the captain merely smiled, coldly. 'You are a lawyer, signor. Our law is here.' He tapped the holster on his belt. 'Now, we will look at your ship.'

He did not seem surprised when he found nothing. But, then, he was looking for guns, not money. 'Now tell me the truth, signor,' he said when his men had scoured the vessel from stem to stern. 'You are not really the business partner of Philippe Desmorins, eh? You are waiting for the appearance of this gun-runner.'

'I assure you, Captain, nothing could be further from the truth. Me, a gun-runner? Do I look like a gun-runner?'

The captain regarded him for several seconds, then signalled his men to embark. 'Let me give you a word of advice, Signor Martingell,' he said. 'I am continuing my patrol up the coast. I will be gone perhaps a week. When I return I do not wish to see you here, nor do I wish ever to see you or your ship in Somaliland, ever again. Do you understand me?'

'Absolutely,' James said. 'I will leave tomorrow.'

As soon as the Italians had departed that evening, James went ashore. 'We are done, finished,' Philippe moaned. He had put away an entire bottle of wine and had just uncorked another; his women were moaning to keep him company. 'Someone has betrayed us, informed against us.'

'Who are you more afraid of?' James inquired. 'The Mullah, or a squadron of Italian lancers?' Philippe swallowed. James pressed his point. 'There is all the difference in the world between being hanged and being staked out on an ants' nest.' Philippe dropped his bottle. 'But there is no need for either of those things to happen,' James pointed out. 'The Italians may suspect what we are up to, but they cannot be in two places at the same time. I am putting to sea, now, to find our ship; she cannot be far if the Italians are agitated. When I return, I wish a signal from you that the coast is clear. Understood?'

'How will I know when you return?'

'You will have your people mount a watch, and wait to spot my topsails. Then you will light a fire if it is safe to come in. If the Italians are here, or have been here recently, you will not light a fire.'

'And you will sail away again?' Philippe was hopeful.

'I will remain at sea for 24 hours, and then try again. And again. And again. Listen, old boy, you set this entire thing up. You simply cannot get cold feet now.'

He had Barents heave the schooner to as soon as the land faded over the horizon, and then mounted extra lookouts. Needless to say the first smoke they sighted was that of the Italian gunboat. Barents hastily had his men drop nets over the side and take on the appearance of earnest fishermen. The gunboat steamed up to within a quarter of a mile, inspected them through glasses, and then steamed away again. 'I do not see how we can avoid capture,' Barents grumbled. 'She is never going to be that far away.'

James was more interested in another plume of smoke, rising out of the northern horizon. The gunboat saw it too, and steamed towards it, while the schooner continued to roll in the swell, her crew hauling their nets. The two steamships closed, and James guessed that they were exchanging words through loud-hailers; he did not suppose both carried the new wireless sending equipment, although the gunboat might well do so. But the Italians had no legal right to search any vessel on the high seas, and Germany was a powerful and friendly neighbour; they were relying upon being able to catch the gunrunners in the act of unloading, inside what might be considered territorial waters. Soon the steamer was on its way again.

By now it was late afternoon, and by

the time the steamer drew abeam of the schooner it was all but dark. James had the ensign lowered and then raised again, the agreed signal, and the steamer proceeded on her way. But James, searching her upper deck with the telescope, had a sudden stab of indigestion; he could see the flutter of a woman's skirt.

The moon was not due to rise until past midnight, and by eight the night was as dark as it was going to get. By then the steamer was hull down on the southern horizon, while the gunboat had disappeared to the north. James had Barents dowse all lights and break out full sail to head south, and an hour later they made out the steamer, returning to them, also carrying no lights. Barents handed his sails and brought the schooner neatly alongside. Before they were even made fast the unloading had commenced. James went up the rope ladder to the deck, and faced Cecile. 'What in the name of God ...?'

'Did you really think I was going to stay away?' she asked, holding his hand to draw him into the deeper shadows of the cabin doorway to hug and kiss him. 'Oh, it has been so long!'

The feel of her, the scent of her, was overwhelming, banishing all his doubts as he held her close. 'You'll be out of here by dawn,' he said.

'Of course, with you.'

'I have to deliver the merchandise.'

'That is what I meant. I have so much to tell you. We have so much to talk about. Besides, I want to adventure with you. I fell in love with you when we adventured in Central Africa. I want to recapture that mood.'

James was torn two ways. Of course he wanted her with him. But he did not want her to experience the discomforts of the desert, not to mention the risk of capture by the Italians, or worse, the risk of exposure to the Mullah. But he knew she was not going to be put off, and she was the boss. The first thing she had to tell him was that she was now Managing Director of the House of Beinhardt; with her mother's support, all opposition had been overcome. 'It is only a temporary position, for me, of course,' she told him, standing beside him to watch the boxes being lowered on to the deck of the schooner; the hold was already full. 'As soon as we return from this venture, and are married, the firm will be yours, my love.'

He still couldn't believe it. But they had to return, first. 'You do realise that this is the most dangerous part of the whole business,' he said. 'We are now totally exposed.'

'I find that exciting!'

'And to the weather as well, begging your pardon, Countess,' Barents said. 'My ship is overladen.'

'The weather is fine. Let's be off.'

They shook hands with the steamer captain. 'How long, Herr Martingell?'

'Be in this position one week from today,' James said.

'I will be here.'

'A whole week in the desert,' Cecile said.

Lisette, who as always was accompanying her mistress, looked even more unhappy than usual.

The schooner was indeed heavily laden, and even with all sail set she made slow progress back towards the coast. Cecile and James spent the rest of the night on deck, while she told him of the many discussions that had taken place before she had obtained everything she wished; and of Anne, who had arrived in Cologne the day before she left. 'She is in the care of Mama and Clementine until we return,' she said. 'She is an attractive child, James, one would never know she has African blood. Her manners are atrocious, but I am sure we can put that right. How I look forward to having one of my own. Now you tell me, how did it go, with Martha?'

'Martha is history,' he said.

'Just like that! How cruel men can be!'

'I don't think they are any more cruel than women,' he said.

Dawn saw the Somali coastline ahead, but also the Italian gunboat, sweeping back down the coast. Those cases which had had to be stowed on deck were covered with tarpaulins. Both James and Barents were worried that she might notice how low in the water the schooner was, once she had identified them, but she did not approach them. 'There is a fire, on the shore.' Cecile was using the glass. 'Close to that cluster of houses.'

'Then it is safe for us to go in,' James said. He stood at her side while Barents as before took the helm himself to con the ship into the little harbour. Sail was reduced to the jib and mizzen, and they crept past the jagged rocks to bring up in the shallow water close to the beach. Philippe was waiting for them, and as soon as the anchor was down the unloading began again, a swarm of Somali-manned boats surrounding the schooner to manhandle the goods. 'Do you think the man who betrayed us to the Italians is in this crowd?' James asked.

'Probably, but I have told them all what happened to that traitor in the Mullah's camp,' Philippe said. 'They will have to think twice about risking their own ... well, we are hardly talking about necks, are we? Will you introduce me?'

'Philippe Desmorins,' James said. 'You know the name, of course, Countess.'

'I am pleased to meet you at last, monsieur,' Cecile said.

'Never has Mareeq been so graced, your excellency,' Philippe said. 'If you would care to come ashore, my house is yours until our return.'

'I am coming ashore, monsieur,' Cecile said. 'But to accompany you.' Philippe looked at James, eyebrows arched.

'She's the boss,' James explained. But he took her aside, while the last of the guns were unloaded. 'Do you have any idea just how uncomfortable this trip will be?' he asked. 'Quite apart from scorpions and snakes and men, all very unpleasant, there is the sun, and the sand. The sand gets everywhere.'

She smiled. 'But that sounds entrancing. You will have to remove it. Every last grain.' She kissed his cheek. 'If you are very good, I will let you do that service for Lisette as well.'

He sighed and gave up; Cecile went below, where her portmanteau had been stowed, and re-emerged a few minutes later wearing a divided skirt, a heavy blouse, a sun topee, and a veil, as well as thick black boots. 'Take me to your Mullah,' she said. Lisette was similarly clad.

Cecile's attitude to life was exhilarating, as always. She even seemed to inspire Philippe with some confidence, while his wives were fascinated by the two glowing white women, surrounded them constantly, getting as close to them as they could, fingering the material of their clothes, even attempting to touch Cecile's hair, none of them ever having seen auburn hair before. 'They do not come with us, I hope,' Cecile said to James.

'Philippe always takes at least one, for his creature comforts.'

'He seems to have a very well organised existence,' she commented. 'And what have you done for creature comforts, these last couple of months?'

'Practised being a monk.'

'Well, then, you must be fit to burst. Is there nowhere we can find some privacy?'

'When the safari actually starts, maybe. How are you on a camel?'

'You'll have to teach me.'

They began their journey at dawn the next morning. Philippe said that there had been no sign of the Italians, but anticipating their return in the near future, James sent Barents and the schooner to sea, with orders to return in five days; Philippe left the same orders for the lighting of the signal fire. Then the caravan headed into the desert. It was a large caravan, some hundred camels, carefully selected and hired, together with their drivers. There was the usual amusement as Cecile and Lisette learned to keep their seats, but by noon the sea and the village and the stream had disappeared behind them, and the sun was scorching down out of a cloudless sky. They stopped for the hottest two hours, until after two in the afternoon, sheltering beneath canvas lean-to's and gasping for breath. 'What do we do for water?' Cecile asked, her shirt stuck to her back and breasts, every curve of her body delineated, and the bandanna she had tied round her neck limp with moisture.

'We'll make a waterhole known to Philippe,' James said.

'Do you think I could have a bath?'

'You haven't brought your tub.'

'Well, I thought it best to travel light.'

'I'm afraid any sort of bathing is out. I did warn you.'

'So I'll stink, like everyone else,' she promised.

Just on dusk, they duly reached the waterhole and were able to slake their thirsts at least, while Philippe saw to the pitching of the camp. Now at last Cecile and James were able to find some privacy, removing themselves some 50 yards from the main encampment and the row of hobbled camels. 'Have you ever slept on the ground before?' James asked.

'Of course.' It was difficult to be sure when she was lying, or just poking fun. But she smiled at everyone during their evening meal, accepting the winks and nudges that accompanied her decision to sleep away from the camp together with her lover.

Then it was a night to remember. It had indeed been a long two months, and to hold a naked, sweat-stained Cecile in his arms after so long was to possess all the treasures in the world. Even the insects which swarmed about them were of no importance until they had both climaxed, and she lay panting on his chest, her hair flopping into his face.

'Tomorrow I am going to be one big bite,' she remarked. 'Why are these little beasts attacking me, and not you?'

'Like me, they prefer soft white flesh to hard brown flesh.' James untied the sleeping bag and allowed her to slide inside. 'We'll protect some of you, at the least.'

'Do you mean we cannot bathe again until we regain the coast?'

'Not unless Mohammed can get us to some flowing water. But I imagine he will.'

'When does he appear?'

'We've a day or two to go yet.'

Next morning they were off again at dawn, Cecile having smothered herself in perfume, which irritated the various mosquito bites she had accumulated, and the scent of which did not seem to please her camel. Philippe's woman—he had brought Atossa—giggled; she also had obviously spent a busy night, and smelt of it. Lisette, who had also slept away from the encampment, but alone, faced the day with grim determination, resisting the attempts of Mbote to be friendly. 'That is some woman you have there,' Philippe confided, as they raised camp. 'Is she yours, or are you hers?'

'It's a question I have been trying to resolve for some time,' James confessed.

'But she owns the firm, eh?'

'Practically. On the other hand, we are going to be married when we get back to Germany.'

210

'Some men are born lucky,' Philippe said.

'You do realise that you are going to be a relatively wealthy man when this deal is completed?' James reminded him. 'You can go back to France and make a good marriage for yourself.'

'I know, and it is tempting. To a Frenchman, there is only one place on earth worth living in, and that is France. But to leave my girls ... it will be hard.'

They had proceeded for an hour and the day was just getting hot when one of the rearguard pushed his way up to the front. 'There are people behind us, effendi.'

The desert undulated, and Philippe and James rode back to the last rise, from whence they could see for a considerable distance. Philippe had binoculars, which he levelled for some moments before handing them to James. James studied the horizon in turn; there was definitely a dust cloud behind them. 'How far?' he asked.

'Fifteen miles, maybe. If they are those lancers ...'

'We'd better hurry. How far are we from the rendezvous?'

'Tomorrow afternoon. They will be upon us before then.'

'Don't you think the Mullah has scouts out, overseeing us?'

'That may well be, but he may prefer to

leave us to our fate, rather than engage a squadron of Italian lancers.'

'Not when we are carrying the rifles he needs to fight his war. But I agree that we should make all haste.'

They rode back to the head of the column, where Cecile waited, she not yet being in sufficient control of her mount to move it more than in a straight line.

'What is the problem?'

'We're being followed. So let's hurry.'

'What will happen if they catch up with us?' she asked.

'If they are Italian soldiers, we will all be placed under arrest and ultimately hanged.'

'They could not possibly hang the Countess von Beinhardt.'

'I wouldn't rely too heavily on that; we're an awfully long way from Berlin. And you want to consider that for a woman as good-looking as you it might be an even longer journey to the hangman's rope.'

'You are poking fun at me.'

'I was never more serious in my life,' he assured her.

'But you will die fighting for my honour,' she suggested. 'Or at least save me your last bullet.'

'I'm hoping we are all going to live.'

They whipped all the camels forward, but there was a limit to how fast the beasts could trot without dislodging some of the boxes of rifles, or worse, James reckoned, unseating Cecile. 'We will not make the noon stop, eh?' Philippe decided. 'We will eat as we go.'

'My teeth will never be the same again,' Cecile complained, chewing the dried meat which was all that was provided for their midday meal, and being jolted by her camel as she did so. 'Or my stomach.'

'How about lower down?' James asked with a sly smile.

'You are a beast. All men are beasts. What was that?'

The sound of the shot hung on the air. 'Effendi!' The rearguard rode up to them. 'They are shooting at us.'

'So much for running,' James decided.

Horses always travel faster than camels,' Philippe said. 'We are done.'

'You are starting to sound like a cracked record. Horses also get thirstier. Would they have known where last night's waterhole was?'

'I think so. They would have followed our trail.'

'But they will still have needed to carry some with them. And where is the next?'

'I had planned to reach it by dusk.'

'Still four hours away. How many

fighting men do you have?'

'From this lot? A dozen.'

'We need to do better than that. Find me 20 men, arm them with these modern rifles and ammunition, and unload one of the Maxim guns.'

Philippe was aghast. 'Those men are regular soldiers. Two hundred of them.'

'We must save what we can. You will take the rest of the caravan and ride like hell for the waterhole. Once you get there, you will set up a defensive perimeter. Use the other Maxims. We will come back to you as soon as we can. The important thing to remember is that the Italian horses will need water desperately by then; keep them away from the water, and they will be lost.'

Philippe pulled his nose. 'And you?'

'I have said, I will come back to you as soon as I can. But we must check them. And when we do, they may well try to bypass us. That is why you must make all haste.'

Cecile was, predictably, a problem. 'If you are staying to fight, then so will I,' she declared.

'Now, sweetheart, don't be difficult. This is men's work.'

'I will wager anything you like that I can shoot as straight as you. Certainly as straight as any of those fellows.'

She glanced at the Somalis Philippe was selecting to form the rearguard, all chattering voices and rolling eyes, fingering their Mausers as if they were solid gold.

'That may be,' he agreed. 'But you are still liable to get hit. We all are. And if we are overrun and taken with guns in our hands ...'

'Do you think I can allow you to risk that?'

'You will, because you must. Now, either you go with Philippe of your own free will, or I will tie you up and send you with him as a prisoner.'

She glared at him. 'You seem to forget that I am the Chairman of the Company.'

'But I am your commander on the ground, Cecile. Now please do as I say.'

She hesitated, then tossed her head and rode away. Philippe had the rest of the caravan ready, and now they moved out. 'I wish you success, James,' he said. 'You are a brave man.'

James had never considered whether or not he was a brave man. He had always known what needed to be done, and had done it without considering the consequences. Up till now that simple philosophy had worked very well. Now it had to work again. He chose his ground carefully, on a ridge overlooking a reasonably flat stretch

215

of desert; there was a hollow behind the ridge, and here he had his men hobble the camels; he left two in charge. Then he assembled the Maxim, and put Mbote in charge of it—he already knew how to handle it—with one feeder. He arranged his remaining men on the reverse side of the chosen slope. 'Keep your heads down,' he told them, 'and mark your targets. Don't worry about being overrun in the first instance; the Maxim will keep them at a distance.'

He levelled his binoculars. The dust cloud was now not more than a mile away, and he could make out the flashes of light from the lanceheads; in another few minutes the pennons came into view, and the squadron flag. The Italians were advancing at little more than a walk. They knew they were within reach of the caravan, and James knew their horses must be feeling the lack of water. And as yet the Italians did not know there was any opposition.

Half a mile, he estimated. Yet he was reluctant to commit murder, as it would be if he merely opened fire on the head of the column. He used his rifle instead, sighted into the ground 50 yards in front of the advance guard, which was itself some hundred yards in front of the main body, six men and a sergeant. He fired, and the sand spurted where the bullet entered. Instantly the column came to a halt, and the advance guard retired. James could see the three officers at the head of the main column sweeping the desert with their glasses, trying both to identify where the shot had come from and what numbers might be opposing them. 'Keep your heads down,' he said again.

The Italian officers were consulting. Then orders were given, and the squadron extended into line. The crazy fools were going to charge. It would, after all, be murder. They simply did not know what they were up against, no doubt presumed it was the usual tribesmen armed with matchlock muskets. 'Remember,' he said. 'Mark your targets.'

A bugle blew, and the horsemen advanced at the trot. Then there was another blast and the commanding captain pointed his sword. James sighed, but there was nothing for it. 'Now, Mbote,' he said. 'Aim at the very centre of the line.'

Mbote began cranking the handle on the Maxim, while beside him his riflemen also opened fire. The Italians were charging, leaving a huge cloud of sand and dust, but the centre of the column, including the captain, one of his subalterns, the standard bearer and the trumpeter, simply disappeared before the hail of bullets. The

217

rest veered off, chased by the firing of the Somalis, and then galloped back out of range, a mile away, to regroup; at least ten men were lying scattered on the sand, some motionless, others writhing, several screaming for help.

'Cease firing,' James commanded, and the Somalis obeyed, reluctantly. Even Mbote sent one last burst after the horsemen; he was highly pleased with the devastation he had wrought. James looked at the sky. It was just past noon, and the day was at its hottest. He allowed his men to drink from their water skins, knowing that the Italians were even more exposed to the heat. Through his glasses he watched them dismount to drink, and to water their horses from the waterskins they carried. But those skins would be all but empty, now.

Then he saw two of the troopers mount and ride back the way they had come. They were sending for reinforcements. At the same time, the remaining officer mounted and advanced, accompanied by a trooper with a white flag tied to his lance. 'Nobody move,' James commanded.

The Italians came up to their wounded, staring at the ridge in front of them. Then they came on again. James sighted his rifle and fired into the sand, and they halted. 'We seek permission for a truce, to tend to our wounded,' the officer shouted in French.

'You have it,' James shouted back. He could almost see the lieutenant's brain working, as he would understand that had not been a Somali voice. 'Ten men,' James shouted.

The lieutenant saluted, and rode back to his men. Then he led ten of them forward with horses, and began picking up the wounded, who were crying out for water. The Italians cast fearful glances at the ridge, but James' men obeyed him, both keeping out of sight and refraining from shooting, although such games as allowing the enemy to collect their wounded were against all their ideas of warfare. 'Now,' James said. 'While they are preoccupied, we will fall back. Slowly and quietly.' He and Mbote dissembled the machine-gun while the Somalis covered them, then they crept back down from the ridge to where the camels waited. They mounted up, and rode off at speed. The Italians could see the dust cloud, but James knew the lieutenant would still have a problem. He did not know what size force had opposed him; he had to expect that a rearguard had been left behind; and he would know it would take him some time to mount his men and begin a pursuit—and what was he to do with his wounded?

All in all, James reckoned he would feel obliged to wait for the help he had sent for; much would depend on how much help there was, and how close.

They rode for an hour, then, in the shelter of yet another ridge, James called a halt and climbed up to survey the desert behind them. His jubilant men were now prepared to obey his slightest command. There was again dust out there, but it was several miles off. He resumed the retreat, and an hour later saw dust in front of him as well. 'I told you to keep away,' he said.

Cecile had 20 armed men with her, and herself carried a rifle. 'And I agreed to go to the waterhole with Philippe. Well, now we are there, and have established a perimeter as you commanded. We can resist an army.'

'We may have to do that.'

'Have you engaged them?'

He told her of the skirmish as they rode back. 'And none of you are hurt?' Philippe was incredulous. 'It was easy, eh?'

'That was easy, because they had no idea we were there or that we were armed with modern weapons. I don't think the next one will be quite so easy.'

He took a long drink of the surprisingly cool water—the well was some 50 ft deep into the sand—then they ate their evening meal, as it was now getting dark. The dust cloud had disappeared. Either the Italians had called a halt or they were advancing very slowly, and by now, James reckoned, they would be desperate for water. 'I think they have gone away,' Philippe said, with a sudden burst of confidence. 'We are too strong for them, eh? *You* are too strong for them, James.'

'I doubt they'd agree with you,' James suggested.

'But you have proved it,' Cecile said, when they again removed themselves from the encampment to find a little hollow in which they could spend the night.

'Don't forget that we still have to regain the coast,' James reminded her.

'You will find a way,' she said confidently. 'Now tell me about this Mohammed ibn abd Allah. Is he as fierce as people say?'

'Every bit as fierce as people say. Don't be taken in by his fine manners, or his personality. He certainly has that. But he has a different concept of ethics from us.'

'I can hardly wait to meet him,' Cecile said.

There was no sign of the Italians next morning. 'They have definitely given up and gone away,' Philippe said.

James was quite sure they had not; they

221

were just not prepared to take any more heavy casualties. But they still remained between the gun-runners and the coast. However, first things first. They proceeded on their way, and that afternoon came in sight of a line of camel-mounted warriors. James halted the caravan, and waited for the Somalis to approach.

'Martingell,' said Sheikh Daoud. 'It is good to see you. And you have brought the guns?'

'I have.'

Daoud looked at Cecile for several seconds, and seemed disconcerted when she met his gaze with perfect equanimity. Then he looked at Lisette, who hastily lowered her veil.

'His Excellency awaits you,' he said.

'I am quite excited,' Cecile confided to James.

They followed the Somalis into the hills, winding in and out of shallow valleys, until they reached the Mullah's encampment. This was far larger than James had anticipated, a small city of tents, approached through a carefully and heavily guarded defile. Once inside the camp they were surrounded by a vast crowd of men, women, children, dogs and goats, as they were escorted up to a central tent which could almost be called a mansion, as it clearly included several apartments. Outside it the green flags of Islam waved in the breeze, and outside it too, waited the Mullah, surrounded by his principal officers. 'James!' Mohammed embraced James, and kissed him on the shoulder, the warmest greeting a Muslim could give. Then he too stared at Cecile.

'Countess von Beinhardt, your excellency,' James explained. 'She is the Chairwoman of the House.'

'Chairwoman?'

'She is the boss.'

Mohammed smiled, and went towards Cecile, who remained standing still, hands at her sides. 'Mademoiselle! It is my very great pleasure.' Cecile extended her hand, and he took it, for a moment, then released it. 'You have made a very dangerous journey.'

'I was well protected,' Cecile said.

'And this young lady?'

'My maid, Lisette.' This time Lisette did not lower her veil, but flushed prettily.

Philippe told the Mullah about the Italian pursuit, and how James had driven them off. 'They will be waiting for you,' Mohammed remarked.

'We must try to evade them.'

'They know you have to return to Mareeq,' Mohammed said. 'We will have to divert them. But first, let me see the guns.'

His eyes gleamed as the boxes were opened. James assembled one of the Maxims for him, and he fired a few rounds. 'These are magnificent,' the Mullah said. 'Now we will carry the war to the enemy.'

'There is just one thing,' James said. 'After our resistance, they will know you have modern weapons.'

Mohammed's teeth gleamed through his beard as he smiled. 'I think that is to our advantage. They will be more cautious, but my men will be more aggressive. Let us eat.'

'You understand that the Countess will expect to eat with us,' James said.

Mohammed smiled again. 'It will be our pleasure.'

James could tell from the glances being exchanged that not all the Somali sheikhs appreciated the presence of a woman at their meal, and certainly the Somali women who were serving did not. Atossa was definitely offended and she ate with Lisette, away from the main body. But as always the Mullah was in complete control. He sat Cecile on his left hand, and invited her to dip into the pot before himself. On James' advice, she had carefully washed her hands before sitting down to the meal, to free her fingers of the least trace of perfume, and now she thrust her hand into the lamb stew with her usual confidence. Mohammed was delighted, and when she had conveyed the food to her mouth, he took her fingers and licked them clean, one by one.

Cecile looked across him at James, who could only waggle his eyebrows. Presumably Mohammed, like any respectable Muslim, had his own harem, but it was impossible to deduce who they were; he could only hope none of the serving women were part of it. Cecile felt called upon to make conversation. 'Have you ever visited Germany, your excellency?' she asked.

'I have never left Somalia,' he confessed. 'Perhaps one day, when we have won our war, and our country is again independent.'

'Ah,' she said. 'You would be very welcome.'

'I am sure of it. But does not Germany also have designs on Africa?'

'Not up here,' Cecile pointed out.

It was Mohammed's turn to say, 'Ah!' He obviously did not believe her.

'I'm in no danger of being raped by that old man, am I?' Cecile asked, when she and James were in their sleeping bag.

'He's not that old,' James told her. 'It's the beard.'

'You should allow yours to grow.' She

225

stroked his chin; on this occasion he had not shaved since leaving the coast. 'I like beards.'

'So you wouldn't object if the Mullah made a pass.' She gave a little shiver.

But Mohammed himself raised the point the next morning, while the sacks of coin were being brought out. 'Is that woman really the head of the House of Beinhardt, James?'

'I'm afraid she is.'

'And she is also your woman?'

'We are going to be married when we return to Germany.'

'Then you will be the head of the House.'

'That's the idea.'

Mohammed stroked his beard. 'What about the other one? The one with black hair?'

'She is the Countess's servant.'

'And therefore will become your servant as well, when you are the Count. Would you sell her to me?'

James' head jerked. 'I hope you're not serious.'

'I am. I find her very attractive. And she has shown that she can live here in the desert. I think we would be very happy.'

'I'm sure you would be very happy, Mohammed. But we Europeans do not sell our women.'

'And you want her for yourself,' Mohammed said, thoughtfully.

'Of course I do not.' He hoped he was telling the truth. Lisette was a very attractive girl, and Cecile did not appear to have any morals at all.

'I would pay very well,' Mohammed said. 'I would pay a thousand gold coins, and any four of my women, to have that woman. You may take your pick from my entire harem. Take Fatima. I happen to know that she regards you highly. And what she does not know about the art of love is not known to woman. Or boys. You would like some boys? Take your pick.'

James restrained a shudder with difficulty; Fatima was the woman who had coated the traitor with honey. 'I am sorry,' he said. 'It is not possible.'

Mohammed gazed at him for several seconds, and James understood that a great deal was in the balance. Mohammed could, if he really wished, take Lisette by force, and Cecile as well. But he wanted a constant supply of weapons and munitions more than even a beautiful woman. 'It is a pity,' he said at last. 'Now, James, are you satisfied with this money?'

'We will have to ask the Countess,' James said.

But Cecile was certainly satisfied. 'Do you have any idea how much it is?' she asked, speaking German.

'I haven't counted it. But I would estimate it is close enough to the full £100,000. If you are happy, tell him so.'

'I am very content, your excellency,' she told Mohammed, who inclined his head graciously. 'Now it is necessary for you to return to the coast. Before you go, we must arrange our next meeting. How soon can you return with another shipment?'

'Three months,' James said.

'That is good. By then you will be married. Will you bring your bride with you?' A sidelong glance. 'And her servant?'

'No, I will not.'

'Ah! Very good. It will be necessary for you to land the guns at a different place from Mareeq. I will have the Frenchman inform you exactly where and when. Now, it is necessary to get you back to Mareeq. To do this we need, as I have said, a diversion. I will send Daoud and a body of my men to the north, where they will seek to attack an Italian fort that has been constructed close to the coast. It will call in all Italian reinforcements in this area. Once this is done you will be able to reach the coast. Your ship will be waiting for you?'

'I hope so,' James said.

'You have no choice now but to accompany us,' James told Philippe. 'You must evacuate Mareeq. The Italians will have no doubt that you were involved in this transaction. But you will have sufficient money to set up somewhere else,' James reminded him. 'Besides, that is what the Mullah wants.'

Cecile, as always, looked spic and span and was heavily scented, despite her inability to have a bath. 'It has been a great pleasure, your excellency,' she told the Mullah.

'Oh, please, call me Mohammed,' the Mullah said.

She raised her eyebrows, glanced at James, and then said, 'Then I will.'

'And there is no need to say goodbye so soon,' Mohammed told her. 'I am accompanying you, for at least part of your journey.'

They watched Daoud and about 500 warriors ride off on their camels. James had spent the previous day instructing them in how to assemble and aim the field guns, and also two of the Maxims. It remained to be seen how well they would do on their own; Daoud indeed would have preferred James to accompany them, but as the object of the attack was to get the Europeans back to the coast in safety that was obviously out of the question.

For the return journey the caravan split up into groups, those camels and drivers recruited from other villages along the coast returning directly to their homes, each man happy with his fee for taking part in the expedition. The main body was thus reduced to 20, all people from Mareeq, but with them, as promised, rode Mohammed and 20 of his personal bodyguard, for the first day. When they reached the first waterhole, they found it blocked by the body of a dead camel. 'What manner of men are these?' Mohammed demanded. 'Do they not know water is God's gift to man?'

His people were scouting about. 'This was a large party, excellency,' they told the Mullah. 'More than a hundred men.'

'Where are they now?'

'They rode off to the north, excellency.'

'That is as it should be,' Mohammed said. 'I am afraid it will be a thirsty trip for you, my friends. Will you make it? You must expect to find other wells blocked.'

'Three days,' Philippe said. 'We have enough if we are quick, and drink little.'

'I feel thirsty already,' Cecile confided. She was certainly looking extremely hot, far more so than Lisette. James began to wonder if she was coming down with something.

'Now it *is* farewell,' Mohammed said, holding Cecile's hands. 'But perhaps I will come to Germany.'

'I have said, you will be welcomed,' Cecile assured him.

'You and Lisette have made quite a conquest,' James suggested, as they trotted their camels to the east.

'He gives me the shivers. And yet, you know ... it would have been an experience.'

'He wanted to buy Lisette,' James said.

'Lisette?' she cried. 'What cheek!'

'I think he would have preferred to buy you, but he knew you were not available.'

'Did he?' Now she was delighted. 'How much did he offer?'

'A thousand gold coins and four of his women. Or boys, according to my taste.'

'And you refused? Then you do love me, after all.'

They reached the next well at dusk, and as the Mullah had predicted it too was choked and poisoned. By then they had used the last of their water. 'Will we make it?' James asked Philippe.

'The camels are no problem; they are good for a few days yet, and it is only 36 hours from the village. Only 12 from the stream.'

'Then let's get to it.'

But the stream had also been dammed, and poisoned with dead animals.

231

'They seek to destroy us,' Philippe said. 'Our crops will all die.'

'You are leaving anyway,' James reminded him. 'You said another 24 hours. That doesn't sound too long.'

'It is very long without water,' Philippe said. 'But as we have no choice we will ride all night, while it is cool.'

They mounted and set off into the darkness, following Philippe's compass, but also his nose, James suspected. They made good progress during the darkness, when the temperature dropped very sharply, but with the rising of the sun they slowed to a walk. No one spoke as they folded their burnouses across their noses and mouths; Cecile indulged in a voluminous silk scarf. Lisette huddled beneath her veil, shoulders hunched. The camels proceeded well enough, apparently not feeling the heat, and certainly not thirsty, while their riders swayed in the saddle, trying to keep awake, and trying not to think of the parched hell into which their mouths were turning.

James insisted they all have something to eat, but none were enthusiastic. 'I could not chew a thing,' Cecile said. 'God, I can hardly speak!'

'Only 18 hours left,' James told her. 'And think of when we get there. Just listen to those saddlebags clinking.'

'And we are being fortunate,' Philippe added, again optimistic. 'There is not an Italian in sight.'

'That is because they have done all they wanted to,' James pointed out.

Just before dusk the first man collapsed, tumbling from his camel and hitting the ground with a dreadful thump. The others dismounted and gathered round.

'He has broken his arm,' one of the men said.

Philippe looked at James. 'We cannot leave him here,' James said.

They bound up his arm as well as they could—he was so parched and exhausted he hardly groaned—and mounted him double with another man. James was more concerned about Cecile, who hardly seemed aware of what was going on, sitting on her camel with her face hidden behind her scarf. Lisette tried to attend to her, and was shooed away. 'I do not like it, Herr Martingell,' the maid confessed to James. 'She has a fever.'

'I think we all have a fever,' James said.

But when the sun grew very hot, about 11 in the morning, and Philippe called a halt, James had to lift Cecile from the saddle, and lay her on the ground; still she hardly moved. But when he kissed her, she stirred, and muttered, 'Are we at the sea?'

'Dawn tomorrow,' he assured her, hardly able to speak himself, so parched and dry were his lips.

Lisette knelt on her mistress's other side, looking very worried. 'She is ill, Herr Martingell,' she whispered. 'She is worse than any of us.'

'She'll be all right when we reach water,' James assured her, refusing to be downcast, at least visibly. 'There will be water, Philippe?'

'We must hope so,' Philippe said.

'But the stream is poisoned and dammed,' Lisette pointed out.

Philippe tapped the side of his nose. 'I have a well in my house.'

'They will have poisoned that as well,' Lisette said disconsolately.

The camels knelt, without apparent discomfort, while the men and the three women lay beside their mounts, being baked as if they were in an oven. James hardly slept. He was too exhausted, while his brain still seethed. There was so much to be done, so much waiting for him, when he got out of this living hell, with something like £100,000 in gold in his saddlebags. It belonged to the House of Beinhardt, to be sure, but he was now the House of Beinhardt. Or he would be when they regained Germany. Would he make this journey again? Mohammed certainly expected him to. But as the head of the House of Beinhardt surely he could send someone else. The rub was that he doubted anyone else could have made it, and got out again. And he wasn't there yet.

But even Philippe was now feeling confident again, as he woke them at four that afternoon, when the huge glowing yellow orb was slowly sinking into the west. 'Dawn tomorrow,' he said. 'Can you smell the sea? Dawn tomorrow.'

'Dawn tomorrow,' James told Cecile, as he manhandled her into her saddle. She gave a half smile in return. He wondered if she would ever wish to make a journey like this again. She was terribly hot, but then, as he had told Lisette, he supposed they all were running fevers of some sort or another.

Through the night they trudged slowly onwards, drooping in their saddles. Then in the half-light before dawn Philippe, leading them, held up his hand. The camels came to a halt. Now they could hear the rumble of the surf on the sand, surely not more than a mile away. And now too they could even make out the cluster of buildings, the mosque, that had been the village of Mareeq. But the village glowed.

Chapter Seven

The Thief

Philippe gave a cry and urged his camel forward. His men followed him, also terrified by what they saw, what they knew must have happened. Even Cecile seemed to awake, to stare into the steadily increasing glow of the rising sun, and at the blackened heap of glowing timbers that lay before it. Only Lisette hung back; perhaps she knew too well.

Now they could smell the scorched remains of what once had been a settlement of human beings; they could smell the sickly sweet stench of burning human flesh, as well. It was broad daylight by the time they actually reached the outskirts of the village. Although it still burned in places, the heat was not intense; the deed had been done at least 24 hours previously. Philippe dismounted to lead his men into the remains of their homes, their loved ones. There were dead men struck down by bullets one or two with weapons still in their hands. The women were far worse, stretched out upon the ground in a neat row beyond the reach of the flames. Every one, young and old, had her skirts around her waist; every one had had her throat cut afterwards. Atossa gave a great howl of misery as she fell to her knees; two of Philippe's other wives had been her sisters.

Cecile slipped from her saddle to the ground, and then also continued to her knees, her strength drained away. Now at last Lisette urged her camel forward, and knelt beside her mistress. Philippe also knelt beside his wives, while his men ranged through the two streets of the village, looking for loved ones. Even the children lay dead, and violated. James went down to the beach to gaze at the harbour. There were several dhows, half submerged in the shallows, their bottoms stove in. But there were no masts sticking up to suggest that the schooner had been taken in the holocaust. Barents was not due back until the day after tomorrow. Meanwhile ...

Miraculously, Philippe's private well had not been spoiled; James surmised that his house had caught fire and collapsed before the Italians had managed to get inside. The men and the two women gathered round it to drink their water, and then feed the camels. 'What is to be done?' Philippe asked, his tone pitiful.

'You were going to have to leave this place anyway,' James reminded him.

'But ... my women ... you do not have blood in your veins, James. It is iced water.'

For which you should be grateful, James thought. 'And you?' he asked the Somalis. 'I can take you on board my ship when it comes, and put you ashore farther along the coast.'

They shook their heads. 'We will go, with our camels,' their spokesman said. 'You will let us keep these weapons?'

'They are yours,' James said, and paid them their agreed fee from the Mullah's gold, together with a bonus.

He was more concerned about Cecile. Like them all she had drunk, but she had refused food, and her temperature was as high as ever. He told himself that she was suffering as much as any of them, not only from the desert but from the horror of the destroyed village, but he worried about her fever. It had to be brought down, but he had no ice. Perhaps water alone would do the trick. She needed a bath, anyway.

With the aid of an embarrassed Lisette he stripped her, while Philippe gazed at the glowing but flushed pink and white skin with equally glowing eyes. Then James stripped off his own clothes and carried Cecile into the sea. Lisette had by now got the idea and she joined him, fully clothed, soon to be followed by Atossa and Philippe, who had also stripped off. Mbote tactfully remained on shore, keeping watch.

It was a kind of game, James supposed, because all three of them were close to hysteria. They held Cecile upright in the water. James could have wished it was cooler, but it was certainly cooler than the air. Cecile opened her eyes and smiled at them. 'I have always wanted to indulge in an orgy,' she said.

James carried her ashore, laid her in what shade he could find, and covered her with some rags that had survived the blaze, while Atossa washed all their clothes, pounding them between stones on the beach as she had no soap; Lisette let hers dry in situ. 'Will the ship come?' Philippe asked.

'If we light a fire.'

They began gathering up unburned wood, stopped when Atossa hurried up to tell them she could see dust on the horizon. The five of them lay in the shade of the burned buildings while the lancers trotted by. They could see the captain scanning the village through his binoculars, but there was nothing for them to stop for. They rode on. 'Do you think those are the ones who did this?' Philippe's hands were tight on the barrel of his rifle, and James was afraid he would start firing.

'No way of telling,' he said. 'They are fighting a war, a war which I doubt they can win, without terrorising the population into abandoning the Mullah.'

'They will never do that,' Philippe asserted.

'And meanwhile they lose their own people, horribly. Can you imagine what happens to one of those captured by the Mullah's men and given to their women?'

Philippe glanced at Atossa, whose tongue came out and circled her lips. James was tempted to ask her if she had ever castrated a man, but decided against it. Their situation was sufficiently extreme.

There was no way they could light the fire until the horsemen were out of sight.

James spent the rest of the day alternately standing on the beach and scanning the horizon through his binoculars, and sitting beside Cecile. 'It is so hot,' she muttered. 'Take me into the sea again, James.'

James did so, although he was realising that the first immersion had not after all brought her temperature down. But the water did cool her a little, and she was able to sleep, while he returned to the beach ... and saw topsails, hull down. He hurried to where Philippe was also sleeping, Atossa in his arms. 'Wake up.

We must light the fire.'

Philippe blinked at him. 'Those soldiers are not sufficiently far away; they will see it.'

'We have to risk that. The schooner is off shore, and we have to get the Countess out of this hellhole.'

Philippe got up, as did Atossa, and the fire was lit. James' principal concern was to control the smoke; he did not think any Italian was close enough actually to see the flames. And the schooner was standing in. Soon he could make out the men on her deck, staring at the shore as they took in the fact of the destroyed village. 'Keep watch,' James told Philippe. 'Mbote, come with me.'

Mbote followed him to where the sacks of coin waited, watched while James counted out two sums of £500 each. 'Are you with me, now and always?' James asked.

'Now and always,' Mbote said.

'Then bring two of those discarded swords, and come.' They took the remaining sacks, two each—each was as heavy as a man—up the beach until they were out of sight of the houses. Then he chose his spot, where he could use a cross reference between an outcrop of the reef standing higher than its surroundings, and a lone acacia tree. 'Dig,' he commanded.

Using their swords, they dug into the loose stones and dust and earth, while watching the schooner approaching. Sweat pouring, they went down several feet, a narrow but deep hole. In this James placed the four sacks. Then they filled the hole again and smoothed the earth across the top. At that moment it was fairly obvious that a hole had been dug, but James knew a few days of the sea breeze at day, and the land breeze at night, blowing across it would completely obliterate any indication that there had ever been digging. Mbote dusted his hands. 'Is not this money for the company, bwana?'

'In due course,' James said.

'But you do not trust them?'

'I do not trust anyone. That is a great deal of money.'

'Not even Monsieur Desmorins?'

'Not even him, Mbote.'

Mbote scratched his head. 'But you trust me.'

'Because where I go, you go, Mbote. Now and always. And therefore when I return for this money, you will be with me.' He held out his hand.

Mbote clasped his fingers. 'Now and always.'

By dusk they were on board, being fed and wined by an anxious Barents, as he listened to what had happened.

'Swine,' he muttered.

'War,' James corrected. 'All wars are dirty businesses. This one happens to be dirtier than most, because of the racial element I suppose. Now let's find the steamer.'

Because of the heat below decks he had a mattress bed made up aft behind the helm, and on this he laid Cecile. There was neither the time nor the material for niceties, and he and Lisette spent their time bathing the half-unconscious woman.

'What is the matter with her?' Barents inquired.

'If I knew that, I might be able to help her.'

'Let us pray it is not a contagious disease,' Barents said, and crossed himself.

Cecile indeed was delirious, and gabbled in German; it was not possible to understand much of what she said. Then she would suddenly sit up, fingers digging into James' arm, while she stared at him.

'We shall do so much, together, James,' she said.

'So much,' he promised her.

Philippe was grave. 'She is dying,' he muttered.

James sighed. 'If we can just find the steamer ...'

They sighted smoke the next day and altered course towards it. But it was the Italian gunboat. 'Signal them that we need help,' James said. Both Barents and Philippe stared at him in consternation. 'We must have medicine,' James told them. 'There is nothing incriminating on board.'

'But they will know we delivered the guns to the Mullah,' Philippe protested, fingering his neck as if he could already feel the rope.

'How can they know that?' James demanded. 'So soon? They can hardly have been in contact with the people on shore.'

'They will be suspicious,' Philippe grumbled.

But he knew there was nothing for it. The distress signal was hoisted, and the gunboat came closer. Soon they were alongside, the gunboat heeling as her men lined her side, armed with rifles. 'What is your trouble?' demanded the lieutenant.

'We have a sick woman on board, who needs attention.'

'Take her to Mogadishu,' the lieutenant recommended.

'That is several days away,' James said. 'The lady will die if she is not attended to, now. Do you not have a doctor on board?'

'Our doctor has more important things to do,' the lieutenant declared, but at that moment he was pushed aside by the doctor himself.

'A sick woman, you say? The plague? I am Dr Inaldo.'

'You tell me,' James said.

'I will come down.' The doctor climbed down the ladder and knelt beside Cecile.

'This is a white woman.'

'She is the Countess von Beinhardt,' James said.

The doctor frowned. 'Of the arms firm?'

'That is correct.'

'There will have to be questions as to what she is doing here.'

'She is taking a cruise on this schooner, which is owned by Beinhardt,' James said. 'It is as simple as that. We put into a fishing village a few days ago, and it must have been there that she contracted her illness.'

The doctor had inserted a thermometer into Cecile's armpit, as she was too delirious to risk her biting one in her mouth. 'This is serious,' he said. 'She has malaria.'

'How can she have got malaria? Isn't it caused by mist and swamp? There was none of that where we have been.'

'Nobody knows for sure what causes malaria,' the doctor said. 'There is a school of thought that says it can be caused by an insect bite.'

James swallowed. 'I shall be one huge bite,' Cecile had complained, jokingly.

'Her temperature is 106 degrees. We must bring it down. I will have to have her on board the ship.'

'Then do it.'

'You are a relative?'

'She is my fiancee, doctor.'

'Then you had better come with her.' The doctor gave the necessary orders. A stretcher was lowered, Cecile hoisted up to the gunboat's deck and carried into the sickbay, a place of pristine whiteness, walls, sheets and orderlies. Lisette accompanied her, ignoring the compliments paid her by the sailors.

James was taken up to the bridge to speak with the captain. 'This is a grave business,' Captain Martino suggested.

'The Countess is very ill, yes,' James agreed.

'I mean this whole affair,' Martino said. 'I would like to know what she was really doing in these waters.'

'Holidaying,' James repeated. 'Fishing. You saw us, a few days ago.'

'That is true,' the Captain agreed. 'But you should know, Signor Martingell, that we have been informed that the House of Beinhardt has been supplying arms to the forces of this Mullah, Mohammed ibn abd Allah.'

'I know nothing about that.'

'You are engaged to be married to the Countess, are you not?'

'Certainly. And I am very worried about her health. I know nothing of the business.'

The captain considered him for several seconds. 'But you deal in guns yourself, do you not, Signor Martingell?'

'I have done so. That is how the Countess and I first met. But I am afraid my activities are very small compared with the House of Beinhardt.'

'The Countess is here,' Captain Martino pointed out. 'Somaliland is over there. The Mullah is over there. And the Mullah has obtained modern weapons for use against our people. That is at least one coincidence too many.'

'Are you proposing to place the Countess von Beinhardt under arrest?' James inquired.

The captain smiled. 'Let us first save her life. It would not be civilised to hang a dead woman, eh?'

Cecile was bathed constantly in cold water, and fed quinine, which made her retch with its ultra-bitter taste. She was also given huge quantities of liquid to drink. The schooner was kept alongside the gunboat.

Barents and Philippe were clearly agitated, but tried their best not to show it; the crew were terrified, as the gunboat's decks were constantly patrolled by armed sailors.

Captain Martino and his officers, however, could not have been more charming, even the somewhat snooty lieutenant who had at first refused to help them. James and Lisette—who had been allowed to bathe and change her clothes—were entertained in the wardroom for dinner and regaled with the story of a great battle that had been fought only just to the north, between the Mullah's army and the Italians. 'They took heavy casualties,' Martino said. 'But then, so did we. This is going to be a long war. It is really very criminal to supply such a man with modern weapons.'

'Even if he is only defending his own country?'

'That is a chauvinist point of view. Do you not know that the French are also claiming part of Somaliland? And the British? The British claim is at least as large as ours. We do not object to this. Surely you do not, either, Signor Martingell?'

'I wish you joy,' James said.

Dr Inaldo appeared in the doorway. 'Signor Martingell ...' his hands were trembling.

James stood up. 'It is the crisis?'

Inaldo swallowed, and took a glass of brandy.

'The crisis is past,' he muttered.

'Then ...' the penny dropped. 'My God!' James leapt from the table and ran along the deck to the sickbay. Lisette followed, stood beside the bed, sobbing. James looked down on the suddenly pale face, composed and beautiful in death.

'What would you have us do, signor?' Captain Martino asked. Gone was any suggestion of investigation into the activities of the Countess; the Italians now offered only sympathy. 'You understand, in this heat ...' the captain said. 'We have no means of embalming on board, and we do not carry coffins. Of course, you could try to make Mogadishu, but that would be at least 72 hours. And I am not sure you would be much further ahead, there. Customs might even refuse to let you land a dead body.'

James nodded. 'I understand, Captain. There are worse places to be buried.'

They stood in a row, James, Lisette, Philippe, Atossa, Mbote and Barents, as Cecile's body, wrapped in the German ensign taken from the schooner, was weighted and dropped over the side of the gunboat. The Italian sailors stood to attention, and Captain Martino had a volley fired over the disturbed water. Then he invited James to his cabin for a glass of brandy. 'What are your plans?'

'To return to Germany and acquaint the Countess's family with what has happened. They will be shattered; Cecile's father died only a few months ago.'

'A sad business. I can put you ashore at Mogadishu.'

James shook his head. 'With your permission, Captain, I'll use the schooner.'

'As you wish.' Martino raised his head as his orderly opened the door and saluted. 'Smoke to the south, Captain.'

'Ah. That will be the steamer. We saw her two days ago.' He looked at James. 'I think she also belongs to your company, Signor Martingell.'

My company, James thought. That was his first priority, now that Cecile was dead. Why did he not feel any overwhelming grief? Simply because he had never loved her. She had fascinated him, and she had dominated him. But he knew she had chosen him to fulfil a purpose, not because she loved him. Now that purpose had gone astray. Or had it? 'Yes,' he agreed. 'She belongs to the firm. My fiancée wished to sail, but she also wished the comforts of civilisation available when she felt like it.'

'I understand,' Martino said. James

suspected the captain understood a great deal more than he revealed. 'Then you must join her. However, before you go, I am afraid I must search your schooner. Necessary procedure, in these waters, you understand.'

'Of course,' James said. 'But what are you looking for? If we were gun-runners, would we not already have unloaded our cargo?'

'Of course,' Martino agreed. 'But if you were gun-runners, you would have been paid for your guns, would you not?'

James shrugged. 'You will find two bags each with £500 in coin, Captain. That is—was—the Countess' travelling funds. Come to think of it, I suppose that belongs to me, now.'

The only additional money on board the schooner was Philippe's satchel. Indeed, Philippe nearly gave the game away he was so terrified when the search began, and equally mystified as to where the bulk of the money had gone. But he pulled himself together when questioned. 'My life savings, signor,' he explained. 'I operated the general store in Mareeq. Your soldiers burned it down when they burned the village, but my money was buried under the house, and I was able to dig it up.'

'Why do you suppose our people burned

the village?' Martino asked.

'I do not know, signor. They may have thought some of the people were supporters of the Mullah.'

'But you were not?'

'I am a French businessman, signor. I have no desire to get mixed up with the Mullah. Now, my wives have been murdered, and I am destitute.'

The captain handed him back the satchel. 'Not entirely, I would say.' He eyed Atossa. 'And you have the beginnings of a new harem, have you not?' He turned to James. 'Very well, Signor Martingell. There is absolutely no evidence that you are anything than what you claim, a fishing party that has come to a very tragic end. But if I may give you a word of advice, perhaps these waters are unhealthy for you. I would hope not to see you here again.'

James bowed.

'What a catastrophe!' Captain Bessers said. James' entire party had transhipped to the steamer, and the *Mannheimer* had sailed south to collect payment from Fessnung in Dar-es-Salaam. 'You say you buried the Countess at sea?'

'There didn't seem to be much choice,' James told him. 'But I still think it is necessary to get back to Cologne with all speed.'

Philippe remained in a state of total confusion. 'There was £100,000 in coin,' he said, as he and James sat on the boat-deck in the balmy warmth of a tropical night, with Aden and the Red Sea due on the horizon at dawn. 'What happened to it?'

'Surely that it my business,' James said. 'You have been paid your share.'

Philippe gazed at him for several seconds. 'You are a crafty devil, James. Does that money not belong to the House of Beinhardt?'

'That remains to be seen.'

Mbote, of course, could be relied upon to keep his mouth shut. But Lisette was also inquisitive and more. 'I saw you and the black fellow take those sacks out of the village,' she remarked, joining James on deck after breakfast the next morning.

'And you have said nothing. That was very thoughtful of you.'

'I am now unemployed,' she commented, at large.

'Will the family not retain you?'

She shrugged. 'They might. But Clementine has her own maid. And perhaps I no longer have any wish to be employed by them. Perhaps I have discovered a taste for adventure. What do you intend to do, Herr James?'

'That depends on what the House of Beinhardt intends to do.'

'They will never accept you, without Cecile. I know this. I have listened to certain conversations. They will even less accept you if you return without either guns or money. They may even have you arrested for fraud.'

'I doubt they will succeed. I will tell them that the money was lost on our return from the Mullah's camp, when we were attacked by the Italians.'

Lisette considered him for several seconds. Then she said, 'You would like me to tell them this, also?'

'I think it would be a good idea.'

Her tongue, small and pink, crept out of her mouth and circled her lips. 'If I were found to have committed perjury, I would be sent to prison. Have you ever been inside a German prison, Herr James?'

'I'm afraid not.'

'They are not nice places. They flog the prisoners. They flog you when you are taken in, and they flog you again the day you leave. As well as whenever they feel like it in between. I do not wish to be flogged, Herr James.'

'I can believe that. The answer is surely not to be found guilty of perjury. Only three people know what really happened to that money: you, Mbote and myself.'

'What of Philippe and Atossa?'

'They will not be in Germany. Besides, they are going to be our partners too. Without Philippe, I cannot return to Somaliland to regain the gold.'

'And when you do?'

'You will get a reasonable share.'

'How reasonable?'

He studied her. 'Are you trying to blackmail me, Lisette?'

'I would not know how to begin.'

'Well, please don't start taking lessons.'

'A girl must think of the future, Herr James. You are asking me to lie for you. And I shall be unemployed. My share of the money is not likely to be very large.'

James began to wish he had, after all, sold her to Mohammed. 'Tell me what you have in mind,' he suggested, 'You surely do not assume that I require a ladies' maid?'

Again. the quick flick of the tongue. 'I would be better to you than that, Herr James.'

'Lisette, your mistress—my fiancée—has been dead only a few days.'

'I know. It is very sad. I am desolated, and I know that you are too, Herr James. Therefore it is fitting that we should comfort each other. I also know,' she went on as he would have spoken, 'that for us to be observed—how shall I put it?—being intimate on this ship, which belongs to the House, would both be unseemly and unwise. All I require is a promise, for the future. When I am unemployed.'

She had clearly learned a great deal from her mistress. James wondered just how much. And she was certainly an attractive young woman, with a good deal of both courage and stamina. And she virtually had him in her power, certainly until he discovered how the land lay in Germany. 'I will promise you, Lisette,' he said, 'that should you lose your position with the House of Beinhardt, I will employ you myself.'

'You have made me so very happy,' Lisette said.

James wondered if she had any idea how many times he had given such a solemn promise to a woman, and various men, and broken it. Easy to say he had never done so willingly, but through force of circumstance. He was still a fairly disreputable character, he supposed, who was now planning to become a thief on a grand scale. But that again was through force of circumstance. He had no doubt that Lisette was right in her prediction that without Cecile the House of Beinhardt would no longer be interested in him. The House of Beinhardt had never been interested in him. Adolf von Beinhardt had considered him a worthwhile investment because of his knowledge of Africa. Cecile had found him an even more worthwhile investment, both as an attractive man and because she had wanted to use him as the figurehead with which she could dominate the House.

He really owed nothing to either of them, and certainly nothing to any of the rest of the family, or the board. But deliberately to rob them of £100,000 ... on the other hand, that money would set him up in England. As what? He knew only one profession. And he had a ready and regular customer in the Mullah. All he needed was a source of supply. But as he kept up to date with events in the arms world, he already had ideas about that. He wondered if that attractive little secretary had ever gone home to England?

He laid his plans with Philippe as they left the Suez Canal and steamed for Marseilles, telling him what had happened; there was no risk of Philippe betraying him—only he and Mbote knew where the money was buried, and only he had taken the bearings. To get to the money they had to return to Somalia. If they could do that as representatives of the House of Beinhardt, they would do so. If not ... Philippe shuddered. 'It is very dangerous,' he complained.

'Think of the rewards,' James urged.

'But only you know where it is buried. You and Mbote,' Philippe grumbled, clearly disgruntled at not being trusted with the original secret. 'And suppose you cannot remember, eh? And if we were to be taken by the Italians ...'

'It is up to us not to be taken by the Italians,' James pointed out. 'And I know exactly where the money is hidden. It is our future, Philippe. All I need is a ship and the backing to get to it. Think of it, £100,000 in coin. Of which you will have a fifth.' From the way his eyes rolled, Philippe clearly was thinking about it.

But he became more nervous yet when they reached Marseilles, where James gave him one of the bags with £500 in it and told him to rent an apartment and wait for word from him. 'We are being followed,' he grumbled, as he and James had an aperitif before lunch. The women were off shopping. 'Watched. Tracked.'

'Oh, come now!' James protested.

258

'I tell you, people are watching us,' Philippe said.

James stroked his chin. He was quite prepared to admit that while he would know instantly if he were being tracked in the African bush, here in this crowded seaport he was like a fish out of water. 'Who is doing this following?' he asked. 'Who even knows we are here?'

'That Italian gunboat had wireless equipment.'

'You think we are that important?'

'The Countess was that important. And then Fessnung would have used the telegraph the moment Barents got to him.'

'So you think the Beinhardts are keeping an eye on us?'

'Someone is,' Philippe insisted.

Yet James was still determined to be forced to commit his crime—as he felt he had been forced to commit all his other crimes. But actually, compared with being Chairman of the House of Beinhardt, £100,000 was not so great a sum of money. As if it could ever be. 'You buried my daughter, at sea?' Hildegarde von Beinhardt positively spat the words at him.

'I had no choice, Countess,' James protested.

'You killed her,' Clementine hissed.

'Now that is a ridiculous statement,' James pointed out. 'There are witnesses as to how and where Cecile died. It was malaria.'

Herr Dorting rested his hand on top of Clementine's, as the girl would have spoken again. 'And no doubt you were, and are, suitably grieved, Herr Martingell,' he said.

'Yes,' James said.

'The whole thing has turned out very tragically, for everyone,' Dorting said. He was speaking, indirectly, to Hildegarde. 'However, life must continue. If you will deliver the payment for the guns sold to the Somali chieftain, Herr Martingell, you will be paid your fee, and we will wish you every good fortune.'

James raised his eyebrows in surprise, even if he was not the least surprised. 'I'm afraid I do not understand you, Herr Dorting.' He looked at Hildegarde; the whole lot of them had to be ranged against him. 'It is my intention to carry out the wishes of my dear Cecile.'

'What wishes?' Dorting asked before Hildegarde could speak.

'That I should take over as Chairman of the House of Beinhardt,' James said. They all stared at him.

'The Will of the late Count von

Beinhardt states clearly that the position of managing director of the House should go to the husband of his daughter,' Dorting said. 'At the present time, Fräulein Clementine does not have a husband.' Clementine gave a monumental sniff.

'Fräulein Cecile and I were betrothed, Herr Dorting,' James said.

'That is not quite the same thing as being married, Herr Martingell.'

Hildegarde suddenly came to life, and pointed. 'I want you out of this house, Martingell. I want you out of Cologne. I want you out of Germany. I do not know how you managed to bewitch my daughter, but I hold you responsible for her death. As for throwing her into the sea to be eaten by sharks ... you revolt me!'

'I am sorry you feel that way, Countess,' James said. 'Perhaps, when you have got over your grief ...'

'I want you out!' Hildegarde shouted, her face red with passion. 'Dorting, have him thrown out.'

'I'm afraid you will have to go, Herr Martingell,' Dorting said. 'But you will be paid your fee. The money, please.'

'There is no money,' James said.

Once again they stared at him. 'No money?' Dorting asked. 'The transaction involved £100,000.'

'And it was paid, by Mohammed ibn abd Allah,' James said. 'But on our way back to the coast we were attacked by the Italians. We were lucky to escape with our lives. It is my opinion that Cecile contracted her fatal illness during our escape. But we had to abandon everything to reach the coast. Including the sacks containing the money.'

'Swine!' Hildegarde shouted. Clementine gave another huge sniff.

'You expect us to believe this?' Dorting asked.

James shrugged. 'There were people with me. Including Cecile's maid. She is with me now. Why do you not ask her what happened?'

Dorting looked at Hildegarde, who gave a barely perceptible nod. He got up and went to the door, opened it. 'Fräulein Uhlmann?'

Lisette had been seated in the outer chamber. Now she got up and came in. She wore a neat dress and matching hat, tilted forward slightly over her forehead and eyes, and looked utterly demure. 'Come in, Fräulein, come in,' Hildegarde invited.

Lisette, who was obviously in awe of the Countess, sidled into the room. She did not look at James, who was half holding his breath. His future depended on this

262

anxious young woman. But then, so did hers upon him. Dorting gestured her to a chair on the far side of the table, sat down himself, sweeping the tails of his coat across his thighs. 'Fräulein,' he said. 'You were Fräulein Cecile's maid. You were with her when she died.'

'Yes, sir,' Lisette said.

'Therefore you have every right to be considered a faithful servant of the House of Beinhardt,' Dorting said, getting as much meaning as he could into his words.

'Thank you, sir,' Lisette said.

'So we would like you to tell us what happened on your journey to Somalia,' Dorting invited. 'You made contact with this, ah, Mullah, did you not?'

'Oh, yes, sir, a very terrible gentleman.'

'What makes you say that?'

'Well, sir ...' Lisette gave a pretty little shiver. 'He wanted to buy me.'

'Buy you?'

'For his harem, sir.' Now the blush was equally pretty.

'Good heavens!' Dorting commented.

'But Fräulein Cecile refused,' Lisette said, acting on the instructions James had given her; he did not wish the Beinhardts to have any idea he might have saved her from that fate.

Dorting fell for the bait. 'Fräulein Cecile was a good mistress?'

'Oh, yes, sir. The best mistress I ever had.'

'But the Mullah paid the money for the guns, am I right?' Dorting asked.

'Oh, yes, sir. There were several sacks of money.'

'Do you have any idea how much?'

'There was talk of £100,000.'

'Some of which had to be paid to the members of the caravan, and the French agent, Monsieur Le Barthe. Is that correct?'

'I do not know that, sir.'

'But you saw several sacks of money.'

'Several sacks, yes. They were on the camels.'

'To be taken back to the coast and placed on the schooner and then on the steamer.'

'I believe so,' Lisette said.

'Tell us what happened on the return journey.'

James found that he was holding his breath. This was where she had to lie, convincingly.

'The journey took several days,' Lisette said. 'We had not gone very far when Fräulein Cecile became ill. She had a fever. Herr Martingell said we should hurry. But then we saw the Italians. Lancers, sir. They had picked up our trail and were close by. Herr Martingell and the men with us tried to fight them off, but there were too many. So Herr Martingell said we must run for it. This is what we did. Oh, how we rode, Herr Dorting! We galloped those camels ...'

For God's sake don't overdo it, James begged, mentally. 'And at last we got away from them,' Lisette said, now herself panting with excitement.

'And you gained the coast?'

'Yes, sir. Some of us.'

'Fräulein Cecile was with you?'

'Oh, yes, sir. Herr Martingell looked after her personally. With me.'

'But not all of your party made it?'

'Not all, sir. No.'

'What happened to the money?'

'The money? I don't know, sir. The camels scattered and ran off.'

'What did Herr Martingell say when he realised the money had been lost?'

For the first time, Lisette looked directly at James. 'I don't think he even noticed, sir. He was too worried about Fräulein Cecile.'

'She is lying,' Hildegarde said. Dorting cleared his throat. 'Lying!' Hildegarde said again, her voice rising.

Lisette looked at Dorting, her cheeks pink and her mouth open. 'Get them out of here,' Hildegarde said. 'They are both liars, thiefs and murderers.'

265

'What about my job?' Lisette asked.

'You? You are sacked,' Hildegarde snapped.

'Countess, you do me a great injustice.' Lisette wiped her eyes with her handkerchief, and James decided that she had a great future as an actress.

Dorting was clutching at straws. 'If you are given your job back, Lisette,' he said. 'Will you tell us the truth about the money?'

Lisette stared at him, eyebrows arched, and once again James held his breath. But, as always, she had her eye firmly fixed upon the main chance. 'I have told you the truth, sir,' she said.

'Out!' Hildegarde shouted.

'You had better leave, Herr Martingell, Fräulein Uhlmann,' Dorting said.

'And my daughter?' James inquired.

'Oh, take the bastard with you,' Hildegarde snapped.

Dorting himself came with them to the door. 'You have not heard the last of this, Martingell. We shall make sure you never work again. Anywhere.'

James bowed. He had won. He could afford to be polite. The door closed, and Lisette would have spoken. James shook his head, and escorted her down the stairs to the waiting cab. Only when they were driving away from the Beinhardt mansion

266

did he allow himself to kiss her hands. In reply, she kissed his mouth.

'Now we are partners, James,' she said. 'You and I, Forever.'

Chapter Eight

The Partners

She was a problem to be solved. But, then, so had been Martha and even Cecile. James' first intention was to get out of Germany before the Beinhardts could begin legal action against him. He hurried first of all to the address he had been given, to collect Anne from her foster parents.

They were reluctant to let her go. Anne was now six years old, fair-haired and blue-eyed, vivacious and intelligent; there was no trace of her African forebears. But as she was obviously *'der Englander's'* child they had no choice. 'She is so sweet,' Frau Glinckel said, 'Such a good girl.' And she glared at James as if certain he would start beating his daughter the moment he got her alone.

'She will be in good hands,' James assured her. 'Fräulein Uhlmann will look after her.'

Which earned him a glare from Lisette. But she was obeying her instructions to keep her mouth shut. At least until they were in the train and rushing towards the French frontier. Then she said, 'I am not a children's nanny.'

'But you are setting up to be my mistress, are you not?' James inquired. 'I come as a complete package.'

'Oh, well ...' Lisette rumpled Anne's hair, and Anne gave her a hug, as she was wont to do with anyone who showed her the least affection. 'She *is* a sweet child. When do I get to be your mistress?'

'When we get to an hotel,' he promised her.

She was content with that, and in the event so was he. Anne having been put to bed immediately after dinner, they enjoyed a couple of brandies, smiling into each other's eyes. Lisette had none of the earthy come-and-get-it allure of Martha, and none of the sophisticated take-me-if-you-dare beauty of Cecile. And perhaps she was not as pretty as Martha or as beautiful as Cecile. But she had a quality all of her own—I-am-yours-if-you-treat-me-right—that was most attractive. That treating her right might mean sharing a large proportion of the £100,000 he had buried in Somaliland was a problem he was quite prepared to face when the time came; he had already sent Philippe a wire informing him that the Beinhardt link was now irretrievably broken, and inquiring as to any progress made towards procuring a ship to return to Somaliland. In any event, the prospect of engaging in a treasure hunt could not help but send the blood racing through a man's arteries.

When they had finished their brandies, their only problem was not to awaken Anne, who was asleep in a cot beside their bed.

Lisette had a tendency to giggle when enjoying herself, and also to giving off great sighs of erotic relief. But she was certainly erotic. 'I have had my eye on you from the moment we first met,' she whispered into his ear when she had subsided, he hoped for the last time. 'But you had eyes only for Cecile.'

'Well, I didn't know she came as a package, as well,' James said.

'You are a wretched man,' she murmured, snuggling against him. 'When do we go to collect the money?'

Apparently she supposed it would simply be a matter of landing on the Somali coast and picking up the sacks. First thing next morning James was out to buy a newspaper and hope to discover

269

if anything was happening down there. A great deal was. The war against the 'Mad Mullah', as everyone was now calling Mohammed ibn abd Allah, had spread out of the Italian claim, which they called Eritrea, into both French Somaliland and the British claim farther north. James read the report twice, sitting at a table outside the hotel cafe, while his brain tumbled. The guns he had sold Mohammed might well be being used against British soldiers. There went a lifetime of resolution.

'Mr Martingell? Good heavens!'

He raised his head, frowned at the woman. She was an extremely pretty woman, of about 30, he reckoned, with soft yellow hair worn in the fashionable pompadour, very good clothes, and a general air of tremendous prosperity. She was also vaguely familiar—and she had addressed him in English! 'It *is* James Martingell?' she asked, with just a touch of embarrassment.

'I am he.' He stood up.

'But you have forgotten who I am,' she said. 'Well, there was no reason to remember, I am sure.'

'Charles Rudd's office!' he exclaimed. 'A secretary ...'

'Anne Horsfall, then, Mr Martingell.'

'Good heavens! May I offer you a cup of coffee, or a cognac?'

Anne Horsfall glanced up and down the street, as if wondering if she should be seen talking with such a raffish character. But she had made the advance. 'I think it is a little early in the morning for cognac, Mr Martingell. I am English, not French. But I would love a cup of coffee.' James signalled the waiter, held her chair for her. 'I am pleased to see you looking so well, so prosperous,' Anne said. 'I had heard that you fell on hard times.'

'You could say that. But I've had hard times before.' He studied her gloved left hand; there were bulges beneath the kid.

She saw his glance. 'Oh, I am married, Mr Martingell. My husband is in Paris on business, and I chose the opportunity to do some shopping.'

'My congratulations,' James said. 'Then your name now is ...?'

'Pennyfeather.' She paused, as if expecting him to recognise the name.

'A South African?'

'Good Lord, no! I was only in South Africa because my father happened to be there on business. He was a friend of Uncle Charles, and I wanted to do something ...' she flushed. 'Actually, I did take a course in shorthand and typing.'

'Very thoughtful of you.'

'But you never married?' she asked.

'No. I was engaged, but my fiancée died, a month ago.'

'Oh, I am most terribly sorry.' She frowned, as he was wearing no obvious sign of mourning. 'But you are still ... well ...'

'I am still in the arms business, Mrs Pennyfeather.'

'Lady,' she corrected.

He raised his eyebrows.

'Winston is a baronet.'

'Oh. Well, then, double congratulations, Lady Pennyfeather.'

'Does your business ever take you to England?'

'It may well do so.'

'Then I'd be delighted if you would call.' She opened her reticule, fumbled through various inside pockets. 'Oh, dear me,' she remarked. 'I don't seem to have any of my cards with me. I'll have to give you one of Winston's.' She held out the small rectangle of cardboard. There were pink spots in her cheeks.

James took the card; glanced at it, and then frowned, It read:

SIR WINSTON PENNYFEATHER
CHAIRMAN
PENNYFEATHER SMALL ARMS COMPANY

The address, in Worcestershire, was in

the bottom right-hand corner. He raised his head as Anne Pennyfeather stood up. 'Do call, if you ever have the time, Mr Martingell. And thanks ever so much for the coffee. What a happy chance, us meeting again like this. Good day to you.'

He watched her walk down the street, bustle swaying gently from side to side. Then he looked at the card again. He was no believer in coincidences. And of course, Cecile's death would have been widely reported, even in England, as would have been the name of her fiancé. Then those odd happenings, both in Marseilles and Cologne ... he had supposed he was being tailed by an agent from Beinhardt. But suppose there were other people interested in him? Once again he looked at the card. But why on earth should a Knight of the Realm seek him out ... and in the person of his wife? Because he needed a salesman for his guns?

'Ha,' Lisette commented, emerging from the hotel with Anne in tow. 'First thing in the morning, and you are out on the street looking for women.'

'You,' James pointed out, 'are setting up to be a shrew. Now ...' he bounced Anne on his knee, remembering that he had named his daughter after the fascinating Lady Pennyfeather. 'We are going for a long ride in a train.'

As James had anticipated, Mbote was delighted to see him again, as was Atossa to see Lisette. Philippe as always, was pessimistic. 'You have seen the newspapers?'

James nodded. 'Some mess.'

'The whole country is at war,' Philippe said. 'I do not think we have a hope of getting back to that money, at least at this time, and escaping with our lives.'

'Without it, we have nothing,' James pointed out. 'I am just about broke.'

'It is better to be broke and breathing, than rich and dead,' Philippe argued. 'In any event, I can find no ship captain who is prepared to risk that coast, certainly without considerable payment in advance. Is there no business you—we can undertake, until this shooting stops?'

'There isn't. I am *persona non grata* in German East, Portuguese East, and British South. Now that the Transvaal and the Orange Free State are part of British South, that takes up the whole of South Africa, save for Rhodesia, and I am *persona non grata* there too.' There is also the matter of the Delgados, he thought, and William's children. There was no prospect of the House of Beinhardt paying those drafts now; he had intended to make up for that with his stolen money. 'Now you say we are *persona non grata* in Somaliland, too.'

'Well, I didn't say that,' Philippe said. 'I have had a meeting with the representative of the Mullah here in Marseilles. They desperately need more weapons.'

'To shoot Frenchmen and Englishmen.'

'Well ...' Philippe pinched his lip. 'Beggars can't be choosers. And it is a way to get back into Somalia, if we can avoid the Italians.'

'I'll not do that,' James said.

'Well, then ... I do not like the look of the immediate future.'

James stood on the balcony of the rented house and looked out at the harbour and beyond, the massive bulk of the Chateau d'If. Beneath him in the garden Atossa, Lisette and Anne were playing, their laughter drifting up on the breeze. They were happy. He wanted them to go on being happy. He had supposed he had the funds to do that—but he could not get at them. A right 'chicken and egg' situation, he thought. I need that money to start up my own arms business, but I need money from my own arms business to get that money. And he didn't have an arms business. Or a client. But ... he turned. Philippe was brooding into his cognac. 'Have you sufficient money left to enable me to make a journey to England? I shall not be gone long.'

'England? You have a contact there?'

'I may well have,' James told him.

He still had some reasonably smart clothes, even after crossing the Channel as a deck passenger on the packet. Needless to say, Lisette had wished to accompany him, but he had insisted that she remain in Marseilles with Anne. 'I go to secure all our futures,' he told her. 'Philippe will look after you until I return.'

Mbote also wished to accompany him, feeling that his boss was doing altogether too much travel without a servant, but James again insisted that he go alone. He had no idea what this venture might bring. But the Pennyfeathers had made the first move. Or at least, one of them had.

A train took him to London, where he changed for Worcester. It was so long since he had last been in England, and then he had been a very young man, that it really was a very strange country to him. Even the language with which he was surrounded seemed strange. But tall, lean, sun-browned, with grey wings to his dark hair, he caught quite a lot of attention himself. He decided to approach via the house and the lady, rather than the arms factory and her husband, whom he had never met. While the lady ... what a good-looking woman, strong-faced, elegant, slenderly voluptuous—no doubt thanks to a variety of corsets and stays—who had clearly had him in her sights for some time. 'Your card, sir?' requested the butler.

'I'm afraid I do not have a card,' James said. 'Is Lady Pennyfeather in?'

He was looking around him at the baronial hall that went well with the grand staircase and the four-storied mansion, as it did with the grounds through which he had been driven in his hired cab. There was certainly money here, if it could be tapped. 'She may be, sir,' the butler agreed, cautiously.

'Well, if you will tell her that James Martingell is calling, I am sure she will see me.'

'Perhaps you'd care to take a seat, sir. Hastings!' A footman immediately appeared, and the butler nodded to him before proceeding down the hall with a stately tread. Hastings gave James a rather apprehensive smile, then stood to attention. His job was clearly to make sure this cardless visitor did not make off with any of the family silver. Not that there was any to be seen.

A door opened, and James, having

sat down, hastily stood up again. 'Mr Martingell. How very good of you to call.' She was cool and utterly entrancing in a light summer frock, and with her hair loose; it drifted down past her shoulders in wisps of pure gold.

'I hope you won't think me presumptuous.'

'I said, it is a great pleasure. Come into the garden.' She led him through the house and out of french doors on to a terrace, where there were chairs and a table, gesturing him to a seat. 'Coffee? Or an aperitif?'

'Well ...'

'An aperitif.' The butler was hovering. 'The Bollinger, Wilson.' The butler bowed and withdrew. 'So tell me,' Lady Pennyfeather said. 'Is this a business or a social call?'

'Ah ... well, I suppose business. But perhaps I should discuss that with your husband. It's just that I felt, as you and I had a previous acquaintance, whereas I have never met Sir Winston, you could perhaps arrange an introduction for me. So that we might do some business together.'

Anne Pennyfeather regarded him for several seconds. Then she asked, 'What business did you have in mind?'

James had not expected quite such a direct approach. Another Cecile? He hoped not. Fortunately he had time to think as the butler reappeared with the tray of champagne. Anne raised her glass. 'Here is to ... *whatever* business you had in mind, Mr Martingell. But do please tell me.'

'I don't know how much you know about the arms trade,' James began, still trying to make up his mind just how far he could trust her.

'I know as much as my husband tells me, which is quite a lot. And about those who take part in it. Let me see ... for the past few years you have been employed by the House of Beinhardt, of Cologne. You have sold their guns to various African chieftains, including, most recently, the Mad Mullah, as he is known, Mohammed ibn abd Allah, who is warring against the Europeans in Somaliland.'

'When I sold him those guns, he was not fighting the British,' James hurriedly pointed out.

'Oh, quite. In the course of your work for Beinhardt you became betrothed to the heiress, Cecile von Beinhardt. But she died of malaria or some such tropical disease some months ago. Am I right?' She showed no trace of embarrassment that she had pretended not to know this when they had met in Paris.

'You have quite a dossier on me.'

'Does that offend you?'

279

'On the contrary. It makes life easier.'

'So, let me complete my dossier. This is of course supposition on my part. But as you are in England, wishing to discuss business with my husband, I would say that your engagement with the House of Beinhardt ended with your engagement to Cecile.'

'I'm afraid you are quite correct, Lady Pennyfeather.'

She gave him a flashing smile. 'Perhaps you should call me Anne, as we are to engage in business.'

'Are we?'

'Well, that is up to you. You wish a new source of arms for your next commitment.' She gazed at him with arched eyebrows.

James took a deep breath. 'It's not quite as simple as that, Anne.'

'Tell me.'

'I have a customer, certainly. But he is the Mad Mullah, who may well use his arms against British troops in Somaliland.'

Anne sipped her champagne. 'An ethical question, to be sure. But you do not *know* that he will.'

'I'd have to pretend to be blind.'

'I see. And is he your only potential customer? Minor chieftains who would be great chieftains all over the world are crying out for guns. In fact, I think I—my husband—might well be able to put you in touch with one or two.'

'If he has the contacts, why should he not sell direct?'

'My husband is a manufacturer, not a salesman,' Anne said. But James knew she was not telling the whole truth.

'Well, of course I should be happy to act as his salesman,' James said. 'Unfortunately, I would need financing.'

She frowned at him. 'You made no profit out of your dealings with the Mullah?'

'Ah, yes. But the money is not immediately available.'

'You mean he has not paid you in full.'

'No. Whatever his vices, the Mullah is an honest man. You may as well know, Anne, that the money is buried, in Somalia.'

'Good heavens!' she commented. 'How much?'

'A hundred thousand English pounds, less a few thousand paid to various locals and a few hundred I have been using for expenses.'

'One hundred ...' she bit her lip, and hastily drank some champagne. 'Wilson!' she called. 'You may serve some more drinks. One hundred thousand pounds. But ... if that was your share, how much did Beinhardt make?'

'Not a penny,' James confessed. 'I

suspected they were going to throw me out on my ear, so I took certain steps.'

'You stole their money!' Anne Pennyfeather threw back her head and gave a tremendous peal of laughter. Then she was suddenly serious again. 'But you have the reputation in the trade of being absolutely honest.'

'As long as people are honest with me.'

'There's a point! Tell me, who else knows about this?'

'My partners. But only I and one other know where the money is buried.'

'And you are quite sure it will be there when you go back for it?'

'I am quite sure.'

'What an intriguing situation!' she remarked. 'Winston will certainly wish to hear of it. You must stay to dinner, James.'

'I'm afraid I have no dress clothes.'

'Ah! Well, then, I shall not dress either. Wilson! Show Mr Martingell to a room, please. I shall see you at lunch, in half-an-hour, James.'

James wasn't quite sure whether he was standing on his head or his heels. It seemed reasonable that, as the Pennyfeathers had been tracking him for some time, they had probably known about the missing money before he had confessed it. That apart, he did not yet know why they specifically wanted to do business with him and no one else, but he was prepared to wait to find out. Certainly if they were prepared to finance an expedition to regain the money. He had hoped to continue the discussion at lunch, but Anne said quite firmly, 'No business during meals. It upsets the digestion. Besides, we can make no progress until Winston has heard your story. Do you ride? But of course, you must. You are South African.'

'Actually, I'm not,' James said. 'But I do ride.'

Lunch was a leisurely meal, followed by coffee and brandy. Anne did most of the talking, about South Africa, which she had much enjoyed, about her uncle, dead so tragically young, ... 'They say he died of a broken heart.'

'I can well believe it.'

'But you were opposed to him.'

James smiled. 'We agreed no business over the meal.'

She smiled in turn. 'But the meal is over.'

'Well, I was never opposed to him. I thought some of his behaviour was high-handed, and I have always been inclined to side with the natives against European encroachment. I would have opposed him had I had the opportunity.'

'As I said before, you're an honest man, James. Well, it is all done now.'

'That isn't so. What he has set up will have to stand the test of time.'

She nodded. 'And it is already crumbling, if the Government goes ahead with its plan to allow the Boers self-government of their own. The horses are waiting.'

Again, it was reminiscent of Cecile. But Anne Pennyfeather was accompanied by neither sister nor grooms as they cantered into the woodland that was part of the estate. 'What does it feel like to own all this?' James asked, when they drew rein.

'You mean the inherited mortgages and responsibilities?' Anne asked. She gave him a sidelong glance. 'Something you don't have to worry about, I suspect.'

'I'm sure your mortgage doesn't amount to more than the value of the estate,' he suggested.

She gave one of her peals of laughter. 'It doesn't, to be sure. But it's there, and can never be eliminated, save by a huge windfall.'

An alarm clock began ticking at the back of his brain, but on such a delightful afternoon, and in the company of such a beautiful woman, he wasn't in the mood to listen to alarm clocks. 'Can you not just sell up, when the burden becomes unbearable?'

'Unfortunately, no. The estate belongs to the family, of which Winston merely happens to be the senior member at the moment. That means he has the right to occupy it. But also that he has the obligation to meet the interest payments on the debts accumulated by his endless list of ancestors. He can never sell it.'

'That sounds something of a raw deal.'

'It's called belonging to the landed gentry.'

'And his heir will inherit this burden? You do have an heir?' Which is what he really wanted to find out.

'Oh, yes,' she said. 'I have a son. That is the first, some would say the only, duty of a wife of the landed gentry.'

'Just the one?'

'Just the one, James. That is *all* the duty of the landed gentry's wife.' She was telling him things every time she opened her mouth; he needed the time to assimilate all that knowledge, and reach a decision about it.

'I have a child too,' he said. 'A daughter.'

'Do you?' She seemed genuinely surprised. 'But I understood ...'

'Oh, I have never married. And Anne is not Cecile von Beinhardt's.'

'Anne?'

He flushed. 'Well ... she was born just after we met, back in 1896. And I ... I was taken with you.'

'Good heavens! What a delightful compliment.' She kicked her horse and rode away from him, cheeks pink. Her turn to do some assimilating of recent information.

He hurried his own mount behind hers. 'I hope you are not offended.'

She drew rein, and slipped from her side-saddle almost in the same movement. James hastily dismounted as well. She released her reins, and the horse waited, docilely. James did the same.

'How could I be offended?' she asked. 'That is the greatest compliment any woman could be paid.'

James wondered if she'd feel the same when she learned that Anne had African blood? Or that she had actually been named after his own mother? But he did not feel now was the time to enlighten her. 'I thought you the most attractive woman I had ever met.'

She turned to face him, taking off her hat as she did so. 'But that was before you met Cecile von Beinhardt.'

'I think the correct way to put it would be that it was before Cecile met me.'

Anne raised her eyebrows. 'You will have to explain that to me. But in any event, she is history, and from your behaviour since her death I cannot believe you loved her.' She took a step forward, so that she was almost touching him. 'Would you like to have an affair with me, James Martingell?' Then she was in his arms, and he was kissing her almost savagely, pressing her body against his, feeling the contours even through the tunic and jodhpurs, realised she was scraping one of her boots up and down his, inhaling her scent, a delicious mixture of perfume and fresh sweat, while her hair tumbled out of its snood and flooded down her shoulders and back. But when he made to lift her into the shade of one of the trees, she resisted, and he let her go. 'I am not really into exposing my arse to the elements,' she said. And kissed him again, chastely. 'I will come to you tonight.'

'But ... your husband ...?'

'We have separate bedrooms.'

'I see.' Suddenly he was angry. 'And that will be after our discussion. So that, should I not agree to do business with your husband, on his terms, you will not come at all.'

'What a fierce man you are, James! I can well understand that your name is feared the length and breadth of Africa. I will come to you, no matter what the outcome of our discussion. You have my word. But I think you will negotiate better without

287

the guilt of just having fucked Winston's wife, and with the promise that you will do so. Do you not agree?' Her words were so incongruous, dripping from those perfect lips, but the more compelling for that. Once again he suspected that his life was being taken over by a woman. But the last time hadn't turned out so very badly.

'So you see,' Anne said, 'it really is a chicken-and egg situation.' Her four-year-old son had been presented to say good-night to his parents, and to their guest, and now Anne sat on a settee in her drawing room. Despite her offer not to dress, she was wearing a pale blue dinner gown, her fingers laden with rings, a pearl necklace plunging into her *décolletage*. She looked good enough to eat. James had to wonder if her intention had been to so befuddle him with desire he would not be able to negotiate at all, whereas if they had already coupled, she might have lost some of her effect. But why? James had another uneasy feeling that he already knew the reason, but had not yet come to terms with it.

'I say, jolly romantic, what,' Winston Pennyfeather remarked. He was a pale young man, not much older than his wife, if at all, James estimated; well built but weak-chinned, the indecisive features accentuated by the mouse-brown hair. But no one could doubt that his dinner suit had been made in Savile Row, or that the sherry served by Wilson the butler was the best Domecq. 'And ... ah ...' he looked at his wife, and although Anne's head did not move James knew a message had been passed from her to him, in response to a question. He was wading in deep water, here.

'So what you would like is for me to finance an expedition to enable you to regain your, ah, ill-gotten gains,' Winston suggested.

'I do need financing, yes,' James said. 'But I was hoping that we could make it part of a general business association. Lady Pennyfeather indicated that you had some prospective customers in mind.'

'Oh, indeed, there are always prospective customers. But none so easy to reach, or so punctual in payment—if what you have said is true—as this Mullah character. If I was able to supply the necessary arms, would he not pay another hundred thousand?'

'He is fighting the British,' James reminded him.

'It is difficult to find anyone in the world today who has not at some time fought the British, or is presently fighting the British, or has every prospect *of* fighting the British at some time in the near future,' Winston pointed out. 'This is one of the penalties we pay for having an empire upon which the sun never sets.'

'So you would like me to resume dealing with the Mullah?'

'I am sure you can control your conscience, old man. But equally, I would like you to regain your money. How much would you need to reach Somalia, dig up the money, and return again?'

'I would need a ship. It need not be a very large or very expensive ship. In fact, the more shabby it is the better, as it will attract less attention. But it will be the principal expense. Chartered for a month, it would cost about £1,000.'

'A thousand pounds,' Winston mused, and looked at his wife.

'I am sure we could invest that much in Mr Martingell's prospects,' Anne said.

'Oh, quite. For what return, Martingell?'

'One hundred per cent,' James said. 'Lend me the thousand, and I will repay you two.'

'Out of a hundred thousand,' Winston remarked.

'I have partners who were with me when I earned that money, and other obligations,' James pointed out.

'That is still a great deal of money,' Winston said. 'Which you cannot reach unless someone supplies you with a ship. I will do that, for a return of £20,000.' James stared at him with his mouth open. 'You may, of course, apply elsewhere,' Winston said. 'But you will hardly get a better bargain. And of course, every moment you delay, everyone else you let into your secret, the chance will grow that either the Mullah or the Italians will get to hear of it, and be waiting for you.' He was smiling as he uttered the veiled threat.

'Why, you ...' James felt the anger welling up out of his belly.

'I think we should eat, and then sleep on it,' Anne said.

She kept the conversation on other matters throughout the meal, drawing James out on his adventures and experiences in South Africa, a subject on which he was quite happy to expound, if only to convey to the always smiling Winston that he was not really a man to be pushed too far. 'And your daughter?' Anne asked. She smiled at her husband. 'She has the same name as I, Winston.'

'How interesting,' Winston said, clearly not the least interested.

'She is six years old,' James said. 'And nearly as pretty as her namesake.'

'Why, Mr Martingell, you pay the sweetest compliments. May I inquire after her mother?'

'Her mother is dead,' James said, deciding the lie would save a lot of more awkward questions.

'How very sad. But I imagined that was the case. I should love to meet your daughter, Mr Martingell. If we are going to be business partners, perhaps I shall.'

She was making a pre-emptive bid. 'If, indeed,' he said.

The meal over, Anne, fully in control of the situation, suggested an early night. James was shown to his room by a footman, just in case he had forgotten where it was. He preferred not to undress, but sat in an armchair and waited. He had no doubt that she would come; not only had she promised, but there was a good deal of unfinished business to be determined. And sure enough, he had not been waiting more than half-an-hour before the door was gently opened, and she slipped into the room, closing the door behind her again in the same movement, and then remaining leaning against it, frowning at him; she wore a négligé, and nothing else, so far as he could see. 'I can see that you are an impatient lover,' she remarked, a trifle acidly.

'I did not know if you would come,' he lied.

'I always keep my word.' She moved

across the room towards him, her body a shimmer of white through the diaphanous material. 'You are not still angry with Winston?'

'I dislike being taken for a fool.'

'I assure you he does not take you for a fool.' She sat on his lap, put her arm round his neck, allowed her suddenly exposed breast to brush his face. 'He knows you to be a hard and dangerous man. But also, at this moment, a desperate one. But he is as desperate as you.'

'Your husband?' But he could not stop himself caressing the soft flesh, while she gave a series of little shudders, presumably of pleasure.

'My husband is bankrupt,' she said. 'Ow!'

His hand had inadvertently tightened. Now he pulled his head back to look at her.

She smiled. 'Well, he is on the verge of bankruptcy. That means I shall be bankrupt, too.'

'You'll have to explain.'

Anne got off his lap and in the same instant allowed the négligé to slip altogether from her shoulders so that she was naked. She walked across the room, sat, and then lay on the bed, one leg up, as if posing for a portrait. He wondered how many times she had done that before. He got up in turn, stood above her and began to undress. Suddenly they were equals. 'He gambles,' Anne said. 'Horses, mainly. But also chemmy. Do you gamble, James?'

'I have never had the time,' James said. 'Or, frankly, the inclination, much less the money.'

'It is a vice, when it gets hold of you.' Anne watched his body appearing, and now she allowed her leg to straighten and lie beside the other. She had quite the most beautiful body he had ever seen, far more so than the slightly angular Cecile. And she was offering all of that beauty ... for what, exactly? He did not really think the £20,000 came into it.

'One keeps making one last bet, in anticipation that one's luck will turn. Until one's creditors run out of patience.'

'Can't he put it on the mortgage?'

'The mortgage was originally incurred by the gambling habits of Winston's great-grandfather. So Winston's father had a clause added to the trust, that no future gambling debts could be supported by the mortgage.'

'Well, then, the business ...'

'Is already also heavily in debt. Now Winston's creditors are suing him. If he cannot raise £20,000 by the end of this financial year they will sell him up. Then we will have no money at all; our tenants cannot even service the mortgage. So you see, he desperately needs both a salesman and a financier.'

'And he does not care how he gets them,' James said. Naked, he got on to the bed and sat astride her thighs. 'But he can raise a thousand pounds or so, to charter a ship.'

'On the guarantee of a payment of the whole debt, yes. I think he will be able to raise that, for a very short term.'

'I have to tell you that I do not altogether trust your husband.'

'He has made you a business proposition. You need him as much as he needs you.'

'And you?'

'I think I need you too. Being married to Winston is not an easy business. It is only tolerable when I can live as I choose, spend as I choose, love as I choose.' Suddenly she seized his shoulders, brought him down on her, and then rolled over with surprising strength, so that she was on top. She kissed him. 'Give me those things, James, and I will be faithful to you, for as long as you wish me to be.'

PART THREE

The Partnership

'By partners, in each other kind,
Afflictions easier grow;
In love alone we hate to find
Companions of our woe.'
William Walsh, *Song: Of All the Torments*

Chapter Nine

The Betrayal

'It is good that we meet at last.' Jean Le Barthe was a short, swarthy man. He had a French name and French nationality, but James suspected he was more African than European. 'My master, *our* master, Monsieur Martingell, is anxious for this second shipment. When he heard that you had parted company with the House of Beinhardt he was concerned. But now ... you have arranged another shipment?'

'That is correct, monsieur. This is through an English house.'

'This shipment will include cannon? This is very important to our master.'

'I have arranged for cannon.'

'Excellent. Our master will be pleased. And when can you deliver?'

'Within two months.'

'The same amount?'

James grinned. 'On the same terms.'

'Of course. I will inform our master.'

'I will also need information as to where I can land the goods,' James pointed out. 'I imagine the Italians have sealed the coast.'

'Why not in French territory?' Philippe, sitting at the end of the table, asked.

Le Barthe shook his head. 'Our master does not war upon the French, nor does he wish them involved in his war. Djibouti is too useful to us, as an entrepôt, a storage depot. But not for guns, which might be discovered and cause an international incident. I assume your delivery will be made by ship. What is the name of this ship?'

'I am not in a position to tell you that,' James said.

Le Barthe regarded him for several seconds. At times he could look very like his self-proclaimed master. 'Well,' he said, 'whatever the name, shape or size of the ship, she will have to proceed to the Horn of Africa. When she is in position inside the island of Socotra, let her fly this banner.' From his satchel he produced a furled ensign, plain green save for a gold embroidered sword in the fly. 'Wearing this flag, your ship will cruise that water until contacted by a vessel flying a matching flag. Is this agreeable to you?'

'Perfectly,' James said.

Le Barthe closed his satchel and stood up. 'Two months. Our master trusts you, Monsieur Martingell.' His tone suggested that he had no idea why. 'I am sure you will not fail him.'

'Two months,' James said.

The agent left the room, and Philippe poured two glasses of cognac. 'These transactions always give me the shakes.'

'As well they might. That is one slippery customer.'

'You do not trust him?'

'I would need my head examined.'

'Yet you do business with him.'

'I do business with his—I beg your pardon—*our* master, and as I believe he is more afraid of Mohammed than he is treacherous, we will do very well. Think of it, Philippe, another £100,000 to add to the first. This one will have to be shared with our new supplier, of course, but there will still be a tidy sum for us.'

'I still do not understand how you secured a new partner so very quickly,' Philippe said.

James tapped his nose. 'I have contacts.'

Just what those contacts were, and where they might lead them all, he was keeping entirely to himself. It was not that he did not trust Philippe, but that he feared the Frenchman's volatility.

'As for the other hundred thousand ...' Philippe grumbled.

James grinned. 'It is there. And once we are back in Somalia, it is ours.'

He felt somewhat volatile himself, had

constantly to remind himself that on two previous occasions in his life he had supposed his future was assured, and on both those occasions he had been brought back to earth with a bump. That would not happen this time, he was determined.

So, then, what about his new partners? Winston Pennyfeather was another man he could never trust; he spent too much time dissembling. There could be no doubt that he knew all about his wife's peccadilloes, but he preferred to do nothing about them. Therefore it was obvious to assume that they worked in harness. Anne's job had been to ensnare James Martingell, the man who could solve their financial difficulties. And she had done so with consummate ease. Yet the odd thing was that James was prepared to trust *her*, not because he was under any illusions that she might have fallen in love with him, however enthusiastic her love-making, but because he believed entirely what she had told him. There were certain things she wanted from life, and she would support and assist and appear to worship any man who could give her those things. At this moment, he was that man. And he would remain so until the new shipment of guns had been delivered and paid for, and the hidden money recovered. Afterwards, well ... there was always Lisette.

He had bought Lisette and Anne presents from England, and while the little girl played with her doll over and over again, Lisette tried on her new gown, in the very latest fashion with its bolero jacket and matching hat, parasol, gloves and boots, over and over again. 'I declare I am quite beautiful!' she said, twirling before her mirror. 'I did not know you understood women's clothes, James.'

'I don't. I gave the assistant your height, build and colouring, and she chose the outfit.'

'Wretched man! But I forgive you. When are we going to get our money.' She had this easy habit of encompassing everything in her own orbit.

'I am going very shortly, as soon as certain arrangements can be made. But you will stay here.'

'I wish to come with you.'

'Someone has to look after Anne. Atossa is staying here. If she is staying then you must stay too. Listen, I will not cheat you. You will get your share. But it will be a highly dangerous expedition. You know the Mullah wanted to buy you. If he sees you again he may decide to take you.'

Lisette licked her lips, not altogether in terror, he guessed. The thought, and their recent separation, made them both

303

anxious to get to bed. Presumably, lying in his arms, she was imagining he was the Mullah; he thought the reality might be a good deal different. But then, lying in Lisette's arms, he could imagine she was Anne Pennyfeather. And there again the reality had been a good deal different. He wondered if it ever would be again?

With such a fortune at stake, Winston Pennyfeather was as good as his word, and on the appointed date, a month after James had left England, a steam-yacht flying the Red Ensign entered Marseilles harbour and moored up. The waterfront was crowded to see her. 'It belongs to an English milord,' explained the Captain of the Port, with whom James had gone out of his way to become friendly. 'We were informed of her coming. She is on a world cruise.' There was no customs interference.

James and Philippe remained at the back of the crowd, drinking in the appointed bar, waiting for the Englishmen to come ashore. In fact, only one did so, a burly steward, who found them easily enough. 'Mr Martingell?' he asked. 'This your gear?'

James nodded. 'And that of Monsieur Desmorins.'

The steward nodded. 'Then I'll be off.

You're expected for dinner. We sail at ten.'

'Cloak and dagger,' Philippe observed. 'It gives me the shakes.'

'But so does everything else, old man,' James reminded him.

They bade farewell to the women. Atossa seemed quite happy to remain in Marseilles; she had developed a considerable appreciation of French civilisation. Lisette was still unhappy.

'Suppose you do not come back?'

'I always come back. But if I do not ...' he did not want to contemplate that, but more from Anne's point of view than Lisette's. 'You must do the best you can. Just remember, when I do come back, all of our troubles are over.'

In fact, he discovered, when he and Philippe went aboard the yacht that evening, that his troubles were only beginning. Waiting for him at the head of the gangplank were not only Sir Winston, but also his wife. Anne Pennyfeather was a picture in a deep-green evening gown with a plunging *décolletage*, and as usual wearing sufficient jewellery to suggest she could liquidate the firm's debts herself if she chose. But perhaps, he thought, like the estate, they were held in trust. 'How good to see you again, James,' she murmured, as he kissed her gloved hand.

'I must confess, I hadn't expected to see you, milady. On such a voyage.'

'How may a man sail round the world and leave his wife behind?' she inquired. 'And is this your associate?'

'Philippe Desmorins.' James introduced. Philippe was clearly star struck.

Sir Winston oversaw them with a cold smile. 'You'll want to see our cargo,' he suggested.

'I think it can wait until we are at sea,' James said.

The yacht actually cast off while they were at dinner, so they took their brandies and cigars up to the flying bridge to watch the lights of France fade into the distance as they steamed south into the Mediterranean. James was impressed. The yacht's name was *Europa,* and she was some 200 ft long, with a crew of 33 including the stewards. Her appointments were superb, her engine purred, and, in the calm of the Mediterranean, at any rate, she rolled but a little.

'Wherever did you find her?' he asked Sir Winston.

'It took some doing,' Pennyfeather said. 'And she is costing me—us—£2,000 a month to charter. I am gambling for high stakes, here.'

'I did suggest an inconspicuous rust-bucket,' James reminded him. 'Do I understand that I am expected to pick up the cost of the charter?'

'The cost of the charter will be laid against the general cost of the expedition,' Winston said. 'Before any share out is considered. Is that agreeable?'

'Entirely,' James said. Was it possible this was going to be an honest transaction?

'You must tell us where we are to go.' Anne murmured. James told them the instructions he had received from Le Barthe. 'And you trust this fellow?'

'I trust the Mullah,' James said. 'He needs our cargo. And,' he added for good measure, 'he trusts me.'

James had no idea what the drill would be for the voyage and lay awake on the bunk in his cabin for over an hour. But there was no soft tap on his door. No doubt while on the ship Anne was required to share a cabin with her husband; there was also the close proximity of her maid, a stolid Englishwoman who bore not the slightest resemblance to Lisette—for which he was grateful—and who clearly stood for no nonsense from anyone including her mistress. More likely, he reflected, having secured his services, Anne felt that she need no longer vamp him. He was not offended. At the end of this venture he would be entirely his own man, and Anne Pennyfeather, for all her attractions, would have become an irrelevance.

The voyage down the Mediterranean was entirely pleasant, the weather fine, the news from South Africa all good; according to the government the war was officially over. It was accepted that there were Boer commandos still roaming the countryside and making nuisances of themselves, but the new Commander-in-Chief, Lord Kitchener, who had replaced Roberts—the senior general having made the announcement that the war was won and promptly departed South Africa—was quite capable of coping with local problems, as he had proved in both the Sudan and India. Once the South African problem was entirely dealt with, he might turn his attention to the Mullah!

Anne Pennyfeather remained an always gracious and beautiful hostess. The afterguard gathered under the awning on the quarterdeck every day just before lunch, and again at six in the evening for champagne. The meals themselves were culinary masterpieces, served by the white-jacketed stewards. 'These people certainly know how to live,' Philippe confided. 'And you know something, James? I think this Lady Pennyfeather fancies you. If you were to play your cards right...'

'Chance would be a fine thing,' James said.

Next morning, he inspected the cargo. 'Lee-Enfields,' Winston said proudly. 'Bolt-action magazine rifles, Martingell, firing .303 bullets. Even the British Army are just taking delivery. This is the most modern infantry weapon in the world, and the best. And look here.' He had the lid taken off another case. 'This is a Lewis gun. Makes your old Maxim look like a pea-shooter. Again the very latest and the very best.'

James fingered the weapons in admiration. He had never seen such killing perfection. But ... 'No big guns?'

'Well, what do you expect, at such short notice? No, there are no big guns. But there will be, in the future, if this deal goes right.'

James grinned. 'If this deal doesn't go right, Sir Winston, there will be no future.'

Three days after leaving Marseilles they docked at Port Said. 'I have some people joining us here,' Winston said, blandly.

'Company people?' James asked, only mildly interested.

'They have worked for the company before, and are now doing so again,' Winston said, and went ashore to greet his associates.

Anne accompanied him, to James' disappointment; he had hoped they might be able to have an uninterrupted chat. But she was playing the game her way, and he sat on the quarterdeck under the awning, sipping champagne, until the Pennyfeathers returned with three men, at the sight of whom James put down his glass and stood up. Survival in the African bush depended on memory more than anything else. One remembered whether or not a twig had been bent this way or that, a leaf fallen when before it had been attached, an animal or bird call that differed from the last heard ... and one remembered faces as much as attitudes. 'Mr James Martingell,' Winston said, smiling as he brought the new passengers forward. 'John Sutherland.'

'Mr Martingell and I have met,' Sutherland said. James looked past him at the other two men. 'You must remember Archie Bell and Tom Proud,' Sutherland said.

'There were four with you when we met,' James said.

'Billy McQuaid,' Sutherland said. 'Poor fellow, he's dead.'

'You surprise me,' James said.

The ship was underway almost immediately, and was already into the canal, with the brown sandbanks to either side as they made their way south, before Anne, for the first time on the voyage, sought James out. 'There's a pleasant surprise,' he murmured as she sat beside him. The quarter-deck was otherwise empty, reasonably cool beneath the huge awnings.

'You understand that it is not possible for us to be, well, intimate, in such limited surroundings,' she said. 'You did not tell me you knew Winston's African people.'

'Is that who they are? I did not tell you, Anne, because I did not know, until I saw them this morning.'

'But you are not happy with the situation.'

'I know that they are three thugs, if that is what you mean. When we met they suggested they were after ivory.'

'That could have been true. Winston was once interested in the ivory business. That was before we married.'

'Just how much do you know about your husband?'

'I know that he is a baronet, who traces his title back more than 200 years.'

'When, if I remember my history, in his efforts to raise money, Charles I decreed that every man in England worth £100 a year should accept knighthood, for a fee, regardless of their backgrounds or characters.'

'That is perfectly true,' she agreed. 'But, after 250 years who's to know the difference?'

'And you've never met these characters before?'

'No, I have not. I have given you my word, James, that you are not going to be cheated. In any way. Please believe that.'

He held her hand. 'Then come to me, tonight.'

'That is quite impossible, and you must accept that. On this ship we are in Winston's power. You need to be patient.'

'And when, after we complete our dealing with the Mullah, and have dug up my money, and are back on this ship with £200,000 in coin under our decks?'

'I have said you will not be cheated,' she insisted, and freed her hand.

He could only wait and watch. He could not even alert Philippe, because he had no idea how the Frenchman might respond. But he had no doubt at all that, for all Anne's promises, Winston Pennyfeather did intend to cheat him, and had now accumulated the manpower to do it. While he had Philippe, an uncertain quality in a crisis, and Mbote. Mbote, he knew, would back him to the hilt, but he was still only one man. And the ship and crew were Winston's. He presumed they were honest English seamen, not into murder on the high seas, but if Winston engineered a situation to suit his purpose they would still have to follow the dictate of their employer. The only asset he possessed was that nothing was likely to happen before the money was recovered. And before then ...

So they made their way down the Canal and into the ocean beyond, sighted the Socotra Islands, and altered course to pass inside them. 'This is bad country, Mr Martingell,' complained Captain Petersen, whom James reckoned was an honest man. 'Where there aren't sandbanks, there are pirates. But you've sailed these waters before, I'm told.'

'Yes,' James said, and handed him the furled Somali ensign. 'You'll fly this from the masthead, if you will, sir.'

The captain held it up. 'Won't go very well with the red duster.'

'It'll only be for a day or two,' Winston said, having joined them.

The flag was set, speed was reduced, and the yacht steamed slowly south. They sighted one or two dhows, but none approached. Both James and Winston studied the little ships through their binoculars, but they were either pirates—who were not about to approach an obviously well-found and probably well-manned ship—or honest traders; none flew the gun-running flag. 'We'll be abeam of Mogadishu tomorrow morning,' Captain Petersen said at dinner, three days later.

'The moment you are, come about and steam north,' James said.

'I hope you're right, and that there are people waiting for us,' Petersen grumbled.

Next day they sighted the minarets of Mogadishu, and promptly altered course to retrace their way to the north; examining the port through his glasses James could also make out the masts of the Italian gunboat; he had no desire to encounter her again. The following morning was stiflingly hot, with only a light breeze and a few clouds. Anne sat on the afterdeck and fanned herself, while sipping iced tea. 'What a climate! I swear it would destroy a woman's complexion in an hour.'

'Or worse,' James said, standing at the rail, and feeling a sudden quickening of his heartbeat; on the northern horizon was a cluster of dhows.

'Telescope,' he called to Mbote, who hurried up with the instrument. James levelled it, but the dhows were still too far distant to make out their flags.

'Shall we reduce speed?' Winston asked.

James shook his head. 'Not till they're identified.'

'Well, I hope you won't mind if I arm my people,' He gave instructions to Sutherland and his associates.

'I suppose we had better do the same,' James told Philippe and Mbote.

Even Anne put on a belt with a revolver hanging from it, a strong contrast to her muslin dress. 'It's terribly exciting,' she confided.

'There's the flag,' James said, again using the glass.

By midafternoon they were surrounded by a dozen dhows, all flying the sword-flag, and James was greeting his old friend Daoud, while the English sailors clustered in an armed but apprehensive group just aft of the bridge, gazing at the hundred-odd bearded Somalis with whom they were surrounded. 'It has been too long,' Daoud said, also embracing Philippe and Mbote.

'This is our new partner, Sir Winston Pennyfeather,' James introduced.

Daoud touched his forehead as he bowed. His eyes were already straying along the deck to where Anne had remained standing, watching them. But apparently he accepted that James would always be accompanied by a pretty woman. Besides, he was here on business, and asked, 'The guns?' James and Winston took him below to show him the rows of boxes, and opened one for him. 'These are good,' he said. 'Oh, very good. Show me the cannon.'

'I'm sorry,' James said. 'None was available. We must hope for better in the future.'

Daoud pulled his beard. 'Mohammed will be displeased.'

'It's a fact of life. You have the money?'

'The money was to include cannon.'

'The deal was for £150,000, with cannon. We will take £100,000 for these rifles and machine-guns.'

Daoud grinned. 'Always the honest man, Martingell. We will transfer the cargo now.'

'I thought for a moment there was going to be trouble,' Winston confided, as he stood with James on the quarter-deck and watched the Somalis, aided by the ship's derricks, transferring the heavy boxes into their dhows. As each ship was filled to capacity she set sail for the mainland. 'But it is all going very smoothly.' He indicated the sacks of coin. 'Do we count these, or would that sheikh fellow be offended?'

316

'I shouldn't think so. But there really is no need to count them; Mohammed ibn abd Allah is an honest man.'

'Well, then, I congratulate you, Martingell, on a most successful venture.'

'Which is only half over,' James reminded him, and went to speak with Daoud, who told him that the Italian grip on the country was no stronger than it had been six months before.

'But that is of no concern to you,' the Sheikh said. 'All you now have to do is sail away, and return here in six months time with a new cargo. Our agent will make the arrangements, as before.'

'We shall do that,' James assured him. 'But Philippe has a wish to return to Mareeq.' He grinned. 'I think he hopes to find some of his wives. Has the village been rebuilt?'

'It is being rebuilt,' Daoud said. 'But I should not go there, Martingell. The people are Italian sympathisers.' It was his turn to grin. 'When there are enough of them, we shall destroy it again. And them.'

'Nonetheless, we must return there. And I would be grateful for your assistance.'

'Mine? At Mareeq?'

James explained the situation, and Daoud pulled his beard. 'That money has lain there for more than six months?

Suppose someone else has dug it up?'

'Only I know where it is buried,' James pointed out.

'And you do not trust your new associates.' Daoud grinned, a gleam of teeth through the darkness of his beard. 'Have you not formed a partnership? Given your words?'

'Europeans do not hold their words in quite such value as do you,' James said.

Daoud stroked his beard some more. 'How many men would you need?'

'No more than a dozen, to cover us.'

'My men will expect to be paid.'

'A hundred pounds a man. Two hundred for their leader.'

Daoud grinned. 'I will lead them myself, Martingell.'

Captain Petersen appeared. 'Smoke bearing 177,' he said.

'The gunboat,' James said.

'Then we must leave you,' Daoud said. Only the one dhow remained alongside.

'Will they not catch you up?' Winston asked as they rejoined him.

'It will be dark in an hour,' Daoud said. 'They will not catch us before then. And after dark they will not catch us at all.' He bowed to the Europeans. 'I will wish you good fortune, and another meeting in a few months time.'

He clambered down the side of the ship

and boarded his boat, which immediately cast off and set its lateen sail.

'What were you and he having such an animated chat about?' Winston asked.

'I was giving him a message for the Mullah,' James explained. 'It is best for all of us if I remain on good terms with him.'

'Absolutely,' Winston agreed, although he was clearly not convinced. He gestured at the gunboat. 'Are we in any danger from that fellow?'

'No, unless we lose our heads. But we had better stow the money in a safe place.'

They cruised slowly north, while the evening faded with tropical rapidity. But they wore all their lights, as did the gunboat, now rapidly coming up astern. 'Will they board us?' Anne asked, standing at the taffrail and looking aft through binoculars.

'They have no right to do so. I'll leave it to you and Petersen to answer any questions, Sir Winston.' The gunboat closed to within a mile of them. By then it was midnight. 'I suggest we all go to bed,' James said. 'She won't approach until daylight.'

Anne and Winston exchanged glances, and James grinned at them both. 'Believe me, I've had all this before.'

James was awake at dawn, to find the Pennyfeathers and their henchmen already on deck, dressed and armed and looking anxious. 'For God's sake put those guns away,' he said. 'They can see us quite clearly through their glasses, and a single shot from that 4.7 in on their bow deck would send us down.'

Reluctantly, and rather sheepishly, they discarded their weapons. By now the gunboat had increased speed and was closing them very fast. But Captain Petersen, as instructed, had taken down the gunrunners' flag, and at dawn the Red Ensign had been set aft, clearly visible in the clear morning air. Of the dhows there was no sight.

'Over to you, Sir Winston,' James invited, making sure he was out of view.

'Ahoy there!' came the call, in English. 'What ship is that?' As if they couldn't see the name!

'Steam yacht *Europa*,' Petersen replied.

'Where are you from?'

'We are out of London, England, on a world cruise.'

'But you are steering north.'

'One of our freshwater tanks has sprung a leak, and it is necessary for us to return to Aden for water and repairs.'

'You can obtain water and repairs in Mogadishu.'

'We prefer to return to Aden. We have an agent there.'

They could see the officers on the Italian vessel's bridge conferring. 'He is going to board us,' Anne muttered. 'I just know he is.'

'He has no right to do so, without substantial suspicion,' James repeated.

'We will wish you a safe journey,' the Italian officer shouted, and the gunboat turned away.

'Wheee!' Anne said. 'I think that calls for some champagne.'

They continued to cruise north for the rest of the day, and the gunboat disappeared. But James knew from experience it would not have gone very far. That afternoon they were in the latitude for Mareeq, and closed the shore until it was just visible. 'Close enough,' James said. 'It will have to be a very quick trip,' he told Winston. 'If we use the yacht's launch we can be in and out before anyone really knows what we're about.'

'The money is that accessible?'

James nodded. 'An hour will do it. But we must be armed, and prepared to defend ourselves.'

'Oh, certainly. That's why I brought

Sutherland and his boys along.'

'As we must be armed and prepared to defend *our*selves,' James told Philippe and Mbote. He had not confided all of his plans.

'I don't like it,' Philippe grumbled. 'We will be outnumbered.'

'Not by much. And we are better men than they, right?'

Philippe did not look reassured, but Mbote grinned.

As soon as it was dark, the steam-launch was put down. 'Two men, to man her and helm her,' James told the captain. 'You will remain here, holding this position, until we return. We shall not be long.'

Winston and his three aides then got on board, carrying with them the money paid by Daoud. 'It's not that I don't trust you and your men, captain,' Winston said with a grin. 'But temptation is a terrible thing.'

'As you say, Sir Winston,' Petersen agreed, not apparently offended.

James, Philippe and Mbote also boarded the launch. And then, to James' consternation, Anne appeared at the head of the gangway, wearing a khaki blouse and divided skirt, and a khaki topee, with her revolver strapped to her waist. But hadn't he known she would? 'Listen,' he said, 'the last woman I took ashore here died.'

'Of malaria, I understand.' She gave her husband her hand to help her over the gunwale. 'But we are hardly going to be ashore long enough for me to catch the disease, according to you, James. And I have as much interest in this treasure hunt as anyone, have I not?' As usual, she was a difficult woman with whom to argue.

Slowly the launch approached the shore, waiting for first light before attempting to pass through the reef. James reckoned he and Mbote were the two calmest people on board, which was no bad thing. When they could make out the surf he had the engine put into neutral, and they rolled in the swell for the next hour, while the first faint glow of light came out of the east behind them. James levelled his field glasses. It was still too dark to make out much of the village, but he could see the break in the reef. 'Slow ahead,' he told the seaman, and the launch moved forward.

The sea remained calm, but with a sizeable swell, which was causing the excessive surf. But the passage was calm, a surge of dark water. Now it was growing lighter by the minute, and they could see that several houses had been rebuilt, that the fields had been recultivated, and water was flowing down the stream into the sea. But the general store remained a burned-out wreck. 'Swine,' Philippe muttered.

James was checking his markers, and was relieved to see the tree was still in place. The launch moved into the entrance and a moment later was in the total calm of the harbour. 'As close as you can without grounding,' James commanded; he knew the launch only drew 3 ft.

At the right moment the coxswain went into neutral, and his shipmate put the anchor over the side. The launch eased to a stop only 20 ft from the beach, riding easily. In the village a dog barked, and then another; there were still no humans to be seen. 'Cover us,' James said, and dropped over the side into chest deep water.

'We're coming with you,' Winston said.

'That would be foolish. We shall be in sight at all times. You are better off here.' Winston chewed his lip. 'Where are we supposed to run to, with four heavy sacks?' James asked.

Mbote joined him, carrying the spades, and the two men waded ashore. Behind them they heard the click of rifle bolts as their support got ready. They waded ashore. 'What will happen if someone has found the money and already dug it up, bwana?' Mbote asked.

'In that case, I have an unhappy feeling that we are dead men, old friend.'

'You do not think we are dead men anyway, bwana?'

'Not if I can help it.' He wondered where Daoud and his people were?

They stood on dry sand and stamped their feet to get the water out of their boots. The houses were some hundred yards to their left. As they watched, a door opened and a woman came out. She stared at them, and then at the launch, and then scuttled back inside and closed the door. 'I think we need to make haste,' James said, and they hurried to the north. When they had reached approximately where the money had been buried, James took his bearings. 'Here,' he said.

He and Mbote looked at each other as they laid their rifles and gunbelts on the ground. Then they grinned at each other, and began to dig. They had hardly removed the topsoil when people came out of the houses to watch them, men, women and children; the dogs were now barking fairly continuously.

James put down his spade, picked up his rifle, and as ostentatiously as possible worked the bolt to send a cartridge into the chamber. The people stopped moving.

James and Mbote resumed digging. They had gone down another foot when there was a shot. Instantly they dropped their spades and grabbed their rifles. The people

325

had started to move forward again, and someone on the launch had fired a warning. The people returned into the village and most disappeared into the houses.

James and Mbote resumed digging, and for a few minutes James felt very uncomfortable indeed; he did not remember going this deep. But of course in the passage of even six months there would have been an additional accumulation of soil, and at that very moment his spade struck something solid, as in that moment dust flew beside him, and Mbote grunted. 'Hit?' James asked.

'Close,' Mbote said.

'Right. Get in there and bring up the sacks.' James himself lay down behind his rifle, listening to another crack. But the villagers were using matchlocks, by the sound, probably more than 100 years old. He returned fire at the nearest house, and was joined by the men on the launch, who blazed away for several seconds, effectively ending the resistance for the time being.

Mbote had been using his fingers, and now, puffing, he brought up the first sack. 'Hallelujah!' he remarked.

'Three more,' James reminded him.

He kept watching the houses. It was impossible to know if any of the villagers had been hit, and he sincerely hoped none had; these people had suffered too much because of his dealings with the Mullah. But at the same time he had no intention of being prevented from taking out his money. In any event, they were being well supported from the launch, from which every minute or so someone sent a shot winging into the houses.

Mbote brought up sack after sack, sweat rolling down his face. When all four were up, James waved at the launch. They would have to make two trips to the beach, and approach much closer to the houses. Instantly Winston's men set up a constant covering fire.

'Let's go,' James said.

They took a sack each, humped it on to their shoulders, and moved down the sloping shore as quickly as possible. The firing was now continuous, and there was no time to determine whether any was coming from the houses. They waded into the water and up to the side of the launch, where willing hands relieved them of their burdens. 'Two more,' James gasped, and waded back to shore, Mbote at his shoulder.

Behind them the men on the launch continued to fire into the houses. But the villagers were recovering some of their nerve, and there were spurts of sand from time to time. Fortunately the shooting was totally inaccurate. They regained the remaining sacks, buckled on their revolver belts, slung their rifles, and saw several men creeping along the edge of the fields, to their right; the Somalis had clearly deduced that the sacks the intruders were removing contained something sufficiently valuable to be worth risking their lives for. Where the devil was Daoud?

'We'll have to discourage them,' James said, dropping his sack and unslinging his rifle as he knelt. Mbote followed his example, and they both emptied their magazines in the general direction of the prowlers. Again, it was impossible to tell if anyone was hit, but the men took cover. James and Mbote hastily reloaded, slung their rifles, and humped the sacks again. They staggered down the beach and into the water, waded back up to the launch. The sacks were taken on board. 'Up you get,' James told Mbote.

Mbote clambered over the gunwale, but then gave a grunt and went down. 'Damnation!' James snapped, jumping into the boat himself 'Keep firing. Cox, get us out of here.'

The anchor was brought in, the engine chattered, and the launch backed off before turning. The firing slowly ceased. James knelt beside Mbote. 'Where?'

'Only my thigh, bwana.'

There was a lot of blood, but a hasty examination indicated that the big artery had not been hit. 'We must stop the bleeding.' Anne was kneeling on Mbote's other side. Now she took off her scarf and offered it as a bandage.

'Good girl,' James said, tying it as tightly as he dared. Mbote managed a smile.

Now they were through the reef and making out to sea; the yacht was indicated only by the glow of light on the horizon. 'What a splendid operation,' Winston said. 'I do congratulate you, Martingell. Pity you've outlived your usefulness.'

James looked round and up, in time to see a scandalised Philippe facing a gun rammed into his waist by Archie Bell. But he was also looking down the barrel of a gun, held by Sutherland. He looked at Anne. 'You said I'd not be cheated?'

Anne did not reply; she was gazing at her husband with a peculiar expression, but whether it was disgust or admiration was difficult to determine. 'So it's over the side with the lot of you,' Winston said. 'You two ...' he nodded to the sailors, 'will stick with my story that these three tried to take over the launch. There'll be money in it for you.' The seamen exchanged glances, but they were unarmed, and this man was their employer. 'You first,' Winston said, gesturing at James.

James sized up the odds. But, supposing Philippe was not capable of action, they were four to one, even supposing the two sailors remained absolutely neutral. What the *devil* had happened to Daoud? Could he make the shore? He was a powerful swimmer, but there were sharks in this sea. And he could not abandon Mbote, who certainly would not make it. Nor, he supposed, would Philippe.

'Do you need pushing?' Winston asked. 'I had always supposed you a man, Martingell.' He jerked his head, and Sutherland and Proud moved forward. James sighed, looked at Anne for a last time ... and saw her draw her revolver.

She was behind the men, including her husband. Now she levelled her weapon ... at Winston's head. 'Just hold it,' she said quietly. Winston turned, as did his companions. 'You said no treachery,' Anne reminded her husband.

'I am getting rid of a bastard who has slept with my wife,' Winston said.

James got over his initial surprise. It was now or never. He stepped forward and struck Proud a scything blow on the back of the neck with the flat of his hand. Proud fell to his knees, firing his gun as he did so. The bullet smashed into the bottom of the launch. Bell promptly turned away from Philippe, and ran into James' fist, which

330

sent him arching backwards to collapse on to the deck. James leapt after him, landed on his chest, and tore the revolver from his hands. In time to face Sutherland, firing as he did so. Sutherland gave a shriek and collapsed into the bubbling water. 'We're sinking!' shouted the coxswain.

Nobody paid any attention to him. Proud was struggling up again, and James turned in the same instant and shot him through the chest. Proud fell backwards. 'You stupid bitch!' Winston bawled, levelling his gun. 'Drop it, Martingell.'

James hesitated, but the revolver was aimed at his head. He let his own gun slip from his grasp and hit the deck, over which water continued to bubble. 'See to Proud, Bell,' Winston commanded.

Bell struggled up and leaned over Proud. 'He's dead.' He looked down at Sutherland. 'They're both dead.'

'Well, now,' Winston said. 'You're as quick and as good as they say, Martingell. But you're guilty of murder. As well as adultery and God alone knows what else. So I condemn you to death.' He levelled his revolver.

'No!' Anne shouted. Winston turned, his face distorted with jealous rage, gun thrust forward, and Anne fired. Her first bullet struck her husband in the shoulder and half turned him round. Her second struck him in the chest. And her third struck him in the face. Sir Winston Pennyfeather hit the deck in a welter of blood.

'Holy Jesus!' muttered the cox. Philippe was past words, as was Mbote. Bell looked left and right as James picked up the gun again. Anne fell to her knees beside the body of her husband. Her shoulders were bowed, but she still held the revolver.

'You,' James said. 'Can you swim?' Bell's head jerked. 'Stop the engine,' James told the cox, and gestured at the darkness. 'The beach is about a mile away.'

Bell licked his lips. 'You can't put me over, Martingell. What about sharks?'

'I'm giving you a break,' James told him. 'We won't put the dead bodies over until you've had time to make the shore.'

'But ... those people will kill me,' Bell said.

'I'd aim not to get ashore at the village,' James agreed. 'That was what I was going to try to do.'

Bell looked at Anne. 'This is murder, Lady Pennyfeather.'

'Get on with it,' Anne whispered.

Bell hesitated, and James nudged him with the gun muzzle. Slowly he climbed to his feet, looked at the two dead men, then jumped over the side with a huge splash. 'We're sinking,' the coxswain said again.

'You have a pump. You ...' he pointed at the petrified crewman. 'Use it. And you ...' he turned to the coxswain. 'Move away from here.' The engine growled into gear, and the propellor turned; white water appeared aft, accompanied by a thin stream from the pump the crewman was working vigorously. Of Bell there was no sign. James gestured Philippe to help him, and then heaved the three dead bodies over the side, Then he knelt beside Anne, who was still staring at Winston. 'That was a very brave thing, you did,' he said. 'And it wasn't murder.'

'I keep telling myself that,' she said. 'But I have killed my husband.' She raised her head to give the cox and the seaman a quick glance, then lowered it again.

'They will be a problem.' Philippe had crawled to be close to them. 'You understand, James, I had no chance. They took me entirely by surprise.'

'I understand,' James said. 'We all owe our lives entirely to Lady Pennyfeather.'

Anne shuddered. 'He promised me ... he swore to me... what was I to do, James? I had given you my word.'

'And I shall be eternally grateful for that.'

'But what do we do now? God, I am sweating!'

'We'll soon be aboard the yacht. Then we'll have to sort out the captain. And the crew. Beginning with these two.' He stood up. He really had no idea how they were going to handle this. Whatever promises they made to the sailors, whatever promises the sailors made back to them, were meaningless in the course of time. The alternative ... 'You understand it was self-defence,' he said, standing beside the coxswain.

'I understand,' the coxswain said.

'And there will of course be a bonus for you and your mate.'

The coxswain turned his head, and grinned. 'If I support your story, eh, Mr Martingell?'

'If you don't,' James said, 'there is liable to be a lot of trouble, and you won't get a cent out of it.' The coxswain nodded. James realised that now he could only play it by ear. He knelt beside Mbote. 'You okay?'

'I don't know,' Mbote said, honestly.

'We'll be having a good look at you in five minutes,' James promised him, and raised his head. The launch slowed as the engine was put into neutral. The lights of the yacht were still some distance off. 'What's the matter?' James snapped.

'There is a boat alongside the ship, sir,' the cox said.

James grabbed the binoculars and levelled them at the yacht. Even at several hundred yards distance he could make out the darker shape alongside the steam-vessel. A dhow! 'Daoud,' he muttered. He had been betrayed twice in one night.

Chapter Ten

The Accomplices

'Daoud?' Anne asked. 'What can he want?'

'This money,' James said.

'Oh, my God! What can we do?'

James looked down. The pump was not quite keeping pace with the water; they were definitely sinking. But even if they were not, they hardly had enough fuel for more than another hour. To return to the shore and the Somalis was out of the question.

'We'll have to see what can be done,' he said. 'Will you go through with it, Anne? No matter what is involved?'

'What are you telling me?'

'We are going to have to kill those men. But as we will be severely outnumbered it may be necessary to distract them. Or allow them to distract themselves.'

She licked her lips. 'I'll go through with it.'

'Philippe?'

'You think Daoud has betrayed us?'

'I have no doubt of it.'

'Well ...' he scooped one of the revolvers out of the water, dried it on his shirt, and began reloading it.

'You two?' James asked of the two seamen. 'Those are your shipmates in trouble.'

'How many, do you reckon, sir?' asked the seaman, by now panting with exertion.

'That we will have to see. But I don't expect more than dozen.'

This indeed was his big hope; if Daoud really meant to make off with the money himself, obviously the fewer people he had to share it with the better. He would know he had the value of surprise entirely on his side, certainly as regards the captain and crew of the yacht. 'We'll back you, sir,' said the coxswain. 'It's that or go down with the launch, eh?'

'Right,' James said. 'Now listen carefully. They'll be waiting for us on board, and will require us to hand over our weapons. Each of you tuck a pistol into your waistband, and surrender them without question. We will conceal the other four guns. He handed one each to Philippe and Mbote. 'Put them behind your back, again in your waistband,' he instructed. 'Which of you two wants the fourth gun?' he asked the coxswain.

'I will take it,' Anne said. 'I can shoot as fast and as straight as any man.'

They couldn't argue with that. James gave her the gun. 'You understand that he may ... touch you before we can begin to fight.' She nodded, released her belt, and thrust the gun inside one of her undergarments. 'Now there is one thing more we need to remember,' James said. 'All of this is pointless if we lose the money. Just be ready to act.'

The launch surged up to the yacht and went round the other side from the dhow. Waiting for them was the captain and first mate. 'We've had trouble,' James called out as they came alongside. 'The launch is sinking. Help us with these sacks.'

The sacks were passed up, and then Anne. 'Milady!' Captain Petersen said. He was in a highly agitated state.

'We saw the dhow.' James scrambled over the side, and Philippe and the crew men passed Mbote up. 'Easy now. He's been hit.'

'Sir Winston ...?' the mate asked.

'Dead. So are the others. Where are our guests?'

'We are here, Martingell.' Daoud emerged from the shadow of the wheelhouse, accompanied by six men, all armed, all pointing their rifles at the newcomers. Only six? That was too good to be true.

'We didn't have a choice.' The captain looked from Anne to James. 'We thought they were your friends.'

'So did I,' James agreed. 'What have you done with the crew, Daoud?'

'They are below. Under guard.'

So, James thought, possibly another four. But he would also have left at least two on the dhow. 'I thought you *were* my friend,' he said. 'What of your word?'

'I did not give you my word, Martingell. I said I would see what could be done. Now I know what can be done.' Daoud stood at the rail and watched the launch, slowly sinking into the gentle waves. The engine had already stopped in a splutter of steam. 'You must have had quite a battle. We heard the shooting.'

'It was quite a battle.'

'Now it is over. You must give me your guns.'

'Do as he says,' James said, and handed over his first revolver. Philippe did likewise, as did the crewmen.

'And you, sweet lady,' Daoud said. Anne gave him her revolver, and James suppressed a sigh of relief. Daoud did not suspect them of double-dealing. Why should he? He appeared to hold all the

338

cards. Daoud was still grinning at Anne. 'You are a very lovely lady. Whenever I see Martingell he is accompanied by a lovely lady. Martingell, I will buy this woman from you.'

Anne caught her breath. 'She's expensive,' James said. 'Not only because she is beautiful, but because she *is* a lady. You know this word, lady? It means she is an aristocrat.'

'Then I will value her the more.' Daoud stood against Anne, ran his hands over the bodice of her blouse, then down her sides to her hips and behind, to grasp her buttocks. Anne seemed to be holding her breath. As was James. If he went for her pubes, where the second gun was resting ... 'To lie between these mounds,' Daoud said, 'would make me very happy. Name your price, Martingell.'

His sense of what was honourable—and what was not—was remarkable, James thought. He was prepared to steal £200,000 worth of coin, but he would not make off with another man's woman without it being a legal transaction. 'Well, shall we say £2,000?' James suggested.

'Then it is done.' Daoud gestured at the sacks. 'Count out the money.'

'I trust you,' James said. 'You count out the money.'

Daoud gestured to one of his men,

who knelt beside one of the sacks and untied it and began taking out the coins; two of his companions watched him with great interest. 'Now you are mine,' Daoud told Anne, with considerable satisfaction. 'I shall bid you farewell, Martingell. My men will see to you. But me, I am impatient for this woman.' He put his arms round Anne, who gave James an imploring look.

The situation would never be better. Daoud was fully preoccupied, and his men were at least as interested in the wealth being revealed to them as in their prisoners, who they appeared to have entirely discounted. 'Hit them!' James commanded, and drew the pistol from his back. Philippe did likewise. But Anne had anticipated them both, thrust her hand into her drawers, drawn her gun and pressed the muzzle into Daoud's side as he sought to lift her from the deck and carry her to the rail, and fired.

Daoud gave a scream of pain and half turned away from her. She fired again and he struck the deck with a thump. By then James and Philippe were also firing. Captain Petersen and his people dived to the deck for shelter as the night exploded. But the Somalis had been taken entirely by surprise, and both James and Philippe were on a killing high, while Mbote also used his concealed weapon to good effect.

The Somalis, dismayed by the fall of their leader, and unused to such close-quarter battle with firearms, sought only to escape. Those on deck tumbled over the side of the yacht to gain their dhow; those on the dhow could think only of casting off; those below, holding the crew at gunpoint, could think only of gaining the deck and thence escape. They were met by a hail of fire, but by now James was calling a halt. Four men lay dead or dying on the decks of the yacht; he reckoned that that, added to what had happened in the now sunk pinnace, was enough killing for one night.

The dhow was cast off and drifted away into the darkness. Philippe sent one or two shots winging after them as they set sail, and someone returned fire, but the shooting was wild. 'My God, Mr Martingell,' said Captain Petersen. 'I thought we were all dead.'

'We may well be, Captain,' James told him. 'If we don't get the hell out of here.'

The engine was started, the yacht moved north towards Aden. James knelt beside Mbote. 'How are you?'

'Bleeding,' Mbote said.

'We must get the bullet out. Philippe.'

'Are you a doctor as well as everything else?' Philippe asked.

'Sadly, no. But I've tended a few wounds in my time.' James summoned the cabin steward, had him dose Mbote with a large whisky and stand by with another. The wounded man was stretched on the saloon table and held there by Philippe and the steward while James probed and Mbote groaned and occasionally writhed. As James had hoped, the bullet had not entered deeply; it had been fired at long range from a matchlock. Once it was out whisky was poured into the wound to act as an antiseptic, then Mbote was bound up and put to bed. 'Will he recover?' Philippe asked.

'If we can avoid infection until we reach civilisation, yes.'

James went below to find Anne, who lay on her face across, her bed. Miranda, who had prudently remained in her cabin throughout the attempted piracy and the shooting, stood uncertainly in the doorway. 'I did not know what to do,' she said plaintively. 'I do not know what to do. Her ladyship will not speak ... Sir Winston ...'

'Draw a hot bath for your mistress,' James told her.

'But, Sir Winston ...'

'Sir Winston isn't coming back. Draw that bath.' He sat on the bed beside Anne. Her eyes were tight shut, but when he held her shoulder, she shuddered.

'I killed one of them,' she whispered.

'Daoud. Yes. He had it coming.'

She rolled on to her back. 'I have killed two men, tonight. My husband ...'

'Both in self-defence. You were magnificent.'

She sat up, pulled up her knees', clasped them. She was trembling. 'Magnificent,' he said again.

She half turned her head, then looked away again. 'I hated him. I always hated him.'

'I had gathered that.'

'If you knew the things he made me do.'

'Don't talk about it. Don't even think about it.'

'What do I tell my son?'

'That his dad died resisting an attack by pirates off the island of Socotra. That is what we are going to tell the world.'

'Those others ...'

'Will not deny it. And if they spread rumours about what might have happened before the attack, it will be their word against ours. Besides, they are accessories.'

'Have you lived all of your life like this?'

'I keep hoping to do better. But ... it's a dangerous business.'

'Did you and Cecile ever have to fight a battle?'

'Yes. We did. But the odds were more in our favour. On the other hand, you are alive.'

Miranda appeared in the cabin doorway; the yacht engine was purring as it drove through the calm sea. 'The bath is drawn, milady.'

'Thank you,' Anne said. Miranda hesitated, looking at James.

'I'll leave, shall I?' he asked.

She held his hand. 'No. I don't want you ever to leave me, James.'

Nothing might have changed as they steamed north. Anne sat on the afterdeck and sipped champagne. She had no black dress on board, but then James doubted she would have worn one if she had. 'Would you tell me exactly what happened, Mr Martingell?' the captain asked, when James joined him on the bridge. 'You understand that I shall have to make an official report. I mean, Sir Winston Pennyfeather dead ...'

'What did your two crewmen say?'

'Well, sir, they say there was a gun battle on board the launch ...'

'Sir Winston and his men tried to murder me and Lady Pennyfeather, and my associates, to gain possession of the money.'

'My word!' Petersen stroked his chin.

'Not a nice entry for the log, eh?'

'Well, sir, no. And afterwards ...?'

'You can tell about afterwards from what you experienced. Sir Winston was actually in cahoots with that Daoud fellow, to take over the ship and the money. However, as you saw, Daoud was not too unhappy about Sir Winston and his people having disappeared.'

'What am I to enter, sir?'

'Well, for the sake of the Pennyfeather family, and the British aristocracy, and all of us, I think you should enter that your ship was attacked by Socotran pirates, and that Sir Winston died gallantly defending both his ship and his wife's honour. There will, of course, be a bonus payment of £500 to every man of your crew, and a thousand to yourself, for the danger in which you were placed and for the manner in which you conducted yourself.'

'And once I make that entry in the log, it will become prima-facie evidence, which cannot be changed.'

'That is my understanding,' James agreed. 'I have also in mind to buy this ship.' He pressed the advantage he saw he was gaining.

'Buy the *Europa*, sir?' The captain was astounded, and sceptical. 'You're talking about £20,000, at the least.'

'Money is not a problem. Will the owner sell?'

'I should think he might, sir. But ... well ...'

'When I buy her,' James said, 'I shall of course employ the entire crew, and yourself, Captain. At improved rates of pay. I hope we understand each other.'

'I would say we do, sir,' the captain agreed.

'How is Mbote?' Anne asked.

'Feverish. I think that is to be expected. But Captain Petersen says we shall be in Aden tomorrow, at which time we'll be able to have a doctor on board and some drugs, hopefully. I think he is going to be all right.'

'I am glad about that. He is a most faithful servant. How long have you had him?'

'Several years, now. You do realise, Anne, that when we get to Aden, the captain will have to make a full report of everything that has happened, of how we were attacked by pirates, and fought them off, but at considerable loss to ourselves.'

'He will do this?'

James grinned. 'He knows he will be adequately paid, as will the crew. And I am going to buy the ship.' She gazed at him with her mouth open. 'Which guarantees his future employment,' James pointed out. 'And that of the crew.'

'But can you, we, afford it?'

'Oh, yes. At the moment. It will make a hole in our capital, but I think it will be worth it, both as a floating home and as a delivery vessel. Of course, the sooner we have something to deliver the better. Anyway ...' he grinned. 'I have always wanted to own an ocean-going yacht,'

'You think in huge parameters,' she muttered.

'As one seldom achieves all one wishes in this life, if you start off thinking small your achievements are likely to be smaller yet,' he pointed out. 'However, in the course of time there will almost certainly be repercussions. One seaman getting drunk, or confiding in his family ... the truth will out, eventually.'

'And then?'

'We must deny that it is the truth. Captain Petersen has written up his log to my instructions. A ship's log is always considered to be inalienable evidence in any future legal proceedings. A good deal of mud may be thrown at you in the course of time, but none of it will stick as long as you keep your head.'

She looked at him. 'Just now you said we.'

'I will say it again, if you would like me to.'

'I have said, I do not want you ever to leave me.'

He held her hand. 'You do realise that I am a murderous, double-dealing, womanising, treacherous scoundrel.'

She smiled. 'Is that all? The same could be said for me. So we will make a good pair. Anyway, you must have a defence.'

'That whatever I have done, I was forced to it.'

'Snap. But there are difficulties. As Sir Winston Pennyfeather's widow, I am entitled to live at Pennyfeather House, certainly until my son comes of age. But should I marry again ...'

'Especially if there are rumours about poor Winston's death. So, we'll set up house somewhere else. Or live on the ship. It's the firm I'm interested in. You have sufficient money to liquidate all of Winston's outstanding debts, and those of the firm.'

'And you would like to take it over.'

'It's always been my ambition, to own my own arms firm.'

'We,' she said. 'Everything must be we. Do you swear that?'

'Willingly. Does that mean you are prepared to trust me?'

'Yes.'

He kissed her. 'There is quite a lot of trusting needs to be done.'

As was to be expected, the news that an English yacht carrying a member of the aristocracy had been attacked by pirates off the Horn of Africa caused a considerable sensation. James and Anne managed to get the yacht out of Aden without doing much more than giving a carefully concocted statement to the local police, but there were press representatives waiting for them in Port Said and even more in Marseilles. Already questions were being asked, not at this time as to the facts of what had happened, so carefully recorded in the ship's log, but as to what the ship was doing in those waters as it was known she was embarking on a world cruise, which suggested she should have turned east after leaving Aden the first time, not sailed south west; supposition was linked to the known facts that James Martingell was a gun salesman, and Sir Winston Pennyfeather a gun manufacturer.

James and Anne decided it would be prudent for him to leave the yacht at Marseilles, and make his entry into England as inconspicuously as possible. In addition, there was Little Anne to be picked up, and Lisette to be sorted out. This last promised to be the most difficult. Anne volunteered to continue back to England with the ship. She would have to field all

349

the media interest as well as any questions that might be asked by the Admiralty or the law. But it would have to be done at some time, and they both knew it would be far better for them not to be together until after the furore had died down. 'Do you trust me?' she asked.

'Absolutely,' he said.

'As I trust you. Well, James, my dearest ... come to me as soon as you can.'

'The very moment.'

But first, there was Le Barthe.

He looked even more Arab than James remembered, as he hunched his shoulders and drank his coffee. 'This is a serious business,' he said.

'Indeed it is,' James agreed. He was drinking cognac, as was Philippe, as anxious as ever.

'Pirates,' Le Barthe said, disparagingly.

'Socotrans.'

'I am not one of these foolish newspapermen, Monsieur Martingell,' Le Barthe pointed out. 'Do you not think Daoud's people made a full report when they regained the land?'

'A full report about what? Daoud tried to make off with our money, monsieur. That was piracy. The money was paid to us in good faith by our master. I suggest he put his own affairs in order.'

'I doubt he will deal with you again, monsieur. Daoud was one of his most faithful commanders.'

'Again, I suggest the Mullah put his own house in order,' James said. 'A few more men like Daoud, and he is unlikely to live to old age.'

'Do you think there will be repercussions from that direction?' Anne asked, when he went on board to say goodbye.

'No. The Mullah has lost nothing—save for Daoud, of course. And when he has had the time to reflect, he may well decide that was actually a stroke of fortune.'

'Then who are we going to sell our guns to?'

'That is something we have to think about. But let's get our own life back on track first.'

There was so much to be done. Mbote was responding to treatment, but he still needed a lot of it, and James put him into hospital in Marseilles. 'You will not leave without me, Bwana?' Mbote asked, anxiously.

'If I do, I'll come back for you, old friend,' James said. 'Wherever fate is taking me, it is taking you too.'

'I believe you care more for that black man

than you do for me,' Lisette declared.

James bounced Little Anne on his knee. 'I care for you all.'

'Because you own us all. So tell me, what is to happen to me?'

'Lady Pennyfeather has very generously offered you a post as her personal maid.'

'Ha! She has a personal maid.'

'I think Miranda is not bearing up very well after her ordeal.'

'*Her* ordeal?'

'She is not so tough as you, Lisette. Anyway, Lady Pennyfeather may have to let her go.'

'And your intention is to fuck us both at the same time, is that it?'

'What an entrancing idea! I should tell you that Lady Pennyfeather is aware of our relationship and will not hold it against you, providing you behave yourself.'

'Lady's maid,' Lisette grumbled. 'I thought all that was behind me.'

'I think you will find Lady Pennyfeather a much more congenial mistress than the Countess von Beinhardt.'

'No mistress is congenial. Suppose I were just to walk out, return to Germany, and tell them the truth? What would you do then?'

'I would not have to do anything. No one would believe you, now. And if they did, there would be nothing they could do about it, as regards me. They would seek to punish whoever they could lay hands on: you. What did you say they do to you in German prisons?'

'You are a beast and a monster.'

'I am a man who is determined to reach the top of the tree. I am perfectly willing to carry those who work for me and with me and support me to the top. If they drop off, well that is up to them.' She collapsed in tears.

'What are your plans for me?' Philippe asked.

'I am hoping you will work with me in the future, as we have in the past,' James told him. 'We have crossed a few rivers together, Philippe.'

'Well, of course, that is what I want too. You have but to give me your instructions.'

'In the first place, I would like you to go back to Africa.'

'Eh?' Philippe's hair seemed to rise.

James grinned. 'Not to the Horn. Farther south, to Beira. I am not particularly welcome in Portuguese East. But there are people there I feel are my responsibility. I had thought to have sorted that out, but recent events may have changed the situation. I wish you to find these people and give them each a thousand pounds. Here is the list.'

Philippe studied it. 'Your brother's wife. Her sister, Her father. Her three children. These are ghosts from the past, *mon ami.*'

'I have too many of those,' James said. 'I do not wish to die and find them all waiting for me.'

Philippe studied him. 'You, James? With the life you have led? I would never have put you down as either a superstitious or a conscientious man.'

'We all make mistakes,' James said.

Philippe studied the list again. 'And this last name? In Dar-es-Salaam? Is she too to get money?'

'I leave that to your judgement. Just find out how she is doing.'

Philippe shook his head. 'Do you know, most people regard you as an unmitigated thug. Up to this minute, I was one of them.'

'And now?'

'Now?' Philippe shrugged. 'I am proud to be your friend. And your partner. But ...'

'Say it. I will not take offence.'

'I do not think it is possible to buy off ghosts from the past, James.'

Perhaps Philippe was right, although James really did not see how any of those ghosts could arise to trouble him in the future. It was, in any event, possible to

354

buy off conscience. And deal with the future. He was actually interviewed by an English Foreign Office official while still in Marseilles. 'Shocking events, Mr Martingell! Shocking events,' said Mr Fordyce.

'More shocking than any I have previously encountered,' James agreed.

'And, you'll excuse me, sir ...' Fordyce thumbed the pages of his notebook. 'You have experienced a few shocking events in your past, have you not? You were engaged in the Jameson Raid. Am I correct?'

'I was not on the Jameson Raid,' James said, carefully.

'But you were arrested by the Boers as an agent for Dr Jameson.'

'That is correct. I was released when they discovered they had made a mistake.'

'I see. Will you deny that you were a salesman for the German arms firm of Beinhardt?'

'I was Beinhardt's agent in Central Africa for a while, yes.'

'Were you not engaged in selling guns to a certain Mohammed ibn abd Allah? Known as the Mad Mullah?'

'I acted as Beinhardt's agent in certain transactions with the Mullah, yes.'

'You, an Englishman, sold guns to this Somali savage for use against Englishmen?'

'That is incorrect,' James said. 'First, the

Mullah may have some savage character-istics, but he is not a savage. Secondly, the guns were for use in defending his homeland against the Italians. At that time the English were not involved.'

'They are now.'

'You will observe that I am no longer in the employ of the House of Beinhardt.'

Fordyce glared at him. 'But you were there a few months ago.'

'Where?'

'In Somalia, selling guns to the Mullah.' He pointed a finger at James. 'Knowing that he is now fighting the British.'

'I'm afraid you will have to prove that rather outrageous statement, sir,' James said.

Another glare. 'Very good, sir. Now tell me the truth about Sir Winston Pennyfeather's death?'

'We were attacked by pirates, and he died defending his ship, and his wife.'

'Very gallant, I'm sure. Do you take us for fools, Mr Martingell? Sir Winston Pennyfeather owns an arms factory, which happens to be in financial difficulties. You are a well-known arms dealer, who, you have just admitted, has had dealings with the Mullah in the past. How odd it is that the pair of you should find yourselves on the same ship at the same time, off the Horn of Africa.'

'I do not find it odd at all,' James said. 'Sir Winston and I were friends. I have been acquainted with his family as far back as 1896, when I met his wife in Cape Town. Sir Winston invited me to accompany his wife and himself on the first part of his world cruise. I'm afraid I must take the responsibility for his decision to go inside the Socotra Islands and see the Horn for himself; I suppose I had told him too many tales about the place. But I can give you my word of honour as a gentleman that Sir Winston never set foot upon the Somali mainland. It was pure bad luck that we were attacked by pirates. And as I say, he died most gallantly.'

'Sir,' Fordyce said. 'You are a prevaricator and a liar.'

'Mr Fordyce,' James said, 'had you not presented your credentials before we commenced this interview, I would knock those words down your throat.'

Fordyce hastily stood up. But he was pointing again. 'Will you deny that your father died an undischarged bankrupt?'

'I intend to pay that debt as soon as I return to England,' James said. 'Or are you trying to tell me that I will not be welcome in the land of my birth?'

'We cannot stop you returning to England, Mr Martingell. However, I should warn you that exporting arms from Great

Britain can only be done under licence.'

'I am sure you're right,' James said. 'I have no experience of exporting arms from Great Britain. That is because I have never had any arms to export. Nor do I now.'

Fordyce snorted. 'Your relationship with Sir Winston Pennyfeather was simply that of friend?'

'That is what I have said.'

'And ... I hate to be indelicate, but would you tell me what is your relationship with Lady Pennyfeather?'

'She is the wife of my friend, But also, as I have explained, an old acquaintance from my Cape Town days.'

'You have no plans for seeing her again?'

'I am sure I shall call, when I am in England. If only to offer her my condolences.'

'Were you aware that Sir Winston was heavily in debt?'

'Good lord, no! In debt? How could he charter a yacht for a world cruise?'

'How indeed, Mr Martingell. Are you aware that since her return to England, Lady Pennyfeather has paid off all her late husband's debts?'

'Has she, by Jove! Well done. He must have been heavily insured.'

'Our knowledge is that he was not insured at all.'

'Was it Alice or the White Rabbit who

said "Curiouser and Curiouser",' James remarked, pleasantly.

'You are saying that you know nothing of Lady Pennyfeather's financial matters, or where she might have obtained this windfall?'

'My dear Mr Fordyce, a gentleman does not delve into a lady's finances. If he is a gentleman.'

Fordyce flushed scarlet and took his leave.

'Oh, my darling!' Anne held him so tightly he thought she was trying to break a rib. 'It has been so terrible!'

'I've had some.' He kissed her, again and again. 'But they can prove nothing.'

'I felt so helpless without you.'

'But apparently you coped magnificently, as you always do. Now, this is Anne.'

Anne released him and dropped to her knees before the little girl. 'Anne. Oh, you are beautiful! Did you know that my name is Anne, too?'

'No,' Anne said.

Anne glanced at James. 'She's a little direct, I'm afraid,' James explained. 'She hasn't really had any upbringing.'

'Well,' Anne said. 'You are going to live with me now. And as we can't have two Annes about the place, we are going to call you ... Lanne.'

'Why?' the child asked.

'Because that is short for Little Anne.'

'Then am I to call you Banne? Big Anne?'

'No. I think it would be best if you were to call me mother.'

'You are not my mother.'

'I am going to be your mother,' Anne said firmly, and stood up.

'She's a little out of her depth,' James explained.

'I would say she is entirely in her depth,' Anne remarked. 'But I am sure we will get to know and love one another.' She gazed at Lisette, who had remained standing by the doorway, and now gave an anxious curtsey.

'This is Lisette,' James explained.

'Welcome,' Anne said. 'I understand that Mr Martingell has explained the situation to you?'

'And to you, milady,' Lisette riposted.

They stared at each other for several moments. Then Anne said, 'If you will take your bag upstairs, Lisettte, Mrs Neale will show you to your room. You may take Lanne with you.' Lisette gave another curtsey, and held Little Anne's hand to lead her from the room.

'I suppose I did not really appreciate just what I was taking on,' Anne confessed, having signalled Wilson to pour champagne. 'In your own way, James, you are quite as much a savage prince, complete with harem, as any Somali chieftain.'

'Put it down to lack of upbringing,' James said. 'Would you like me to make other arrangements?'

'Definitely not,' Anne said. 'We are yoked together, James, by mutual crimes and mutual ambitions.'

'And mutual love?'

'I hope so. Do you intend to go on sleeping with that woman?'

'Only when I am not sleeping with you.'

'Well,' she said. 'No one could ever accuse you of dissembling. So, as you are now lord and master of everything you behold, what is your first command?'

James wondered if she had truly accepted the situation, however much she was prepared to wear it. But then, there were so many things about Anne Pennyfeather that were worth wondering about. She had killed her own husband. Why, exactly? To save the life of the man she loved? Or to safeguard her own future? Or because, as she claimed, there had been some long-running hatred between them of which he knew nothing? He suspected that it was a mixture of all three, however much he wanted to believe only the first. Yet she had done it.

Equally had she sworn to be faithful only to him, if he gave her what she wanted. And he had done that. Yet he did not doubt that she had her own agenda for the rest of their lives. Of her life, anyway. He began to wonder if the only truly loyal female he had ever encountered was poor Martha. If she had betrayed him, it had been purely a matter of the flesh.

But circumstances were different to the relationship he had had with Cecile. Here he held the purse strings, as Anne well understood. Even after he had liquidated his family's debts as well as the Pennyfeathers', and made payments to Philippe, Lisette and Mbote, and bought the yacht *Europa* for himself, he still had the whole £100,000 for the second shipment. Swiftly invested, it made him a reasonably wealthy man for life. But he wanted so much more.

It was necessary for Anne and himself to hurry slowly in their relationship. The death of Sir Winston Pennyfeather, gallantly defending his wife's virtue against a horde of Somali pirates, was hardly more than a nine days' wonder to British society—where he had not been all that popular anyway—or to the British press, which had more important matters to

362

think about as the rivalry between France and Germany reached a full-blown crisis which resulted in the humiliating dismissal of Delcasse, the French Foreign Minister. One result of this when he returned to office was a concordat between Britain and France, two nations which had been at loggerheads for nine centuries. Most people hailed the political milestone; James regarded it as an example of the way the world was shrinking, as far as possible clients were concerned.

While the crisis was boiling, and the Pennyfeathers were quietly being forgotten, he kicked his heels at a house he had bought in Worcestershire and not far from the Pennyfeather Estate. Here he kept in close touch with Anne and was able to spend at least one night a week with her; the fact that they were lovers was by now widely known, and she was being ostracised by the 'county'—but this did not seem to concern her. Lisette seemed to have settled in very well, and was caring for Lanne with much enthusiasm; there was no suggestion that she move in with James. This would have been vetoed by Anne in any event, but James had by now sized up Lisette as much as any other of the women who had played so large a part in his life: she would use her sex as and when necessary to obtain what she wanted, but it did not interest her that much. She still had her eye on the main chance, and had deduced that the main chance lay with Lanne. Again, James was content. He had Mbote, now fully recovered, as his servant and his friend.

He also had Atossa, who lived with him as his housekeeper pending Philippe's return.

It was in fact some months before Philippe returned from his journey to Beira. But his news from there was reassuring. 'The Delgados managed to raise the money to remove themselves from Portuguese East back to Portugal,' he said, pausing briefly in his hugs and kisses to Atossa, and gulping glasses of cognac. 'My God, but it is good to be home!'

'You mean they had left before you got there? Who paid for this? Beinhardt?'

'I do not know. And I thought it best not to ask too many questions. The name of Martingell is still remembered in Beira.'

'And in Dar-es-Salaam?'

'Oh, indeed. It is not a place I would ever revisit, if I were you. I called on Herr Fessnung, pretended I was a journalist gathering material for a book on African tribal wars, and mentioned your name. He was quite offensive, described you as a liar and a cheat, said there was some talk of your having murdered your fiancée.'

'The devil!' James remarked.

'But of course, no one could possibly prove anything. They are also very certain you stole the money.'

James grinned. 'But there again, they cannot prove anything. Tell me about Martha.'

'Gone,' Philippe said.

'Gone? You mean she's dead?'

'I do not think so. There is no record of it, and your friend Fessnung had no idea what had happened to her. But she is definitely not in Dar-es-Salaam.'

Well, well, James mused. It was very tempting to suppose that she had at last found a wealthy man who would support her for the rest of her life. It was far more likely that she had been persuaded to go off with some man who would abandon her as soon as he was tired of her, leaving her to walk the streets. He sighed. Supposing the Beinhardts had not betrayed him and then employed him, but instead he had returned to Beira with his 25 per cent share of that original shipment, might he not have settled down in perfect harmony with his half-caste mistress-cum-wife, and lived very contentedly ever after?

The answer was almost certainly no. He would have continued selling guns for the House of Martingell, which would have involved lengthy absences, and in those absences, as had actually happened, Martha would seek company. That was her nature. But he wished her well.

'So what do we do now?' Philippe asked. 'We have no clients, and even if we did, we have nothing to sell them.'

'As always, you are a pessimist, old friend,' James told him. 'We do have things to sell.'

During the waiting period, Anne had persuaded her husband's manager to continue running the Pennyfeather Small-Arms Company. The firm already had a small but consistent clientele, for their range of sporting guns, which were very popular, combined with the odd order for a dozen or so rifles for various Eastern potentates who wanted to arm their palace guards with the latest in modem weaponry. These were all very legal affairs, the arms only shipped under licence from the British Government. 'We really only just tick over,' Anne explained to James, as they sat at dinner together. 'What we need is another big kick in the rear to move us up a few notches. I have had to let go all of the extra people we took on to fulfil the Mullah's order. Can you do that for us?'

'Yes,' James said.

'Just like that?'

'I have been putting out feelers, making contacts. Next week I am meeting up with a representative of a prospective customer in London.'

'James! That sounds tremendous. Who is this customer?'

'An Afghan prince, or sheikh, or whatever it is they call themselves.'

She frowned. 'Who does he intend to fight?'

'The Amir, I believe. Afghan politics are a little complicated.'

'They always have been. But ... what of the British involvement?'

'It's a problem. I understand that Habibullah Khan is on the verge of signing an agreement with the Indian Government, which will virtually make Afghanistan another Indian province. The British feel this is necessary to prevent Russian encroachment. But naturally the idea isn't very popular with a large number of Afghans, who would rather run their own affairs.'

'And if you start a civil war, will the British not send troops through the Khyber Pass?'

'I've an idea they won't. You'll agree that previous British miltary expeditions into Afghanistan have always turned out disastrously, save for Roberts' dash in 1878. Anyway, I won't be starting a civil war. A chap wants to buy our rifles, and we need a client. What he does with the guns is up to him.'

She stroked her chin. 'It would be simpler to deal with the Mullah.'

'Not again,' he said. 'Will you agree that I should see this fellow?'

'I agree that you should do whatever you wish, James. I have said I will back you, always.'

He blew her a kiss. 'You'll be able to up production, and employment. There is one small problem. I may have to go to Afghanistan myself. That will mean a fairly long absence from England.'

'Can I come with you?'

'That is up to you. It will be arduous. And it could be dangerous.'

'I should like to come with you,' she said.

He had expected nothing different. 'Well, then,' he said, 'don't you think that for the sake of propriety we should get married?'

She gazed at him with her eyebrows arched and her mouth slightly open. 'I was beginning to wonder if you'd ever ask.'

They both wanted a quiet ceremony; Anne decided they would be married in the manor as soon as James had paid his visit to London and met with the Afghan agent. 'Would you believe,' he said, 'that

I am 44 years old and this is the first time I will have been married.'

'It hasn't happened yet,' she joked, shifting her sweat-wet body from beneath his. 'But the first thing we must do is have a child. I want your child, James.' That surprised him. She was passionately fond and protective of her son, and he liked the little boy as well. Equally, she seemed fond of Lanne, even if the little girl continued to move through life with a generally suspicious attitude. James wondered if this was not encouraged by Lisette. 'I agree with you,' Anne said. 'And will be worse when we are married, I have no doubt. Can we not get rid of her?'

It was the first time she had raised the matter, after some three years. 'Let me think about it,' James said.

'You mean you are genuinely fond of her? Do you still sleep with her?'

'I have not slept with Lisette since we came to England.'

'Well, she certainly hasn't taken up with anyone else, to my knowledge. She concentrates all her energy on Lanne. I think it is unhealthy. So what is the problem?'

'She knows rather a lot about my murky past.'

'Your murky past is history. I do not see how she can harm you. She was an accessory after the fact of stealing the money. And she has been well paid. I really think we should get rid of her, James.'

He rose on his elbow to look down at her. She had the most innocent of faces—which disguised the most active and persistent of brains. 'Perhaps I am reluctant to add to the list of people, men and women, who have reason to wish to revenge themselves upon me and mine. There are quite a few, you know.'

She smiled. 'There is no one in the whole world can harm you, James, and you know that. Firing Lisette can be your wedding present to me.'

It would have to be done, he knew. Just as he knew that all the very valuable help Lisette had given him in the break with Beinhardt had been pure self-interest, and nothing more. For which she had been paid. He owed her nothing. Yet it was a distasteful prospect. 'You do not know how lucky you are, Philippe,' he said, as the two men sat over their cognacs at dinner. 'You are a faithful lover, and Atossa is a faithful mistress.'

Philippe grinned. 'That is because I once had more than enough. Every man should start off with 12 wives, or concubines, or whatever you wish to call them, and slowly whittle them down to the one he values the most.'

'There wasn't anything very slow about the way yours were whittled down,' James pointed out.

'I know. I shall never forget that. Yet did I manage to retain the best.' He looked up as Mbote came in.

'We have a visitor,' Mbote said.

James raised his eyebrows. 'Someone you don't much care for, I'd say.'

'That is right,' Mbote said. 'It is Monsieur Le Barthe.'

Chapter Eleven

The Vengeance

Philippe rose to his feet like a startled pheasant. James remained seated. 'You'd better show him in, Mbote,' he said.

Mbote withdrew and returned a moment later with the half-caste. 'Monsieur Martingell. Monsieur Desmorins.' Le Barthe bowed. 'You are difficult gentlemen to track down.'

'Then I congratulate you on finding us,' James said. 'Have a seat. Cognac?'

'Thank you, monsieur.' Mbote brought

the goblet to him. 'Ah, such luxury,' Le Barthe said.

'I assume you are here on business,' James said.

'Sadly, yes. There is much business. The Mullah has been distressed that he has not heard from you for so long, that he, or rather I, have been unable to find you for so long. He desperately needs guns and ammunition. His position has grown serious because of the lack of supply.'

'I am not the only arms dealer in the world,' James pointed out.

'Our master prefers to deal with men he knows and feels he can trust.'

'You'd better say what is on your mind,' James suggested. Philippe was trembling but Mbote stood by the door, as massively calm as always.

'Well, you see, Monsieur Martingell, there are so many questions to be answered. When our master sent me to find you and place another order, this was six months after Sheikh Daoud's unhappy death ...' another pause, but as James did not reply he continued. 'And when I discovered that you had left Marseilles, as had Monsieur Desmorins ...' he gave Philippe a contemptuous glance, 'and that no one knew where you were, he then instructed me to resume dealings with the House of Beinhardt, direct. I did this, and was informed by the House, in the person of a Herr Dorting ... is that correct?'

'Probably,' James agreed.

'Herr Dorting informed me that while the House of Beinhardt would be perfectly willing to supply our master with arms, they must first be paid for the last shipment. This payment, in the amount of £100,000, was made to you, Monsieur Martingell. But you never passed it to the House of Beinhardt.'

'It went astray.'

'You mean you stole it.'

'One needs to be careful what one says, especially in the house of the man to whom you are saying it,' James suggested, quietly.

'You stole it, monsieur,' Le Barthe repeated. 'And hid it, and returned to reclaim it, when you brought the shipment of arms from England. It was in trying to prevent you from doing this that Sheikh Daoud was killed. Am I not right?'

'Sheikh Daoud,' James said, 'attempted to take Sir Winston Pennyfeather's yacht by force in an act of piracy, and was prevented. In the gun fight that ensued, both he and Sir Winston were killed, as you may have read in the papers. I was unable to ask Sheikh Daoud what moment of madness drove him to such an act, because he was dead.'

'You expect us to believe that?'

'I will tell you frankly, monsieur, I do not care whether you believe it or not.'

Le Barthe finished his cognac, and Mbote hurried forward with the decanter to refill his goblet. 'No doubt it will remain a mystery,' Le Barthe said. 'Our master accepts that Sheikh Daoud acted oddly, and is prepared to forget the business. However, he requires both a shipment of guns, and the original £100,000 which he paid you for the Beinhardt shipment. He offers you two alternatives. One is to make the payment to the House of Beinhardt, now, following which they will make another shipment of guns to our master; or two, make another shipment of arms now, for which you may regard that original £100,000 as payment. Do you understand this?'

'It's a little garbled, but I get the meaning.'

'So, which will you do?'

'Neither.'

Le Barthe's head came up, and he all but choked on his cognac. 'I do not accept that I owe either the Mullah or the House of Beinhardt a penny,' James said, still speaking in a quiet voice. 'Nor, as the Mullah is now openly waging war upon the British in British Somaliland, despite his assurances to me, can I consider selling him any more arms or ammunition. Will you stay to dinner, or have you somewhere to go?'

Le Barthe looked aghast. 'Do you think you can defy Mohammed ibn abd Allah?'

'I am not defying him, Le Barthe. I am simply terminating our business relationship. Happens all the time.' Again Le Barthe goggled at him, then he got up without a word and left the room. 'Make sure the gentleman closes the door behind him, Mbote,' James said.

Philippe refilled his glass; his hand was shaking so much James feared for the safety of the decanter. 'What are we to do? Might it not have been better to repay him the money?'

'I couldn't, even if I wanted to; there is not £100,000 left. Anyway, I consider that he has betrayed me, not the other way around.'

'He will be very angry. When I think ...'

'That was the Horn of Africa. This is England. We're short on nests of stinging ants, or women who are experts with a honey pot. Quit worrying. And, Philippe, our chat with Le Barthe goes no further, right?' Philippe gulped at the brandy.

Next day James took the train to London and met up with Azam-ud-Ranatullah, the representative of Yunis Haidar, the Afghan warlord who was planning the downfall of his cousin Amir Habbibullah Khan. He did not altogether take to Azam, who had none of the charisma of the Mullah. But his requirements were straightforward enough. 'This is a sizeable order,' James said, sipping coffee.

'The cost will be met,' Azam said.

'I have no doubt of it. I was thinking more of getting it to you. I assume you wish the transhipment made in secret?'

'We do not wish the British Government to know of it,' Azam agreed.

'I will need a guarantee that the guns will not be used against the British.'

'It is not our intention to fight the British.'

'A guarantee,' insisted James. Azam bowed his head. 'Now tell me how we get the guns to your lord, several hundred miles from the sea, without the British learning of it?'

'Persia,' Azam said. 'We have friends in Persia. They will assist with the passage of the guns.'

James considered, but as usual he had to rely on the fact that these people needed the weapons. 'You understand that to export guns from England I need a licence from the British Government.'

'You do not have to state the destination.'

'I'm afraid I do. With small shipments it is possible to, as we say, fudge it. With a shipment this size, that will not be possible.'

'You are saying the transaction is impossible?'

'No,' James said. 'I am saying that it will have to be illegal. If I am found out it will cost me a heavy fine and perhaps even a gaol sentence.'

'And you are not prepared to risk this?'

'I will risk it. But the cost will be doubled.'

Azam looked at the figure James had scrawled at the bottom of the list. '£200,000,' he mused. 'That is a very large sum of money, Mr Martingell.'

'This is a very large transaction,' James pointed out.

Azam nodded. 'You talk about money. It is our lives that are at stake.'

'I assumed you had taken that into consideration.'

'Yes. Very good, you shall have your money, when the guns have been delivered.'

James grinned. 'No, no, Mr Azam. The money will be paid in four instalments.' Azam's eyes narrowed. 'You will pay £50,000 into my bank now,' James said. 'A further £50,000 will be paid when the goods have been assembled, and inspected for quality by you or whoever you wish to employ for that purpose, and are satisfied that it is as you ordered. A further £50,000 will be paid on arrival of the goods in the seaport designated by you, before they are unloaded. The final payment will be made when you take delivery.'

Azam stroked his chin. 'Almost you make me feel that you do not trust me, Mr Martingell.'

'I have accumulated too many scars from trusting people, Sheikh Azam.'

'Very good. Now, transport. You are able to arrange a ship?'

James smiled. 'I think I can arrange that, Sheikh Azam.'

'Good heavens!' Anne remarked as she surveyed the list. 'Can we do this?'

'Over half from stock,' James said. 'We have three months to find the rest. I believe that by going into overtime we can manage half of the remainder, and I'm negotiating with Brentham's for the rest. This is a big one, darling. A really big one.'

'Of course, I understand that,' Anne said. 'I'm only bothered about the legality of it. Can you possibly keep it a secret?'

'Long enough to ship it. If there's a problem before I get back, well ... you'll have to hold the fort.'

'And go to prison?' But she smiled. 'I

thought I was coming with you.'

'And I know you cannot.'

Her head came up. 'I cannot?'

'Lisette told me that you had missed your period.'

'That abominable woman! I thought you were going to dismiss her?'

'All in good time. But are you going to risk it? You did say you wanted my child.'

'I do, more than anything else in the world. But missing one period doesn't necessarily mean a thing.'

'It could mean a lot. I won't be away more than a couple of months.'

'And by the time you come back I shall be in prison and looking like a house. Ah, well, it'll be an experience.'

'The case won't come up before I return. What you need to do is tell everyone that your husband handled the whole thing, and you know nothing about it. You're a beautiful woman, and an aristocrat. They'll handle you with kid gloves. Especially when they realise you're pregnant.'

'And you?'

'As you said, it'll be a new experience.'

'My trouble is,' she remarked, 'I don't actually have a husband.'

'But we're going to put that right, tomorrow.'

There were only a handful of guests. Anne's train was carried by Lanne, and she utilised Lisette as her maid of honour, to the German woman's delight. She had not been fired yet, and James and Anne had decided that she would not be until James returned from Afghanistan. 'I may need the support,' Anne said.

James had Philippe and Mbote as his groomsmen, somewhat to the alarm of the parish priest who was performing the ceremony, while Atossa and young Winston were the other guests. Both Lanne and Winston were now approaching their teens, and both were most attractive children, even if they did not really seem to take to each other. Anne put it down to Winston's being at the masculine age where girls were sissies, and to be avoided. James was more concerned about Lanne's continued and visible discontent; she only seemed to come to life in Lisette's company—another reason for putting off dismissing the nanny until the last possible moment.

'Well?' Anne asked, as they lay together in the huge bed. 'What is it like to be married, my love?'

'At the moment, heavenly.'

'You realise that once the trustees get to know of this they will probably require me to move out of the house, and Cousin

George will take over.'

'Then you'll move down to my house.'

'Oh, I wish I were coming with you! You will be careful, James?'

'I have every intention of coming back.'

Then it was time to work. There was a lot to be done. The initial £50,000 had duly been deposited, and James was now gathering the full cargo. He considered it best that he had as little as possible to do with the factory, and left that to Anne's manager. Globurn was obviously both amazed and a little disturbed at the size of the order he was required to fill. 'For export, milady?' he inquired.

'I am no longer your lady, Mr Globurn,' Anne reminded him. 'I am Mrs Martingell. Yes, the guns are for export.'

'There'll be a certificate, then?'

'I am sure there will be, Mr Globurn. But that need not concern you. Simply have the goods ready for movement, by the end of the month.'

Also by the end of the month James had the extra weaponry assembled at the Pennyfeather warehouse close to the factory. By then, as she had predicted, Anne was embroiled in negotiations with the trustees, who were requiring her to move out of the family home. James regarded this as good cover for the operation, however personally distressing it was for her. He had laid on a caravan of wagons, into which the arms were loaded, as they were inspected by Azam himself. 'Where do they go now?' the Afghan inquired.

'To where they will be shipped.'

'And that is?'

James grinned. 'My business, Azam. But you are welcome to accompany us, if you are going to stay with us throughout the voyage.'

Azam snorted. 'I have no wish to spend several weeks at sea. I will travel across country and meet you in Persia. I will bid you *bon voyage.*'

'I would say you have forgotten something,' James pointed out. Azam gave another snort and produced a cheque for £50,000. 'You realise that if this is not honoured I shall simply dump the goods overboard and return home,' James told him.

He had fitted out the *Europa* with the latest in wireless equipment, as he had done the same for his Worcestershire home, so that he could be in constant touch with Philippe and Anne—Mbote would, as always, be accompanying him—although he left strict instructions that they were to await his calls, and not try to contact him at sea. Then it was down to the secluded, and carefully reconnoitred, Welsh cove where the cargo was to be loaded. Captain Petersen and his crew were by now quite happy to follow James anywhere, especially as they were guaranteed big bonuses for the voyage. The arms were loaded without mishap, and the yacht steamed into the night.

As it was obviously imperative not to place themselves in a position where they could be stopped and searched, James opted to forego the Mediterranean and the Suez Canal and round the Cape of Good Hope. This necessitated a fuelling stop in Luanda, but he surmised that the Portuguese in Angola would not be interested in a British ship, so long as he kept a low profile.

The fuelling was completed and they were away again before anyone realised that the owner was the notorious James Martingell. Then they had to guess where he might be going next. It was a great relief to James that he and Captain Petersen would not have to navigate the Persian Gulf; the guns were to be put ashore at the port of Chah Bahar. This was more an open roadstead than a harbour, but a small armada of luggers and dhows was waiting to tranship the guns ashore. There were port officials about, and a few soldiers, but these merely looked on politely.

Now it was necessary to perform the usual drill, and having placed the third cheque in the ship's safe, James despatched Petersen to sea with orders to return in a fortnight. He was pleasantly surprised to discover that it was only about 200 miles from Chah Bahar to the town of Duzdab, which was within a few miles of the Afghan border. But the road not only led through some fairly high mountains but was also in places very close to the borders of British India. Not that he supposed the British in Baluchistan would risk an international incident by crossing the border to seize a cargo of guns—even supposing they knew the guns were there.

Persia was at the moment undergoing a severe political crisis. The finances of the country were so bad that they had been taken over by foreign experts, which had resulted in a revolution only the previous year. The Shah had realised he was beaten and had allowed a constitution to be drawn up, but had then promptly died, and his son and successor Mohammed Ali Shah was attempting to reverse recent events and reassume direct rule.

'But this is good for us,' Azam said. 'They have no time to worry about these outlying districts.'

There was certainly no attempt to

interfere with or even inspect their caravan as they set out.

'All is turmoil here in the heart of the world,' Azam explained over their campfire that night. They had already climbed over 1,000ft, and it was distinctly chilly.

'It is the British and the Russians, you see. They both want Persia, because it has oil. But the British have secured the rights to the oil, and the Russians are angry about this. Then, you see, the Russians wish to expand into India. That is why they want Afghanistan. But the British refuse to allow this, which is why they have secured controlling powers in Afghanistan also.'

'But if you do manage to mount a successful revolution and depose the Amir, will that not mean the end of the arrangement with Britain?' James asked.

'Of course. That is our intention.'

'Then you will have no one to defend you against the Russians.'

Azam grinned. 'We do not need anyone to defend us against the Russians, Martingell. We will defend ourselves against the Russians.'

James hoped he was right. But he found the Afghan sheikh growing on him. Azam might lack charisma, but he was a distinctly tough and, James reckoned, loyal man.

'Now,' Azam said, 'we have a journey of several days ahead of us, and these hills soon become mountains. It will be very chilly.'

'And nothing to drink,' James murmured. The entire caravan was Muslim, with the exception of himself and Mbote.

'But there are women. You wish one?'

James looked across the camp at the cluster of women gathered round their own camp fire. He rather did feel like a woman, not having had any creature comforts for over two months. And several of the girls, as he had observed on the march, were sensually attractive. But as always, he was reluctant to jeopardize his position as being a man apart, without apparent weaknesses, when dealing with these people. 'I'll manage,' he said. 'But Mbote might care for some company.'

Being away from the yacht and the radio he was of course out of touch with Philippe. But he had spoken with the Frenchman only four days before reaching the Persian coast—he had not risked it after that just in case anyone was listening and might be able to deduce his position and therefore where he would be landing the guns. On that occasion all had seemed well at home; the second cheque had been honoured, and no one outside of the firm seemed to be aware that he had left the country, or that he might be carrying a cargo of guns. Of course that fortune could not last, but it was at least saving Anne any embarrassment.

She was, Philippe had told him, about to move into his house, having finally lost the battle to retain the occupancy of the Pennyfeather mansion. 'We shall make her as comfortable as we can,' Philippe assured him. But James was in a desperate hurry to get home.

A week later they reached the Afghan frontier, and he found himself surrounded by bearded, turban-clad warriors armed with old firearms and great curved *tulwars*, who stared at the Lee-Enfields with awe, touched them as one of Arthur's knights might have stroked Excalibur. Here too there was another emissary from Yunis Haidar, with the final payment, as before a cheque drawn on a British bank. James had insisted upon the paper rather than gold, to evade the risk of encouraging anyone to attempt to rob him on the way home. Of course it was entirely possible that payment on the last two cheques might be stopped, or that there would no longer be funds to meet them. The fact that the two earlier cheques had been negotiated meant nothing now that the guns had been delivered.

But those were risks he had to take when dealing in illegal merchandise. As with the Mullah, he put his faith in the certainty that the Afghans would need more guns in the course of time—if they were setting up to oppose both British and Russian interests—and they would have to come back to him.

Rather to his surprise, but also his relief, Azam elected to accompany him back to the coast, along with a troop of his Afghan warriors, all now armed with the new weapon, and very proud of them too. 'We would not wish anything to happen to you, Martingell,' the chieftain said. 'After all, we are in business together, are we not?'

The two men were on the way to becoming friends, although James constantly reminded himself that he had considered Daoud his friend, until temptation had proved too much for friendship. But it was reassuring that the Afghans wanted him kept alive. They made much better time going down the hills, unladen, than going up with the guns. And there in the harbour was *Europa*, waiting for him. 'You'll come on board to say goodbye,' James invited.

'It will be my pleasure.'

Azam's previous visit had been merely a brief one, and he had been more interested in seeing the guns than the ship. Now he was eager to be shown over her, and fascinated by her appointments. James left Captain Petersen to show him everything he wanted, and went to the wireless room to call Philippe. But there was no reply.

Anne had of course visited James' house on several occasions, so she knew what to expect: considerably less space, for a start. Fortunately Winston was away at school, but he would be home soon enough. On the other hand, with both James and Mbote also away, the house was at its emptiest. 'You and Lanne will continue to share, for the time being,' she told Lisette.

'And I will share with Atossa, of course,' Philippe volunteered.

'Well, then, we won't get in each other's way, will we,' Anne said brightly, and went off to inspect the kitchens, which were under the control of a formidable woman named Mrs Perchard.

'Mr Martingell left all the arrangements to me, milady,' Mrs Perchard said.

'And I am sure you do everything very well,' Anne agreed. 'But I would like to inspect the lunch and dinner menus every morning at breakfast.'

'Yes, ma'am,' Mrs Perchard said, clearly disgruntled.

That night there were five of them for dinner, and Anne was amused as she looked around the table. An English aristocrat, a French gun-runner, a German maid, a Somali mistress, and a half-caste African little girl. Quite a gathering of the nations, she supposed. But another aspect of the way her life had whirled entirely out of control since Winston had inaugurated that crazy and fatal plan to get them out of debt. She had been all for it, in the beginning. She had remembered James Martingell as a romantic, unlucky figure from her girlhood. Uncle Charles in Cape Town had often spoken of the hunter-cum-gunrunner. Anne had a suspicion that Charles Rudd had always rather admired the lean man of action—not that he would ever allow admiration to get in the way of business. Even more than Napoleon's attitude to generals, Uncle Charles had rated a lucky business associate higher than a talented one. James Martingell was unlucky, and there was an end to it.

Save that James had then started making his own luck. By stealing £100,000? That was luck-making on a grand scale. When he had laid his plans, Winston had not known about the money. But he did know that James Martingell had been selling guns to the Mullah, as agent for the

House of Beinhardt. When he had also learned that Cecile von Beinhardts was dead, and that the links between James and the Beinhardts might be said to be on the verge of snapping, his eyes had gleamed. Arms for the Mullah meant big money.

Thus they had had an agent waiting to shadow James when he had arrived in Marseilles, and their people had followed him all the way to Cologne and back. Save that she had taken over halfway along the line. To her, it had all been half a joke, then, although she was well aware of the seriousness of the Pennyfeather financial situation. And James was a handsome, well-mannered, gallant man, even if clearly out of his depth in a country as civilised as France: she did not suppose they would have found it so easy to track him and snare him in the African bush.

Besides, with that handsome German fräulein in tow, she had not been at all sure he would take the bait. When he had, bedding him had seemed the obvious thing to do. She and Winston had always had an open marriage, as did so many of their social class, even if it would never be admitted by either party. The other golden rule was that one should never become pregnant by anyone save one's husband. Of course mistakes were made, when the husband usually had to pretend the child was his anyway. But the system worked very well in a society where so many marriages were contracted for family rather than personal values. Theirs had certainly been a business arrangement. Winston, due to the death of his strait-laced father having been pitchforked into attempting to manage the arms firm light years before he was ready for it, and already cursed with the lust for gambling, had sought the hand of the daughter of someone he had supposed to be a South African millionaire. When he had discovered that Daddy's weakness for bad investments had left his only daughter with a pittance, he had been very angry indeed. They had then been married a matter of months, and she had feared Winston might kill her when he had entirely lost his temper, slapped her face to and fro, and then hurled her from the bed.

At that moment she had started to hate him. But she was his wife, and he was her entrée to high society. She had gone her own way, emotionally, as had he. Even their joint production of young Winston had been a perfunctory matter; every so often he invaded her privacy, and she had had to put up with it. But since her pregnancy he had ignored her sexually. Thus seducing all of that lean, hungry manhood that was James Martingell had been fun. It was only when she was already embarked upon her adventure that she had learned that the man was, literally, sitting on a pot of gold, with the utterly innocent confidence that no one was going to stop him getting it. She had never seen such a gleam in Winston's eyes, not even on the first night of their honeymoon. But then, he had always counted money more important than sex.

Had there been a gleam in her eye as well? Because here was the salvation she had long sought ... perhaps. Of course, to run off with James Martingell would be the scandal of the century. She would never again be accepted in polite society. But £100,000 was worth a lot of sacrifices, especially with a man she knew she could very easily love. It had never crossed her mind that Winston would attempt to steal all the money for himself, or that he would, quite cold-bloodedly, have determined to kill James and his friends. Nor had she ever considered how she might react to such a scenario. Well, she was a civilised—even if amoral—woman. She still trembled when she remembered what she had done, and trembled more at the thought that young Winston might ever find out about it. But when it had come to the simple choice between James and the husband she hated, she had not hesitated a moment. Anne Pennyfeather, *femme fatale!*

And now her life had been entirely taken over by that lean, hungry, sexy man. Perhaps that had been fated since their meeting in Uncle Charles' office ten years ago. Perhaps that had always been her destiny. It was not something she had any intention of now challenging.

'Thank you, Miranda,' she said. The maid gave a little curtsey. She was the most loyal of servants, had never questioned her mistress's account of what had happened on the dreadful night three years before; Anne had decided against letting her go and submitting to the grooming of Lisette. Now she closed the door behind herself. Anne remained seated before her mirror for several more minutes, gazing at that calm, resolute, handsome face that gazed back at her. Had she looked like that at the moment she had shot Winston? She knew she had not looked like that at the moment she had shot Daoud. She had killed two men. Hardly an occupation for a lady!

She sighed, got up, shrugged off both negligee and nightgown, gave her stomach a little rub—was there really James' child in there?—and lay down on the bed. James should have reached Persia by now, have unloaded the guns, and be on his way to

Afghanistan. He had called six days before, when nearing the end of his voyage. As usual, he was on a high. James was always on a high. She was surprised at how much she was missing him, how much she wanted him home. But was it so surprising, after all, she had killed for him? She turned off the fight, fell into a deep sleep, awoke with a start, for a moment uncertain where she was, unsure of what had awakened her. A noise, certainly.

Then she heard a scream. She sat up, throwing back the covers, leaving the bed and crossing the room to the dresser in long naked strides. She pulled the drawer open, took out the loaded gun that always waited there, and turned to face the door. Just the one scream. But there was movement in the house. And who had screamed?

She bit her lip as she gazed at the door, only half visible in the darkness. Naked, she could not face the unknown. She moved to the bed, pulled on her negligee, and as she did so the door opened. Anne was aware only of men, several of them. In the gloom their identity or nationality was impossible to tell. But they were running towards her.

She levelled the revolver and fired, and one of the men screamed and fell; she did not know if he was dead. Then they were on her, hands seeking to grasp her body, others seeking to tear the revolver from her grasp. Now it was she who screamed!

'A wonderful ship,' Azam said, emerging from the engine-room and looking slightly dazed. 'You understand, that for someone like me, born and bred so far from the ocean, the very idea of sea travel is strange and wonderful. When I came to England by ship, I was continually amazed. But to own such a vessel ... you are a fortunate man, Martingell.'

'Yes,' James agreed, absently. There should have been someone at the house to take his call. Those had been his instructions.

'And now I must take my leave,' Azam said. 'I will contact you again in a few months, should, as I am certain will be the case, we need more weapons and munitions. I will wish you a safe voyage home.'

'Thank you,' James said, accompanying the sheikh to the rail, where he was checked by a call from the bridge.

'There is a radio message, Mr Martingell.'

'Excuse me.' James hurried up the ladder, where Petersen was waiting, his face grave.

'This has just come through, Mr Martin-gell.'

James scanned the paper.

MARTINGELL. I WISH MY MONEY
AND I WISH MY GUNS. DO YOU SUP-
POSE YOU CAN OPPOSE THE WILL
OF MOHAMMED IBN ABD ALLAH?
FOOLISH MAN. I POSSESS YOUR
WIFE. I POSSESS YOUR DAUGHTER.
I POSSESS YOUR ENTIRE HOUSE-
HOLD. CROSS ME AGAIN, AND THE
ANTS WILL FEED WELL. BE INSIDE
SOCOTRA WITH YOUR SHIP IN ONE
MONTH, OR YOU WILL HEAR THEIR
SCREAMS IN HELL.

'Can he be serious, sir?' Petersen asked.

'He's a serious man,' James said.

'But it has to be a bluff.'

There had been no reply from the house.

'We can't be certain of that, Captain,' James said. 'But have your operator keep calling on our wavelength.' Slowly he went down the ladder. Of course it was not a bluff. Not for the first time in his life he had been caught out by his own over-confidence, in this case, his certainty that Anne and the others could not be harmed while living securely in England. But had he not recognised, almost from the moment of their first meeting, that Mohammed ibn abd Allah possessed tentacles which could reach to every quarter of the globe?

Then what was he to do? He could pay the ransom, he supposed, with the money he had just received from the Afghans, and virtually bankrupt himself—not for the first time. But there was no prospect of obtaining another cargo of guns for several months. Besides, his entire being rankled at the thought of surrender.

But what was the alternative? Return to England and leave Anne and Lisette, and Anne and Philippe and Atossa, to their fates? Fates which were really quite unthinkable. With the exception of Mbote, they were all the friends he had in the world.

And their fates, even if they escaped the ants, would have been already unthinkable, he was sure. He was aware of a powerful and growing anger, a burning desire to avenge his women. And then get them back? Well, then, take on the Mad Mullah? The Italians and the British had been doing that now for several years, without a glimmer of success.

But he knew the Mullah, and the Mullah's habits, and the Mullah's country, better than any Italian or Britisher. What he needed was sufficient men. 'Is there bad news?' Azam inquired, waiting for him in the gangway.

'Yes,' James said. 'Do you read English, Azam?'

'Indeed.' James gave him the telegram. Azam frowned as he read. 'Can this be true?'

'I am very much afraid that it is true.'

'What are you going to do?'

'I am going to get my wife and daughter back.'

Azam pinched his lip. 'You have an army?'

'I have a nucleus. Did you really like the ship?'

'I have said I think it is marvellous.'

'Would you like to sail in her?'

Azam gazed at him for several seconds. 'With my men, I presume, Martingell.'

'As many as care to come.'

'To take on this Mullah? His reputation has even reached Afghanistan.'

'You and your people would be well paid.'

Azam pulled his beard. 'It would be a great adventure.'

'Then give me your hand.'

Azam hesitated a last time, then grinned, and held out his hand. 'I will raise you an army, Martingell. How many men can your ship carry?'

'Sixty will be sufficient,' James told

him. 'Providing every man has a modern rifle.'

'And a desire to fight, eh? It will indeed be a great adventure.'

Chapter Twelve

Coming Home

'Listen,' Anne said. 'We have stopped moving.' The ship was rolling gently in a smooth sea, no longer surging ahead. After so many weeks, so much memory.

She had been gagged and blindfolded when taken from the house, together with the others, and had remained blindfolded, her hands tied behind her back, until, after a most uncomfortable journey in a wagon, they had been carried on board this ship, and locked away in a special compartment within the hold; their kidnapping had been long and carefully prepared. Then sail had been set—she estimated it was a schooner—and they had gone to sea.

Only then had their blindfolds been removed. By then Anne had had a fairly good idea of who were her companions; now she could verify her instincts. Lisette, Atossa, Lanne, and Philippe. They all remained dressed in their scanty night-clothes, and apparently had not been interfered with, if one allowed that being manhandled like sacks of coal did not count as interference. Thus they were being reserved from some other fate.

Her only relief was that Winston had been away at school; she could only pray that their kidnappers did not know about the boy. Her real fear was that her baby might have been harmed in the manhandling; but she felt no extreme discomfort in her womb. But who were their kidnappers? 'The Mullah,' Philippe had mumbled. He was very frightened.

'In England?' Anne was incredulous.

'His people are everywhere.'

'I am so thirsty,' Lisette complained, and banged on the hatch. 'Water!' she bawled. Remarkably, water had been brought. Philippe had tried to speak with the sailor, using an African dialect, but the man had not responded.

'What is going to happen to us?' Lanne asked.

'I don't know,' Anne told her. 'But as we are English gentlewomen, we must be brave.'

'The Mullah will stake us out on an antheap,' Philippe said dolefully. 'He will coat our privates with honey, and let the ants eat us.'

'Do you mind shutting up?' Anne requested coldly. The idea was revolting. But ... she looked at Lisette.

'It is I he wants,' Lisette whispered. She licked her lips. 'For his harem.'

'You are hallucinating,' Anne told her, even more coldly.

That had been six weeks ago. Now she supposed she hallucinated herself, from time to time. They had still not been in any way ill-treated, physically. They had been fed, amply, if the food, consisting mainly of couscous liberally mixed with hot peppers, had not been very edifying. They had been given water to drink. And they had been allowed to visit a crude lavatory once a day and go on deck for an hour every morning.

She was sure they had all put on weight, and recalled with a shudder that Arab—and thus presumably Somali—men liked their women plump. But they had not been allowed to bathe or change their clothes—they had no change of clothes anyway.

Being on deck had at least meant that she could form some idea of where they were going. But the ship's captain would not risk the Mediterranean, and the possibility of being held up and perhaps searched while passing through the Suez Canal;

he opted to sail right round the Cape of Good Hope, which was why their voyage had taken so long. How she had stared at the distant sight of Table Mountain as they had rounded the Cape. But there was no reason for anyone on shore to inquire as to the purpose or destination of a vessel that kept well outside the three-mile limit.

But by now, surely James would have delivered the guns to Afghanistan, and regained the *Europa,* and be calling home. What would happen then? She had no idea what had happened to Miranda or Mrs Perchard; she only knew they were not on the ship with them. Would he know what had happened? Could he? And even if he did, would he do anything about it? Why should he? With her disappeared the whole business had fallen into his lap.

He would only come after her if he loved her, and she had no proof of that. They had been business partners who had found it mutually agreeable to share their bodies. Even their marriage had been a business proposition. And she was pretty sure that he had no great paternal affection for Lanne. What *would* he do? But then, what was she going to do?

And now, at last, after six weeks at sea, the sails had been lowered, and the schooner rolled in the gentle swell. The prisoners looked at each other and made

403

no comment. They knew where they were, for they had all sailed these waters before, save for Lanne, and they had been on deck five days earlier when the minarets of Mogadishu had been sighted. 'Looks as if you were right, Philippe,' Anne remarked.

She had come to know him very well during their captivity, as he had come to know her; they might as well have been married. But apart from their forced intimacies, she had been able to estimate his character, which was essentially pessimistic. So was Atossa's. Both had been so weighed down by the fate that had overtaken them that throughout the voyage they had shown no sexual interest in each other, or in any of the other women. Lisette was more buoyant, but at the same time had a generally gloomy opinion of life, although Anne suspected that she was hoping for better things when they finally reached the Mullah. Lanne was young enough to be curious and resilient; she complained about the food and about her inability to have a wash, but she regarded each day with the hope of something better.

While she ... she kept telling herself that things could be a lot worse. She had not been raped, as yet—she did not suppose there was a man who would wish to rape her in her present condition—and she had not been beaten, and she was alive and even reasonably healthy. But she was a prisoner of the man James had defied. It was for him that she was being preserved. To be staked out on an ant-heap, smeared in honey? The very thought made her skin crawl. But as she was a husband-murderer, was it not what she richly deserved?

There was a bump on the hull, followed by voices. She looked at Philippe. 'Somalis,' he said, as dolefully as ever.

The hatch was opened, and their captors beckoned them on deck. Philippe went first, then handed up the women one after the other. Anne was last, inhaling the warm sea air, feeling the sweat trickle down between her shoulder blades, looking around her at the empty sea, and then at the dhow which bobbed alongside the schooner. What memories that brought back. Not for the first time she wondered if all this was merely a punishment for her crimes. But if that were the case, why should little Lanne be involved? The girl, as always, was clinging to Lisette.

They were pushed to the side, where Philippe was already clambering over the gunwale to get down to the deck of the dhow. Atossa followed him, and Anne suddenly became terribly aware of eyes. The women were filthy, their nightclothes and hair were filthy, but as the breeze

405

caught the thin material and exposed even a fraction of leg, the eyes seemed to come together, staring at them. She was not the only one who felt the sexual hostility with which they were surrounded. Lanne began to cry. 'They will not harm you,' Lisette assured her, and lifted her over the rail to pass her down to Philippe.

As always, Anne was last, dropping on to the deck, and being seized by the shoulder to be pushed aft, to where the others were gathered. She lost her balance and sat down with a thump, beside Lisette, and the dhow was cast off. The lateen sail was hoisted as they drifted away from the schooner's side. There too sails were being hoisted, and a moment later she was on her way, making to the east. The captain of the dhow, a swarthy Arab in a burnous, came aft to look at them, He stood above them, with his hands on his hips. 'Martingell's woman,' he said, in English.

He was looking at Lisette, who opened her mouth to protest, then glanced at Anne, flushing, but seeking a lead. 'I am Martingell's woman,' Anne said quietly. 'I am his wife.'

The captain stared at her, then threw back his head to give a shout of laughter. 'Martingell's harem,' he commented. 'This will be sport for our master. And you?' He squatted before Lanne, who drew up her legs in apprehension.

'Martingell's daughter,' Anne said.

The captain nodded, 'She will be sport. When our master says.' Lisette put her arm round the girl's shoulders. 'And you,' the captain stood again, this time above Philippe. 'You I have seen.' He looked at Atossa, who was trembling. 'And her. Perhaps I will have her, when our master permits it.'

Atossa huddled closer to Philippe, who looked as if he might be prepared to give her away there and then, if it would preserve his own life. By now the dhow was under sail, making for the coast. 'Are we going back to that place Mareeq?' Anne whispered to Lisette, who squinted over the side at the fast-approaching shore, as uncompromisingly brown as was most of this coast. 'I do not think so. I do not see anything I recognise.'

The land certainly looked empty, but as the sail was lowered and the anchor was thrown over the side a large number of men emerged from behind the low sand dune on the shore. With them were camels. 'You go with these men, eh?' the captain told them.

'How do we get ashore?' Lisette asked.

The captain grinned. 'You have feet, eh?' He bent, grasped her arm to drag her upright, threw his other arm round her knees, and hurled her over the side. Lisette screamed as she flew through the air, lost her breath as she plunged into the sea, thighs first, to be totally submerged for a few moments before emerging, spluttering and staggering to and fro, but standing, waist deep in the water.

Lanne had also screamed as her friend and mentor had been literally thrown away from her. But before she too could be manhandled, Anne had scrambled up. 'Come on,' she said. 'We could do with a bathe.' She didn't want to be thrown, still fearing for her baby.

She held the girl's hand, dragged her to the rail, and jumped over, carrying Lanne with her. They entered the water feet first, and although their nightdresses ballooned around them, they received quite a jar as their feet hit the sand. A moment later Philippe and Atossa joined them, and they waded towards the beach and the waiting bearded, heavily armed men, one of whom stood at the water's edge to greet them. 'Martingell's woman?' he inquired.

Here we go again, Anne thought, as her companions all looked at her. 'I am Mrs Martingell,' she said.

The man grinned. 'Our master will be pleased to see you, Martingell's woman,' he said.

It took several days for all of Azam's men to be rounded up and got on board; few of them had any knowledge of the sea, and they looked about them in consternation at the yacht's appointments; but none was prepared to challenge Azam's authority. There was also the matter of provisioning them, and the yacht's own crew, for some time; there would be no opportunity for replenishment in Somalia, other than Mogadishu, and that had to be avoided.

By the time they were all aboard, *Europa* looked an overloaded troopship. James could only hope that the weather would remain fine until they could be disembarked in Somaliland. To go to their deaths? Some of them, certainly. And how many others? He remembered being accused a dozen years ago of wishing to start a war by Adolf von Beinhardt. Now he was doing just that. For a wife he was not at all sure loved him, or even truly desired him. And for a daughter who would probably grow up to be no better than her mother. Yet he had every intention of taking on the Mullah. Perhaps he had known from their first meeting that it would one day be inevitable.

His biggest problem was lack of information. Loaded as his ship was with Afghan soldiers, he dared not stop at any port, much less a British one, and thus could obtain no news of what might actually have happened. Had all his friends, Philippe and Atossa and the servants, been murdered? Had the English police done anything about the crime? The fact was, he knew, that the English police would be quite out of their depth in dealing with someone like the Mullah.

'May I ask, sir, what exactly is your plan?' Captain Petersen inquired, sitting at table with James and Azam and Mbote; these last two were equally curious, although they would ask no questions.

James spread the chart in front of them. 'We are to rendezvous with the Mullah's people here.' He prodded the spot on the map just south of Socotra. 'This is where we offloaded the guns, remember, Captain?'

'And got attacked by pirates.'

'Well, these people will also certainly be pirates,' James agreed. 'But with the firepower we possess I do not think we need fear them. What we must do is turn the tables on them, and use them to find our way into the Mullah's camp. So here is my plan.'

'My God, what a country!' Anne muttered through parched lips. Her lips were not the only part of her that was both parched and uncomfortable. The brief relief of being submerged in the seawater off the beach was several days in the past, and she had come to the conclusion that riding a camel was not a pastime ever intended for women, although both Lisette and Atossa seemed capable enough, and even Lanne was making a better job of it than herself. But none of them was pregnant.

At least they had been given additional clothing to wear, the Arab *haik*, which was actually very like an additional nightdress. although of much thicker material. She felt she could have coped with the camel, had all else been equal. But the unceasing heat, the scarcity of water—they were allowed one swallow every two hours—the unchanging brown sand and rock, the vultures which hovered it seemed only a few feet above their heads, combined to make her feel that she was tracking through the valley of death.

Now she thanked God for the presence of Lisette, who had made this journey before. 'It will not be long now,' Lisette said.

'Was it not a journey like this killed your mistress?'

'I think it must have been something she ate,' Lisette said. 'Maybe she was poisoned. Nobody knows.' Despite the heat, Anne shuddered.

But the next day, as the country began to rise and even show the occasional trace of green, she realised that they were surrounded by horsemen, armed and with flowing robes. 'The Mullah's men,' Philippe muttered. He was more agitated than ever.

'Do you not know him well?' Anne asked.

'Too well.'

'Then what are you so afraid of?'

'He thinks I have betrayed him. What he will do to me ...'

'Well, listen,' she said. 'Tell him that everything you did was on orders from James.'

Philippe shot her a glance. 'And if he ever gets hold of James ...'

'Do you think that is likely? We must each of us look to our own salvation.'

She was certainly determined to do that, as she could see no way in which James could help her now, even supposing he wanted to. Why should he? He had everything, the money, the arms factory, a new outlet for his guns, all to be set against a wife she knew he did not altogether trust, and a daughter he felt was a duty. It was clearly a case of every man, and even more, every woman, for herself.

The horsemen did not approach until the caravan had camped for the night and the camels had been hobbled. Then they came into the perimeter, dismounting to stare at the captives, who had been brought together by the caravan master. Thus far, as on the ship, the women had been offered no physical violence, save by the very presence of these desert marauders, and the gleam in their eyes as they stared at the white flesh. They awaited the command of their master. And now he was very close. Anne felt Lanne's fingers biting in hers, and responded, grateful that the little girl had turned to her rather than Lisette.

Words swirled around their heads. 'Do you know what they are saying?' Anne whispered.

'We are to be taken to the Mullah's camp,' Atossa said. 'It is not far.' Apparently it was to be done immediately, although it was now growing dark. And they were to ride horses rather than camels, although Anne discovered to her consternation that there were no side-saddles.

Then they were away into the night, escorted now by only a few Somalis. They rode for little more than an hour, through a series of defiles between the mountains, before topping a rise to look down on the glow of myriad campfires. 'The Mullah's army,' Philippe said, dolefully.

They descended the slope and were surrounded by people, women and children as well as men and barking dogs. Anne was more interested in the tents, some of which were quite elaborate, although none matched the huge tent in the centre, before which there stood several guards. It was indicated that they should dismount before this, and Anne slipped gratefully from the saddle; her bottom was not the least painful part of her exhausted body. But now she would need all of her energy, both mental and physical, because emerging from the tent was the Mullah.

Although she had never seen him before, Anne recognised him immediately, from his air of total confidence, total command, as much as from the eyes which glowed even in the night. He gave an order and torches were brought, held above them while he peered at them. He began with Philippe. 'You dog,' he said in English. 'You have betrayed me.'

'Hear me, oh my master,' Philippe begged, following Anne's instructions. 'I obeyed the orders of Martingell.'

The Mullah looked him up and down. 'And you will suffer for it,' he said. He gave orders to his men, and four of them seized Philippe's arms to drag him away.

'Have mercy!' he screamed. 'I will do anything you say. Have mercy!' His shouts ended in a gulp, and Anne presumed someone had hit him.

'He spoke nothing but the truth,' she said.

The Mullah only glanced at her; he was looking at Atossa, who was trembling as much as her lover. 'You,' he said, 'I give to my men.'

Atossa seemed to stiffen. Whatever the excitements of her youth, over the past few years she had become used to a life both sedentary and that of a lady. 'I will tell them to fuck you till you die,' the Mullah said. 'But not until tomorrow. Your husband must watch.'

Atossa licked her lips, and looked as if she was about to scream. Instead she allowed herself to be led away. 'Are you a man or a monster?' Anne demanded. 'My husband told me that you considered yourself a representative of God on earth.'

'And is not your god also a God of wrath?' Mohammed demanded, for the first time looking directly at her. 'You are Martingell's woman?'

'Yes.' Anne tossed her head.

Mohammed gave a little bow. 'Then you are inviolate, both as another man's wife, and as a hostage. I have made certain demands of your husband. When he obeys those demands, you will be set free. You and your daughter.'

Anne decided now was not the time to argue about Lanne's parentage. 'And if he does not obey?'

Mohammed gave a slight shrug. 'Then, no matter where he takes refuge, he must hear your screams.'

She could not prevent herself from catching her breath.

Mohammed smiled. 'But I am sure, as he is an English gentleman, he will not wish to risk that.' He turned to Lisette. 'And you,' he said. 'Are you also Martingell's woman?'

'Certainly not,' Lisette said, without hesitation.

'You were with him, when last he visited my camp.'

'I was my mistress's maid.'

'And then your mistress died.'

'And then Martingell employed me as the nanny to his daughter.'

Mohammed looked at Lanne. then he snapped his fingers, and Anne realised she was holding her breath. 'I am sure you are hungry and thirsty,' Mohammed said. 'I would dine with you.' His gaze shrouded all of them. 'But you are also filthy and wearing rags. My women will attend to you, and then we will sit together.'

Anne found it hard to believe that she was not dreaming. She, Lisette and Lanne were taken by the Somali women into the interior of the vast tent, past drapes and cushions of the richest embroidery. When they had traversed several low doorways, they found themselves in a small chamber furnished principally with a huge tub of steaming water. Before they could gather their wits they were stripped of their clothing by the chattering, curious women, and made to get into the water. That commodity might be scarce in the desert, but there was no lack of it here, and it was sweet-scented and warm. To Anne's consternation, however, several of the woman also stripped and got into the bath with them, giggling at one another as they soaped and massaged the white bodies.

'Mother!' Lanne gasped, as sensuous fingers slid over her flesh. Anne was aware of similar sensations; none of the two men in her life had sought quite such intimacy. But Lisette merely smiled and enjoyed it. So why not do the same? How strange that she should be learning about life from the German maid? Lisette was clearly anticipating the fate that was in store for her.

The bathing girls paid particular attention to their hair, both on their heads, clearly exclaiming over the texture and being particularly interested in Anne's golden tresses, but equally astonished and even concerned that her pubic hair was of a much darker colour. Far more disturbing, these girls' pubes were shaved. 'I think it is a hygiene matter,' Lisette said. 'Out in the desert, with sand, and bugs ...' she rolled her eyes.

'I hope they will not attempt to shave us,' Anne said. Lisette rolled her eyes some more.

But that fate, in any event, was not to be immediately theirs. The bath took some time, but when the women were satisfied that they were clean, and they went about their business in a most methodical fashion, sifting each hair in their search for dirt or insects, and to Anne's horror actually extracting more than one tick to be squashed between the fingers with a snap and a spurt of blood, they were wrapped in towels as sweet-smelling as the now filthy bath water, and gently pummelled dry. 'What is going to happen to us now, Mother?' Lanne asked.

'I have no idea,' Anne confessed. Their own clothes had been removed, presumably to be destroyed, and now they were given but a single haik to wear, which tied at the neck but was unsecured everywhere else. On the other hand, there was sufficient material to conceal them completely so long as they remembered to hold it shut. Anne wrapped her fingers in the folds and hugged them across her body, showing Lanne how to do the same. Lisette was less concerned with total concealment, and allowed her legs to escape from time to time as they were led back through the tent. But Anne understood that Lisette was following her own agenda, now; they might have been light years apart.

Mohammed ibn abd Allah sat by himself in one of the outer compartments. He did not rise as the women were led in, but gestured them to sit, Anne on his right and Lisette on his left. Lanne sat beside her mother. 'You understand,' Mohammed said, as the huge earthenware dish was brought in, 'it is not the custom of my people to dine with their women. But for you, I make an exception. I was taught this by Martingell. Are you hungry?'

For all her exhaustion, Anne realised that she was actually very hungry, 'Yes, my lord,' she said. 'Is that how I should address you?'

'That will do, Mrs Martingell.'

Anne tossed her head. 'In my country, I was addressed as milady.'

'But that was before you married Martingell. Eat.'

He seemed to know everything there was to know about her. And hunger was overcoming her desire to preserve her dignity. Lanne and Lisette were already digging their fingers into the stew. She followed their example, and had swallowed her first mouthful of the lamb before she realised the Mohammed was not actually eating with them. 'Are you not hungry, my lord?' she asked.

'I have already eaten,' he said.

Memory of various things James had told her about the Arabs came back to her. 'And if you eat with me you cannot execute me. Is that not true?'

'A little knowledge,' Mohammed said, 'is often a dangerous thing. Certainly depressing.'

Anne ate some more and began to feel almost human again. Lanne and Lisette were tucking in as fast as they could. 'How long do we have to wait?' she asked.

'For your husband to obey my instructions? He must first make the rendezvous I have given him, and he must then come to me with what he owes me. I estimate that he should be at the rendezvous now. Today is the appointed one. Then it will take him a week to get to us here. That is not so very long.'

'And when will you decide that he is not coming?'

They gazed at each other. 'I am a generous man,' Mohammed said. 'I have allowed him a fortnight from today to be in my camp.'

'And then?' Once again Anne held her breath.

'At the end of that time,' Mohammed said, 'You will be executed. I am sorry, Mrs Martingell, but I have said this will happen, and I do not ever alter my decisions.'

Anne licked her lips. Her appetite was less sated than lost. 'How will I die?'

'You are a beautiful woman, and that is a pretty child. I will give you and her to my men, as I have done with Atossa.'

'And Lisette?'

'Lisette has not betrayed me. Rather do I wish her for my own.' He stood up and held out his hand. 'You have eaten enough. Come.' Lisette hastily got up as well. Her gaze, as it flickered over Anne, was scornful.

'Reduce speed,' James commanded, and Captain Petersen rang the engine telegraph. The growl of the engine dwindled, and the yacht slipped quietly through the calm water. There was no moon, but the sky was clear, and visibility was quite good. James, Petersen and Azam swept the horizon with their binoculars, port and starboard. Far away to the west a light winked, but that had to be on the shore; they were some ten miles off. 'There!' Azam said.

He had the keenest eyes, but now the other two men could also make out the dark shape on the water, approaching them silently under the light breeze. 'Stop engines, Captain,' James said. 'But maintain steam.'

The order was rung down, and the *Europa* came to rest, rolling gently, her engine now only a slow rumble. James took another sweep of the horizon; he did not want any ship close enough to hear the sound of firing. But the sea was empty, save for the yacht and the dhow. 'There will be at least 40 men on board that ship,' James told Azam. 'So arm your men and have them concealed on deck. However, it is essential that at least some of the Somalis are taken alive. You understand?'

Azam nodded and hurried off to place his men. 'My people will play their part, Mr Martingell,' Petersen volunteered.

'I was sure of it, Captain. But your business, and that of your people, is to keep out of trouble; we need you to handle the yacht, eh?' He checked his own revolver, and joined Mbote on the main deck.

Slowly the dhow approached, and the sail was dropped, to leave it as still as the yacht. 'What ship is that?' someone called in English.

'The yacht *Europa,*' Captain Petersen replied.

'We seek Martingell.'

'He is on board, waiting for you,' the captain said. 'Come alongside.'

There was a muttered discussion on board the dhow. Then the English-speaking Somali called, 'Put down a boat, and send Martingell to us. With the money and the guns.'

James and Mbote looked at each other. 'He is not stupid,' Mbote said. James wished he had killed all the men with Daoud.

'How can the guns be loaded into one boat?' Petersen was demanding.

'Send us Martingell and the money,' the Somali said. 'Then we will tranship the guns.'

James ran up the ladder to the bridge. 'Get alongside him, Captain.' Petersen threw the telegraph forward, and within seconds the yacht was moving through the water. 'Don't ram him,' James reminded the captain. Petersen himself took the helm.

From the dhow there came shrieks of alarm as the much larger ship moved rapidly towards it, and several shots were fired, but these were submerged in the volley from the yacht's decks by Azam's tribesmen. The dhow rocked as the bullets smashed into it and several men fell overboard. 'Hold your fire!' James bawled, as the yacht swirled alongside in a sudden flurry of foam. 'Grapples and board.'

The irons were thrown, as the yacht's engine again went into neutral. It took her some distance to lose way again, but several of the grapples had lodged, and the dhow was dragged along beside her, gunwale creaking and breaking under the strain. James himself, sliding down the ladder with his revolver drawn, led the boarding party, Mbote at his elbow, but it seemed as if all the Afghans were behind him, and in a matter of seconds the dhow was secured. Apart from those who had fallen or jumped overboard—some were calling out to be rescued from the shark-infested waters—there were a dozen Somalis dead or badly wounded, and another dozen who had surrendered, and were now kneeling on the deck, hands above their heads.

'Who was your spokesman?' James demanded, speaking English. Heads turned, and the man indicated began to shiver. 'What is your name?'

'Affan, your excellency.'

'Right,' James said. 'Affan, you will come with us. As for the rest ...'

'They should all die,' Azam said.

'No doubt,' James agreed. But he wasn't

into cold-blooded murder. 'Fetch those fellows out of the water,' he said, and returned to the yacht to give his instructions to Petersen.

He had not lost a man.

James reckoned that to load all his Afghans on board the dhow would be an even tighter squeeze than on board the yacht, but it would only be for a short while. 'Now listen very carefully,' he told Affan. 'You are going to take this dhow into the shore exactly where you would have landed me had I surrendered. Any treachery and I will cut your throat. How many people will be waiting for us?'

'There will be a caravan,' Affan said. 'Many people.'

'How many,' James said. 'And remember, if I discover you are lying, I will cut off your balls before I cut your throat.'

Affan rolled his eyes. 'Maybe 20 people.'

'All men?'

'Yes.'

'Then we'll need the clothes.'

He had the dead and captive Somalis stripped to their loin cloths, so that his Afghans could wear their robes.

Then, as instructed, Petersen put down one of the yacht's lifeboats. In it he placed all the surviving Somalis, apart from Affan. They were given food and water for three days. Then he towed them out to sea, to where there would be three days hard rowing to the mainland. They cursed and swore, but were helpless.

Meanwhile, James and Mbote, assisted by three of the crew of the yacht, got the dhow under way; the Afghans were not sailors. The breeze remained light, and James knew they would not make the shore before dawn. He set the Afghans to work to conceal the splintered wood where the bullets had struck so they would not be visible until close to; by the time any Somali got close enough to make out the damage, the matter would have been settled. Slowly the sky lightened, and as it did the beach came into sight. It was an open beach, with no shelter, but there were people gathered there, with camels. 'Again, please remind your men that we need those camels,' James told Azam, who, with his people, were crouching in the bottom of the dhow. Affan was aft, with Mbote.

James now joined them. 'Go forward and drop the anchor,' he told Mbote. 'Now, Affan, remember that your business has only just begun. If you wish to go on living, do exactly as I tell you.' Affan sweated.

The anchor plunged into the water, and James put his plan into operation. He gave the appearance of being manhandled over the side by two of the Afghans and dropped into the water, Affan beside him. A dozen of the Afghans followed, swathed in their captured robes; the remainder waited on the dhow, still out of sight. The people on the shore shouted questions, as the apparent crew of the dhow waded towards them. Affan did the answering. James had no idea what he was saying, but he did not fear betrayal; Azam walked immediately behind the Somali, his knife pressed against Affan's ribs. Certainly the waiting men did not seem alarmed, and with the rising sun behind the Afghans and the dhow it was difficult to see clearly—until the Afghans reached dry land. Then the Somalis suddenly realised that they were looking at strangers. And at death.

'Now,' James said, drawing his revolver and shooting the man who appeared to be the leader of the caravan. A fusillade of shots rang out and several men fell. Fortunately the camels were hobbled, for they roared and kicked in terror as bullets sang about them.

The skirmish was over in seconds; the Somalis had been taken entirely by surprise; half had been killed and the other half were wounded and afraid. 'I presume you intend to spare their lives as well,' Azam said, sceptically.

'They can walk to wherever they wish

to go.' James summoned the remainder of the Afghans from the dhow, and also Mbote and the sailors. 'One week,' James reminded them. 'And if we are not here, then every day after that.'

'We'll be here, Mr Martingell,' the coxswain agreed.

There were only 30 camels, and James had 60 men; it was necessary to double up, and so as not to overburden the beasts a good part of each day's march had to be on foot. This kept progress slow. But Affan knew where the waterholes were, and as he had no desire to die of thirst himself he was quite happy to lead the caravan to them. 'What happens when we reach the Mullah's camp?' Azam asked when they were camped for the night on the second day.

James had been afraid someone was going to ask him that. 'We should gain entry to the camp easily enough,' he said. 'The Mullah's people are expecting a caravan, and we will be a caravan. The moment we are in the camp, however, we will be discovered, and we must then act very quickly. We will charge the Mullah's tent, regain the women, and hopefully capture the Mullah as well. Then we will leave, making sure that we have a camel for each man.'

'Will the Somalis not follow? Even supposing we can get out?'

'Possession of the Mullah is our trump card,' James told him. 'They will not risk the Mullah's life.' Azam pulled his beard; no doubt they did not value mullahs so highly in Afghanistan.

It was just after noon on the third day, and they had stopped for their midday meal, when one of the Afghan lookouts reported dust to the west. 'If those are the Mullah's people,' Azam said, 'our plan will be discovered now.'

'If those are the Mullah's people, they must all be destroyed,' James told him.

Azam gave his men the orders to load and check their weapons, while James and Mbote went forward to see for themselves. They lay in the shelter of a rise while James inspected the advancing horsemen through his binoculars. 'Italians.'

'Coming straight for us,' Mbote pointed out.

James estimated there were two squadrons of cavalry, say 300 men, but this time he had no Maxim guns. Nor did he care to risk losing any of his own people this early in his campaign. They hurried back to the encampment. 'Italian soldiers,' James told Azam. 'Heading this way. We must pack up and get out of their path as quickly as possible, and hope that they are in a hurry and will not stop to pick up our trail.'

'Then what of those?' Azam asked. James turned, and felt vaguely sick. Behind them was another cloud of dust. And this was a bigger force, perhaps three squadrons. He was virtually surrounded, by 600 professional soldiers. 'Are we lost?' Azam asked.

'Perhaps not,' James said, his brain working overtime. The Italians had now spread out and were advancing in five separate squadrons; each squadron outnumbered his own small force by at least two to one. 'Let's have a burnous,' James said, and mounted the white garment on the end of a rifle. Then he walked away from his small body, having instructed no man to move. Once clear of them, he faced the oncoming cavalry, the burnous held high.

Orders were given, and the Italians came to a halt, horses snorting, pennons waving in the breeze. A subaltern walked his mount forward. 'You wish to surrender?' he asked in French.

'I wish to speak with your commanding officer.'

'He does not wish to speak with you. He wishes your surrender.'

'Tell him my name is Martingell,' James said. 'Tell him that I have an important subject I wish to discuss with him. Tell him to speak with me and there will be no bloodshed. Tell him if he refuses this, my people will sell their lives dearly. Every man is armed with a Lee-Enfield magazine rifle and ample ammunition. To destroy us will cost you a great many men. Tell your commanding officer this.'

The subaltern gazed at him for several seconds, his hand twitching next to his revolver holster. But James met his stare unwaveringly, and at last the young man wheeled his horse and rode back to the main body. James remained waiting for some half-an-hour before several horsemen approached him. Riding in front was an officer wearing the insignia of a colonel. He came to a halt before James, his escort behind him. 'Martingell!' he said. 'There is a warrant for your arrest, monsieur. They are waiting to hang you in Mogadishu.'

'I thought your war was against the Mullah,' James said.

'The man you have been supplying with arms.'

'I do so no longer, He is as much my enemy now as yours. I can give him to you.'

The colonel's lip curled. 'You?'

'Do you know where to find him?'

'Of course I do.' The colonel waved at the mountains to the west. 'But he cannot be approached. Once my men enter those hills they are overseen by the Mullah's lookouts, and he either moves his camp, if we are in strength, or he attacks us, if we are weak.'

James in turn pointed at his own people. 'Those men are not Somalis. They are mine. But they are dressed as Somalis, and the Mullah is expecting me. I and my people will be allowed into his camp. Once there, we intend to rescue some white ladies he has taken prisoner and leave again as quickly as we can—with the Mullah. If you and your horsemen were to follow us, at night, you would be able to attack the Mullah's camp while he and his men are distracted. I have a guide who will take you clear of the Somali lookouts.'

The colonel stroked his chin. 'How do I know this is not some elaborate trap, laid by you and the Mullah, to destroy my command?'

'I suppose you do not,' James agreed. 'Everything in war is a risk. But you will never have a better opportunity to end this war, now.'

Once again the colonel considered. Then he nodded. 'You are right. I have heard it said you are an honest man, Martingell. We will support you.'

James grinned. How that tag had stuck to him, through all the years of dishonesty!

'When do we march?' the colonel asked.
'Tonight,' James said.

The Mullah as usual sat with Anne and
Lanne when they ate. Lisette was not
to be seen. She had been absorbed into
Mohammed's harem and was no doubt
enjoying herself. Anne did not wish to
think of Philippe. He remained trussed
and waiting to be sacrificed, should James
not come. Atossa had been subjected to
continuous sexual assault before her lover's
eyes, until she had died. 'This is the last
day,' Mohammed said gravely, when she
had finished her meal. 'At dawn tomorrow
Martingell's time is up. So is yours. Believe
me, dear lady, I am very sorry about this.
But I am Mohammed ibn abd Allah. What
I say must come to pass. I have told my
men that they may have you if Martingell
does not come. This is how it must be.'

Anne licked her lips, her stomach light.
But to tell him she was three months
pregnant might be to make matters worse.
'But perhaps,' the Mullah said, 'there are
worse ways to die. The Frenchman will
die first.'

Anne had to cough before she could
speak. 'And the little girl?'

'My men will share her with you.'

'You are a devil incarnate.'

'I am a man fighting for his country

and his people. The Italians, the French and the British have more guns than we. They will only go away if they are made to realise they can never conquer us. Was there not a Frenchman who once said, "The kings of Europe threaten us? We throw them the head of a king"?'

'You estimate me too high, my lord,' Anne said.

'Your death will tell the world that I am not to be meddled with, only feared. I will wish you a good night.'

'What did he mean, Mother?' Lanne asked. 'Giving us to his men?'

'It will be a game,' Anne said, hugging the little girl. 'Oh, just a game.'

Was it possible to strangle her now, she wondered? Of course she had the physical strength—but did she have the mental? Over their weeks of captivity, with Lisette gone, they had at last struck up a relationship. Anne now truly felt that Lanne was her daughter, at whose side she must die, horribly, tomorrow. She could not believe she deserved that, any more than the little girl. She could not deny that she had been a promiscuous woman in her time. She had always claimed, at least to herself, that Winston's mistreatment had made her so. She had never looked at another man since James had entered her life, but to be at the mercy of several hundred ... the thought could not be tolerated. But it was going to happen.

Eventually Lanne slept, and to her surprise Anne also dozed from time to time, as the night wore on, and the dogs ceased barking ... but she was wide awake when the animals started their cacophony again and an enormous rustle seeped through the camp, followed by a steadily growing noise. Lanne woke up. 'Is it time, Mother?' The child certainly knew that something was due to happen this day.

Anne stood up as the tent flap was thrown open. 'Well, well,' the Mullah said. 'Our lookouts have signalled that Martingell approaches. It seems that he has marched all night in his determination to reach you.' Anne's strength gave way and she fell to her knees. 'Indeed, milady, you may well offer a prayer of thanks,' the Mullah said. 'Come outside to greet your husband. And continue to pray, that he has brought my money and my guns.'

Anne held Lanne's hand as they stumbled out into the sudden, bright sunlight, to watch the camels coming through the defile to the east. Mohammed was watching them too, and now he spoke to his aide. Anne did not understand what he was saying, but she knew what had upset him; there were

30 camels, but every one carried two men. The men were all wrapped in burnouses and had dark complexions, but every one carried a rifle. And James was riding in front, not apparently bound or in any way a captive. Mounted behind him on this first camel was Mbote, also armed.

Mohammed barked a command, which was repeated by his aide. A few seconds later there was the blare of a bugle, summoning the Somalis to arms. But even as the alarm was sounded, the intruders charged, firing their rifles. The Somali camp erupted into pandemonium, men, women, children and dogs running to and fro, screaming, gathering weapons, taken entirely by surprise in the absence of any warning from their guard posts.

For a moment, the Mullah stared at the charging Afghans in consternation, then he gave a growl of anger and turned to Anne, drawing his sword as he did so. 'No!' she screamed, and kicked him as hard as she could on the ankle. He fell with an exclamation of pain, and Anne seized Lanne and ran with her into the tent, throwing her weight against the pole to bring it down in a flurry of goatskin beneath which they lay huddled on the ground; at least they would be more difficult to find here.

She listened to the shooting and the

shouts and screams from all around her, gasped in terror as the skins were pulled off her, and she looked up ... at James! 'Sweetheart!' He knelt beside her, and put his other arm round Lanne.

'My God!' she said. 'My God! I did not think you would come. But ...' she looked around her. Parts of the camp were on fire, but the Afghans had ridden straight for the centre, and were now gathered in a circle round the Mullah's tent, some 50 armed and determined men. But they in turn were surrounded by the Somalis, who had recovered their nerves. From their ranks there burst a horde of women, wailing and screaming.

'Lisette is there.'

'She must fend for herself.' Lisette had made her choice, as the women ran into the Somali ranks.

'The Mullah!'

'Somewhere in that mob, I would say,' James said.

'But now we are trapped,' Anne said.

'Not entirely. You've never actually met Sheikh Azam ud-Ranatullah, have you?'

Azam touched his forehead. 'A lady as beautiful as you, Mrs Martingell, is worth risking death for. But James, if those Italians let us down, we are all dead men.'

The Somalis were being given orders,

and were forming ranks, while machine-guns were being brought forward. Anne clutched James' hand. 'Listen,' Mbote said.

Heads were turning in the Somali ranks as the notes of a bugle call cut across the desert. A moment later the Italian lancers debauched from the next valley to the south, where they had been guided by Affan, out of sight of the Mullah's guard posts. They made a splendid sight, lances couched, pennons flying, dust rising from their horses' hooves as they broke into the charge. Certainly they were too much for the already disturbed Somalis, aware only that there was treachery in their midst, and that their 'impenetrable' camp had indeed been penetrated. They broke and fled as the horsemen thundered into them, their camels, always reluctant to face horses, also running as hard as they could. Colonel Massimo pulled rein before James and his people. 'I congratulate you, Mr Martingell.'

'As I you, Colonel, on a famous victory.'

'But where is the Mullah?'

'Somewhere in that mob.'

The Colonel wheeled his horse and rejoined his men to lead them in pursuit. James hurried to where Philippe was still tied to his stake.

'*Mon Dieu!*' the Frenchman cried. 'But

I never thought to see this day.'

'You'll live forever, old friend,' James told him. 'Atossa?'

Philippe sighed. 'They murdered her.' James rested his hand on his friend's shoulder. Atossa had been the very last of his harem, and he supposed she had always been the favourite. 'Will they catch the Mullah?' Philippe asked.

'I doubt it. But we are not going to hang about here to find out. Where is Lisette?'

'She went with Mohammed,' Anne said.

'Quite a carve-up!'

'James, if he gets away, won't he come after us again?'

James looked around him at the desolated, burning camp. 'If he gets away, he's going to have a few things to think about before he can pursue any more personal vendettas. And the next time, we'll be waiting for him. Or his thugs.'

'It has been a great adventure,' Azam said, as his men disembarked at Chah Bahar.

'I could not have done it without you,' James acknowledged.

Azam clasped his hand. 'Then we are friends, for evermore. And partners eh, James? Will you sell me more guns?'

'If I can.'

Azam nodded. 'I will be in touch.'

'There was quite a to-do,' remarked Inspector Larchmount.

James surveyed the wreckage of his house. But at least it had not been burned. 'Both maidservants?' he asked.

'Throats cut like chickens. You understand no one found them for several days. It was the postman reported that the mail hadn't been collected for some time. That was when we got the order to break in. Horrible, it was. Your lady is lucky to be alive, sir.'

'I know that.'

'She wasn't here, I understand.'

'No,' James said. 'She wasn't here.'

'Can you tell me where she is now, sir?'

'She's in an hotel.' He had considered it best to leave them all out of sight until he had discovered how the land lay. Anne had, in any event, been principally concerned with regaining young Winston, and reassuring him that she was all right.

'And you have no idea who could have done it?'

'No,' James said.

'It's strange, you see, sir. Nothing appears to have been taken, although, as you can see, the place is a little smashed up, as if there was some kind of fight. Two women, fighting for their lives. But you see, sir, they hadn't been,

440

well, interfered with. Strange.'

'Very strange,' James agreed. 'Now, Inspector, if you'll excuse me, but I have to start putting this place back together.'

'Oh, yes, sir, of course. But there's this gentleman wishes to have a word.'

James had assumed the other man in the room was also a policeman. Now he realised that he was very well-dressed, wore a carnation in his buttonhole, and looked altogether superior. 'Thank you, Mr Larchmount,' he said.

The police officer almost curtsied as he left the room.

'My card,' the stranger said, offering it.

James looked at the small cardboard rectangle. 'War Office,' he remarked. 'Colonel Marks.'

'It was reckoned I would be the best person to handle your affair, Mr Martingell.'

'I did not know I had an affair, at the moment.' James went to the sideboard, which, surprisingly, had not been damaged. But the people who had ransacked his home had been Muslims and not interested in strong drink. 'Whisky?'

'You may pour me one,' Colonel Marks said, indicating that he would drink if their business came to a satisfactory conclusion.

James poured two, gestured his visitor to a seat as he took one himself. 'I imagine you consider me a bad boy.'

'Selling guns to Africans, possibly in arms against Great Britain. Selling guns to Somalis, definitely to be used against British soldiers. Selling guns to rebellious Afghan tribesmen, in full knowledge that Great Britain has an interest in maintaining the present Afghan government. Exporting arms and ammunition without a licence. That is a considerable list.'

'The guns I sold in Africa were on behalf of a German company,' James pointed out.

'Not entirely. You also handled the sale on behalf of the Pennyfeather Arms Company.'

'I was the agent, not the principal.'

'No doubt. But both that sale and the one to Afghanistan were undertaken without a licence from the British Government. You do understand that you can be gaoled for that, apart from suffering a heavy fine.'

'I am not responsible for what Sir Winston Pennyfeather did,' James said. 'As for Afghanistan, you may have a difficult job proving that I sold them any guns.'

Marks snorted. 'Do you really suppose you can hoodwink His Majesty's Government, Mr Martingell? You have a considerable ledger against you.'

442

'Are you sure you won't have this drink?' James got up to refill his glass.

'Yes, I will have that drink,' Marks said, surprisingly. James gave him the glass. 'I should also inform you that the Beinhardt Company is preparing a massive claim against you, for fraud and, indeed, downright theft.'

'They too will have a job proving that,' James said.

'But one suspects they will, except in certain circumstances.'

James sat down again. 'I'm interested.'

'I suppose it is possible that you spend so much of your time stoking up minor wars on the fringes of our Empire that you are unaware of what is going on at the heart. However, your behaviour in conjunction with the Italian forces in Somalia, even if it did not actually result in the capture of the Mullah, indicates that your *heart* may be in the right place. The Italians are talking about giving you a medal in honour of their victory. However, if it has so far escaped your notice, you should understand that in the not very distant future there is going to be a war between Britain and Germany.'

'I assume that is a confidential reflection.'

Marks gave a grim smile. 'Not in the least. We know it. The Germans know it.

Just about every war office in the world knows it. The Germans would prefer not to have a war for the time being. Their dream is to fight when they have a High Seas Fleet equal in strength to our own. We have no intention of allowing them to gain such equality. It is simply a matter of when we fight, and on what grounds.'

'Or pretext,' James suggested.

'As you say. But it could happen any day. The Kaiser, with due respect to someone who is, after all, a member of our own royal house, is so unstable a character that at any moment he may provoke a crisis that will prove impossible to remedy short of arms. He has already come close to this on more than one occasion in the past few years. Agadir, Baghdad ... the list is growing. Now, the situation is that while our fleet has nothing to fear from the Germans, fleets do not win wars; they can only prevent the enemy from winning, over us, at any rate. To beat Germany we need men and arms. We will have the men when the time comes, there can be no doubt about that. The arms are not quite as guaranteed. We need every arms manufacturer in this country to supply us, on a full capacity, from now on.'

James raised his eyebrows. 'Are you suggesting that I should work for the

British Government?'

'Exactly, my dear fellow.'

'You surprise me.'

'Well, let me surprise you some more. Consider the advantages. You would be legal, for the first time in your life. The charge of exporting arms from Britain without a licence would be dropped. Any charges brought against you by the House of Beinhardt would be most strenuously resisted—by His Majesty's Government. You would be acting in the interests of your country, for the first time in your life. Your company, and therefore you, would receive a considerable profit.' He smiled, and drank some of his whisky. 'There might even be a British gong in it, at the end of the day.'

'Now you amaze me,' James said. Poor William would roll in his grave.

'So?' Marks inquired.

James considered. The whole thing had a faint ring of a bad joke. But for all the reasons Marks had outlined, it could turn out to be a very funny joke indeed. Certainly he had nothing to lose. And Anne would be delighted. 'If you will convey to me everything that you have just said, in writing, Colonel, I'm your man.'

'I think that can be managed. Although the writing will be, shall be say, diplomatically arranged so as not to cause offence. To anyone.' He raised his glass. 'Here is to the future of the Pennyfeather Arms Company. Or will you change the name?'

'Oh, yes,' James said. 'I prefer Martingell to Pennyfeather. Do you know, Colonel Marks, after damn near twenty years ... I think I've come home.'

This Large Print Book for the Partially sighted, who cannot read normal print, is published under the auspices of

THE ULVERSCROFT FOUNDATION